"We've got a problem," Malgi said. "Those guys want to kill us."

Tuttu tapped his laptop PC. "We can last, half rations, six days. That's if we play the defensive."

"I know," the old man said. "But I think we should wait."

Tuttu looked, daring the *angatkok*. "We have to settle this. It's Mick's way or ours... we have to take care of him if we want to survive." Malgi smiled, then nodded.

Claudia caught the unspoken dialogue. Settle it: Mick's way of greed and *tanik* values—wait for rescue, every man for himself—versus Malgi's way of sharing and Inupiaq values—work together, survive together.

Malgi smiled again. "I did not mean wait forever, Grandson." He held up a finger. "One day, two days."

"Let them think they have the upper hand." Tuttu's voice got deeper, lower. "Grandfather's right. Let them come. Let them use up their bullets. And when they think they have us"—he rubbed his palms together—"we will kill them."

AGVIQ

WAR
AT THE TOP
OF THE WORLD

Also by Michael Armstrong

AFTER THE ZAP

Published by
POPULAR LIBRARY

AGVIQ

THE WHALE

MICHAEL ARMSTRONG

POPULAR LIBRARY

An Imprint of Warner Books, Inc.

A Warner Communications Company

POPULAR LIBRARY EDITION

Copyright © 1990 by Michael A. Armstrong
All rights reserved.

Popular Library®, the fanciful P design, and Questar® are registered
trademarks of Warner Books, Inc.

Cover design by Don Puckey
Cover illustration by Jim Warren

Popular Library books are published by
Warner Books, Inc.
666 Fifth Avenue
New York, N.Y. 10103

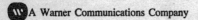 A Warner Communications Company

Printed in the United States of America

First Printing: July, 1990

10 9 8 7 6 5 4 3 2 1

To my mother,
Sylvia Jane Jander,
and to the memory of her mother,
Anne Hughes Jander

Acknowledgments

Through the Individual Artist's Fellowship Grant program, the Alaska State Council on the Arts provided generous financial assistance to me during the writing of *Agviq*. Conversations with numerous people helped me shape this book. In particular, I am indebted to the contributions made by Helen Armstrong, Charles Barnwell, Gregory Reinhardt, Jennifer Stroyeck (especially!), and my editor, Brian Thomsen. Chris Morris and Janet Morris, the godparents of this book, were immensely supportive from *Agviq*'s early beginnings. I am especially grateful to them for enthusiastically praising *Agviq*'s predecessor, "Going After Arviq" (first published in Janet Morris's collection *Afterwar*, Baen Books, 1985). Without them, this novel would not have gone beyond that short story that no one seemed to want to publish. Thanks to all.

—Michael Armstrong
Anchorage, Alaska
April 1989

"I learned to fight the pain of living."

> —*Quin Slwooko, 13,*
> *Gambell, Alaska, walrus hunter,*
> *after being lost for 21 days*
> *with his father and brothers*
> *on the ice near St. Lawrence Island.*

Preface

For the sake of the narrative, *Agviq* assumes that sometime in the late twentieth century the Inupiaq, or Northern Alaskan Eskimos, have lost any sense of cultural identity. *This is not now the case*. Although their culture is threatened and in danger, at the time of the novel's writing the Inupiaq, or "real people," retain a language, traditions, stories, and ways of living that distinguish them from the dominant culture of the United States of America. Among the things that make the Inupiaq different from other cultures, including other Eskimo or Inuit cultures, is their reverence for and their hunting of agviq, the bowhead whale (*balaena mysticetus*).

However, the Inupiaq, like other Native American peoples struggling to preserve their cultural identity, must cope with many threats to their way of life, including attacks on subsistence hunting and fishing rights, the spreading influence of Western ideas, and abuse of alcohol and other addictive substances. It is not my belief that the Inupiaq should or will return to their ancient, pre-Western contact traditions. However, I hope that they continue to preserve traits that make them different from non-Inupiaq, and that non-Natives respect their right to become whatever kind of culture they choose to be. *Agviq* is written out of a deep respect for the Inupiaq people and as a warning against the things that threaten to destroy not only their culture, but all cultures.

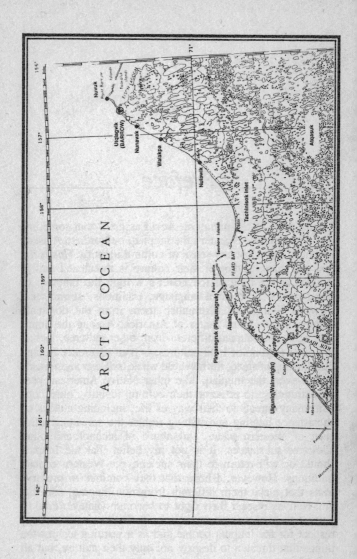

Chapter 1

CLAUDIA peered down into the thin muddy soil and saw agviq. With the tip of her trowel she gently scraped back the dirt from the fins and exposed the rest of the object. The soil slid away from the dull yellow artifact, ancient rootlets shrouding it and ripping away in one small clot. She brushed a blond hair off her forehead, leaned back and rocked on her knees, and let the joy of discovery wash over her.

"Agviq," she whispered.

Removing her light polypropylene gloves, Claudia reached out and touched the artifact. Time fell away from her, the two organic layers she'd dug through fading away, and her present merged with the past of the person who'd dropped or lost or hidden the carving of the whale. She had found the artifact in what she called "the pure level," below the layer of brass cartridges, pop can pull tabs, and plastic tampon inserters: the stuff of the ubiquitous Western culture, the junk the presence of which marked a culture as post-contact. The artifact had been below the floorboards of the old Inupiaq Eskimo house she had excavated a day earlier, frozen into permafrost, locked in the layer of soil between floor and supporting bottom logs. Someone—a whaler, an ancient Inupiaq man?—had dropped the object and now she picked it up, held it to the light, a baton passed between two generations, across two hundred years.

She felt his strength, his power, that long-gone whaler, felt him struggling to stay alive on that narrow spit between sea and bay. Claudia imagined the early Inupiaq, the Real People, living their lives before the whites, the Yankee whalers, had brought Western civilization: rum and oil, smallpox and steel. The whites had thought the Inupiaq a simple people.

No, she thought. Not a simple people, no, she knew they couldn't have been that. She had seen their artifacts, seen the innumerable gadgets and widgets no one could ever figure out: a tool for everything, complicated devices wondrous in their manufacture, deadly efficient for killing the sea mammals that made the Arctic a paradise, not a desert. *Whales*. With stone blades and skin boats and no steel or gunpowder these people had killed sixty-ton whales. *Agviq*. She felt the old culture, tried to imagine every detail, tried to think what it would be like to become them, become a coastal people who lived almost exclusively on the bounty of the sea.

Agviq.

The low Arctic light of the summer evening caught the whale, bathing it in diffuse orange-yellow rays, the incised lines of the lips, the eyes, the flukes clear. Claudia blew away bits of dirt, already drying in the sun, and clicked the carving against her front teeth. Yes, ivory, she confirmed, not antler, not bone; it had that decisive clink of ivory. She held the object up against the southern horizon, backlit by the sun, Peard Bay between her and the flat tundra turning red in the distance.

The ancient village of Pingasagruk, the site—*her* site— spread west and east of her, a cluster of mounds at the end Claudia worked on, a series of brackish ponds to the east. Beyond the ponds, toward Point Franklin and Barrow far beyond, two towers shimmered in the waning heat of the day. As she stared at the taller of the towers—a metal tower, near a point marked "Seahorse" on the U.S. Geological Survey map—it caught the light of the setting sun, and glowed bright silver. A red flaming dot, like a meteor, separated from the apex of the tower and fell over the horizon. Jet, she thought, hearing the boom follow seconds later. The jet to Barrow.

Behind her, ocean. Claudia turned, faced the Chukchi Sea. A line of ice loomed on the horizon: the threatening pack ice. Distantly, two derricks from a passing barge flickered through the haze, seeming to be a mirage; the diesels from the barge tugs thrummed. She'd watched its slow progress up the coast since early afternoon—fuel oil and four-wheel ATVs and snowmachines for Barrow and Kaktovik, one last run before freeze-up. She held the whale carving against the sun, blocking most of the light, nothing but a pinpoint shining through the hole drilled in the object's center.

"Claudia?" a man said from behind her. The weak signal of a distant station hissed from the radio in his hand.

Guiltily, she turned, laid the artifact back in its depression in the excavated pit, knowing she should have measured its provenance before she'd pulled it.

"Break time, Rob?"

She glanced at her watch, buckled on its strap around a loop in her daypack. Nine oh-four P.M. With the digging season coming to an end, they'd been putting in twelve-, fourteen-hour days since the weather had cleared two days earlier.

"*Claudia*, uh—" He held up the radio in explanation.

Right, she thought. KBRW's Tundra Drums. They had made a habit of listening to the messages sent out from the Barrow radio station every night at nine. "Let me write up this artifact," she said.

Claudia measured in from the sides of the meter-square pit, jotted down the numbers with pencil on the smooth plastic pages of her write-in-the-rain notebook. *Artifact 534*, she scribbled, *ivory object of bowhead whale (?), four lines incised ventrally, radiating out from a central drilled hole. 218.34 m North, 134.23 m East*—She extended a string attached to a stake at the high point of the excavation area, ran it out over the artifact until the bubble of the line level on the string wavered straight. With her tape, she calculated the depth of the artifact, wrote *2.56 m below datum* next to the other figures.

And then she picked the artifact up again, feeling less guilty: its location had been accurately recorded in three dimensions, its pinpoint position plotted relative to the site datum—a convenient USGS bench monument. She had identified the artifact's position relative to all the points of the world, and its position in space, and hence in time. Claudia copied the same information out on a manila coin envelope, and put the carving of the whale into the brown bag, into her pocket.

She laid a scrap piece of clear plastic over her pack and her notebook, and walked across the site and down to the tidal beach on the inland side of Pingasagruk. Their orange tent nestled in an indentation against the dune, guy ropes taut in the wind and the tent's fly flapping softly. Rob knelt before a camp stove and a driftwood fire he'd kept going since supper. The smoke from the fire rose up and away from Rob, swirling away from a blue tarp stretched across a driftwood frame. Rob picked up an enameled tin pot from the campstove, and poured her a steaming mug of scalding, bitter camp coffee.

"Ahhh," she said, sipping the coffee; it cut through the slight chill from the waning arctic summer, hot coffee, black and straight.

The KBRW radio announcer read off the evening's messages. In a village where everyone had a phone and hardly anyone went out hunting or fishing, the Barrow people still sent out radio messages, mostly birthday greetings or stern admonitions from mothers to teenage daughters to come home. But Claudia and Rob had set up a system through their bush pilot to send them a message on Tundra Drums if she had to tell them anything, and they listened faithfully every morning and evening. The radio cut the monotony of fieldwork and reminded them that the world existed beyond the edge of the tundra, even beyond Barrow.

"Found some ivory," Claudia said as the messages ended and the radio deejay put on an old reggae tune, Bob Marley's "Stir it Up." She reached in her pocket, handed Rob the whale carving. "Under the floorboards of the house, maybe from some sort of cache. I've found sixteen ivory objects in the same level, in the same ten-by-ten centimeter area.''

He turned it over, following the incised lines with his fingertips, then clicked the ivory against his teeth. "Yup, it's ivory," he said. "What do you think? What period?"

"Classic pre- or early-contact Inupiaq—late Thule," she said. "You can see the old Birnirk tradition reflected in the incised lines, the little hole in the middle, but it's not as busy as some of that Punuk or Old Bering Sea stuff to the south—no holes with dots, nothing like that."

"But it's a contact period house?" Rob asked. "We're sure of that now, aren't we?"

Claudia gazed across the fire, south and out to sea, to where the smoke drifted. She nodded. "Forgot to tell you—you were working on the northeast house. Yeah, the floorboards to the house aren't adze-cut; they're sawn." She picked up a plank of driftwood, a modern piece of two-by-six lumber that had been washed up on the tidal beach. "Like this: see the circular saw cuts? Same thing on the floorboards of my house; they've been milled. Oak, I think—from whaling ships. I haven't found any brass spikes, but there're some holes and stains that look suspicious."

"But you said you found this whale object under the floorboards?" Rob asked. "Maybe it's not related to the house—maybe it predates it." The radio droned on in the background, the deejay putting on another Marley song, "Buffalo Soldiers."

Claudia shook her head, sipped her coffee. She sighed. "I don't think so. I don't think anything left here predates those floorboards. There might have been some older stuff thirty years ago, but that's all eroded, all gone. These guys built their village from the wreck of whaling ships—most likely, from the disaster of 1871 when thirty-two ships got caught in early pack ice. Shit, this place isn't so ancient after all."

"But you haven't found much anything else modern, have you?" he asked.

She glanced at him, saw his eagerness, and smiled. "No. No, you're right. It's a pure site in that respect, maybe the last time the Inupiaq lived almost free from Western traditions,

Western trade goods. After that...the Yankee whalers came, and guns, and whiskey, cholera, syphilis, TB—''

"*Tee-Vee*. Four-wheelers. Cigarettes. Cocaine. AIDS.''

"Yeah. The world's shit.'' She snorted. "After that, it's one big happy family, one global cesspool, all the same kind of government—rich on top, poor on bottom, commissars and capitalists, proletariat and peons. Before that, decent human beings just struggling their damnedest to stay alive.'' Claudia stood, finished the rest of her coffee. "Oh, well, Rob. What's done, is done. Let's finish up, get in a few more hours of digging tonight.'' She reached to turn the radio off, but as she touched the volume knob, a piercing screech wailed from the radio, from KBRW, from the station in Barrow.

The noise stayed her hand, and she let her arm fall to her side. She knew that noise. Everyone knew that noise, knew it from radio tests: a long, drawn-out hum, a two-tone scream. *"This is a test of the emergency broadcast system,"* the radio would say. *"This is only a test."* She waited for the words, waited for the reassuring voice of the announcer to come on. The screeching ended, and someone spoke.

"Initiating emergency broadcast system,'' said a different announcer—not one of the KBRW regulars, but some man with a slight Southern accent. "System on. Please stand by for an announcement from the Office of Emergency Management.''

Claudia looked at Rob. He'd stood, staring up at her. "What? Not that Germany reunification thing?''

"Fuck no; they settled that before we left,'' she said. "I think.''

"Please stand by for—'' The announcer fell silent.

Claudia grabbed the radio, whacked its side, dialed the volume up higher. "*Noooo!*'' someone screamed from the radio. "NO!'' The announcer's voice had become hysterical, like a boy's voice cracking from puberty, but she recognized it as the announcer who had easily read the messages minutes before. "They fucking did it!'' he yelled. "They did it goddamnit they did it they did it they did it.'' The man panted, his breathing a drumbeat in the microphone, and then he calmed down, and his voice shifted from hysteria to a dull, almost whispering monotone.

"They did it, brothers, they did it. This came over the wires, over the EBS." Dead air hung on for half a minute, and then he spoke again, slight Inupiaq accent clicking over the syllables of the words, over and over. "Anchorage: nuked; Fairbanks: nuked; Tok: nuked; Attu, Adak, Shemya, Kodiak: nuked; New York, Los Angeles, Chicago, Tampa, Atlanta, Denver: nuked, nuked, nuked, *nuked*. Omigod" —his voice broke again—"they fucking did it they fucking did it they—"

"My God," said Rob.

Claudia grabbed the radio and hurled it down. She snatched the whale carving from Rob—he still held it in his fist—and stormed away from the radio, away from the fire, across the dune. She stopped next to her pit, stared out to sea, running her fingers over the ivory carving.

"Agviq," she whispered.

"*Claudia.*" Rob shouted after her. He came up behind her. The radio dangled from the strap, wrapped around his wrist. His arms hung against his body, hands balled into tight fists. "Claudia." He reached out to put an arm around her.

"It's over, Rob. Over. *Tampa* . . . shit." She thought of her hometown, of old friends. "*Over.*" She pushed away from him, whirled around, and looked northwest to the setting sun. August second, she thought, the day the sun first sets after the endless summer. She ran across the dune, across the sod burying the old village of Pingasagruk, down the sedges creeping in on the ocean edge, over the sand speckled with coal, and to the shore of the Chukchi Sea. She waded in, cold water rising over the tops of her felt-lined shoe-pac boots, raised her hand to throw the whale back in the ocean, to the walrus from which it had come— then stopped.

She had imagined the world ending a million times, had seen the holocaust of unleashed nuclear weaponry play over and over in her mind. Nuclear war had been an article of faith for her, a certainty Claudia had endured from childhood: this *is* the way the world ends. Arm cocked back to throw the ivory artifact to the walruses, Claudia paused as she saw a mushroom cloud rise up like a mirage from the ocean, a ghost of a cloud flickering against the sun.

Against the horizon, against the line of white icebergs pushing their way to shore, against the harsh glow of the sun setting into the first summer night, the cloud rose up, a fountain of mist. The mist rose up from the water, droplets making a faint rainbow. A second mushroom cloud, a second fountain rose next to it. She grabbed for the binoculars in her parka pocket, pulled the Nikons over her head, turning the foggy lenses and focusing on the spray.

A dark shape materialized in the binoculars; two dark shapes. Clouds; spray. More spray. A nuclear submarine—a boomer?—she thought, blowing itself up? The mushroom clouds faded away, and the dark shapes slid under. Claudia counted to herself, one thousand one, one thousand two, on and on, up to thirty. The dark shape rose, booming again, blotting out the sun, breaching, huge bomber head taking up most of its body, long fins curving back, flukes spread out like wings. She focused the binoculars again, then smiled to herself. Not nukes, not submarines, not an explosion. As the dark shape hit the sea, a great spray rising up from under it, a flash of light rippled across the ocean, across the sky.

"Agviq," Claudia whispered. She let the binoculars dangle from the strap around her neck, felt the effigy still clutched in her left palm, opened her hand, traced the figure. "The whale." Running her tongue over her lips, she tasted the brine of tears around her mouth, remembered the taste of the old muktuk she'd eaten in Barrow years ago, before they'd stopped whaling. Agviq, she thought, watching the two whales play in the ocean. Agviq lives, agviq will go on. She turned and walked back to shore.

Rob stood at the edge of the water, sea lapping the bottoms of his leather-and-rubber boots. "Claudia?" The radio crackled in his hand, the announcer screeching something about Prudhoe Bay.

She smiled, stroking the whale object. "It's not over, Rob. It's not over." She turned, looked back at the breaching whales. "It's just begun."

* * *

Claudia and Rob sat before the fire. Chunks of coal scavenged from the beach smoldered in the flames, her boots drying soles-up on sticks jabbed into the sand by the fire. Behind them the blue tarp on the driftwood frame flapped in the wind, and little eddies of smoke rose up at them. A piece of plywood with a map of Alaska pinned to it lay across her lap. A new emptiness burned within her, a hard coal of despair ready to be fanned into flames, and Claudia kept wanting to wade back into the ocean and let the chilling water wash over her and suck her under. She rubbed the carving of agviq—looped through a nylon cord now around her neck—and the old ivory gave her strength. There will be time, there will be time, Eliot's lines from *Prufrock* reminded her, and she slowly convinced herself that it was too soon to die.

"Anchorage," she said, drawing a teardrop shape looping northeast from a dot on the southern edge of the map. She winced at the name; she had friends there. "Fairbanks." Another loop in the center of the state. The university, the museum—Froelich Rainey had done his early work there, the Ipiutak stuff. And Larsen's and Giddings's stuff, a lot of it in the museum. Gone. All gone. "Galena." A loop west of Fairbanks.

"The radio didn't say anything about Galena," Rob said. "Why do you think the Russkies would hit Galena?"

Claudia looked up. Rob bit his lip, glared at her. "It has a forward fighter squadron out of Elemendorf in Anchorage," she said. "If the Soviets followed up with bombers . . ."

"My brother's in that squadron," Rob said softly.

Right, Claudia thought. "Okay; Galena's a question mark." She erased the teardrop. Give him hope? Sure, stupid as it was: Rob's squadron could have been rotated back to Anchorage. But give him that, anyway. Hope's all that's left. "Attu, Shemya, the sub base at Adak, the PAVE-PAWS radar at Clear, the backscatter radar at Tok . . ." More teardrops. "Anyplace else?" She barked the questions at him.

"Prudhoe. Kaktovik."

"Right." Two more teardrops. The old oil fields at

Prudhoe, the DEW line—North Warning System—station and the newer oil fields around Kaktovik in the Arctic National Wildlife Refuge that had never amounted to much. "What about . . . Barrow?" she asked, thinking of the DEW line site at Barrow—except that should have been hit first, before any of the lower-48 cities.

Rob shook his head. "We'd have seen it."

"Yeah," she said. Fifty air miles south of Barrow, they would have *felt* a nuke. "So Barrow made it. But if they got Prudhoe . . . What are the prevailing winds now?" she asked.

Rob tapped the two locations west of Barrow, the point at the top of the state. "Southwest—away from us." He traced a finger down the map, and she drew in two more teardrops.

Claudia held the map away from her, looked at the long ellipses, the worst edges of radiation. Damn, she thought, the state's *huge*. The nukes might not get everything right off. "Okay, southwest," she said. "What about stuff from Canada, Siberia?"

Rob shook his head. "Too far east, too far south. There's a sub base at Petropavlosk on the Kamchatka Peninsula in the Soviet Union—we'd hit that for sure. Some stuff in Central Siberia, but nothing to worry about."

"Yet."

Rob nodded. "Right—yet. So what do we do?"

Claudia tried to smile. The edge in his voice prevailed. Rob sat close to the fire, shoulders shivering, his face pale. Not from the cold, she thought, not from the cold of the air.

Their relationship had flipped back. Over the last week he'd worked his way through his shyness, begun to overcome his insecurities. Rob had begun to forget about the rank academia subtly imposed: he, the undergraduate, helping the all-but-dissertation graduate student complete her thesis. She'd begun to let him get close, had even been tempted to violate her pact of not having sex on a remote site. But then . . . They were back to the old relationship: she was boss, she had to make the decisions. And why? Not because she was a woman—she had to laugh at that, the old stereotype of women being the secret rulers of the world—

but because she had the knowledge, she was the one almost done with her Ph.D., because it was her site, damn it.

"Wait," she answered. "Wait at Pingasagruk."

"Maybe we should go to Wainwright," he said, "Walk down the coast." His voice began to rise. "It's only thirty miles. Those hunters we saw two days ago, maybe they'll be back from Point Franklin and can take us back to Wainwright. There'd be people there."

She shook her head. "No. We can't go there—not yet."

"But *why*?" he said. "They could help us. How long can we stay here? Wainwright would be just as safe—the fallout won't hit us. What are we going to do here to survive—hunt eider ducks?"

"When the time comes, yes. But no place on this coast is going to be safe, not for the next few weeks."

"But—?"

"You remember Chernobyl? No, maybe not—I was only fourteen, you would have been eight. I did a report in high school on it. The way the weather works, the Arctic gets it up the ass from radiation. Northern Europe, the East Coast, Moscow . . . all that's going to hit us pretty soon. Now, do you think Wainwright's going to have fallout shelters?"

"We could build one there . . ."

"Right. And we'd take at least three days hiking to Wainwright, it might take us another day or two to build it, and then we'd probably have to share everything with half the village."

"So what do you want to do—build one here?"

"Christ, *yes*, Rob." She stood up, moved around from the windbreak behind her, into the swirling smoke of the fire. The rising sun—still a short night—cast long ruddy shadows on the smooth sand. "We've got at least three weeks of food here, plenty of water, fuel. We'd have to build a hole or something for a shelter, I don't know—"

Rob jerked his head up, smiled at Claudia, then stood and gazed up the dune toward the site. "A hole," he mumbled. "A pit. We need a pit." He turned to her. "We *have* a hole, Claudia. What the hell have we spent the last five weeks doing?"

"Digging"—she grinned—"digging a pit! Rob, you're a genius."

"Digging a pit!" His voice rose, and he almost squealed in delight. "We've exposed almost sixteen square meters, and we're nearly down to sterile. Dig a pit! The house!" He waved up at the supply tent, pitched in the wind on top of the site, next to the house mound. "It's a classic Inupiaq semi-subterranean house, complete with entrance tunnel, katak, and floorboards. Damn it, Claudia, those old guys didn't know it, but they were building perfect fallout shelters."

His voice settled, became calm, and in that calm, she saw him go from hysteria to hope. Good, she thought. He'll need that.

"—except for one thing," Rob went on. "And we've got that. Toilet paper."

"Toilet paper?" Claudia stared at Rob like he'd just leapt over the edge into insanity buck naked and without a parachute. "Toilet paper?"

Rob walked over to their tent, began rummaging through his gear. "Toilet paper," he called back. "Toilet paper."

They had laid the last of the floorboards back in the house pit when they heard the whine of an all-terrain vehicle coming down from the Point. Claudia stood, scanned the beach to the northeast with the Nikons, handed the binoculars to Rob. Three four-wheelers kicked out dusty plumes against the early-morning sun.

"Those the guys who came by before?" Rob asked.

Claudia grunted. "Yeah." She glared at him. "Maybe they didn't hear about the . . . bombs," she said to Rob. "We'll see if they know, but don't tell them if they don't." He scowled back at her, nodded. The men on the ATVs turned inland, rode up over the sand dunes encroaching on the ocean side, and drove over to them.

Claudia shook her head, pissed that they'd ridden on her site. No, not her site now, she thought. Their land. She looked at the three men on the Hondas, jet black hair whipping out from under their caps, dark brown eyes half-hidden behind the fatty folds of their eyelids. Their land, it had always been their land. The blood of the people who'd built Pingasagruk, who'd named it, flowed in these men.

"Jim," she said to the man with the sea otter fur cap.

He killed the engine of the motorcyclelike vehicle, swung his leg over the seat, stood up, stretched. Jim nodded, glanced at Rob, then Claudia. The other two men—Horace with the glasses, skinny Oliver, she remembered—leaned back in their seats. Their parkas were patched, dirty, scraggly wolverine ruffs around the edge of their hoods. Horace had a long-barreled .22 revolver strapped to his side, and Jim had a rifle stashed in a plastic scabbard on the ATV. She shuddered, recalling her initial unease a few days ago when the three Eskimo men had stopped by the site. With their guns, their big ATVs, their dark eyes, they had intimidated her, almost scared her. They were hunters, sure and powerful and in control. But once she had made it clear why they were there, Jim and Horace and Oliver had opened up, as if they had come to an informal and unspoken understanding with her, with Rob: this is our land and you're just visitors. Now, she thought, now we aren't visitors; Rob and I are refugees. She didn't want to find out what that meant—not yet.

Jim lit a cigarette, walked to the edge of the pit, leaned down. "You finishing up?" he asked.

"Yeah," Claudia said. "Backfilling."

"I thought you guys weren't leaving for another week?"

Claudia glanced at Rob, shook her head slightly. "We aren't. We still have some mapping to do, but the backfilling has to be done first." She smiled at Jim. "So we don't forget, you know? Got to be good to the land, right?"

Jim nodded. "Right."

Claudia stepped out of the pit. "You guys want some coffee? Some Pilot bread?"

Jim shook his head. "Nah, we've got to get back to Wainwright." He jerked his chin down the coast, sucked on the cigarette. "Horace has to work tomorrow."

Work? Claudia relaxed. They didn't know.

"Your family still at the Point?" Rob asked Horace, the guy with the thick glasses on the orange ATV. Claudia jerked around to face Rob, stared down at him, suddenly remembering: Horace's family had a boat, they had seen them cruise by earlier in the summer.

Horace smiled. "They've gone to pick up some gear at fish camp, over at Kugrua River. Left yesterday."

She grinned, shook her head at Rob. The boat . . . if they were coming down the coast, he might have asked to get a ride with them back to Wainwright. But the Kugrua River was inland, on the other side of Peard Bay.

"You"—Rob looked at Claudia, nodded back—"you guys have a good trip back."

"Yeah." Jim flicked his cigarette at the tundra, got back on his ATV and kicked the engine over. The ATVs spat out blue smoke, and the three men gunned their engines. Horace nodded at them, and they drove back to the beach and down the coast, back to Wainwright, back to the village.

"We could have gone with them," Rob said.

"Yeah, maybe," she said. "They're nice guys, you know? But think about it, Rob. You want to tell them that their world's ended, too? Maybe they've gotten used to some of the stuff we honkeys brought them—four-wheelers, guns, cigarettes. Maybe they *like* being part of that universal, homogeneous culture: everybody speaking English, everybody swilling Coke, everybody smoking Camels, everybody wearing jeans. Maybe they *like* leaving that shit you find in the top levels of every site you see in the world: rifle cartridges, aluminum cans, cigarette butts, plastic tampon inserters.

"You want to be the one to tell them they can't get that stuff anymore? You want to be the one to tell Jim there won't be anymore smokes, anymore shotgun shells? You want to tell his wife she's going to have to cram tundra grass inside her every full moon 'til she's an old crone? Maybe they won't want that. Maybe they'd get mad. Maybe they'd shoot us. Not Jim, or Horace, or Oliver maybe. But someone."

"Yeah, but—"

"Dig, Rob," she said, jumping down into the pit. "Let's get this thing built before our hair falls out, okay?"

With the floorboards back in place, the house appeared as it had a month ago when Claudia had scraped back the last bit of dirt and exposed the structure. Smooth planks—salvaged, she guessed, from the wrecks of nineteenth-century whaling ships—covered an area about eight by ten feet. At the south end of the house a hole about two-and-a-half feet in diameter had been cut in the floor. Vertical planks, their ends snapped off when the house collapsed on itself, rose up perpendicular to the floorboards. Claudia had wanted to excavate the sidewalls, to dig beyond them and determine the house edge, but then... She sighed to herself as she looked at the exposed house. No time. No time.

When Rob and Claudia had first exposed the house, the edges of their meter squares had not come down precisely on the rectangle of the floor plan. Some units overlapped the house in narrow triangles, with side wall planks left standing in the middle of the squares. They shoveled dirt on the outside of the house, into these excavated triangles, and tossed bright pennies in the bottom of the pit so if they ever—ever?—wanted to re-excavate the house, they would know where they had stopped.

Something in Claudia kept her from destroying her precise digging, from ruining what science had already ruined. I have to build this shelter to survive, she thought, but I'll do it so I don't wipe out the past.

The ancient house, what Arctic archaeologists called a "Point Barrow-type house," had originally been covered with sod, top and sides; with driftwood scavenged from the beach and bay, they would rebuild the house, new sod protecting them not from the cold, but from the radiation. Sidewalls would hold back the loose dirt of the pit; six posts would support the sod roof to go on overhead.

Working through the twilight of the new night, Claudia helped Rob dig down into the hole in the floor—the *katak*—and excavate the entrance tunnel. As they dug, an arctic ground squirrel, what the Inupiaq called a *siksrik*, for the sound it made, dug his own house on the mound next to them. The siksrik built a warren of tunnels, little entrances popping up all over the site. Claudia watched him scurry across the dune, clutching in his mouth a tangle of her fine blond hair stolen from her hairbrush. Tan with black spots, a white chest, the siksrik had built up a good summer's worth of fat; his coat was glossy, and his hips wobbled as he ran down into his tunnel. Run little siksrik, run, she thought. Hope you survive too.

The old entrance tunnel of the house had been exposed in their archaeological excavation, a six-foot section of tunnel, mostly filled with yellow ice that reeked of piss and seal oil. Point Barrow-type houses melted in the brief summer, filling with water that froze in the fall; as the Inupiaq inhabitants would have done if they'd come back to this house, Rob whaled away with an ax, chopping out the old ice. He sloped the tunnel down from the house, then up to the surface, making a cold trap.

The walls of the house and tunnel dripped water from the melting permafrost. Claudia hoped that once covered, and with the decreasing air temperature, the melting would slow down and stop, else they would be awash in water. Out from the side of the entrance tunnel, where the kitchen of the original house would have been, they dug another short tunnel and a pit: their latrine.

Rob tacked sheets of butcher paper on the inside of the shelter—his idea. The paper had originally been used to make crosses for an aerial photograph session shot earlier in the summer. Now, as Rob had explained, the wax-lined paper should make their shelter airtight and keep the radioactive dust out. She laid out her orange three-man tent on the floorboards while Rob finished up, then they both climbed out of the pit.

On a tarp spread over the ground Claudia and Rob sorted through their supplies. In the middle of a pile of supplies before them was what she called her paranoia pouch. On every trip she had taken—backpacking, driving, canoeing—the little nylon pouch had come with her. She'd carried it with her since she was ten, when she had sat terrified watching *The Day After* on the family's VCR. She had kept the pouch handy, a talisman against the nuclear war she had been convinced would someday come. Modified and altered over the years, she had developed a tool kit that might keep her alive: wire and fishing line, hooks, waterproof matches, her Swiss Army knife, needle and thread, and a crystal scintillator, for detecting radiation. Paranoia, she thought. You're only paranoid if what you believe isn't true.

Rob flipped through a dog-eared paperback book, a bright orange mushroom cloud exploding behind the Golden Gate bridge on the cover. *Pulling Through*, by some guy named Ing. He'd found it in a used bookstore, Rob explained, and had brought it with him on the trip to read. It was all about some people who survived a nuclear war, but half the book was a bunch of stuff about how they did it.

Holding the book open with two rocks, he carefully examined a diagram in the appendix. Rob punched an inch-wide hole in one end of a coffee can, then taped the hose of a foot-operated air pump to the can—the pump for an inflatatble raft they had brought with them, thinking if they had time they could try to recover a whaling ship's anchor spotted the summer before in Peard Bay. He laid the can next to six rolls of toilet paper set out along an eviscerated cardboard box, rolled the cardboard around the can and tissues, and taped it together with duct tape in a long tube. Another coffee can, both ends opened up, went on at the other end, and then he wrapped the whole thing in a plastic garbage bag split in half.

"Ah," Claudia said, "so this is what the toilet paper's for."

Rob nodded. "An air filter. We don't want to be breathing radioactive particles, do we? Watch." He stuck a loose piece of flagging tape over the hole marked "inflate" on the foot pump, then screwed the tube from the toilet paper over the "deflate" hole. Squeezing the bellows on the pump with his foot, the action sucked air through the toilet paper, and the flagging tape over the "inflate" hole flapped in the small breeze.

"Ing's idea," he said. "An econo air filter for a homemade fallout shelter. We'll build an air shaft just above the entrance tunnel, make a rock filter using the dirt screen at the top of the shaft, and suck air down with this. The rocks will get the coarse stuff and this will get the fine stuff."

"What about the stale air?" she asked. "How will you get rid of that?"

"Ah." Rob picked up a tin can, triangular holes punched

along the bottom. "Bounty of the sea," he said, tapping a piece of sun-bleached Styrofoam and strapping it with a tape hinge over the open top of the can, a penny stuck on top of it. "Simple valve: suck air in with the pump, it closes. Stop pumping, and the stale, hot air rises enough to open it slightly and push out. Ing's idea again."

Over the tin can and at an oblique angle he stuck a slightly larger length of plastic pipe—more junk from the sea—and stuck the pipe through a hole in the north wall, just above the level of the floor, so the open end of the pipe would be exposed to the surface. Rob then laid the toilet paper filters in a shallow trench outside the house walls and above the entrance tunnel.

They took a nap in the early morning, shortly after the sun came back up, and finished the shelter by the next day. The blue tarp stretched behind their cooking area reminded Claudia of the wind direction; as long as the wind didn't shift, and kept coming from the northeast, they would be safe—until the winds brought the deadly clouds in over the poles. Claudia had tried to calculate how long that would take, tried to remember the wind patterns of the Chernobyl accident; about two days was what she figured, two days before the first fallout hit. Within forty-eight hours she and Rob had to be in the shelter.

While Rob shoveled dirt around the sidewalls of the shelter—backfilling the excavated triangles beyond the house— Claudia pitched the orange tent inside the shelter. Two tubes of nylon poked out at either end of the tent. One tunnel went around the air valve, the end cinched tight like a sphincter. She crawled out the other tube, down into the katak, out the entrance tunnel and up to the surface. With three ragged planks of plywood she and Rob built their roof, the windbreak's tarp placed over that, with random boards and sticks supporting.

A small piece of wood went over the trench with the air filters, the end of the filter tube poking out into a narrow shaft rising to the surface. On top of the air shaft they laid the wire screen, and sprinkled loose gravel on top of that. Loose dirt got packed around the air vent, another tin can with holes on top of the tube. The sod they'd cut to first expose the ancient house went back over the new roof. More sod was peeled back from the tundra and laid in three courses on top of the original sod, a foot thick. Enough? Claudia thought, trying to remember how dense dirt walls would have to be to block out the hard radiation. Is a foot enough?

All the artifacts, all the gear they wouldn't need in the shelter, everything not necessary for the next weeks of their life, they put inside the collapsed supply tent, buried in another ancient house only partially excavated. When they had finished, the site looked the way it had when Claudia had first seen it: low sod mounds against the sea.

"Ready to go down?" Rob asked.

Claudia looked out at the Chukchi Sea. No whales. Had she seen agviq, or his larger cousin, agviqulaq, the gray whale? She didn't know. No barge—the tug had probably gone on to Barrow, to whatever fate awaited it there. The ice hovered off the coast, miles out still, but she knew that same ice could come rushing into shore, like it had in 1871 when a freak storm trapped the whaling fleet, which probably provided the timbers for Pingasagruk's houses. The ice could come rushing in, and with it high winds pushing pulverized, deadly bits of Europe at them.

"Yeah," she said, "ready to go down." Claudia crawled down after Rob into the entrance tunnel. She pulled a heavy board across the entrance, and followed Rob's flashlight up the katak, into their shelter.

When he sealed the tent's tube around the air pump and turned off the flashlight, they were plunged into darkness, and into night.

_____ *Chapter 2* _____

FROM the stink of their sweat and piss and feces the archaeologists emerged three weeks later into the Arctic night. Huddled in their dark shelter, Rob's and Claudia's pupils seemed to have dilated to the edges of their irises; it had been Rob's idea that they come out at night, so as to not blind themselves with the dawn. Dressed in fallout suits made of butcher paper, visqueen, and duct tape, they looked like astronauts from a bad B-movie.

A light snow had fallen, and Pingasagruk seemed to glow in the moonlight. Claudia squinted through her scintillator, watching for the tracks of gamma rays. The square crystal flickered briefly, and as she held it against the sky, it shimmered with a blue-green light. She sucked in her breath, yanked the scintillator away from her face, glancing back at the open hole of the shelter. Still hot? she thought. It should be over. Claudia looked back up at the sky.

Through a break in thick clouds a curtain of blazing light rippled down from south of Polaris, violet rays like cracking whips shooting out from the fluorescent sheets. The edges of the curtain rose and fell, crinkling and expanding, out and back and in, the lungs of the heavens breathing. In her fallout suit Claudia heard the slight pants of her own breathing, the roar of the skies echoed in the hiss of her heart. She peered through the scintillator again, watched a brief burst of flashes in the crystal, then smiled.

"Is it okay?" Rob asked.

Claudia nodded, pointed up. "The aurora borealis—it's just cosmic rays, an ion storm." She handed the square crystal to Rob, shrugged. "The hard rays won't get us now."

"Made it?"

"Well—yeah, for now." She ripped the butcher paper suit off, tore off the cardboard box helmet, and turned to go back into the shelter—their house. "A hot meal—that's what we need: canned stew, coffee, nothing cold. Real food." She smiled. "And hot water. Let's wash this stink off; let's get drunk and make a roaring fire."

Rob grinned back at her, ripped his suit off, tossed it on top of hers. "And then?" he asked. "And then?"

She looked out to the ocean, at the surf frothing as it hit the shore, at chunks of ice lapping in the surf, and at the pack ice moving in closer. "No more 'and then,' Rob. New rule for survival: no more 'and then.' Take it as it comes."

"But we've got to plan, figure out how to last the winter. Our food—"

Claudia turned, shoved his chest. "No more 'and then,' Rob, you got it? We're alive; take that for now, okay? *Alive.*" He stepped back from her, frowning, eyes squinted nearly shut. "Aw, Rob." She put an arm around him. "I'm sorry. We'll figure out what to do." They stared up at the borealis, at the majesty of ions shedding their charge in their upper atmosphere. Wisps of clouds spread across the auroras.

"We'll figure out what to do."

Dawn came suddenly, swiftly, not the gentle easing of light earlier in August, but the raising like a shade of the fall equinox: one moment, darkness, the next, light—but a strange light.

The sun rose up from behind the two towers to the east, almost directly behind the shorter tower—the signal tower—whose sides were oriented to the compass. Light reflected off the freezing thaw ponds at the northeast end of Pingasagruk. A haze permeated the horizon, deep purples and orange reds glowing in thick bands. Like the 1883 eruption of Krakatoa, Claudia thought, sunsets would be colored differently from so much ash in the upper atmosphere. A blue-green sun pushed its way through the red bands and seemed to burn with half its usual brightness. The sight of that oddly colored sun confirmed in her what the radio had insisted was true. The tremendous amount of debris in the sky—enough to turn sunrises into alien events, enough to turn the sun blue—convinced her of what she had before only intellectually accepted: her world had ended.

Claudia stared at the sun until even its pale beams hurt her eyes, and dug out her glacier sunglasses. Rob pulled a baseball cap with the KBRW logo low over his forehead, put his own sunglasses on. Day. Daylight come. Claudia turned to face the new day.

"Okay," Rob said. "Should we go to Wainwright?"

"Yeah." She shrugged. "Longer hike to Barrow."

They had laid out their supplies: a dozen cans of food, a gallon can of stove fuel, two boxes of Pilot bread, miscellaneous spices, two jars of peanut butter, her twelve-gauge shotgun, some freeze-dried food, two rolls of fresh toilet paper—the filters had been buried in an old test pit—a box of shotgun shells, a first-aid kit . . .

"We can't take all this stuff," Rob said.

"Take all the food, all the gear we can, leave the rest in the house. Cache it." She opened her backpack, stuffed in her sleeping bag, selecting clothes that she had to have, clothes she could do without: socks, lots of socks, yes; shorts, no, T-shirts, no; heavy rain suit, yes—no; wind parka, yes; long johns, yes . . . What she didn't take she double sealed in two big plastic garbage bags. On top of the pack she lashed her shotgun, the old Winchester Ranger she had inherited from her dad. She ran her hand down the barrel, brushed away a bit of sand.

"What about the artifacts?" Rob asked.

"Take a few—for models." *Models* she thought. Models for what? "Leave the rest." She picked up her notebooks, the site map. "I'll take the notes." Agviq on a thong around her neck; yes, that she'd take. The notes, of course, Murdoch's 1892 report, *Ethnological Results of the Point Barrow Expedition*—the Arctic archaeologist's Bible—the maps, the drawings . . . Claudia looked at the small mound

of paper, sat down. "Damn. I'll never write this site up."
She jerked her head up, realizing what she had said.
"*Never*. No Ph.D., probably no fucking university, my
thesis committee's probably not even alive . . . damn, damn,
damn." She balled her fists, pounded the notebooks, scattering
them to the ground.

"Claudia . . ." Rob knelt next to her, held her. "It's only
a piece of paper."

"It's not!" She whirled, gripped his shoulder. "It's a
process. It's grabbing fucking nature by the throat and
making her tell her secrets! I had it, I had it . . . this site, I
began to understand it. And then—" She let go, wiped her
eyes.

"But you understand Pingasagruk?"

Claudia stood, looked northeast, up the dunes. "Yeah, I
think so. Yeah."

"Then the process . . . ?" Rob shrugged. "Maybe you did
it. Knowing how these people lived . . . maybe that's still
worth something?" He squeezed her shoulder. "Maybe it
will be worth something?"

She smiled, a thought occurring to her. Keep the artifacts
for models? Models. "Yeah," the anthropologist said. "*Yeah*.
Maybe it is."

They left Pingasagruk as they had found it, a series of
mounds hiding the cast-off tools and toys of people who had
used the land: the ancient Inupiaq, and now, them. Everything
they couldn't take—the rubber raft, the pump, the supply
tent, extra clothes, extra gear—got left in the old house, the
fallout shelter. Rob placed a piece of plywood over the
tunnel entrance, piled loose sod—frozen stiff like bricks—
over the intake air vent, and poked a driftwood pole wrapped
with flagging tape into the little vent. Maybe they'd come
back some winter or fall, Claudia thought—use it as a
hunting camp.

Southwest. The beach stretched flat and straight almost to
the horizon, a few mounds off in the distance. A little
frozen finger of Peard Bay poked along the southern edge of
the beach. Tromping through the light snow, they walked

away from Pingasagruk, back to where the bush pilot had set them down two months ago.

Claudia stopped at their old staging area, on the firmer sand as far as their bush pilot had dared to go, and looked back through her binoculars at the site. From the southwest, Pingasagruk seemed higher, the taller mounds clustered at the point where the dune narrowed to a point. Blocks of sod and earth, timbers jutting out of the edge, lay in piles at the point. Early explorers had said it had been haunted, had said spirits had wailed screeches at hunting parties hiking by the abandoned village. Let it rest, she thought. Let the people be. Past is past and future is future. She put the binoculars back in their pouch, fingered the carving of agviq. Thank you for this knowledge, she said to the land. Thank you for the opportunity to share your secrets.

She turned and left Pingasagruk behind.

The coastline rose and fell in low dunes, sometimes a flat expanse of narrow beach between Peard Bay and the sea, sometimes a series of hummocks like Pingasagruk. Claudia and Rob plodded on, the internal frames of their packs digging into the smalls of their backs. Despite the below freezing weather, Claudia stripped to a turtleneck, her jacket and sweater draped over the top of the pack. She couldn't get away from the archaeologist's habit of staring down at the ground as she walked.

Pingasagruk's relics had been scattered well beyond the site's edges. Reinhardt had written about that, had developed a theory about how the artifacts were distributed by wind and wave action as they eroded out of the site. Depending on its specific gravity, some artifacts settled out near the site. The heavier material, the denser material, got carried hundreds of meters off site.

Claudia walked through the heavier stuff. Whipped by the wind, the light snow had blown away, revealing hundreds of bleached bones: caribou, seal, walrus, bear. She picked up a driftwood stick, and as she walked she idly flipped over bones, yanking them out of the slightly frozen sand. One bone in particular rolled over less easily than the lighter caribou bones, or even the walrus bones. The underside glowed golden in the morning light. She reached down, picked it up.

"Look at this, Rob," she said.

He came up beside her. She held out a twenty-centimeter chunk of ivory, the sharp end of a tusk, fat end broken off. Like a new moon, one side of the tusk was dark and yellowed, the other end bright white. Along the keel of the tusk, where the bleached and unbleached sides met, someone had sliced away a section of ivory, so the point of the tusk came together like the prow of a ship. Where the tusk had been sliced away the cortex was porous, rougher, not smooth like the outside of the tooth. Claudia hefted the tusk, handed it to Rob. It seemed to weigh about half a pound.

"Ice probe?" he asked. "Murdoch describes one, I think—a *nauligaq*: a retrieving seal harpoon, with the probe at the end of the shaft to test the ice." He turned the tusk over and over in his hand. "Nice piece."

She nodded. "Nauligaq? Richard Nelson calls 'em *unaaq*. Same idea." Claudia took the tusk from him, imagined it fixed to the end of a staff and used to judge the weight of ice. "Or it could be a root digger." She hunched over, dragged her foot behind her like a mad scientist's assistant. "*Ivory, ivory,*" she mumbled.

Rob mimicked her, continuing the game: early in the season they had gone beachcombing, and had played fools mad with ivory lust. "*Ivory, ivory . . .*"

Claudia giggled, shook her head. "Ivory. It's a keeper, Rob. You take it."

"You don't want it?"

She fingered the carving of agviq on its thong around her neck. "No."

"Well," he said, taking the tusk from her, "maybe I'll *make* it an ice probe." He reached back, shoved it in an outside pocket of his pack.

Beach. Sand and beach. They walked on, past hunks of dense oak timbers—relics of century-old whaling shipwrecks— where vegetation had taken root in the lee side of the timbers, the first step in the construction of a dune. Fibrous mats of pale orange rootlets had packed the soil hard around the timbers, and now the drifting snow settled where the sand had built up: frozen pockets of moisture for the spring. New life, Claudia thought, seeds of villages being born. Copper spikes stuck up from the dark brown wood, the copper weathered to a bright green patina. Occasionally they'd kick up copper plates a foot square, one side dusky reddish brown, the other side gleaming green like the spikes, ice frozen into little windows in the dents of the metal. Things last up here, she thought. The cold preserves them.

The beach rose up to another dune complex, like the slightly elevated terrace Pingasagruk had been on. Rob and Claudia hiked over the tundra, up and over frost cracks cutting like little gullies in the dune. Claudia had a theory about such cracks, that they acted like black holes for artifacts, slight depressions that storms pushed things into. She'd tested the theory at Pingasagruk, and found beneath the more recent driftwood a little treasure trove of harpoon points, bolas balls, even a set of delicate ivory earrings.

On this dune the cracks trapped fragments of plywood, fishing nets, tampon holders, whiskey bottles, and millions of little Styrofoam packing beads. She flipped over one piece of plywood and saw faded, stenciled Cyrillic lettering.

"*Zavod imeni,*" she read aloud, recalling her college Russian. "'Factory named—'"

"Factory named what?" Rob asked.

Claudia shrugged, set the Soviet plywood down. "Doesn't matter—it's probably gone anyway."

One large frost crack led to a square thaw pond, rusty-colored mud on the bottom and edges, clear ice six inches thick on its surface. They took their packs off, sat down and leaned against them.

"I wonder if the water's good," Rob said.

Claudia stared at the pond, shrugged. "We used stuff like that to bathe in at Pingasagruk. Got to drink sometime." She rummaged in her pack, unstrapped an E-tool—a folding shovel—from the side, then pulled out a little plastic pump attached by a short tube to a little plastic cylinder. "Filters out giardia parasites and radioactive particles," the label on the little cylinder read. She shook her head. Let's hope, she thought. With the E-tool she broke through the ice, then pumped and filtered the pond water into two Sierra cups, and handed a cup to Rob.

"Cheers," she said, and drained the cup. The water tasted cold, brassy, but not bad, not salty or briny. She pumped another cup, drained that. Rob dug through his pack and handed her a piece of grape fruit-leather.

Claudia stuffed the wad of thin pulp into her mouth, chewed it quickly. She repacked the filter, reached down, strapped the E-tool back on her pack and tightened the straps holding her shotgun across the pack's top. Jerking the backpack up, she backed into the straps and snugged the pack tight around her shoulder. Claudia looked out at sea, at the sun below high noon and sinking toward the west.

"Burning daylight," she said. "You want to camp here for the night or keep going?"

Rob leaned back against his pack, staring south across Peard Bay, at the flat and shiny new ice. He turned toward her, looked up at her pack already on her shoulders. He looked down the coast, down the dune complex. "Dunes seem to go a ways. We can camp anywhere—might as well keep going. That site down the coast, Ataniq? How far is that?" He stood, reached down to pick up his pack.

"A few miles—six miles from Pingasagruk. It's where Peard Bay narrows and the barrier dunes meet the coast."

"A few miles . . . You want to try to make Ataniq?"

She smiled. "You got it, babe."

The greenish light of the setting sun shined on the bleached driftwood cabins at Ataniq. Claudia's main adviser at the State University of New York at Binghamton, a Professor Cassell, had done his thesis work there; it had been a passing reference in his dissertation that inspired her to excavate Pingasagruk. Ataniq, he'd written, might have been contemporaneous with Pingasagruk. If they were, he'd wondered, why were they so close? Cassell had postulated that shifting leads in the ice had caused the ancient inhabitants to move from one site to another.

"A close analysis of house types, ownership marks on harpoon points, and other comparative features," he had written, "would answer the question of whether the same people lived at both places within a generation." Cassell told her he'd put that in there as an open invitation for another dissertation, but she'd been the first person to bite at the bait.

More modern buildings had been built over the ancient ruins, an old trading post. Cassell said he'd found whiskey bottles under one corner of a building, but Claudia never knew if he had been kidding or not. Wind off the ocean whistled through the collapsing buildings, shreds of gray canvas from someone's more recent tent whipping in the wind. A caribou skull and rack glared down at them from one shack's cross beams.

Claudia shuffled up from the beach, around the lee side of the largest cabin. She stared down at her feet, out of habit scanning the tundra for bits of chipped chert and idly noting a profusion of recent .30-06 rifle shells, still-shiny golden brass. Rob came up behind her. She looked around for bones, curious what else the hunters who had been here had killed; so intent on the ground was she that she didn't see the aviator until she almost stepped on his body.

His right leg folded back in an unnatural hinge, and his bare, swollen feet poked out from a ragged flight suit. Claudia stopped, jerked her head up, one hand reaching back for the shotgun strapped across the top of her backpack. Rob stopped short behind her, glanced down at the body, then began to help her with the gun.

The man's face had been ripped or shot away, and his belly had been chewed open and the entrails removed. Enough remained of his flight suit and insignia to identify the man's nationality: a red flag on one sleeve, the letters CCCP stitched over a remaining pocket. Soviet. Claudia looked up from his shoulders, above his face, to where frayed ends of parachute cord flapped in the wind from the loops of a chest harness. A Soviet flier. Good, she thought, good that he's dead.

Something had chewed off his left arm, so that the end of his scapula poked out from his shoulder, little strings of muscle still attached. Footprints the size of Frisbees led away from the body. Claudia backed up, bumping into Rob.

"Give me that goddamn gun," she said, holding her left hand out to him. He slapped the shotgun into her hand, and she pulled it forward, clicking the safety off, sliding the action back and forth, ejecting three rounds, the first two number-four buckshot, the last one a rifled slug. Shaking, she reached down, picked up the rounds, pocketed the buckshot, and slid the slug back in the shotgun.

"A polar bear's been here," she said, "there's a polar bear around. We are not camping here, Rob, we are absolutely not camping here. Did I load slugs in this thing?"

Rob put a hand on her shoulder, steadied her. "You had it loaded two buckshot, three slugs, like we decided. You ejected the buck and one slug, and put the slug back in."

"Three sluggers left?"

"Yeah. You want me to take the gun?" he asked.

"I can handle it," she said. "Better put more slugs in."

"Good idea," a voice said to her right.

She whirled around and raised the gun, her finger starting to squeeze the trigger; then she relaxed, clicked the safety on, and let the shotgun hang from the crook of her arm.

"Jim," she said.

Jim, Jim with the sea otter cap and the wolverine-trimmed green parka, stood on the dune edge. A .30-06 rifle hung from his shoulder, his right hand tugging at the strap.

"It's the anthropologists," he said. "What are you doing here? Shouldn't you be in Barrow?"

"The, uh, bush pilot never came, Jim," Claudia said.

"Probably had a lot on his mind." Driving up the beach behind Jim were Horace and Oliver on four-wheelers, something large and white strapped to the back of Horace's Honda.

Claudia tried to smile at Jim, but couldn't shake his grimace. His lips looked pale, light pink, and a thin trickle of blood oozed out from his mouth. Little sores dotted his forehead. "Yeah," she said. "I guess the bush pilot got preoccupied."

Horace and Oliver stopped their four-wheelers, got off, walked over and stood next to Jim. The strap over the holster of Horace's .22 revolver had been unsnapped; Oliver held a .375 Ruger rifle by the butt of the barrel. Claudia could identify the white thing on the ATV: a bear skin, a polar bear, *ursus martimus*, she thought to herself. She nodded at the two men, and they nodded back.

"So where you headed?" Jim asked.

"Wainwright," Rob answered. "Your village."

"Uh-uh," said Jim. "I don't think you want to go to Wainwright. Wainwright's had a little trouble."

"I guess," said Claudia.

"There was a war," Horace said. He smiled. "You know, huh?"

"We know. Heard it on KBRW," Rob said.

"Ain't no KBRW anymore," Horace said. "You see our Russkie?" He walked over to the dead aviator, kicked the body. "Nanuq got the Russkie. We got Nanuq. Like winter, you know? Winter's going to get Russia, but we'll get winter."

"Right on," said Oliver. "We're *Eskimo*, man. Big winter coming, that's what my old man says. Freeze-up's never come this early. Big winter coming, but it don't mean shit to us. We're Eskimo, you know?"

"Inupiaq," Jim said silently.

"Right, Inupiaq. The Real People, you got it?"

"Sure," said Rob. "So things are bad in Wainwright, huh?"

Jim shrugged. "Lots of people dying from the radiation." He picked at his sores. "A little hungry, yeah. We got a polar bear, though." He kicked at the Russian. "Better off than him." He glared at Claudia and Rob. "You don't look so bad. Smile."

"Huh?"

Jim tugged at the rifle strap. "*Smile.*" They both smiled, foolish grins like in old family photos. "Yeah, you look good. Your gums aren't bleeding? Your hair isn't falling out? No sores, no shits? How come?"

Claudia shrugged. "That house we dug up? We filled it in, made sort of an iglu, and stayed underground." She looked down at the ground, shuffled her feet, looked back up. "Wainwright—we were heading to Wainwright. We . . . well, if there's anything left, any—"

"*No*," said Jim. "You can't go to Wainwright. Wainwright doesn't want you."

"But, we . . . maybe we can help," said Rob.

"*Fuck you*, honkey," Horace said. "We don't want your goddamn help."

"Jim," Claudia said, "Jim, I know—well, where else can we go? Rob's right, we *can* help, we'll hunt, fish, whatever. We're stuck out here, Jim. *Stuck*."

"You want to help, woman?" Jim asked. "Sure, *you* can help. Make babies, sew parkies, chew hides: women stuff. Him?" He jerked his head at Rob. "He's a dumb shit. He's no hunter. He can't help. You want to come? Fine. Horace will give you a ride. But him? We don't need him."

Claudia glanced at Rob, smiled at him. Dumb shit? No, she didn't think so. "We can't do that, Jim. You know that."

"Our terms, lady, our terms. This has always been our land, always, even when the whites took it, even when our own people sold it. See? We've always controlled this land, and now . . . now we *rule* this land, understand? If you want to come to Wainwright with us, it's on our terms, got it? You want to come to Wainwright, woman?" Jim walked toward Oliver's orange Honda, and Claudia shook her head and turned away.

"But where will we go?" Rob asked. "We can't survive on our own. We *need* you."

Jim turned and smiled, showing his bleeding gums, the empty holes in his mouth. "It makes me feel good to hear that, honkey. 'We need you.' No white man has ever said that to us. But it's too late, man, it's too late. Where can you go? Go back to Pingasagruk and crawl back in your iglu and see if you can survive. Or"—he paused, jerked his chin north—"go back to Barrow. Bunch of assholes up there, maybe they'll take you."

"Barrow?" Claudia asked.

"Barrow," Jim said. Horace and Oliver had mounted the four-wheelers. Jim waved his arm around, up and down the coast. "All of Peard Bay, Kugrua River—this is our land, and we don't want you here. We're going back to Ulguniq— Wainwright, to you—because our people need this meat.

But we'll be back, and if we find you here, or any place south of Ataniq, we'll shoot you. You understand?

"We'll shoot you."

Jim got on the four-wheeler, Oliver and Horace started up their Hondas, and the hunters roared down the beach.

Chapter 3

GREEN sky, brown ice: the mouth of Kugrua Bay stretched a mile wide before Rob and Claudia, colored by sediments and scoured by snow and sand into a glossy brown plain. The sun rose from straight-on east, over the bay, sneaking between the ashy clouds and the horizon, turning the sky pea green, searing the band between land and clouds a brilliant orange: green sky, orange horizon, brown ice.

At Ataniq they had buried the dead Soviet flier in a shallow depression, piling gravel and loose timbers over his body. A peace made with their enemy, and with polar bears who might be attracted to the smell of raw flesh, Claudia and Rob then hiked as far from the old trading post as they could before darkness enveloped them and cold stopped them.

A swampy hunk of land sprawled south of Ataniq, from where the easternmost tip of Peard Bay poked into a little inlet between Ataniq and the sea, and to Kugrua Bay, a smaller bay off Peard Bay. From Ataniq the long spit of land began that ended in Point Franklin, and from Point Franklin the Seahorse Islands extended down in a chain across the mouth of Peard Bay to the mainland. The archaeologists had thought of hiking back up to Point Franklin, stopping at Pingasagruk to retrieve the rubber raft, and then hopping across the Seahorse Islands if the sea ice hadn't frozen. Too long, too risky, they'd decided; after camping for the night, they had gone south instead.

Walking down the coast of the swamp, over the frozen marshes and puddles, they had come to the mouth of the bay, where the Kugrua River expanded into a bay that looked like an embryo on the map: head a little bay to the east, body a blob, the Kugrua River a long umbilical cord connecting the bay to the heart of the tundra. Claudia had studied and studied their maps, three one-to-quarter-million USGS quadrangles of the coast from Wainwright up to Barrow, and she'd thought, No way around it, the only way to walk to Barrow is to hike around the south—and mainland— side of Peard Bay.

But to get to the mainland and the broad beach stretching north to Barrow, Claudia and Rob would have to cross the mile of ice between the bit of beach they stood on and the safety of Eluksingiak Point across the bay. Rob walked up to the edge of the ice, to the ice that looked like frozen, weak coffee, dirt and sediment trapped in the ice. After they had discussed crossing the ice the night before, Rob had made an *unaaq*, an Inupiaq hiking stick, by attaching the ivory tusk Claudia had found to a five-foot piece of driftwood. He stared down at the ice, tapped it with the unaaq.

"I don't know, Claudia," he said. "Looks mighty thin."

"You want to wait a few days? Maybe Jim will come by and give us his opinion. We could discuss ice conditions right before he blows our heads off."

"Shit, I didn't say that . . . If we'd gotten the rubber raft, we could just slide over the ice, safe and sound."

"Would have taken us two days to get the raft and come back, Rob. We've been over this."

"I know, I know: 'We don't have enough food, we have to take the risk, blah, blah, blah.' But it's a *mile*, Claudia. You know anything about ice? I don't."

"One *unaaq* thrust and it's safe, that's what Richard Nelson says. *Coastal Subsistence in Wainwright*, right out of the elders' mouths. Try it."

"But what's 'one unaaq thrust?' A hard thrust? A light thrust?"

"Just hit the fucking ice, Rob, and see if the damn stick goes through, okay?"

He pulled back his arm, raised the staff down, and hit the ice with the ivory point. It dug in, chipped a hunk of ice away, but did not penetrate. Rob shrugged. "That's a thrust. It didn't go through. But I'm still not convinced . . ."

"*Shit*," she said. "Why don't we just pretend we're skating?"

"What?"

"You want honkey folklore? I'll give you honkey folklore."

She took her pack off, dug out the E-tool, and started whacking away at the hole started by Rob. The little chunks of ice cracked away, the point of the collapsible shovel biting into it, until she had made a fist-size hole in the ice. Water splashed up, spreading across the ice. Claudia enlarged the hole, evening out the sides. She put the E-tool down, grabbed her measuring tape from her pack, and calculated the ice's thickness.

"All right," she said, "how's this: 'One inch, keep away; two inches, one may; three inches, small groups; four inches, okay.' Skating rules-of-thumb. It's three inches thick. I think we can go across." She repacked the E-tool and tape, slung the pack over her shoulders.

"If you think it's safe . . ."

"I don't think it's safe. I think it's a little risky. But I think doing anything else is just as risky, so I'm going across." She turned from him and started across the ice.

"Claudia . . ."

"You coming?"

"Claudia—Jesus, bitch, quit being so goddamn superior, okay?"

She turned, stared at him, mouth agape for the moment. "What?"

"Just cut the damned know-it-all crap, okay, and listen. If we don't go and get the rubber raft, fine. But let's not plunge merrily into the darkness, all right? Cool it a moment."

She smiled, giggled. He's got a spine in him, doesn't he? she thought. Claudia walked back to him on the land, put her arm around him, hugged him tight. "You're so cute when you're mad, Rob, you know that?"

"Oh, fuck off, Claudia." He tried to pull away, but she held on to him.

"Look, I'm sorry. It was a good idea, the raft."

"Yeah . . ."

"So we'll be careful, okay?"

"Sure, sure."

"What's your idea?"

"Rope up, like with crossing glaciers. Keep our packs loose, and go across spread out, one at a time. That way, if the ice breaks and one of us goes through, the other can pull 'em out."

"Okay." She squeezed him, let go, then unbuckled the snap on her hip belt, leaned back, and lowered her pack to the ground.

Rob took a fifty-foot skein of rope from his pack, looped it around his shoulders, tied it in a knot at his chest, then repeated the procedure with the other end of the rope around Claudia. He took a quarter from his pocket, held it heads-up in his palm.

"Flip for point, okay? Loser goes first. Call it."

"Heads."

Rob stared at the coin, positioned on his thumb. "Man, that's all these are good for now." He flicked the coin in the air, caught it between his fingers, and opened his hand: tails. Rob smiled. "Lead on, MacDuff."

"Give me the unaaq."

He handed her the staff. "This ol' root pick, Claudia? Or is it an ice probe?"

"Root pick, ice probe, hunk of ivory . . . We create our own artifacts now, don't we?"

"Yeah," said Rob, "we do."

She led the way across the ice, rope unwinding behind her. Rob followed, and they walked across Kugrua Bay.

Eluksingiak Point beckoned to them, a fingertip of sanctuary thrusting out into the ice. Claudia kept her eye on the point and a little island slightly to the northeast. Walking in a zigzag route to spread their weight evenly, she marked their passage with jabs of the ice, like a dance diagram: scuffle, scuffle, slide, slide, jab, jab; scuffle, scuffle, slide, slide, jab, jab. From her readings she knew the Inupiaq had developed an art of ice walking, and she wished she had spent more time on the ice with the old guys when she had done ethnographical research years ago. Nelson wrote of a walk some of the hunters had developed, a crablike gait for crossing thin ice, a crouching walk for crossing questionable ice.

Hell, she thought, an Inupiaq wouldn't even try to cross bad ice; they'd just wait until it froze, chewing on little bits of blubber to pass the time. But they had to cross; she didn't want to test Jim's anger, didn't want to test her limits of hunger. And, she realized, she wanted to get to Barrow, get to a place she at least knew somewhat well, surround herself with people who had treated her as a friend. If I can get to Barrow, she thought, maybe I can make it.

The red rubber ball of the post-holocaust sun glared in her eyes and then rose up into the low cover of the ash cloud. The long flat shadow of the point fell away into an even light that made the cracks and crevices of the ice easier to see. Scuffle, slide, jab ... Claudia worked her way across the ice. She glanced down at the bay, noticed that the ice had turned deep black, jet black, so clear that she could almost see to the bay's bottom. A clear spot, she thought, trying to figure out why the ice had gone from silty brown to black. A deep spot in the bay, a place where the Kugrua River flowed out to sea, or perhaps a point where the tide surged in ...? She jabbed down with the unaaq, a quick, sure thrust, and the ivory point of the staff broke through the ice. As water bubbled up from the little hole, as she fell forward slightly, cold fear rose up her veins, fear like fatty tissue surging through her arteries to clog her brain: a stroke of mischance.

"*Rob!*" she screeched, the ice cracking behind her like a cannon shot. Slide, shuffle, jab, *crack*. Claudia pulled an arm loose from the pack, switched the unaaq to her free hand in a quick pass, shucking the pack off and hurling it in front of her. It skidded across the ice, then stopped. She grasped the ends of the staff with both hands, fell to her knees, spreading her weight across the unaaq held out in front of her. She spun on her right knee, a ninety-degree turn, like she remembered reading a hunter had done once. Turn away from the breaking ice, don't go forward, can't go back, go to the side.

Gray ice, brown ice loomed before her. She scuttled to it, feeling the ice crack, running like a mad crab. The line around her waist pulled taut, and she hoped that Rob had kept up with her, that he was still in firm ice. Claudia stopped, unable to pull the rope, and caught her breath. The ice was gray beneath her, the warmth of her breath melting a little window in the frost on the ice's surface. Gray ice, gray with bubbles that had risen up from the bottom: hard ice. She shifted the unaaq to her right hand, stuck the point down, and stood. She jabbed, one quick thrust; the unaaq did not break through. Claudia turned, pulling on the rope, and looked back.

Like a long, straight pole the yellow plastic rope stretched across the ice. There, to the right of the rigid rope, was the small hole where her unaaq had broken through the ice. Spreading from the hole two cracks radiated north and south, one toward firm ice, the other back along the direction of the rope. The crack ended in a hole, a man-size hole, a Rob-size hole, Claudia noted. The rope like a pole went down into the hole, held underwater by some oppressive weight.

"*Rob!*" she yelled. Claudia pulled, digging her heels into the gray ice, leaning back into the rope, its end looped to her, another section looped around her right arm. She fell into the rope, pulled into the rope. "Rob," she whispered, willing the end dipping into the ice hole to rise up, to come over the edge. "Please, Rob, Rob, please."

Hand over hand she pulled on the yellow plastic rope, wrapping inches gained around her wrist. A foot of damp rope came out of the water. Another foot. Something bright blue rose to the top of the circle of water. Another foot. A head rose up, then a limp arm, two limp arms, his back. She pulled, scrambling onto firmer ice, dragging him out of the deep, dark water.

The ice bent before him, and she slid him across the breaking black ice, pulling him to firmer ice before he fell through again. His dark hair hung over his eyes, his hat gone. Claudia jabbed with the unaaq to keep from sliding, watching the ice crack away, pulling and pulling until he was on firm ice. She stopped, caught her breath, yanked one last time until she was sure he was safe. Reeling in the rope, she carefully walked back to him, took his pack off, turned him over, then grabbed him underneath his shoulders and dragged him to shore.

Fifty yards to shore; they had been fifty yards to shore. They'd almost made it.

Claudia set Rob on the bare gravel of a beach, looked down at his calm face, his eyes staring up, an ugly purple-green bruise on his forehead. She tilted his head back, listened for the hiss of his breath, watched for the steam in the air. Nothing. Tearing her gloves off, she felt his carotid artery, cool to the touch. Nothing. She opened his mouth, blew four quick breaths through his cold lips, then placed the heel of her hand four fingers up his sternum, other hand laced on top, and pushed down. His body arched up with each relaxation of a stroke, then fell down with the violence of the cardio-pulmonary resuscitation. Down, up, down, up, fifteen times, breathe, breathe. Again. She felt his artery. Nothing. Again, *again*. She pushed air into his mouth, gasping, shoved his heart against his spine, feeling the firm muscle compress and expand. She could almost see the blood flow through his arteries, could see the warmth spread into his cheeks. Hold on, she thought, hold on, Rob, help is coming.

Claudia looked out at the ice of Kugrua Bay, at the flat tundra, nothing and no one for miles and miles. What could she do? she thought. Call up search and rescue, frequency 123.45 on the ground-to-air radio in her pack? Dial 911 from the handy phone booth conveniently located at Eluksingiak Point? Push, push, push, breathe, breathe . . . "They're not dead until they're warm and dead," she remembered an EMT instructor saying long ago, but that presumed hospitals to warm the bodies, machines to pump blood and air into him, people to spell her until help came. Sure, maybe the mammalian diving reflex had kicked in, and maybe like a torpid seal life still hovered in Rob's brain. Maybe. How long can I do this? she thought, and she pushed and breathed and pushed and breathed until her arms and lungs could pump and breathe no more.

The snow and ice and the loneliness fell upon her, and she slowed down, quit pumping. She breathed one last breath into him, his lips warm from her lips, and then pulled her mouth away. Claudia felt his carotid artery, hoping for even a slight pulse, felt nothing, and then let him go.

Claudia undid the rope from Rob's body, walked out one last time on the ice, and lassoed and retrieved her pack and then Rob's. She sat down on the hard sand beach of the point next to him, and cried until her tears turned to ice.

And then, like the Soviet flier, she buried him.

Chapter 4

CLAUDIA buried Rob in a shallow hole chopped into the sand, buried him like the Soviet flier and the gear they had left behind in their fallout shelter: beach timbers his casket, ice his headstone. She promised herself that someday she would come back and bury him properly, if the siksriks left anything behind, if the wolverines hadn't gnawed his bones into dust.

She buried him with his pack, with the things he had brought with him she could not use: a collection of keys, ratty underwear, a broken trowel, his journal scribbled on write-in-the-rain paper. She took his sleeping bag, took some socks, took his knife and the food he had carried. And when she was done she covered him as best she could, turned her back on him, and walked north with the slightly heavier pack to Barrow, never looking back, never thinking of why he had died and not her, because she knew why: luck.

Luck. The world ran on luck now, on fate, on the fickleness of ice that took one and not the other, on a plunge into cold swift water that knocked you senseless, on accidents of chance that put you in the middle of a nowhere where no one bothered to send bombs. Luck, fate, it was all chance, except for what you could steal, except for what little you could do to beat the inevitable: death and more death, like the footsteps she took to Barrow, like their paces across the ice, each day a step, and if one day the ice took you, well, that was it, you could walk the long journey but one day the journey ended.

One day's hike north of Nalimiut Point, where the Seahorse Islands circled around the east end of Peard Bay, Claudia came across a fishing camp—"Tachinisok Inlet," it said on the USGS map. A gravel road ran due south from the inlet, and ended, she remembered from her flight over earlier in the summer, at a steel tower by an airfield. An aluminum boat had been dragged up on the beach by the road, next to a plywood shack with blown-out windows; a loose door flapped against the side of the house in the wind.

Claudia shrugged off her pack by the boat, pulled out her shotgun, and entered the shack. Midday light fell through two small windows into the shack, the panes jagged and hanging from shredded visqueen plastic stretched over the window frames. She let her eyes adjust to the light, and as the details became clearer, she quickly inspected the room. A smell like old walrus blubber pervaded the place, and for a moment she worried about bears. Something skittered on the floor, then stopped.

She jacked a shell into the chamber, clicked off the safety; the orange warning paint of the safety button glowed almost phosphorescent in the low light. Her eyes adjusted further, revealing the scene: leaning against the wall, hand clutching a wooden spoon, was a woman, her dark brown hair hanging over one side of her head. Little slivers of glass stuck out of the right side of her face, the side toward the window, and brown-red blood had dried on the yellow-and-green flower print of her *kuspuk*, her dress. More shattered glass littered a green Coleman stove on a table before the woman, a black charred pot on top of the stove.

Something chittered from the woman's throat.

In one quick move Claudia raised the shotgun to her shoulder, sighted down the barrel, and fired at the thing gnawing at the woman's chest. A small brown creature about the size of a squirrel, but with a short tail and black spotted fur, flipped back from the woman, chittered again, then fell silent. *Chik-chunk*, Claudia ejected the shell. Bare patches of pink skin dotted the ground squirrel's coat, and its bared teeth gleamed white against bloody gums. Fucking siksrik, she thought. She set the safety, laid her shotgun down.

A curtain, its flowered print the same pattern as the woman's *kuspuk*, flapped next to the window. Claudia yanked the curtain down, rolled the dead woman onto her side, and covered her head with the curtain. Looking out the south window, Claudia stared down the road to the steel tower; some force had snapped off the top two-thirds of the tower, twisting and bending the steel struts of the base into hunks of spaghetti.

"Shit," Claudia said.

She grabbed her shotgun, ran out of the shack, up the road a mile to the tower. She passed two more shacks, their windows blown out, too. A body lay next to one shack, but she passed it by, running toward the tower. Some sort of harsh warmth passed over her—from exertion, she hoped. Panting, she stopped at the tower, looked up at its apex.

The tower looked to be a twin to the steel tower near Pingasagruk. One weekend she and Rob had done a survey of the north end of the site, walked well beyond the site edge. They'd come across the keel section of an old whaling ship, found a Yankee grave next to the wooden signal tower north of the site. Beyond an open stretch of sand with no dunes they had come to the steel tower, the tower barely visible from camp. It wasn't a radio tower, like she had figured, but some sort of *radar* reflecting tower, with steel four-by-eight-foot mesh panels at the peak. Something to do with the DEW-line station at Barrow, she thought. This tower at Tachinisok Inlet must have been the same kind— she couldn't remember what it looked like the first time they flew over—except that all but the base had been sheared off.

South of the tower a low crater had been blown in the tundra, and a little frozen pond—the blast excavating down to permafrost—gleamed from the bottom. Claudia looked up at the tower, at the way the top had been shredded but the base still held, then looked down at the crater. Little pieces of metal stuck out of the crater's edge. She picked a piece up, turned it over, the fabric of her gloves catching on the sharp edge. Arabic numbers and Cyrillic lettering had been etched into one side.

Slowly, carefully, as if the steel could still bite, she set the metal down. Patting her pockets for the scintillator, she pulled it out of the inside pocket of her down jacket, and with shaking hands squinted through it and looked at the pit. A few stray flashes flickered through the crystal—cosmic rays—but it otherwise remained blank.

A *dud*, she thought. This was a dud. A missile had hit the earth without exploding, a big bullet pounding down from the heavens and blowing only kinetic energy. She remembered the light disappearing over Pingasagruk's steel tower, the glowing red light she had seen the day of the war. A nuke. This had been a nuke—Barrow's nuke, she was sure of it—that had failed to fire.

What was that nuclear strategy—the decapitation attack? She had read of it once, some esoteric discussion of hypothetical nuclear attack plans. First thing you do, you take out the other side's command, control, communications, and intelligence systems—you take out their early warning system. Barrow. Barrow had a DEW-line station, Kaktovik had a DEW-line station. Boom, boom. Kaktovik had to have been hit, Barrow *should* have been hit.

But why would the Soviets hit Barrow *after* they'd already gotten the lower-48? she thought. That's what the radio had said: all those cities attacked. Unless . . .

An engine whined out from sea. Claudia whirled, ran to a rise in the road, a slight hill where she could see the ocean. Rounding Point Franklin and the Seahorse Islands to the northwest, an aluminum boat droned its way up the coast. She waved her arms at the boat, and it turned toward the inlet. Smiling, Claudia ran to meet the boat.

Almost a mile out, the boat picked its way through small icebergs floating near shore. Just on the edge of the horizon, the larger ice pack loomed; over the last week the pack had moved in, then out, as if the sea were breathing. Claudia grabbed her binoculars from her pack and stood on the low bluff above the beach, watching the boat come toward her. A man piloted the boat, a tarp-covered pile of gear in the bow of the skiff. He wore a white anorak, a dark ruff pulled up around his collar, and a blue cap snugged tight on his ears. She waved at the man, but he didn't seem to notice her. Then the boat turned, following the coast north. The bow of the skiff slammed into the low waves, making a harsh din: the whine of the outboard motor, the slapping of the boat on the sea.

Claudia raised her shotgun, thinking to fire it, but then lowered it. He wouldn't hear me, she thought. No need to waste a shell. Her eyes wandered to the aluminum boat pulled up onto the slight bluff above the beach. She smiled. Why signal him anyway?

Peering under the boat, she discovered an almost-new seventy-five horsepower Evinrude motor under a tarp, a red twenty-five-gallon gas tank laid next to it. Claudia reached under the boat, rocked the gas tank. She heard the reassuring slosh of liquid—gas, she hoped—inside.

"All right," she said to the disappearing boat, "no more walkin'—I'll follow you."

Up the road, inside the shack by the other body, she found a five-gallon blue-and-white drum of Blazo kerosene, another five-gallon can of gasoline next to it. Luck's holding out, she thought. Hanging from a rack on the wall was a Ruger 30.06 rifle with a scope. She ransacked the house next to it, too, piling into wood crates a box of shotgun shells, another box of rifle cartridges, some cans of beef stew, half a box of Pilot bread, matches, a pouch of rolled-up tools, a life vest, a tarp . . . It took her three trips to get all the stuff down to the shore. On the last trip she looked at the man, the only other body there, seeming almost to be asleep in the snow.

Okay, she thought, but dreading another burial. Okay, I owe you that.

She dragged the man's body to the seaward shack, the one with the dead woman in it. The man hadn't been hit by flying glass—he had been outside the house. Nothing pierced his pullover parka, but when she rolled him over to drag him on his back, she noticed a hole in his forehead, a little sliver of shiny steel sticking out of the hole. Shrapnel from the tower, Claudia thought. Dumb luck. The nuke hadn't been a total dud.

Laying the man inside the shack with the dead woman, Claudia looked around. Slim pickings. The Coleman stove looked shot, and the pot on it was a charred mess of burned stew. From the shack's pantry she took a few cans, but that was it. Claudia looked at the man's parka—trimmed with wolverine around the hood and waist and lined with sheepskin—and at her own grungy down parka. The woman had on a pair of caribou hide mukluks, bottoms made of ugruk skin. She felt like a grave robber, but Claudia pulled the parka off the man and took the woman's shoes. They smelled a little, but if she aired them, she figured, it wouldn't be too bad.

"Sorry," she whispered.

With a little grunting and levering with an oar, Claudia tipped the aluminum skiff over on its keel. She dragged it down the bluff and to the beach, then put all the scavenged gear in the bottom of the boat. The outboard motor was too heavy to carry, but she managed to drag it down to the boat and set it in the stern. Fuel lines, gas tank, all looked okay. She topped off the tank, found another tank by a piling under the dead woman's shack, and transferred the remaining gas into the spare tank.

A gust of wind blew through Claudia's hair. She glanced up, took a glove off, and licked her finger. Wind from the north. Shit, she thought. The ice pack will move in. She tossed the man's parka, the woman's mukluks, and her pack on top of the other gear in the boat and covered it with the tarp. Her shotgun she wrapped in a plastic trash bag and set next to the stern seat. Got to hustle. She pushed the boat down the beach, then looked up at the shack with the two bodies.

"*Okay*," she said, "all right, all right."

Bury them? No, not so the siksriks can dig them up. The lady had had enough of that. Hustling the can of Blazo back up the bluff, she dragged it into the shack. She sloshed kerosene on the bodies, on the walls of the shack. With a scrap of ripped curtain, she made a torch, wrapping the cloth around a stick from the beach, soaking the cloth in kerosene. She tipped the drum of kerosene over in the doorway and watched the gas pool on the floor.

Claudia walked down to the beach, stopped below the

bluff. She lit the torch, gauged the distance to the shack, then hurled the flaming torch at the doorway of the shack. Just before the torch hit, she ducked down, the low bluff shielding her; a cloud of hot gas roared overhead, a satisfying *whoosh* erupting from the house. She poked her head over the edge. Flames licked from the doorway of the shack, thick black smoke belching out from the broken windows.

"I'm sorry," she said again. "Thank you. Rest in peace."

Pushing the skiff out in the water, the bitter cold water lapped at the bottom of her shoe pacs. The boat bent and cracked new ice, slush ice as she pushed it out to sea. Waves and wind kept nudging the boat back to shore, and Claudia had to dig in with the oar, until the boat was in water deep enough to lower the outboard. She set the choke, opened the gas line, and pulled back on the starter cord. The engine kicked, spitting out black smoke. She yanked the cord again. More smoke. Again. On the third try, the motor roared into life.

"*All right*!" Claudia yelled, twisting the throttle on the motor and steering into the waves. "All right."

The bow of the boat rose above the waves, spray rising up in her face, the boat slamming up and down in a monotonous drone, the sound boats made in the open sea, a sound you could hear for miles. Wind in her face, water sliding by her . . . Claudia smiled, glad to not have to walk. Watching the water for ice, she gained the feel of the boat, figured out the proper throttle speed to keep the boat riding the waves smoothly. The land and the burning shack slipped away behind her, and she made her way north to Barrow.

It took her the rest of that day and all of the next to get to Barrow. At Nulawik, about twenty-five miles up from Tachinisok Inlet, the ice pack creeping south forced her to camp; the light had dimmed and it became too risky to dodge icebergs. But the next day the wind had shifted, the pack had blown back out, taking with it the young slushy ice and opening up a wide lead along the shore. She made a quick run up the coast, the water almost smooth, hardly enough 'bergs to make her even get nervous.

With hardly any experience running boats, Claudia had

no idea how long the gas would last, but when she passed Walakpa, eighteen miles south of Barrow, with fuel still remaining in the first tank, she relaxed. No problem. She recognized Walakpa by the narrow pyramid on the bluff, the memorial to Will Rogers and Wiley Post—that had been where their plane had crashed. Ford had dug there, too, a few years after the crash.

Just south of Barrow, something shiny glinting from the bluff in the late afternoon light caught her eye. She pulled into shore, beaching the skiff at the mouth of a little gully. Hundreds of fifty-five-gallon drums spilled down the gully and onto the beach. The light snow that had dusted her tent the night before partially covered the rusty, orange-red barrels. The sides and tops of some of the drums had corroded away, so that the drums looked like the vertebrae of some enormous snake. A gust of wind blew, and the shiny object on the bluff glinted again. Claudia grabbed her unaaq, her hiking staff, and walked up the beach to the gully.

Working her way up the ravine, she climbed over the fifty-five-gallon drums and over pieces of junked machines. The wind blew the snow away from the hollows of rotted barrels, and pale white objects remained. She reached down, picked up one such object, turned it over in her palm: a squat, dense bone, with a little knob at one end, a narrow shaft, an oblong hole just above the distal end—a seal humerus. She noticed more bones in the trash heap: the dog-faced vertebrae of caribou necks, the mashed and misshapen leg bones of walruses and seals, the thin arches of ribs, great bleached racks of more caribou. The butchered bits of hunted animals had wound up in the ravine, tossed among the steel barrels flaking away into oxidized chips. More recent bones had bits of fur stuck to them, long strings of cartilage, sometimes hunks of skin. Claudia searched for that shiny thing, saw it again as the wind blew.

Red strands blew back from in front of the shiny thing, two pieces of teardrop-shaped glass, mirrored sunglass lenses. A crack split the left lens in half. The wind gusted again, and the red strands fanned across the glasses again. Claudia reached up, grasped the red hair, and the glasses skittered down the side of an upturned half-barrel. Two hollow sockets, like black marbles, stared back at her, lips stretched back over white teeth grinning at her.

"Oh, shit," Claudia said. She dropped the head, watched it flop back down. Long red hair whisked over the head, hiding the dead face. Inch-wide holes, the edges of the nylon fabric curled back in scorched and melted strands, dotted the back of the woman's parka. Standing, she gazed beyond the woman, at a jumble of rusting red drums piling up onto the tundra, and the litter of bones and bodies and dead human beings.

MNI—minimum number of individuals—was the term faunal analysts used for the calculation of body counts. Count the number of femurs, of humeri, of crania, of atlases and axes, and divide by the number of such bones an animal was known to have. Skulls worked best, because every animal only had one skull. Claudia counted human skulls, human heads lying like spilled billiard balls—*chance again*— on the felt of the tundra. Thirty, forty, fifty, a hundred—she quit counting after a hundred, didn't want to count after a hundred. She guessed that there had to be at least a hundred skulls: big skulls, little skulls, medium skulls. Hair and flesh still clung to the skulls, skin stretched tight across the faces, hair hanging in hanks from crown or nape or chin. Skulls with flat foreheads were women, she remembered, skulls with rounded foreheads were men. Men, women, children, all dead, dead from the radiation, she thought, though some still had their hair; dead, maybe, from starvation, from disease. Dead, maybe—she looked at the body of the red-haired woman with the mirror shades again—from violence.

As Claudia stared at the skulls, at the bodies thrown randomly among the junk, some buried in the bottom of the ravine, others hanging over the edge, she thought of Rob, of the Soviet flier, of the man and woman struck dead by the dud nuke, of her sisters and parents and family caught in the fury of a war that should not have been. Dead. All dead. She looked at the faces of the bodies, skin stretched tight over skulls like someone had grabbed their hair from behind and yanked. With her unaaq she gently poked the bodies, turning them faceup to see if she recognized anyone. One skull had pale blond hair like her sister, cut in the same pageboy style.

"Susanne," Claudia whispered.

She set the unaaq down, reached for the body and dragged it away from the edge of the ravine, laid it out on the hard ground. Susanne, she thought, No, not Susanne, but like her, it could be her. Claudia ran back to the boat, dug through her gear, and pulled out the E-tool. Her shotgun, wrapped in plastic by the stern seat, clattered to the deck. She reached for it to put it away, then thought better of it, and took it with her, back up to the bluff and to the blond body.

"Got to bury them," she said. "All dead, nobody gave Susanne a decent burial. Got to bury them."

Striking the frozen ground, chipping away little hard divots, Claudia whaled with the E-tool at the snow, at the dirt. Flakes of cold dirt flew up into her face, into her eyes. Sweat beaded on her forehead, and she took off her cap, shed her wind parka and pile jacket. She dug again, panting. The catch between the blade and the handle slid loose, and the blade bent back. Claudia sat down, E-tool in her hand, staring at the foot-wide hole, barely an inch deep, at the blond woman's body, at the bodies in the ravine.

"So many bodies," she said. *"So many."*

She allowed herself tears then, the salty brine coming down her cheeks, mixing with sweat and flakes of icy dirt. She cried for Rob, cried for the Soviet flier, cried for her lost dissertation, cried for her thesis committee, cried for her university, her home, her family, her nation. She cried for the world and the people who would never be buried, who would never be mourned. She cried for herself. Then, breathing hard, sobs coming between pants, Claudia laid the E-tool down, bent the blade into the shaft, and collapsed the handle. She took a bandanna from her pants pocket and wiped her face. Then she stood and faced Barrow, the bodies behind her.

A mile or so to the north, Claudia could make out the outline of Barrow against the horizon. The airport runway stretched to the south of town, to the east; a small group of buildings clustered at the western end of the runway. About halfway between the airport and the ravine a group of satellite dishes ringed a small rectangular-shaped building, the dishes angled almost even with the horizon and pointed due south. Some taller buildings, the highest just four stories, gave relief to the Barrow skyline; otherwise it was a series of squat, one-story structures. A half dozen plumes of smoke rose from the village.

So, thought Claudia, someone still lives there. She looked up the coast, at the sun falling below the dust clouds, ready to make its brief bright appearance for the afternoon. She looked at the bodies in the ravine, some—like the red-haired woman—with bullet holes. Maybe Barrow won't be so welcoming, she thought, Or maybe it *will* be welcoming, like the welcome Jim and Oliver would give.

She went down to her boat. An end of the tarp flapped in the wind, an evening breeze blowing up. The wind would cover her tracks in the snow. She smiled. Can't hide the boat if someone heard me and comes to investigate, but I can hide *me*.

From her gear in the boat she pulled out her daypack, stuffed her sleeping bag in that, along with a flask of water, a few candy bars, and a box of shells. She sniffed the dead woman's mukluks; not too bad, she thought. The man's parka—with a white cover over the sheepskin hide—was no worse. Off with the shoepacs, on with the dead people's clothes. They're dead, maybe I'm dead, maybe we're all dead soon, she thought strangely. Push the boat high above the water, tie the tarp down good. She laid her unaaq back down in the boat, next to the E-tool, and slung the shotgun over her shoulder.

Claudia Kendall, ABD, girl guerrilla, she thought, and hiked up above the bluff, toward Barrow.

She walked toward town along the road from the lake where Barrow got their water, south of the edge of the airport runway, just past the cluster of satellite dishes. She remembered the road from a hike earlier in the summer, remembered finding a snowy owl's nest on a high mound, remembered also finding a more ancient human burial, two skulls and crossed leg bones laid out on the ground. Thaw ponds dotted the land, little frozen skating rinks on either side of the gravel road. As she walked by the satellite dishes she came upon more bodies.

"*No*," she said.

These bodies had been placed on wooden racks, one or two to a rack, laid out in corduroy parkas, with tools and guns and cooking pots leaning against the rack posts or hanging from nails. These bodies all had chestnut skin and black hair, though some of the women wore their hair in curly little caps. Well, perms aren't diagnostic, Claudia thought, but looking from body to body she could still hazard a guess: Inupiaq. She thought back to the bodies in the ravine, the archaeologist in her pondering the mystery: why were some dead laid out here with such care, while others had been tossed into the ravine with animal bones?

The beginnings of a more sinister thought occurred to her, confirming her suspicions, but Claudia did not want to consider it, did not dare explore the idea. But something did change in her, a curtain falling down, a relay clicking. No tears *now*; she felt no tears, she had no tears left. Something hard and cold and mean streamed through her, not anger, not fear, exactly, but something more basic. She stopped, the downy hairs on her body puffing out, her heart beating faster. Fight or flight, she intellectualized, that old dread reflex surging through her soul; only it was something more, she thought, something almost rational. Revenge, perhaps. Anger. Okay, she thought, something's wrong . . . *Snick*, she slid the receiver back on the Winchester Ranger and chambered a round. Gripping the pump of the shotgun in her right hand, she held the shotgun in the crook of her elbow, forefinger on the safety ready to click it off.

Claudia walked around the west side of the runway, alongside the pond road into town. Another road cut off to the west, down through an old gravel pit and to the beach. Two tugboats had rammed a barge up onto the beach—the same barge that passed by Pingasagruk? she wondered. Broken packing crates littered the beach and road, and one of the tugs had been run aground, while the other tug bobbed in the slush ice at the barge's stern.

A cluster of buildings was to her left, on the sea side of

the road, and to her right a jumble of empty wood packing crates the size of refrigerators had been stacked behind a big blue steel building, the old Arctic Cash 'n' Carry store. SKI-DOO was printed in big faded red letters on the sides of the crates, a treasure trove of snowmachines: SKI-DOO, SKI-DOO, SKI-DOO. SKI-DOO, Claudia thought, skedaddle, ski-doo, skedaddle. Working her way along the side of the building, she crept around the edges of the snowmachine crates. The sun set behind a building across the road to her left, blinding her for a second as she came around the corner.

"Maybe you should stop," a man said from in front of her.

Shading her eyes with her left hand, Claudia looked for the man. She heard the snick of a rifle bolt, smiled to herself—one rifle against her shotgun—bent her knees, and twirled around to her left, leaping toward a broken crate, an old snowmachine inside the box. A shot cracked and a bullet whizzed to her right. Duck, twirl again; she cowered down behind the snowmachine, hidden behind the remaining panel of the crate, and looked for the man. He stood about fifty feet away, a handsome Inupiaq in his thirties, dressed in a white atigi, dark brown wolverine ruff around the hood, a blue baseball cap pulled low over his eyes—the same man she'd seen in that passing boat at Tachinisok Inlet, Claudia realized. She raised her shotgun.

A chest shot, she thought, easy, line the sights up, pull, blow him away from fifteen yards. She held the gun steady, moved it quickly to her right, and fired a shot to the man's left, trying to remember how narrow the choke was on her Winchester.

"Sonofabitch!" the man yelled, hitting the dirt and scrambling for the cover of a pile of lumber.

Good, thought Claudia, got him pinned down. "Don't shoot at me!" she yelled. "I don't want to hurt you!" She pumped another shell into the chamber, rose up from behind the snowmachine crate, and raised the shotgun at the man.

"Goddamnit," he yelled, "give me cover!"

Oh, shit, she thought. She heard another *snick* of a rifle from the building to her left, caught the glimpse of a shape blotting out the sun from the roof. Claudia bit her lip, kept the shotgun aimed at the man; he looked pitiful as he tried to slowly crouch behind the small stack of old gray boards.

"I'm covering *you*," she said. "They can cover me, but I'm covering *you*."

The man looked up at her, pushed his cap back from his face and the hair out of his eyes. He smiled at her, stood, holding his rifle barrel down. "*Claudia?*" he asked.

Claudia squinted at the man, tried to ignore the other two men she knew had to be to her right and left. "Simon?"

"*Tuttu*," he said. "It's Tuttu now."

What's that mean? she asked herself. "Caribou?" Claudia giggled nervously. "That because you're good to eat? Or because you're fast?"

Tuttu ejected the round from his rifle, locked the bolt back. "It's my name," he said. "Tuttu's my *inua*, you know?" He jerked his head left and right. "Natchiq, Kanayuq, cool it. This chick's not going to hurt anyone." He pointed with his rifle at the shotgun leveled at his chest. "Okay?"

"I don't know," she said, thinking of all the bodies in the ravine, thinking of how Jim had been at Ataniq. She kept the shotgun on him.

"We found your boat," Tuttu said. "Got all your gear. Nice stuff. It should come in handy for us."

Damn, she thought. No way back. Barrow—she had to stay in Barrow, no matter what, no matter how. They had her. "Okay," she said. She lowered the shotgun, ejected the shell, and put the safety on.

"Damn waste of a round," Tuttu said. He walked toward her. "We've been looking for you. Why didn't you let us know you were coming?"

Claudia smiled. "Looking for me? Was that you who passed by Tachinisok—you know, where that tower is?"

Tuttu nodded. "You were there? Natchiq wanted me to stop there, but the ice was movin' in. I missed you; you should have signaled."

"No radio, Sim—*Tuttu*. I guess I could have used the pay phone at Nunavak, but I didn't have a quarter."

"Aw, shit, Claudia, that's not what I—"

"Lot of dead people in that ravine, Tuttu," she interrupted. "Maybe you can understand why I was a little jumpy."

Tuttu glared at her. "Yeah. Maybe you can understand why *we're* a little jumpy."

Claudia glared back. Tuttu looked good, she thought, not like Jim and the others from Wainwright: he had all his hair, even a thin little mustache, and there weren't any sores on his face or lips. "Things been pretty bad, *Tuttu*? Barrow get some nasty radiation?"

He nodded, one slow nod: up, down. "Not Barrow—we use the old name now," he said, "*Utqiagvik*." Tuttu shrugged. "Yeah, we got some hard radiation. The war, the damn war . . . You hear?"

"Rob and I picked up the news on KBRW, right before . . . before it went off the air."

"Rob?" He looked around her, down the road. "That kid who was workin' with you? Where is he?"

"Dead." She looked down at her feet. "Fell in the ice." She looked up. "Kugrua Bay." Claudia picked up the spent shotgun shell.

"You *crossed* Kugrua Bay? Shit." Tuttu blinked, then shook his head. "You didn't hike all the way up here?"

She shook her head. "Hiked to Tachinisok Inlet; found the boat there, at that camp." Claudia shrugged. "The boat had a little gas. I motored up the rest of the way."

Natchiq and Kanayuq came down from their hiding places, stepped up to her side. She glanced over at them. Marvin and Arnold, right, Simon's old hunting partners. Good names for them, she thought: Marvin—Natchiq, the seal—sleek and at home on the ice; Arnold—Kanayuq, the bullhead fish—stubborn and quick to dart off. Marvin grinned at her, patted his thirty-ought-six rifle, slung it over his shoulder. Claudia grinned back.

The Three Stooges, she called them, when she first met them, because the three cousins had been awkward and fumbling and shy. That was before she had done that subsistence study and found they were the only real hunters left in Barrow, the only ones who even tried to keep the old ways. Brothers, Marvin and Arnold had both worked as heavy-equipment operators, when they could get work; she remembered them as quiet, soft-spoken, but with a subtle sense of humor. Marvin and Arnold's parents, and Tuttu's mother, had all been killed in a house fire. They'd been partying and someone left a toaster oven on and the smoke alarm didn't go off and the drunken parents died. The kids had been at their grandparents, at Malgi and Masu's. Orphaned together and raised together. Simon's father, Claudia had heard, had died on the streets in Fairbanks shortly after the fire—passed out cold in below-zero weather.

Simon grew up and became a good corporate Native who had been a rising star in the Arctic Slope Regional Corporation: she had remembered him as cool and articulate, proud of his ability to work with the white lawyers and engineers of the Native corporation. Claudia had met him the first summer she was in Barrow, back when the North Slope oil still gushed and the money flowed and everyone thought that the new wells in the ANWR would be another Prudhoe Bay. The North Slope Borough Office of History and Culture had hired her to work on a dig at Nuvuk, an old village near the point; Simon had set up the computer program they used to crunch their data. He had a good head for numbers, the kind of mind that could see patterns and put them together, the kind of mind that could remember a lot of tiny little details: lines of machine code, tricky little sub-routines buried deep in a program, the numbers of artifacts and the computer abbreviations for them, stuff like IVOBJ, NID; Ivory object, non-identifiable.

A few years later, when Claudia had updated Helen Hughes's 1982 whaling subsistence study, she'd come into contact with Simon again. The Slope had changed and Simon had changed. Flying to Kaktovik to set up a computer program, his plane had crashed and the pilot had been killed. The emergency locator transmitter didn't go on—the pilot had forgotten to check the batteries—and Simon had been stranded on the tundra for a month. He walked a hundred miles back to Barrow; he shed all his fat and dropped his Western ways like an old suit that no longer fit. The trip changed him, turned him all spiritual and mystic, and with his cousins Marvin and Arnold he went back to the old ways, what little their grandfather could remember. He had quit programming computers and started carving ivory:

weird, abstract whale figurines that had started to gain some attention back East. Simon—Tuttu. Alive. It figured.

"Anybody at that camp?" Natchiq asked. He stared at her parka, at her mukluks.

She sighed. "Yeah." She ran her hand over the parka, scuffed the top of one mukluk with the toe of another. "A man. A woman. I, uh, borrowed these. They're dead. That tower there, you know? I think a Soviet missile homed in on it."

"A nuker?" Tuttu asked. The three men shifted slightly back.

"No—yes." She shook her head. "Well, we got lucky. It was a dud. Nuke didn't go, and I think it self-destructed on impact. I couldn't detect any radiation." Claudia pulled the scintillator out from its chain around her neck, waved it. "The uranium or whatever's pretty well shielded, I guess. There was a big crater and anything radioactive could have survived the impact and been slammed down into the earth."

"So how'd they die?" Natchiq asked.

Raking a hand across her face, scratching her cheek, Claudia remembered the woman. The smell of their death came back to her, came back from the parka and the boots. "Air blast, I guess. The missile made a big hole in the ground, like a meteorite, and it knocked most of the tower down, shredding it. The man was outside. He got a piece of steel in his head. The woman . . . the woman was standing by a window. The glass . . ."

"Ai," Natchiq whispered.

Claudia shivered, imagining the death. *Ai.* A thought occurred to her, explaining why Natchiq was so curious. "You . . . Natchiq, you knew them?"

He nodded. "My sister . . . those mukluks. She made the parky, too, for my brother-in-law."

"I'm sorry." The smell of the parka suddenly repulsed her. She began to pull it up. "Do you want—"

"No," he said. "No, it's okay."

"The rifle—in the boat," she said to Tuttu, "I found a rifle in one of the cabins there. If you want it . . . ?"

"Yes," said Natchiq, nodding. "Yes, I would like it very much."

Tuttu stared at her, then shook his head. "You walked," he said. "You *walked* across Kugrua Bay. You took a boat up through new ice. *Huh*. Well, that might count for something with the elders. Malgi really wants to see you. Come on—we got to take you to see 'em."

"What we got to see the elders for, Tuttu?" she asked.

"To see if you live," he said, as if he were talking about a driver's license exam. Natchiq and Kanayuq came up to the left and right of her and Natchiq took her shotgun away. "To see if we don't put you in that ravine," Tuttu continued.

The ravine, Claudia thought, Oh: *the ravine*.

Chapter 5

TUTTU walked Claudia down Apayauk Street, the gravel road that paralleled the coast, heading northeast toward the main part of town. Low mounds dotted an open field along the bluffs to the east, diagonal from the Cash 'n' Carry. Snow whirled around the mounds, settling into the lee sides. White arches of whale jaws stuck up from a few small hills; great lumpy whale skulls looking like mutant boulders clung to the bluff edge. Claudia smiled at the complex of mounds, the small area ringed by weather-beaten houses to the north, south, and east, with an electrical line running down one edge.

" 'The High Place,' " she said, "old Utqiagvik." She stopped, paused to look at the archaeological site.

Natchiq and Kanayuq, following them, stopped behind Claudia. Tuttu turned to her, waved at the mounds. "You ever dig that, arky? Seems like every damn archaeologist who's been through here dug that at some time."

She shook her head, thinking. Ancient Utqiagvik, the Arctic archaeologist's dream, an entire town of mounds, enough mounds for a decade of digging . . . She ran through the list of people who *had* dug there: Ford, Stanford, Dekin, Chang, and, of course, Reinhardt, before he'd done his study of Pingasagruk. "A professor of mine did," she said, remembering, too, that her adviser, Cassell, had dulled his first trowel there. "But I never got the chance. Too many other projects.'' Ford dug in, what, 1936? she thought. And Dekin in 1981, '82? ''That site will outlive us all, Tuttu, but the sea will take it someday.''

''Yeah,'' he said.

Claudia pointed at two men who pounded away at a roofless shack with ax and maul, dismantling the old house into neat piles of wood. ''What're they doing?''

''Firewood,'' Tuttu said. ''Takin' it down for firewood.'' He jerked his head to his left, toward a big log chalet, an old corporation officer's house, Claudia remembered, half its walls torn away. '' 'Bout all a house like that is good for. Too big to heat. Happens a lot these days.'' He took her elbow, nudged her forward.

They moved up the street, past the rows of houses that always reminded Claudia of Cape Cod, the neat saltbox houses with whitewashed sides, red trim, gables at either end. But the usual Barrow junk cluttered the lawns: fifty-five-gallon drums, old snowmachines, old trucks, scraps of sheet metal, packing crates, dead dogs . . . Apayauk turned into Stevenson Street, and they went past the old Polar Bear Day Care Center, by the community center, past the dancehouse. Claudia whirled, looked back at the dancehouse.

''You finished it,'' she said. ''You got the *qaregi* built.'' When she had left for Pingasagruk, Tuttu, Natchiq, and Kanayuq were just getting the frame in, and had begun to lay the sod walls. The North Slope Borough Office of History and Culture had given them a grant to build a traditional dancehouse; the qaregi was going to be a *real* dancehouse, a showplace for tourists, but also a center for teaching young children the old ways.

Tuttu shrugged. ''It saved our ass, arky. You did a good job with the plans. We crammed nearly twenty people in that during the . . . after the attack. Me, Natchiq, Kanayuq, our families, some elders. Those things make damn good fallout shelters, you know?''

''I know,'' she said. Claudia looked at the sod-covered dancehouse, at the double-glazed skylights, the door thirty feet away leading down like a cellar entrance to the entrance tunnel. The qareqi—yeah, it made a damn good fallout shelter, she thought, just like the house at Pingasagruk. A puff of smoke curled out from a pipe in the ceiling. It made a damn good house, too. Twenty people in that little room. Amazing.

They continued beyond the dancehouse, up the street by the Top of the World Hotel, and then took a left past the Arctic Slope Regional Corporation offices and Stuaqpak—"the big store," its Inupiaq name meant. Trucks and cars were parked along the street, in the lots by the hotel, next to little clusters of four-wheel ATVs; some of the headlights and windows of the vehicles were broken. But no one was on the streets, though on a normal day, Claudia thought, there would be dozens of people hanging out at the store, kids smoking cigarettes at the bus stop in front, a relic of wealthier days when the village could afford bus service.

A man with a little goatee and a red baseball hat stumbled out of the covered walkway by Stuaqpak, wobbled over to them. BLACKROCK CONSTRUCTION had been printed across the brim of the hat, and below that the acronym CMFIC. The man pushed the hat back, squinted at Claudia, and stumbled back. He burped, and she could smell the cheap whiskey even at three paces. She shook her head; *some* things were still the same.

"Hey, Simon," the man said, "hey, how ya doin'?"

"You're drunk, Edward."

"Yah, I am." He straightened up, stared at Claudia again. "It's a tanik. A blond bitch. Hey, Marvin, Arnold, where'd you find a tanik? You gonna *fuck* her?"

"Go away, Edward," Tuttu said. He kicked at the freezing gravel road, reached down, scraped up a handful of pebbles and threw it at Edward's feet. "Suck up your booze, Edward. Drink it all, you hear? Drink it all."

Natchiq and Kanayuq grabbed more stones, threw them at Edward's chest. "Get out of here, drunk!" they yelled.

Edward scuttled away, back to the shelter. "I'm th' mayor," he screamed. "Chief Mother Fucker in Charge! I'll arrest you! You jus' watch."

Claudia shook her head. "Some things don't change, eh *Simon*?"

"Damn drunk," Tuttu muttered. "I didn't think anyone had any booze left. I'd thought we'd got it all." He jerked his head at a three-story white building next to the hotel, with a bank in front, and a neat little sign set in the gravel that said NORTH SLOPE DISTRICT COURTHOUSE. "In here," he said, taking her elbow.

Inside the courthouse a woman screamed.

Claudia pulled away from Natchiq and burst into the courthouse. Tuttu and his partners followed her, crowding behind her in the doorway. She ran down the halls of the building, to an open courtroom.

As she came in, all the heads in the room turned toward her. Several dozen people sat in the public chambers, and three older men and four women sat in the jury box. Another elder, a thin, deeply tanned man with a jutting chin, sat behind the judge's bench; Claudia recognized him as Tuttu's grandfather, Oscar. Oscar smiled at her as she came in, a strange, knowing smile. Two younger men held the arms of a white woman squirming before the bench, some sort of black stuff dripping from her wet, blond hair onto her face. The woman leaned forward, hanging from the men, and let out a horrid yell, the scream rising up from her chest in a banshee howl.

Claudia recognized the woman; she had been one of the ticket clerks at the airport, a thin, stylish woman with bleached blond hair named Barbara or Belinda or Betty. Claudia remembered asking her why she had come up to Barrow, and her reply had been quick and to the point: "Big bucks, hot fucks," she'd said.

Belinda whirled around, broke loose from the guards, rushed toward Claudia. The two men grabbed her, held her. She struggled, her hands tied behind her back. "Help me!" she screamed at Claudia. "You've got to help me! They want to kill me. Tell them to let me go, just let me go!"

Claudia turned to Tuttu, jerked her head at the woman. "What is this, Simon?" she asked.

"Tuttu," he reminded her.

"Yeah, *Tut*-tu. What the hell's going on?"

He shrugged. "Elders meet now and then to decide

how . . ." He paused, bit his lip. "To decide how someone's talents can best be, well, used."

Claudia felt that chill she'd felt at the ravine, at the edge of town. "Go on."

"If someone's talents are not particularly . . . useful, particularly if they're, uh, not Native, they, uh, might go see nanuq." He glanced at Belinda, looked away quickly.

"Go see nanuq?" Go see the polar bear? she thought.

"You know, Claudia. Like in the books. The old ways. They take a walk on the ice."

Shit, she thought. The long walk . . . No Inupiaq had done that for decades. "How many Inupiaq have gone to see nanuq?"

Tuttu glanced at his hunting buddies, at the elders, at the small crowd. "Uh, a few, it's been mostly—"

"Mostly whites." She thought of the bodies in the ravines. "Taniks."

"No, not just taniks . . . Blacks, some Koreans, but not that many."

Claudia loosed the straps on her daypack, set it down, stepped up close to Tuttu, shoved him in the chest with her fingers. "Not *many*? *Not many*? I counted at least a hundred bodies in that ravine. Two hundred! Three hundred, maybe!"

Tuttu pushed her back, shoving her into Natchiq and Kanayuq. "You weren't here, tanik! You didn't have to go through what we did!" He rubbed his shoulders, let his arms fall to his side, clenching and unclenching his fists. "When the war came, when that bomb hit Prudhoe Bay— you could see the flash!—the whole town went nuts. Lots of people, a lot of the pilots, just took off. A seven-thirty-seven of tourleys had just loaded up and it . . . it got out, quick. Then the madness started.

"At first, it was like one big party, almost everyone got drunk. And *you know* how we are when we get drunk. We never could hold our booze, right? Edward—you saw Edward. Imagine two hundred people like that, half the town. Whites drunk, Inupiaq drunk, blacks drunk, Koreans drunk, little children drunk. And every other person's got a gun, a pistol—even Uzis, someone had an M-sixteen—and all those years, all that hatred that had been building up . . . It just came out.'' Tuttu slammed his hand on a table to the right of the jury box. ''Bam! You ever hear a firefight? My uncle, he was in Vietnam, he had a good description. 'Firecrackers,' he said. Like firecrackers, dozens and dozens of firecrackers, popping and popping in an orgy of explosions and you think they'll go on forever, a century of Fourth of Julys. And then it stops, it stopped. Silence, and so many dead, most of the village—a hundred, two hundred dead. We didn't count, we didn't *want* to count. *So many dead!*''

''Tuttu, I—'' Claudia turned from him, looked at the elders, at the people seated behind Tuttu. They all stared at her, cold, hard looks on their faces—except for Oscar, who had a silly grin on his face. Belinda squirmed in the arms of the guards, sobbing. *''Why?''*

''You don't know, Claudia!'' Tuttu yelled. ''You weren't there! *Why*, you ask? Why did we do it? You know why. You said so yourself, in that report you wrote. I read it, again and again, in that long wait during the fallout. The whites destroyed our culture, our language—Christ, hardly any of the elders even speak Inupiaq. The taniks brought up alcohol, destroyed subsistence hunting. They wrecked the caribou herds, wrecked the walrus and the seals . . . Finally, they took away the whales. You said that. They told us we couldn't hunt agviq. You said that. You said they had quote 'almost completely destroyed anything remotely resembling the Inupiaq culture.' ''

Claudia nodded. ''Yeah, I did. But such a revenge—''

He slammed his hand on the table again. ''Revenge? No, more than that—*madness*. We went crazy! God damn us all, we went crazy! I—'' He leaned against the table, held his hand to his forehead. ''Some of those bullets . . . I probably fired them. I don't remember, I don't *want* to remember. But we'd *already* gone crazy, our culture changed too fast. In less than two hundred years we went from a stone-age society to—to what? We changed too fast. First you whites destroyed our subsistence way of life, telling us what we could and could not hunt after you'd wiped out anything worth hunting, then you got us hooked on a cash economy, yanking that out from us, too, with promises of oil fields that never worked out. Finally—*damn you*—you turned us into some welfare culture, livin' off the BIA and our almost worthless corporation dividends. Any good job the whites got, and any stinking job the Koreans took, and all we got was free cable TV. *Fuck.*'' Tuttu spat.

"But to kill, still . . .'' Claudia waved her hand at Belinda. "To kill *her.*''

Tuttu shook his head, took a deep breath. "That's not how it is now, you don't get it,'' he said softly. "When the killing stopped, when that horrible night ended, the village, Barrow, picked up the pieces and figured out what to do. Man, *we* knew about the radiation, so a lot of us made shelters—the qaregi, the high school gym, Stuaqpak—and crammed as many in as we could. Some of the taniks left, took the rest of the planes south. Okay; we let them go. And some whites stayed—not a lot, 'cause a lot of the whites just ran and never came back, but a few, mostly the cronies of our dear ex-mayor. You know what, though? A lot of people—Inupiaq, tanik, whatever—didn't go into the shelters. They just kept drinking, lived like nothing had happened and there wasn't a cloud of radiation comin'. And they died. *They died.* Those are most of the bodies you saw: Inupiaq, tanik, Korean, black. So now what we've got is maybe two hundred alive, less than a tenth of the population when I was a boy. A lot didn't even survive in the shelters.'' Tuttu pointed at the elders in the jury box. "Man, that's about all the old folks left. So now, you see how it is? People got to be useful, okay? They got to pull their own weight.''

Claudia shook her head. "So Belinda isn't useful, and for that she'll die?''

The elder, Oscar, smiled at Claudia, leaned forward. "This woman . . . She is a parasite, see, anthropologist. A parasite. She lived off us. She tried to hide, tried to cover her true coloring with black shoe polish. Hah!'' He rubbed his own blue-black hair streaked lightly with gray. "She stole our food. What good is she?''

"I'll cook,'' Belinda said, sobbing. "Anything, anything. My boyfriend's the one who smeared this shit in my hair, he snuck me into the shelter. I was going to go on that plane south, but he wanted me to stay. He took care of me, he'll take care of me now.'' She pointed with her bound hands at a man, an Inupiaq in the front row. ''Right, James, please—*please*?''

James lowered his head, refused to look up at her.

''She is useless,'' the old man said. ''There is not enough food for the winter for useless people.'' He stared at James, and under his gaze the man, barely out of his teens, looked up. ''A woman has to take responsibility for her actions. But a man has to take responsibility, too.''

The eldest of the women in the jury box said something to Oscar that Claudia couldn't catch, and Oscar smiled, then nodded. The woman got up, went over to a small girl, whispered something to her. The little girl ran out of the courthouse.

''Release her,'' Oscar said.

''What?'' asked Belinda as her guards untied her hands. She rubbed them, then wiped at her face with the sleeve of her shirt. ''What . . . what are you going to do?''

''This . . . this anthropologist is right,'' Oscar said. ''There has been too much killing. Masu''—he motioned at the old woman—''Masu says that if you are so intent on looking like an Inupiaq, then you should act like one, too.''

The little girl ran back into the courtroom, panting slightly. She handed Masu a purple spray canister and a towel. Masu came out from behind the jury box, stepped up to Belinda. She snapped the cap off the can, an image of a dark-haired woman on the side of it.

''No shoe polish,'' Masu said, ''do it *right*.''

Masu reached behind Belinda's head, swept her hair over her face, and pulled it down. Shaking the can, she touched the nozzle, spraying thick globs of brown foam into Belinda's hair. The old woman massaged the tanik's hair, spraying more foam in, and then she wound the towel around the woman's head. She rubbed the towel, then whipped it away. Belinda's hair fell over her shoulders and face, a tangled mass of jet black. Masu wiped her purple-stained hands on the towel.

Belinda reached up, rubbed the damp hair, held a lock in front of her. ''I . . . I wasn't really blond anyway.'' She blushed.

"Belinda . . . No, *Paula*, that's what we will call you," Oscar said. "*Soot*. Hah! Paula, you will stay in Masu's house, in our house. You will work hard, you will do whatever Masu tells you, do you understand? And James . . ." He pointed at the young man. "You will live with her as her husband, and you will become a hunter, and you will take care of her as she takes care of you." He waved at the door. "Ai . . . Go. Go before I change my mind."

James rose, took Belinda's—Paula's hand, and the couple left the room.

Claudia watched them leave, then stepped up to the elders. "So?" she challenged them. "How will you judge me?" She pushed a hank of blond hair back from her face and glared at Masu, at Oscar, high in his seat. "Will you dye my hair, too, and make me some crone's slave? Is that what my worth is? Let me know my worth to you, if you think you're entitled to that."

Oscar rose, held out his hands. Raven beaks rattled from the white anorak he wore over a turtleneck shirt. A raven's head, bound with sinew, swung from his neck, tangled up with a pouch stuffed with some lumpy material. He came out from behind the bench, beaming.

"I am known as *Malgi* now," he said, standing before her. "And I judged you long ago."

"The loon?" Claudia asked, translating the Inupiaq word. The arctic loon, the loon with the pale gray head, the piercing red eyes—but "to give birth to twins," the word meant as a verb base. Her heart seized at the sight of him, at the raven's head, dried and rotting. An *angatkok*, she thought. He's become a shaman. Malgi: the loon, who gives birth to twins. Yes, it fits, it fits.

Malgi nodded. "The loon." He waved his right hand, shook it at her. "I saw you coming, saw your long walk up the coast from the house in the ground. It was I who sent Tuttu to look for you, and it was I who heard your boat, like a farting seal." Kanayuq and Natchiq stepped back from Claudia. She stood, frozen before him, barely able to breathe. The elder stroked her face, ran his fingers down her hair, yanking slightly on it. "You are in good health? You were able to hide from the sick sky?"

She nodded slowly, whispered, "Yes. Yes—we lived in an old house."

"Ah: *we*," the elder said. "Your student? That young man who fawned over you? He did not come with you? He died?" Claudia nodded. "I feel sadness for you, but great joy that your friend's burden has been relieved." Malgi smiled. "I imagine he felt guilt that he survived—that he didn't know how to love you."

"Yes," Claudia said, thinking, It's true, yes.

"And now you have come to us, anthropologist, come to Utqiagvik. This pleases me." He waved his left hand at the other elders, who smiled back at her. "It pleases us. You will be most useful to us, you see? I wanted you to come here, prayed that you would be brought to us. And you have. Once I taught you, told you much of what I knew, but it is obvious now that you are a great teacher yourself. You have learned much of our old ways, know more than even I could know."

"I . . . I do not know all that much," she said, thinking of Pingasagruk, of the mystery she still did not completely understand.

"It is good to be humble, daughter," Malgi said. "But now, now you must accept your strength." He reached down, lifted the carving of the whale around her neck, held it, stroked the whale's fins, flukes, the incised lines. "Agviq brings you to us. Agviq has guided you here, kept you alive."

"I—" What could she say? Claudia thought. This horrid, great fear tore through her, not the cold fear she'd felt coming into Barrow, but the fear of the unknown, the fear one feels upon coming up to a high cliff, before descending down a winding trail into the darkness of a canyon below.

"You will teach us!" Malgi yelled. His right hand gripped the carving of agviq, twisted it tighter and tighter around her neck, until the thong bit into her skin. "That is your value! You, anthropologist, will teach us how to regain our pride, to once again become *Real People*!" She felt the blood rush from her head, the air die in her mouth, the world grow black before her. Malgi let go, pushed her back into the arms of Natchiq and Kanayuq.

"Or you will die," the elder said. He looked down. "Or we will all die."

Chapter 6

LIKE a child bursting into the world, Claudia climbed up through the katak and out of the entrance tunnel into the qaregi. Natchiq and Kanayuq followed behind her, carrying her gun and her gear from the boat. The tunnel floor rose slightly toward the dancehouse, and as she walked up into the main room, passing small anterooms off the entrance tunnel, the air grew warmer. When Tuttu slid back the trapdoor to the room, a cloud of steaming chicken stew washed over her. The back of her pack scraped against the katak, the hatch door, so that she had to lean forward slightly to enter.

The early afternoon light barely shone through the skylight high up on the room of the underground sod dancehouse. Claudia smiled at the gut skin stretched across the inside of the light; plastic skylight on the outside, gut on the inside: she liked the authentic touch. One big room, the dancehouse measured twenty by twenty-five feet, with four timber posts in a small square in the center. Planed cedar boards had been laid out for a floor, and rough-hewn wall planks angled up slightly from the floors. But the qaregi's design had been changed from that of a ceremonial meeting house, its purpose in the nineteenth century. Essentially a large iglugruaq—a sod house—Tuttu and his cousins had remodeled the qaregi into a communal home for their extended family: smaller chambers had been partitioned off on the sides, but the main area had been left open. Benches were arranged around a wood stove that hissed and crackled at one end of the central area. A pipe rose up from the iron stove to the ceiling, a few feet away from the skylight.

Standing over the stove, a young woman about Claudia's age stirred a big pot of chicken stew; her long black hair was cut into short spikes at her crown, and she had stripped to mukluks, jeans, and a black T-shirt that said ROAD KILLS on the back in dripping blood lettering.

"Tammy!" Claudia shouted.

Tammy turned, fishing lure earrings jangling in her left ear, squinted at Claudia, then broke out into a huge smile. "Goddamn," she said. "Goddamnit . . . Claud-ya."

Tuttu glanced over at Claudia, his eyes wide. "The woman-who-loves-women knows you?"

"Tammy!" she shouted again. "You made it!"

Tammy made it, she thought. Why should she be surprised that Tammy had survived? The tough Inupiaq had come to Barrow from Oregon, where she'd been raised by white parents—they'd adopted her as a child, in a celebrated case that had tested the Indian Child Welfare Act. Tammy. Claudia had met her that summer, amused by her quaint, slightly archaic tough-dyke punk act. At first she'd made the mistake of thinking Tammy had been raised in Barrow; she asked her if she spoke any Inupiaq and Tammy replied that she spoke a little French. They used to joke that Claudia was Eskimo on the inside and Tammy was white and between the two of them they might make a real Inupiaq. Tammy. Bitchin', as she might say, Claudia thought. Bitchin'.

Tammy put the spoon back in the pot and came over to Claudia, hugged her. Claudia pulled back, cocked her neck. "Damn Mepps earrings." She unhooked an earring from her hair, looked at Tammy.

"*You* made it," Tammy said. "Man, I thought—"

"*I made* it," Claudia broke in. She glanced over at Tuttu, Kanayuq and Natchiq snickering behind him. "I met Tammy early in the summer," she explained to them. "She was working at Stuaqpak and we used to get high together. You got any of that killer dope left, Tammy?"

She jerked her head at Tuttu. "The federales confiscated it. No drugs, he says."

"Makes you crazy," Tuttu explained. "Though with the lesbian, how can you tell?" He rubbed the thin mustache on his lip, pointed a finger at Tammy. "What corner you sleeping in? You mind if Claudia shares your space?"

Tammy nodded. "Shit no. All *right*. Let me show you." She shoved the pot of stew to the back of the stove, licked her fingers.

"Good," said Tuttu. "Little Nuna, you tell her how things work now, okay?" He patted Claudia's pack. "She'll tell you what you can keep and what goes into the village stores."

Claudia frowned. "You're appropriating stuff?" Inside, she smiled. It'd be the right way under the circumstances.

"Ai," he said. "Well, I'd like to. I'm trying to get the other families to pool their resources, put everything at Stuaqpak, but right now it's voluntary. 'Communism,' my old Eskimo scout buddies call it, but it's the only fair way I know. We pull together. Maybe when we're better off . . . if agviq's willing." He waved at a corner of the dancehouse. "Nuna will tell you. She'll let you know what women are expected to do, what you can keep and not keep."

"What about my shotgun?" Claudia asked. She glared at Natchiq. "You going to give me my Winchester back?"

Tuttu looked at his hunting partner. Natchiq gripped the gun stock, shook his head slightly, then shrugged. "We'll talk about that later, okay?" Tuttu said. "Nuna will explain things." Natchiq and Kanayuq set down the crates of supplies, and the three men went back outside.

Tammy put an arm around Claudia, helped her with her pack. "He calls me that: 'Nuna,'" she said after Tuttu had gone. "Dirt."

"Earth," Claudia corrected.

"*Dirt*," Tammy insisted. "Doesn't matter. I'm still good ol' Tammy to you. Here." She pointed at a three-by-five area in the corner to the right of the stove. "Shove this shit over; this is the single girls' dormitory." She waved at the wall to the right.

Claudia squinted, got her bearings. The east wall. The

katak was to the south, the stove to the north. The men were to the west, wives to the south, old people by the stove. Was that the old way? she asked herself. She tried to remember what Reinhardt wrote on that. Did they even have huge houses back then? Claudia couldn't remember.

"How'd you hook up with Tuttu's family?" she asked.

"Got me," Tammy said. "I think because my parents— my natural ones, not my adopted parents—are supposed to be from Kotzebue, and Tuttu's got a second cousin from there or something. He took me in after the . . . you know." She helped Claudia drag the wooden crates over to her area. Tammy rummaged among some junk against the wall, pulled out two cardboard boxes, and set them on the floor. "Let's see what you've got."

Setting her pack down, Claudia undid the straps and knelt next to it; she started emptying pockets. Tammy sat next to her in a yoga squat, and pulled out the two sleeping bags and their sleeping pads.

"We'll keep those," she said. "Anything extra's supposed to go to Stuaqpak, but let's just get this stuff hidden away real fast . . . You mind? Why do you have two bags? Get a little chilly?"

"That kid I went down to Pingasagruk with? Rob? It's his."

"Why'd he give it to you? He stay there?"

"Yeah. He died."

"Oh." Tammy pushed the bag toward her, touched her arm. "Oh, I'm sorry. You want the bag?"

"No, no, take it. And the pad."

"You sure?" Claudia nodded. "Okay. My bag's a little shot. We can lay it out beneath us, and I'll use Rob's." She patted the plywood, laid a hand on Claudia's knee. "You don't mind sleeping next to me?" She jerked her chin over at Masu sewing next to them. "Some of the women get a little nervous around me—they think I'll fondle them or something. Although . . ." She grinned.

Claudia shook her head. "The body warmth will be welcome on cold nights. But if you want to fondle me . . . just don't wake me up, got it?"

Tammy sighed. "Yeah." She began poking through

Claudia's supplies. "All right, let's see what else you got ... Oooh." She slid Claudia's last two bars of Cadbury chocolate under her pillow. "I never saw those. Did you see those?" Claudia shook her head, grinning. "Good. The rest of the stuff"—she threw the canned and freeze-dried food into one of the boxes—"is Stuaqpak's."

"What about the camping gear?" Claudia pointed at a pile of backpack pots and pans, a small stove, the flask of remaining fuel.

"Our supplies." Tammy shook her head. "Tuttu and the old man have some weird ideas about sexual equality," she said. "See, it's kind of like the bad ol' days: men hunt, women cook and sew."

"And have babies?"

"Yeah—they're getting around to that, too. See, the cooking gear ... Well, that's yours, but it's camping gear, so some of the men—hunters—will want that. If you had a husband ... you don't have any old flames here, do you?" Claudia shook her head. "Okay, so this stuff belongs to our qaregi, and someone like Tuttu will use it." Tammy picked up the camping gear and put it in the other box.

She shrugged. "That's okay, long as I can use it when I go out."

Tammy snorted. "You ain't *goin'* out. Men hunt; women cook and sew." She rubbed her cheek, and Claudia noticed a fading bruise, still an ugly greenish yellow. "Least, that's the way I had it explained to me."

"We'll see about that." Claudia thought about what Malgi had told her. Teach them? How could she teach them if she had to stay in the house, tending the lamps, scraping hides, and sewing mukluks?

"Whatever." Tammy moved on to the packing crates. "You carried this stuff down from that site, too?"

Claudia shook her head. "Found it at Tachinisok Inlet— uh, at a camp there. Same with this parka and the mukluks." She explained about the tower and the boat and the dead people and the nuke.

"A dud then? I remember seein' something to the south that day." Tammy pulled out the boxes of crackers, canned goods, tossed them into the cardboard boxes. The wooden crates were deep and narrow, four feet high, six inches wide, two feet deep. From the side of the crate Tammy slid out the rifle. She picked it up by the stock, slid the bolt back, opened up the chamber, and nodded. "Empty—nobody home." She sighted down the barrel. "Oooh—nice piece." Tammy hefted the Ruger. "For damn sure you won't get to keep this."

Claudia grabbed it back. "I don't want it, but Natchiq's got my shotgun. I told him I'd give this to him—I found it in one of those cabins down there, I think it's his brother-in-law's. Maybe we can trade, huh?"

"Maybe." Tammy snorted. "Don't count on it. I know these guys, they'll keep your shotgun *and* the rifle."

"Fuck that," she said. "It's my shotgun, like my boots and my sewing kit—I get to keep the sewing kit, don't I?"

"Yeah, yeah, that's cool, Claudia . . ."

"That Winchester's my dad's gun. I didn't have any brothers. I was the oldest. When my father died, I got the gun, see? It's not the greatest gun, it's no damn over-and-under Weatherby, but it's my dad's. He taught me to hunt, taught me to shoot. Are we clear on that?" She raised the barrel of the rifle up, pointing it at the ceiling.

Tammy held her hands up, waved Claudia back. "Hey, hey, chill out, bitch. That's fine by me, but I don't make the rules. Talk to Tuttu, or Malgi."

"Maybe I will."

"Fine." She glared at Claudia, shook her head, and then began poking through her other things: her clothes, her books, her notes, the artifacts. "I guess the rest of this is yours. I'll have to tell Tuttu about the rifle, though." She rubbed her cheek again. "Sorry."

"He knows about the rifle. *I'll* remind him."

"Okay." Tammy rose, grabbed her atigi, a sheepskin pullover covered with floral-print cloth. "Let's take this stuff over to Stuaqpak. Uh"—she pointed at Claudia's parka, wrinkled her nose—"I can show you the bathhouse. Water's a little scarce, but I think with the stuff you've brought in, they'll let you clean up. Okay?" Tammy put an arm around her, squeezed her shoulder. Claudia stiffened, pulled away. *"Okay?"* She squeezed Claudia's shoulder harder.

Claudia relaxed, smiled, put an arm around Tammy, and squeezed back. *"Okay."*

Tammy and Claudia walked past Stuaqpak down Stevenson Street, to where it followed the coast into Browerville. The bluff fell sharply to the beach just north of town, and the road ran between the beach and a lagoon north of Utqiagvik proper. Claudia remembered that the ancient village of Utqiagvik and the system of mounds ended with the bluffs, though there were a couple more old villages farther up the coast: Pigniq near the old Naval Arctic Research Lab, Nuvuk at the point.

Smoke rose from a few buildings in Browerville, the neighborhood of Barrow on the other side of the lagoon. One white building, an old New England saltbox design, stood out above the others: Brower's Café, the old signal station.

"What do they call Browerville now?" she asked Tammy. Claudia recalled a linguistic dispute that always arose when identifying Barrow. Utqiagvik, she had been told, translated roughly as "the high place" and technically referred to the main part of Barrow—the bluffs, the mounds. But some called the whole area, including Browerville, *Ukpiagvik*, "where they hunt snowy owls," and her informants said that meant the general area. She imagined a Venn diagram where Utqiagvik could be part of Ukpiagvik but Browerville couldn't be Utqiagvik, and thought that simple enough. But it didn't help that the old explorers called the area *Utkiavik* or *Utkiavie* or *Utkiavwin*.

Tammy shrugged. "Some of the old guys call it 'Ukpiagvik,' I guess, but it's still Browerville, though, if you know what I mean." She held the tips of her fingers to her lips and lightly kissed them. "Bunch of *umialiks*, you know?"

"Yeah." Umialiks, Claudia thought, meaning "rich," not in the old sense of "a whaling captain." Even when she had first come to Barrow, Browerville had been a little snobbier, a little higher status. It had grown up around the rescue station and expanded into the Cape Smythe Whaling and Trading Company, an operation established in the late nineteenth century by Charles Brower, namesake of the neighborhood. Sometimes considered a separate village, sometimes not, Browerville had a different character from Barrow; the houses were newer, more modern, fancier. Claudia often thought of Browerville as something separate from Barrow; the real Barrow, the real Utqiagvik, was the village built over the old mounds, the old houses—the village on the bluffs.

"What's Browerville like now?" she asked.

Tammy stared off at the houses on pilings perched between the beach and the great tundra. "Scared," she said. "Desperate—like us. Lot of whites live there, what's left of taniks." She moved down toward the beach. "Let's get some water."

The icy wind blew hard from the west. Claudia shivered in her light down parka, pulled the neck of her jacket tighter—she had washed the sheepskin parka and already missed its warmth. The great black clouds still covered the sky from horizon to horizon, the same clouds that had hung over the sky since she and Rob had crawled out of the shelter. Sliding below the clouds, the setting sun shone in their faces, a purple red globe. Yet another glorious sunset, she thought.

A line of larger ice moved in from the northwest, still about a mile out from shore. The new sea ice Claudia had worried about a few days before had come back in, closing the brief lead of yesterday. Interspersed among the new ice were small icebergs, old ice, deep blue or smoky green. That's it, she thought, it's freezing up now. Another few weeks or a month and we can walk on that, the newer ice freezing the older ice solid, and the pack ice rammed hard against the shallow sea bottom.

She helped Tammy roll a large chunk of blue ice from the ocean shallows and onto the beach. Using a small hatchet hung from her belt, Tammy broke the blue ice into smaller chunks and then piled them in two white plastic buckets. *Piqaluyak*, it was called, Claudia remembered: blue ice, frozen saltwater compressed so hard the salt had percolated out and the water had become pure. The ice would sit in a pan on the back of the wood stove and melt. Drinking water. The two women hefted the buckets of ice and headed back along the beach to the qaregi.

Rounding a bluff below the Polar Bear Daycare Center, Claudia and Tammy saw three men walking down the beach from Browerville toward them. In the low light of the setting sun, it was hard to distinguish figures, but in the alpenglow one man's red baseball cap stood out. The three men came closer and Claudia's guess was confirmed: the man in the red hat was Edward.

A trail up to Stevenson Street and the qaregi snaked around a burnt-out apartment building on their right. They moved toward it, but the three men angled toward the trail, blocking their way. Tammy put her bucket down, ran a gloved hand through her hair, cocked a hip at the men—her tough dyke pose, Claudia thought. The plastic handle of the bucket dug into her palm, and Claudia had built up momentum moving up the low slope. She glanced back at Tammy, kept moving, letting the weight of the bucket pull her forward and through the men. It was an old trick she'd picked up in New York City: move ahead, eyes front, ignore any human obstacle before you.

"Where you goin'?" Edward asked.

He stuck out an arm, pushed her right shoulder, and she spun around clockwise, the bucket swinging around and into him. He pushed her harder, falling back a step, and she had to set the bucket down. The other two men cut her off from Tammy, and Tammy, Claudia noticed, had straightened up, chest slightly forward, hunkering down in a slight crouch.

"Goin' to see your little Toot-Toot, tanik?" Edward asked again.

She glared at him, studying him like she would a bad piece of sculpture or an ugly mound of dung: slowly, contemptuously, deliberately. Her gaze moved up from his worn-out shoe-pac boots, rubber glopped with Shoe-goo, to his greasy black jeans, to the oversize North Slope parka half-zipped, to the mangy wolf ruff around the hood, to Edward's dirty face with its scraggly Ho Chi Minh beard. Claudia stood two feet back from him, rocking on her feet.

"Fuck off," she wanted to say, but she knew that to say nothing would be best.

"Gonna go screw your little Toot-Toot?" Edward asked. "Gonna be his little honkey bitch? Or you gonna maybe dig up some dead Eskimo bones, like a good little archaeologist?"

Claudia glanced back at Tammy, at the two men between her. Taniks. She didn't recognize them at first, but when the shorter man turned to her, she recognized him almost instantly by his droopy eyes, the weak chin, and the walrus mustache: Mick, the bush pilot who'd flown her to Pingasagruk the first summer of her fieldwork.

The fat guy next to him she guessed was Karl, Mick's boss, the head of Naataq Airlines; he'd been involved in some kickback scheme with Edward a few years back and there'd been a big stink in the Anchorage papers, Karl's fat face immortalized in one classic photo of him coming out of the Anchorage federal courthouse with the hood of an Eskimo parka half-lowered over his eyes. Damn war did him a favor, Claudia thought.

"She's gonna dig up *your* dead bones, motherfucker," a voice said from up on the road, "if you don't watch your goddamn mouth."

Tutter stood up at the top of the little trail, a Winchester Ranger shotgun—*her* shotgun—in his hand. He slid the receiver back for emphasis, but Claudia didn't doubt he already had a shell in the chamber; a shell popped out, which struck her as somewhat curious. Had he ejected buck for a slugger? she thought.

"Hey, Simon," Mick said. "Chill out, man. It's cool. We were jes sayin' hello to the little ladies." Karl turned to Tuttu, his fat little hands waving in front of him.

"Sure," Tuttu said. He snorted. "Well, since you're being so polite and all, why don't you help the little ladies with the buckets?" He pointed at the buckets with the shotgun.

"Ah . . ." Edward said, then sighed. He picked up Claudia's bucket and carted it up the little rise. Tuttu nodded, jerked the gun at Tammy's bucket. Mick looked at Karl, Karl shook his head, and Mick took her bucket up.

"Thank you, gentlemen," Tuttu said, stopping them at

the top of the path. "You're so kind." They set the buckets down.

Edward turned to Tuttu, looked at him, started to open his mouth.

"Save it," said Tuttu.

Mick and Edward went back down the path, joining Karl. Claudia and Tammy watched them go by, standing where they had been. When the men got to the bottom of the beach, Tuttu called out after them.

"Hey, Edward, big shortage of blond pussy, huh?"

Edward ignored him, and the three men walked off, south down the beach, toward the beached barge.

"*Blond pussy*?" Claudia whispered to Tammy.

"Edward has a thing for blond taniks," Tammy explained. She looked up at Tuttu. "I guess it's catching, huh?"

Claudia shook her head. When they joined Tuttu, he had reloaded the shells and slung the shotgun over his shoulder—*my shotgun*, she thought. He stood by the buckets, motioned down at them when they came up.

"Thanks," Claudia said, a bit sarcastically. "Why didn't you kill those assholes before in that big firefight?" She wanted to bite back the words as soon as she said them. Idiot, she thought.

Tuttu scowled at her. "All I could do to keep them from killing *me*," he said. He shook his head. "Edward won't bother you again."

" 'Preciate it," Tammy said.

Tuttu nodded. "I was getting hungry. Wondered what was taking you so long to get water." He turned, patted his stomach. "Shouldn't you be makin' supper tonight?"

"Eat shit," Tammy mumbled as they walked back to the qaregi.

My shotgun, Claudia thought, staring at the Winchester slung over Tuttu's shoulder. *My shotgun*.

Chapter 7

MOVING in and out like bashful suitors, the slush ice had come in and gone out six times from the shore. One day a thin sheen would cover the open water from the beach to the pack ice a few miles out, and then a westerly wind would blow the pack ice to the horizon and fracture the slush into little pans. But each time the pack ice moved back in, it had grown thicker, higher, whiter.

Claudia had hiked down to the beach to dispose of the contents of the qaregi's honey buckets. Tuttu had never gotten the qaregi hooked up to the city sewage system—just as well, since Tammy said it broke down the first day after the war, and the engineer who could have fixed it had been killed—and so they had to poop in a little bucket in a little room off the entrance tunnel. The poop got dumped in a drum on the beach, and when the ice got thick enough to walk on, the drums would be dragged out on the ice and left to float away in the spring.

She'd heard that was how the villages took care of sewage after the previous world war. In one of his articles Reinhardt had written of the legacy of such waste management: "And as we flew up the coast to Kaktovik, we saw thousands of little orange rusty fifty-five-gallon barrels littering the beach like so many seashells." So many seashells full of shit, she thought he might have added.

After Claudia emptied the honey bucket, she wiped out

the tin pail with snow, dumped the snow in the barrel, and then set the little bucket down; she would pick it up on her way back. Claudia walked up the bluff to the old archaeological site. She often went there when she needed to get out of the qaregi, went there to "meditate on the mounds," as Tammy called it.

The newer village had expanded on the remains of the old, but a five-acre parcel at the south end of the town had been kept open, leaving the twenty or so mounds undisturbed. In the summer tourleys had come down to the site, tripping over whale skulls, and gazed out to sea, so that they could go home and say to their grandchildren: "I saw the Arctic Ocean." Periodically some squad of archaeologists would dig up a mound or two in the search for an ever elusive Ph.D. The Holy Grail of that hunk of Utqiagvik had been to prove continuous occupation back to the time of the Arctic Small Tool Tradition, circa 4,500 years before the present, but no one had ever done it.

She'd never spent a winter in Utqiagvik, but everyone said that the postwar winter seemed to be living up to their worst nightmares. A thickening cover of snow, that rarity in the Arctic desert, blanketed the mounds, so that they looked like a plain of giant melted marshmallows. Sloppy, giant melted marshmallows, she thought, noting the drifts building up on the leeward side of the mounds.

She liked the mounds at sunset, because from them the view south was relatively unobstructed. The big log house that had always blocked the south edge of the site had been carved down to pilings, and an equipment yard she remembered from a few years back had disappeared, a chain link fence and a flattened construction shack the only remaining ruins. On one high mound—Mound 16, according to one of Dekin's reports—Claudia tried an experiment.

Lining up sticks with the point where the sun set, each day she came down to watch the sunset and mark its passage across the southwest horizon. Tammy would come down in the morning to catch the sunrise, and each day the two sticks—sunrise to the southeast, sunset to the southwest—moved closer and closer. Claudia had figured it out, time of sunrise and sunset, and one day, she knew, she and Tammy would come down together and mark the last day, when the sticks would be almost touching and the moments of sunrise and sunset would be barely fifteen minutes apart.

A man came walking up the bluff from the beached barge, and as he got closer Claudia recognized Tuttu's white canvas atigi, the sunlight sparkling silver off the little tips of the wolverine ruff around his hood. Tuttu walked in long, smooth strides. He tended to slide his feet, too, pushing out, like skating. As he came closer she tried to hear his footsteps, but his feet made soft padding sounds in the snow, calculated, almost, as if he pulled up with one foot just before the other touched, the crunch of hide against snow barely a whisper. As he came up to her the orange ball of the sun fell below the horizon, and she marked its passage with another stick, six inches closer to Tammy's sunrise sticks.

"You shouldn't be out alone," Tuttu said.

She shrugged, then stood. "I can handle myself. Edward hasn't bothered me in a while."

"You shouldn't be out alone," he repeated. He walked off, stopped, looked back at her.

"Right," she said, following him.

She fell into step to his right, trying to match his walk, but his legs were longer than hers. His footsteps sounded like the crushing of butterfly wings and hers like the death throes of crackers being pounded into bread crumbs. They skidded down the face of the bluff to the beach, and as they got to sea level the wind hit them straight on. The cold found all the little gaps in her down parka where the feathers had clumped up or the nylon had torn. For the tenth time that day she wished that the sheepskin atigi she had salvaged off the dead woman would hurry up and dry—the fourth washing and it still smelled.

"The pack's moving in," she said. "It's early, I guess."

"Ai," he answered. Tuttu waved out at the line of white. "Soon, a great storm will come and make the *tuvaq*, make the ice solid against the sea bottom. Malgi says it should never happen this early. The tuvaq usually comes in December, but Malgi thinks it will come by November, when the sun finally sets. He says this will be a blessing, because by then we will be low on food and we can then hunt seals.''

"The nuclear winter," she whispered.

"Nuclear winter? Malgi spoke of that, too." He stopped on the beach, looked out to sea. "What is this? *More* war?''

Claudia shook her head. "Not more war—the continuation of war. An old theory that had become a little discredited. The logic was good, but no one really had the data, and you know scientists . . .'' Tuttu squinted at her, and they continued on up the beach. "Well, maybe you don't. Anyway, the theory goes that a nuclear war, even a little one, would put a hell of a lot of ash and debris in the atmosphere— remember how that volcano blew near Anchorage a few years back?''

"Iliamna? Yah, holy shit, that was a big one.''

"Right. Well, like an umbrella, all that ash would block the heat of the sun from getting in. Some said that was okay, because it would keep the earth's heat from escaping, too. Anyway, it would make the planet temporarily colder.'' She shivered. "I guess the theory's right.''

"Another spot on the seal," Tuttu said. "It's winter anyway. Come November, there won't be any fucking sun anyway.''

"Yeah." She thought of that. Damn good luck, at least for the Arctic. "So it won't really matter, will it?''

"It *will* matter." He raised the shotgun, sighted on an iceberg, mimed shooting it. "It will matter because we can get the seal earlier.''

Something growled from the beach ahead of them. Claudia squinted, tried to make out the shape in the light. Nothing white—she'd see that, if it was nanuq, a polar bear. She reached up for the gun at her shoulder, felt the emptiness, then held out her left hand to Tuttu.

"Give me my gun, Tuttu," she said calmly. She pulled off her left mitten with her teeth.

He hissed—he heard the sound, too—then turned, but by the noise his feet made as he shifted his weight, Claudia didn't know if he was lining up his shot or turning to her. She squinted harder, and made out a dark shape against a patch of snow: something smaller, not a bear, about fifty yards away and moving fast toward them.

"I know how the gun shoots, Tuttu," she said. "I know how to hit that thing."

"No way, woman," Tuttu said. "I can hit it."

Claudia glanced over at Tuttu. As he brought the gun to his shoulder, he slid the receiver back, sliding a shell into the chamber: click-chunk. She moved slightly to the right, giving him room. The animal growled, stopped, and she saw its head shift from Tuttu to her and back. Good, she thought, confuse the critter. She moved a little bit more to her right. It clacked its jaws, shut up, ran, and leapt at her.

Tuttu fired. A flash of flaming gas burst out of the barrel, and a slug shot through the air. Yes, slug, Claudia thought, not hearing the sound of shot spreading; she heard the sound of one big slug ripping the air, not the sound of many pieces of lead. Tuttu grunted. She watched the animal tumble toward her, heard and saw the slug hit it just as she heard something clatter to the ground to her left. The slug hit the animal, at fifty feet a firm thunk; it expelled air—whoof! —then rolled, crunched into the snow.

Something black moved behind the animal on the ground, a second animal, a hundred feet behind it, then fifty. Claudia looked over at Tuttu. He had fallen to the ground, and was now sitting up, rubbing his shoulder and shaking his head. Her gun lay on the snow between them, the stock of the shotgun pointing toward her. The animal clacked its jaws, whoofing.

Claudia stepped to the gun, swung down, grabbed it by the barrel with her right hand, and put her left hand around the stock. Slug or shot? she thought. How did Tuttu load it? No time to ask. Sliding the receiver back, hearing the comforting click of the second shell moving up into the chamber, Claudia put the butt of the stock to her shoulder. She spread her feet slightly, braced for the kick of the slug, hoped to hell Tuttu had loaded shot second. Deer shot. As she settled the stock into her armpit she brought the barrel up, looking quickly for the animal, aiming toward where she had heard it stop clicking its jaw.

The thing was black and the light was dim but its teeth were a white flash through the air. She put the teeth in her sights, lowered the barrel slightly, and pulled the trigger— pulled like her dad had taught her, slow, smooth, with the whole finger, not the fingertip.

Another flash of flame and smoke spat out the barrel, thrilling in the twilight. The Winchester kicked slightly, not hard like the slug, gentle like with shot. She chambered another round, braced to fire again.

The shot sang out of the gun, dozens of bits of steel whirring through the air. It hit the black beast, and the animal quivered in mid-stride. It flipped around, stopped, fell. Another? she asked herself. Claudia looked into the night, up the beach. No more. She lowered the shotgun, walked up to the two animals.

They were each barely four feet long, not quite three feet from front paws to top of head. She rolled the first animal over with the tip of her boot. A dog. A thin, emaciated dog, ribs poking through its skin, a wet, red wad of hamburger where its chest had been. She ejected the third shell, caught it as it came out, loaded it back into the magazine. Tuttu came up to her.

"That gun's got a kick," he said.

"Why the hell didn't you load buck first?" she yelled at him. "Of course it's got a kick if you load a slugger." She clicked the safety on, kneeled down to look at the dogs.

Tuttu shook his head. "I had it loaded to kill," he explained. "Slug, then shot. Slug to stop it, shot to finish it off. They don't make a lot of shells anymore," he explained. "First shot's got to count these days."

"*Second* shot's got to count, too." Claudia rolled the dog back over. "Poor thing."

"Could have been a polar bear," Tuttu said. "Ya know?"

"Yeah." She slung her Winchester over her shoulder, adjusting the strap so it rubbed against the little silver piece of duct tape; its weight felt good on her shoulder. "*A dog*. The village lets dogs run loose?"

He shook his head. "We've been eating most of 'em. I

saved three bitches, two studs—got 'em in an old house next to the qareqi. Going to need sled dogs someday." Tuttu kneeled down next to the second dog, the black dog, and felt its neck. "This one slipped its collar. It's not mine, though." He pulled his knife out, began gutting it. "Good eating, dog—the Koreans are right about that."

"Shit." She turned away, walked down the beach from him, felt the shotgun on her shoulder. Claudia sighed, slipped it off. Holding it in both hands, she glared at Tuttu. "Guess I shouldn't have this, huh? Here." He ignored her, kept gutting the dog she had killed. *"Here."*

"I don't know, *anguguq*," Tuttu said, glancing up. "Hunter."

Claudia stopped at the word, set the butt of the shotgun on the ground. *"Hunter?"* She rolled the Inupiaq word around in her head, translated the phrase: *one who has grown into a hunter of small game.* She smiled, touched the strap of the shotgun.

"Hunter," he said. He turned to her, held up the liver, no bigger than his hand, steaming in the cold. "Your shot, you get the good parts."

Claudia kneeled next to him, reached out to take the liver, then shook her head. "Uh, I think . . ." Christ, she didn't want to eat raw dog's liver. "I think, *Masu*, yes, she is the old woman, we should honor her with these kills . . ." *What the hell are you saying?*

Tuttu grinned, stuffed the entrails back in the dog's body, then lifted it up by its legs. He held her kill out to her. "Take it," he said. "Take it back to the house and show them what you have done."

Claudia slung her shotgun over her shoulder, grasped the thin legs of the dog. Tuttu stood, picked up the dog he'd killed, and they walked back down the beach. At the path up to the qaregi, he stopped and rested, putting the dead dog down.

"You know," Tuttu said, "some of the men say that a woman should not hunt." He held up a hand as she started to protest. "But you *are* a good shot. Perhaps it is better that our hunters be good shots."

Claudia nodded. "Perhaps—"

"Anthropologist . . . I spoke of this problem to Malgi, and he said . . . He said I should ask you." He bit his lip, and his voice cracked a little. "*Should* women hunt?"

Christ, Claudia thought, had he *planned* this, dogs and all? Had Malgi seen it? It didn't make sense. The dog dripped blood at her feet, and its weight grew heavy in her arms, the weight of the shotgun digging into her shoulder . . . She wanted to scream, "Fuck yes, women should hunt, what did I just do?"

Instead, she mulled the question, cleared her throat, feeling herself go into "lecture gear," Rob used to call it. "In the old days, I have heard, *some* women hunted"—she hefted the dog—"if that is what they were good at. We—in these days, Tuttu, I think we will have to follow the ways of the old days. And they say, I think, that if women can hunt well"—she raised the dog high—"then they can damn well hunt."

Tuttu listened, his face solemn as he absorbed the idea. He raised his eyebrows, and then squinted his eyes, a hard look on his face that made Claudia tremble.

"It is good that women can hunt," he said finally, "because then they will also be able to shoot. They can have guns"—he waved at Claudia's Winchester—"and I think we will want some women to have guns."

She squinted at him, shrugged. "I don't understand."

"Soldiers," he said. "Warriors. We might need warriors."

The weight of the gun, of the dead dog, felt heavier still, and the strap seemed to cut deeper into her shoulder. Warriors? Claudia thought. That was not what she wanted with the gun, not that, not to *kill*. Who would she have to kill, why?

"But to hunt," Tuttu added. "Women hunting?" His eyes opened wide, his mouth a little *O*, as if some imp had snuck up behind him and whacked him on the back. "Even *whales*?" he asked, whispering.

Claudia smiled, thinking of the great mammals, thinking of the spring when the leads would open and the ocean would team—she hoped—with the leviathans. God, yes, she thought. *Whales*. Agviq.

"Even whales," she said. And she said the phrase she would say a thousand times again. "If agviq is willing."

"Ai," said Tuttu, standing, and they went back to the qaregi.

A few weeks later, when the time between sunrise and sunset was no more than a few hours, Claudia and Tammy walked at the foot of the bluffs to the beached barge, scavenging for firewood. One of the tugs had been pushed over onto its side, keel high out of the water. The barge itself rested solid on the beach, mooring ropes still attached to bulldozers high up on the bluff, the ropes rubbing across the name of the barge: MERCURY. Portable lights had been set up to light the barge's unloading, but they had been knocked down. Broken shipping crates littered the deck of the barge, cardboard boxes and canned goods spilling out of the crates. Pieces of the crates had been washed up on the beach.

Tammy stopped, pointed at a red pickup truck, its front wheels hanging over the edge of the barge. "Had a little looting there after the radiation came," she said. "Tuttu tried to organize an unloading crew, but things got, uh, crazy. There's still some stuff there, though: drums of flour and a whole bladder of fuel oil. We've been meaning to salvage it all."

Claudia remembered the *Mercury* moving by Pingasagruk in early August, the day of the war. The first barge of the short shipping season—the narrow window of opportunity when the shore ice had broken up and the pack ice had moved out to sea—there should have been half a dozen barges after that. She didn't have to wonder what had happened to the rest of the barges; if the crews had had any sense, they would have landed at the first village and gotten out of the fallout. She marveled at the courage and dedication of *Mercury*'s crew. It would have taken another day or two to get to Barrow after the war day.

"What happened to the barge crew?" she asked.

Turning to Claudia, Tammy shook her head and pointed at the tug beached next to the barge. Its pilot house was scorched, its windows had been shot out. "A waste," she said, "a damn waste. Those people may have saved our ass by coming here, and for what?" She jerked her head up the coast. "The ravine; they're in the ravine."

Somebody fired a rifle from the top of the bluff, the bullets pinging maybe twenty feet over their heads.

Tammy and Claudia looked at each other after the first shot, hit the dirt when a second bullet whizzed by, and by the third round they were down on their bellies crawling toward the base of the bluff. At the bluff they hugged the side of the hill, burrowing into the slight dusting of snow that had fallen the night before. Claudia slipped her Winchester off her shoulder; since Tuttu had given her back her gun and they'd run into the dogs, she had carried it whenever she walked around town. She released the safety and started to slide back the receiver. Tammy held her hand, put a finger to her lips, pointed up. Claudia nodded.

She couldn't see the person firing from the bluff; he or she must have been back a few feet from the edge. The rifle fired again, and Claudia tried to identify the rifle by the sound, a brief *pock-pock-pock*. Tammy cocked an ear at the noise, too, then visibly shivered.

"Assault rifle," she whispered to Claudia. "Military— heard a lot of them in that madness after the nukes." She pointed at the barge. *Pock-pock-pock*: the windows on the red truck shattered.

"Sounds like three-round bursts," Claudia said. "What's that old assault rifle the Army used?"

"M-sixteen," Tammy said. "Uh-uh—those are full automatic only. This guy's firing bursts."

Claudia stared over at her. "You some kind of gun nut, girl?"

Tammy blushed. "Worked at a rifle range once." She glared back at Claudia. "Hell, it's a living. Was." The shooter fired again. *Pock-pock-pock*. "Could be some kind of selective fire model, maybe a Ruger Mini-fourteen," she added.

"Mini-fourteen," Claudia said. "Eskimo scouts sometimes used Mini-fourteens." She remembered a footnote to some research she had done on subsistence hunting. Back in the 1980s the Eskimo Scouts wanted a selective fire assault rifle, since as hunters they were used to shooting single shot; they wanted a military gun they could use for hunting, too, if they could con the National Guard into supplying it. "What's he doing?" Claudia asked. "Target practice?" That would be stupid, she thought; everyone knew bullets were in short supply.

Tammy shrugged, pointed at the barge again. *Pock, pock, pock,* the bullets flew through the air and hit the barge. One hit a pallet of plywood sheets, and the plywood began to burn. The line of bullets danced along the barge, through packing crates and tipped-over four-wheelers, to a big gray rubber bag that looked like a deflated whale. As the bullets hit they briefly flared in the early-morning light.

"Incendiaries," Claudia said, realizing what the bullets were. "Flamers."

"Flamers?" Tammy asked. *"Shit, the fuel bladder."* She looked up, at the bare face of the cliff edge, the hard sand and snow and pea gravel sloping up to the top. Tammy shoved Claudia around, pushed her up. "You've got to stop him—he's going to blow the fuel!"

"What?" Claudia looked back at the barge, at the fiery bullets hitting more pallets of wood, then up at the cliff. Tammy shoved her again. "No," she said, "not that way." She imagined them coming over the bluff edge, scrambling up, the shooter hearing the sound and cutting them down as they came up. "No—*this* way."

Claudia scrambled north up the beach, back to where a cluster of houses lined the bluff edge. The shooter would be south of the houses. She ran up a narrow cut in the bluff, where spring snow melt had carved a vee in the face, like walking up a rock chimney. *Pock-pock-pock,* the man—if it was a man—fired. She came to the top, Tammy behind her, ran over to the north side of a house, the man still firing. Christ, she thought, couldn't he get his range? Tammy stopped behind her; Claudia held a finger up to her lips, pointed north along the bluff, toward the qaregi.

"Get Tuttu," she whispered. Tammy nodded, ran off.

The east wall of the building, the side away from the ocean, slanted south, so that the wall hid her from the shooter. Sliding along the wall, Claudia jacked a shell into the receiver, a slug, she remembered—Tuttu's idea of a load. She shook her head, ejected the slug, and loaded the buckshot: one-ounce buck, enough to stop a man, and easier to aim. Better.

Pock-pock-pock, the shots continued. What the hell, what the hell, she kept thinking. He was firing three-shot bursts, and she didn't know if he would switch to full automatic or what. Claudia tried to imagine the man's distance, his height, tried to line up the shot before she came out of cover. She had hunted small game before, tracked them and hit them on the run. She had killed ducks and one time even a coyote that had been harassing the family cattle. But rabbits were rabbits, ducks were ducks, and this was a man. Combat, she thought, this was combat, and she'd never done combat—not stalking combat, that encounter with Tuttu had been pure reaction, adrenaline moving her, not this conscious attack. And for what? Maybe the guy was target shooting. So she would shoot him for that?

No, she argued with herself, that wasn't it, she knew he was trying to blow the barge, blow the fuel bladder. Someone with a grudge, she thought, someone who wanted to wreck their fuel supply. She hadn't even known about it before—Tuttu hadn't told her, and she wondered what else he hadn't said—but she didn't have to think hard to figure out the importance of fuel. Fuel would power generators, if they needed electricity, it would power four-wheelers and outboard engines, give them the range to hunt, to feed themselves. That fuel bladder might mean death or survival. But she wasn't sure she could kill him . . .

Claudia set the butt of the shotgun against her armpit, barrel pointing down, ready to fire the gun as she came around the building. She checked that the safety was off, rested her finger against the trigger. Breathing in slowly, calming herself, she took one long breath, held it, stepped around the corner of the building, and raised the shotgun.

The fuel bladder exploded. *Pock-pock-pock*, she heard another burst. An expanding cloud of flaming gas rose up from the barge, a man backlit by the explosion. Warm air washed over her, the stench of unexploded fuel pushed toward her. Claudia lined up the gun sites, the man—yes, it was a man—two hundred feet away. Take him, she thought, pull the trigger. No, she thought again, the damage is done, why kill him? The man turned to her, turning from the blast, a skinny rifle dangling from a strap wrapped around his arm. A red hat pulled low over his forehead concealed his eyes, but for a brief moment she could see the lower half of his face: clean-shaven cheeks and chin, a thin little mustache over his lip. Then he saw her and raised the assault rifle, the quick movement pushing the hat back as the stock of the gun came up to his shoulder.

She pulled the trigger. As her finger pulled back, as her fingertip folded back to her palm, a barrel of fuel exploded on the *Mercury*. The sound startled her, and she jerked back, the tip of the shotgun rising up as she fired. The man pitched forward, crouching, and the buckshot screamed over his head. Something red fell to the earth, the man rolled, and Claudia ducked back behind the building. She jacked another shell in. Bullets hit against the side of the house, one bullet tearing through the thin wall at the corner two feet above her head. Claudia scurried back along the side of the house. Somebody moved behind her, footsteps crunching in the snow, and she whirled, shotgun ready, then relaxed. It was Natchiq, Tuttu's cousin.

"Natchiq," she said, lowering the Winchester.

"Where is he?" Natchiq held up the thirty-ought-six she had given him days ago, loading a shell. Claudia waved down toward the side of the house. Inside the house, something caught on fire.

Natchiq ran along the west wall of the house, crouched, rolled, and disappeared around the corner. Claudia swallowed her fear, followed him. She ducked down, peered around the edge. Natchiq looked along the bluff, fanning his rifle out in front of him, toward a building on the other side of Stevenson Street.

"Where'd he go?" he asked her.

Claudia shrugged. "I don't know." She looked down at the ground, at a red hat in the snow, pointed.

Natchiq picked up the hat, held it out to her. The crown of the hat had been shredded, opened up. BLACKROCK CONSTRUCTION, it said across the brim of the hat, and below that, CMFIC. "Edward's hat," Natchiq said, " 'Chief Mother Fucker in Charge.' *Sonofabitch*."

She took the hat on the end of her shotgun barrel, let the hat slide down the gun through the hole in the crown. Lucky bastard, she thought. Another inch and she'd have shredded his face. "Edward?" she asked, remembering the guy who had harassed her. "The mayor?"

"Ex-mayor," Natchiq said. He looked out at the burning barge. "*Anaq*. Shit. We were going to try to off-load that fuel tomorrow, get those barrels of food out of there."

Tuttu ran up with Tammy and Kanayuq; the two men had their rifles. Claudia let the hat slide off the barrel, locked the safety. She picked the hat up and handed it to Tuttu. He took it, pushed his fist through the hole, looked at Claudia, at her shotgun, at the brim of the hat.

"You could have shot a little lower," he said. She shrugged. "This is our old mayor's hat, isn't it?" he asked. Natchiq nodded. "Mayor Ed got this hat from one of the companies that, uh, charged the Borough rates somewhat in excess of the market price," he explained to Claudia. "The guy you and Tammy saw shoot up the barge, the guy you shot at, he was wearin' this hat?"

"I didn't see anything," Tammy said. She looked at Claudia. "Just heard the rifle firing. What'd the rifle look like?"

"He wore the hat," Claudia said. "Uh, it was a skinny rifle, a long thing—a magazine—coming out of the stock." She glanced over at the burning barge, the house burning on the bluff. No one tried to put the fires out; they just stood there arguing hats and guns.

"No handle at the top?" Tammy asked; Claudia shook her head. "That'd be a Mini-fourteen then. Incendiary bullets. Where'd he get incendiary bullets?"

"Same place Edward got a Mini-fourteen," Natchiq said.

"Scouts," Tuttu said. "Alaska National Guard, Eskimo scouts. We used to do maneuvers together, 'til he got drunk and they yanked his commission."

Groups of villagers came down the road from town, down from Browerville. The flames on the *Mercury* were dying down, though some had spread to the tug moored alongside;

the flames of the house leapt up the roof, and they had to move away from the heat. Natchiq jerked his chin at the approaching people.

"We'd better take care of Edward quick and easy," Tuttu said.

"Ought to clear it with the elders—" Natchiq protested.

Tuttu stared at Natchiq, smiled at Kanayuq. "You want to go pay our respects to the mayor?" he asked. Natchiq shook his head.

"Right on," said Kanayuq. "Let's do it." They both looked at Natchiq, he looked at Claudia, and then, sighing, he slowly nodded. The three men turned, laid their rifles across their arms like they were hunting, and walked off.

A few minutes later, Claudia heard the shots echoing across the town—*crack, crack, crack*—and she knew that they had found their game.

Later, she checked Edward's body in the ravine, counted the bullet holes, and felt the top of his head. She thought that there should be some cuts in his scalp, at his crown, but found nothing. He'd shaved recently, she saw, using a bad razor; cuts sliced his jaw, his chin, his upper lip. She stared at the smooth face, tried to match it with the face she saw shooting in the dusk, but something seemed wrong. Edward's face was too wide, his eyes too narrow, his hair or something like that was wrong. She shrugged, stared at the hat, and after a while convinced herself that it had been Edward, yes, Edward had fired those shots, he'd been the one to blow the barge.

I guess, she thought. *I guess*.

A few days later, long after the barge had burned out, and the house on the bluff burned to the ground, Tuttu called the heads of the various families together and met at Stuaqpak. About twenty people stood around at the front of the store, by the checkout counters, by the magazine racks and the paperback book displays and the empty trays that had held candy and bubble gum and cigarettes. The rows of canned goods and over-the-counter drugs and toothpaste and camping supplies filled the main part of the store, boxes of older equipment set on the racks next to new camp stoves in plastic shrink wrap, or faded yellow coils of rope hanging next to new spools of shiny polystyrene cord. Tacked to the shelves were little yellow inventory lists, a strict accounting of every item.

Tuttu held a wad of such lists in his hand, the food lists, the fuel lists, the lists of essentials. Stuaqpak had row upon row of cosmetics—home perm kits and more cans of hair dye like Belinda had used—but no one cared about that; you couldn't eat eyeshadow and lipstick. Representatives from the various houses hung together in groups, whispering among themselves. Claudia didn't recognize half of them, but some of the families looked familiar. One group consisted of mostly taniks, a couple of guys and a chubby woman in her late forties with frosted blond hair. They looked vaguely familiar, and then she recognized Mick, the bush pilot, again. Karl sat on a counter, a big hideous gold nugget watch on his beefy wrist, talking to the woman. She wondered how they had survived the little massacre and then remembered seeing Mick and Karl with Edward; right, they must have been in his family's house.

"We got a problem," Tuttu said. He held up the lists, as if that explained everything. "The problem is, we're runnin' out of food."

"Got lots of food," a short, stocky guy sitting on one of the checkout counters yelled. He waved at the store shelves.

Tuttu shook his head. "*Had* lots of food, Uugaq," he said. "Would have had, if the ex-mayor hadn't shot up the barge."

"He didn't shoot it up, Toot-Toot," Karl yelled. "I was with him. Drinking." He squinted his eyes at Tuttu. "You know that."

"Yeah, we found him drunk," Natchiq said. "You're right about that."

"Fuck off," Karl said. "Eddie was an asshole but he couldn't have shot that barge. He was so smashed he'd be lucky to find the right end of a gun."

"Doesn't take much skill to shoot up a barge," Tuttu said. "Claudia shot his hat off him and we found him with a Mini-fourteen, the barrel hot and a half-empty magazine."

Karl squinted, shook his head. "All he did was go out and take a pee. I didn't see him take the rifle."

"Lot of things you never saw, Karl," Tuttu said quietly. "Edward blew the barge and he blew a lot of fuel and some food. We could have used the fuel to go down to Atqasuk and check the store there." Tuttu looked at Karl and Mick, then sighed. "I crunched some numbers, man. Looked over the old Stuaqpak records, and did a new inventory. Lot of stuff got looted after the war. Counting what should be in town, what probably is gone—well, I powered up my old laptop PC and did some calculations. It's going to be close, and I'm not sure we'll make it."

"Make it to *when*?" the white woman asked.

"Yeah," Mick said. "How long we got to last? The war might have ended and help could be coming any day now."

Tuttu shook his head. "Get real, fucker. We've been monitoring the radio, and there's *nothing* out there. Tell 'em, Natchiq."

Natchiq rose up from next to the magazine rack, where he had been leaning against the wall. "Nobody's home," he said. "We've been listening at the cable station, monitoring three times a day. Nothin' coming in, UHF, VHF, AM, FM, shortwave, you name it. No Russkies, no Japs, no lower-48, it's just one long hissing."

"And even if there is someone alive," Tuttu added, "you think they got time to come take care of us? What you want, *tanik*, a goddamn seven-four-seven to swoop down and take you back to Houston? Come on."

They argued on like that, back and forth, and Claudia listened to the discussion, analyzing, intellectualizing. Basic shock, she thought, death 'n' dying on a big scale. Denial, bargaining, acceptance, death, that's what they were going through on the village scale, over and over, little stages, little deaths. The death of civilization, the death of a country, the death of a town, and now maybe the death of humanity itself. They were bargaining, trying to cut deals, not coming to the acceptance that their way of life was over. It shocked her, because it seemed so obvious.

She'd hit acceptance almost automatically, it had come to her when she'd seen the whales breach that first day at

Pingasagruk. She'd figured it out, all right. Her world had ended, she knew that, it had seemed so obvious, but here some still hadn't made that connection. It didn't make sense, since Barrow had to have seen more death than she could possibly have seen. Wouldn't that have made it all so obvious? Or had the village become numb to death, and now they were waiting for rescue like Santa Claus?

"It's over, asshole," Tuttu was yelling, and Mick—his voice gruff and stubborn—was yelling back, "It ain't over 'til it's over," and they weren't getting to where they should be, which Claudia knew because Tuttu had told her was the pooling and confiscation of every supply, and rationing, and acceptance of his plan. Then Malgi got up, and the room went quiet, because he talked in a whisper and when an elder talked in a whisper, you shut up.

"I think," Malgi said, "I think that it does not matter." He waved his hands left and right and smiled at Tuttu, at Mick. "It does not matter if we are all alone or if help will come, not now, because there is no help *now*, is there?" He looked at Mick.

"Well, no," he admitted.

"And even if help comes, will we want it?" Malgi asked.

Mick frowned. "What do you mean?"

"What if the Russians won the war?" he asked. The angatkok grinned. "What if someone *else* won the war? We might not want their help. Think of those long years before the white man came, all those years we waited for their help, not knowing we really wanted it. Think of the great help we got: measles—"

"—penicillin," Mick said.

"—alcohol," Malgi said.

"—cable TV—"

"—BIA homes—"

"—freezers—"

"—pollution—"

"—cigarettes—"

"—lung cancer—"

"—rifles—"

"Okay, rifles," Malgi admitted. "And outboard motors

and sno-gos and computers and four-wheelers and pickup trucks and VCRs and planes and a bunch of other shit that's really great but which we can't use—''

''—because Edward blew up the barge,'' Natchiq said.

''Yes,'' said Malgi, ''because *Edward* blew up the barge, and because someday all that fuel would have run out anyway, all the bullets will have been used up, all the metal will have rusted, and then where will we be? Where will we be?''

''Back where we were,'' said Tuttu.

Malgi smiled. ''That was a rhetorical question,'' he said, and Claudia remembered suddenly that Malgi had been a deacon in the church, he'd even delivered a few sermons, and he'd been in the Toastmaster club, so he could throw out phrases like that. A rhetorical question, she thought, but that was the answer, yes, that was the one she had seen.

Back where they were. Back to a time where infants were lucky to live to adulthood, where being an elder meant you'd lived to forty and if you were a woman your teeth had been ground to nubs from chewing hides, where people starved regularly and where a child born in winter sometimes got left out on the ice. She'd read the nineteenth century accounts and she wasn't going to glorify it one damn bit: the life of a pre-contact Inupiaq had been rough as hell.

But, she thought, but they *had* lived totally off the resources of the Arctic, and you couldn't take that from them. *They lived.* Damn it if they hadn't survived in a place most taniks thought impossible to survive in, and damned if they hadn't done it for nearly seven thousand years.

''So that's what we're going to do?'' asked Mick. ''You're going to go back to being savages?''

''No,'' Claudia whispered, her quiet voice filling in the silence. ''No, no going back. Not to that which the Inupiaq were or had become. Something else . . . something *better*.'' She saw it in her mind, then, saw the great thing they could do: Utqiagvik held great riches, metal that wouldn't rust for centuries, ideas that could be used and adapted. She saw the thing they had almost become in the mid-twentieth century, a synthesis of old culture and new technology, before they had blown it in the nineties.

"*Yeah*, anthropologist?" Mick asked. "You some kind of romantic, are you? Is this all that noble savage crap I used to read about?"

"*Listen to her*," Malgi shouted. "The anthropologist knows." The elder nodded at her, prodding. "Go on."

She shook her head, not sure how to explain. "The Inupiaq are—are *becoming*," she said. "And I don't know what." But she could taste it, taste the flesh of the whale, of agviq. That was the taste of the future, she knew, the taste of the sea and the brine and the blood. "Or how," she added.

Tuttu stepped forward, arms crossed on his chest, defiant. "She's right. We're becoming . . . something." He lowered his arms, shook the yellow list. "But for now, we can't think of that. Yet. For now, we have to think about . . . about how we're going to feed two hundred people for the next two months."

The people in Stuaqpak grew a little silent, and then started talking among themselves. She could feel the idea taking hold, Tuttu's romantic vision, her vision, Malgi's vision. They'd seen what she had seen, and what they had seen was hope. Denial, bargaining, acceptance . . . Claudia knew there was one thing wrong with that scenario, though: *sometimes you didn't die.*

Back in college a friend of hers, Phil, an old lover, had gotten testicular cancer. It used to be fatal but they had come up with a new treatment and Phil had told everyone that "fuck if I'm going to die, I'll beat the damn cancer." After they had cut off one of his balls and pumped him full of cancer-killing drugs, she'd visited Phil with a touchy-feely friend of hers, Ellen, and Phil had sat there in his hospital johnnies making jokes about how "they can't say ol' Phil has balls now." In the elevator going out Ellen had whispered to Claudia one word: *denial.* And a year later Phil flashed a slip of paper in Ellen's face (because Claudia had told him the story) with NERD spelled out on his lab results. *No Evidence of Recurrent Disease.*

Sometimes you didn't die, Claudia thought, and she kind of had a hunch that *not* dying sometimes meant believing that you wouldn't die, even if you really ought to. Hope.

Utqiagvik had to have hope, because if they had hope, then they might make it. She watched them argue and chew on the idea, and then she saw something else flash across their faces, something ugly.

"Well, I don't know," said Mick. "What do you want us to do?" It was a challenge, Claudia saw, not really a question.

"Put everything in Stuaqpak," Tuttu said. "I know a lot of the houses have supplies of your own, that you haven't put everything here." He paused. "That you haven't put everything back."

"We've put a little in," Uugaq said. "Didn't I bring in that case of toothpaste?"

"Sure," said Tuttu, "and Karl brought back a whole crate of foam cups. And we've got enough paper plates for a century of picnics. *Good idea*," he sneered. "We can run a contest, see what the best recipe is for Styrofoam mousse and baked Crest."

"Man, we need some of that stuff," said a short, fat guy Claudia remembered as John. "You think I'm going to give up my supplies if everyone else does? So that you can ration it out, they get fat, and we starve? *Bullshit*."

"You're right, Siqpan. I don't think anyone should give up their supplies"—he looked around the room, staring at each person—"unless *everyone* does."

"How you going to make sure no one holds out?" Mick asked. "Strip search 'em?" He groped toward the frosted blonde, and she squirmed away. His wife, Pat. A couple of men laughed at that.

"Pick a day," Tuttu said. "Everyone brings all their food to Stuaqpak. And then we go around to each house, and search it. Anything left behind—I'm sure people will *forget* things—gets taken."

"Fuck that," Mick said.

"Bullshit," Karl said.

"Communism," Siqpan added.

The group starting arguing, voices rising, and Claudia looked to Tuttu, he to her, at Malgi, and she saw where it was going. They wouldn't do it. They were too used to owning, too used to having possessions, not used to sharing.

That's what got lost with the hunting, she thought. People owned things then, sure, that's how an umialik got rich, but a good hunter shared his game. He might get the best parts, but the meat got shared, passed from his hunting partner, who might be his brother-in-law, to his grandma, to his uncle, around and around, in a complicated network based on family connections, so that no one starved, no one went without unless everyone starved. But when people quit hunting, when they quit sharing food, it all fell apart, and it became *mine, mine, mine*.

Natchiq moved around to Tuttu's right, and Kanayuq to his left, and out from underneath their atigis they pulled not their rifles, but Mini-14s with big magazines, and she bet they weren't set on three-shot bursts. The two cousins slid back the bolts on their assault rifles, locking and loading the guns, and at the sound the room suddenly shut up.

"Okay," said Tuttu. "We won't *ask* for donations anymore, and we won't *tell* you to contribute. But we're taking Stuaqpak now, it's my qaregi's, because we've put *everything* in it, and if you want anything . . . Come and get it."

"*Hey*," Mick said, "I put shit in here, I'm not going to let you keep it."

"Sure, Mick," said Tuttu. He flipped through the inventory sheet. "Some lipstick, right? And I think you donated a box of bubble gum." Tuttu reached down to the candy rack, picked up the last remaining box of gum there. "*Here*." He flung the gum at Mick. "Anybody *equally* generous can have their stuff back. We don't mind." He flipped through the list again. "Toothbrushes? Yeah, someone turned in some toothbrushes. Twenty cans of hair dye? That might be worthwhile when we all get gray hair, huh? Plastic forks? Deodorant? Toothpicks? This is valuable crap, right?"

Karl and a couple of the men moved forward, but Natchiq and Kanayuq lowered their assault rifles to chest height, and the men backed off. They moved back to the door, shaking their heads, and the crowd broke up.

"Bring it all in!" Tuttu shouted after them. "Bring it all in or nobody gets anything." Mick turned at the door to say something, glared at Tuttu, shook his head, and walked out.

"Nobody gets anything," Tuttu whispered.

The cousins lowered their guns, set the safeties. As they got down off the checkout counters, Claudia noticed their hands were shaking.

Gonna be trouble, she thought. Gonna be *bad* trouble.

Chapter 8

STUAQPAK was black, brown-black, the black that a room got when the sun set and the lights had been out and eyes adjusted to night sight, pupils dilated so that the irises were little rings. A candle lantern dangled from a rope on the ceiling, casting a pool of light a body wide on the first floor. The lantern swung back and forth in a narrow arc, a pendulum, making the circle of light dance around. Every now and then the candle caught a glint of glass or steel: display cases tipped over, racks of sunglasses strewn on the floor, the barrel of a rifle poking out from cover, the small circle of a hunting scope.

Silent soldiers, Claudia thought, peering out from her position along the ledge of a balcony looking down from the second floor onto the first. They're damn good at waiting, at being still in an uncomfortable position for an uncomfortable amount of time. "Oscar's Army," Tuttu called them, using Malgi's tanik name. Natchiq, Tuttu, and Kanayuq, of course, and she and Tammy and a boy named Puvak. Six pairs of eyes peering into the darkness.

Well, seven eyes, she corrected herself. All but Natchiq wore black eye patches over one eye, their shooting eye; Natchiq wore dark glasses, the rubber cup on his scope folded back. It was Tuttu's idea, the eye patches. The shooting eye would get adjusted to the dark behind the patch. If someone came into Stuaqpak carrying a flashlight—

and they probably would—Natchiq in the dark glasses would shoot out the light, Tammy would shoot out the candle with a kid's water pistol—an Uzi water gun—and when it got dark again, they'd flip the patches back and shoot with the night-dilated eye. "The poor man's night-vision goggles," Tuttu called the trick.

Boxes and crates cluttered the west side of the second-floor balcony, the odd angles casting triangular shadows. Trademarks of famous brand-name televisions and appliances had been printed on the boxes, but Tuttu had pulled a shell game: inside the boxes were food, essential supplies, the unnecessary stuff stored downstairs in food boxes. Like a Marxist physician doing triage, he'd separated the Stuaqpak goods into three categories: that which was necessary for survival, that which might help them live longer, and that which was totally useless. It was amazing how much junk in the store fell in the latter category: all the vanity items, innumerable little knickknacks, and things like clothes that did not cover or keep you warm, tools that performed no useful function. Waste. All waste.

Cold pervaded the room, a clean, pure cold, the cold of a place that had been without heat for some time, so that every object had cooled to the same temperature. A thermograph of the room would have shown the candle lantern glowing orange-red, six bodies red, and everything else blue or turquoise or green. No heat, all cold, all waiting. Claudia thought of the guard duty as training, training for that time when the tuvaq had formed and they would sit on the ice waiting for seals.

Now they waited for brigands, scoundrels, and thieves: whoever was determined to raid Stuaqpak. Tuttu had laid down the gauntlet, had scratched the line in the snow: those who share with all share what is in Stuaqpak, and those who share with none get none. Claudia saw what he had done, knew as well as Malgi and Tuttu the importance of it. If they were to survive beyond when the store food ran out, they had to learn to share. Put-up or shut-up time, she thought.

Claudia sat at the southwest corner of the balcony, with a clear view down to the checkout counters. To her right

Kanayuq stood up, stretched, then quickly ducked down behind a row of sand-filled fifty-five-gallon drums at the top of a stairway connecting the two floors. Racks of souvenir T-shirts for the tourleys hung along the south wall, with sayings on them like LONDON, PARIS, ROME, BARROW, or MY GRANDMA WENT TO THE TOP OF THE WORLD AND ALL SHE GOT ME WAS THIS DAMN T-SHIRT.

Over where appliances used to be sold, to Claudia's left, Tuttu guarded the main stash of supplies; he had a good shot at the main door. A little armory had been set up in the northwest corner, all the shells and cartridges and guns packed behind boxes of books and more fifty-five-gallon drums of sand. Tammy hunched down in the armory, ammo laid out before her, ready to toss shells and cartridges to anyone who needed them, extra guns and rifles before her if someone's weapon jammed. Natchiq, the man in shades, set up position at the northwest corner of the balcony, and between him and Tuttu was Puvak, a thirteen-year-old boy who'd turned out to be a hell of a shot with a .22 rifle.

Puvak had come from his father's house, the house of Amaguq, a second cousin of Tuttu. Amaguq's family had been the only other villagers to go along with Tuttu's plan. Shortly after he'd come over to Tuttu's side, Amaguq's house had been burned to the ground and he and his son had moved into the qaregi; they split watch duty between Stuaqpak and the big house. Amaguq's watch had fought off an attack the night before, and Claudia knew there'd be another raid that night. Amaguq had taken a bullet in the arm—fortunately, just a .22 bullet and hardly a wound at all—and like his namesake, the wolf, he had been all for taking the offensive, fangs bared. But they didn't know who had attacked, and it was only two houses against maybe twenty, so all they could do was defend what they had.

And wait.

Claudia didn't think they could keep holding off attacks much longer; they had only so much food, though they had a lot of bullets. A *lot* of bullets. She'd asked Tuttu about this, and had been surprised at how quickly he agreed. His strategy wasn't to fight them off; his plan was to wait the brigands out.

"They know there's stuff in Stuaqpak," he had explained earlier in the day. "So when stuff runs out they'll come here. But they'll also think their neighbors have stuff, and if we make it hard to get at Stuaqpak, they'll steal from their neighbors. When the bullies take all the food from the victims, the victims will come to us."

But Claudia hadn't been so sure the victims wouldn't just start fighting for the bullies. She knew bullies, knew that once a bully defeated someone, he could make that person do what he wanted. Tuttu was a little more confident. "If the victims come to us with anything they've got left," he said, "they get an equal share of what we have. But if they go to a bully, all they get are handouts. They'll come to us. When we've got a real army, we'll crush the bullies."

So they waited, waited for the bullies to be bullies, and waited for the victims to become soldiers. Claudia looked at the meager supplies on the second floor of Stuaqpak and knew that when everyone joined together there'd barely be enough to share. But that wasn't the point, she saw: the point was to get everyone to share, and like the parable of Christ and the loaves and fishes, they'd find the food from there.

The big heavy exterior door creaked open, and several sets of footsteps—Claudia counted at least three—thudded down the arctic entryway, the hall connecting the main floor of the store to the outside. Around her she heard the dull clicks as rounds got chambered into firearms. She slid the receiver back on her own shotgun, hand trembling a bit as the first shell rose up in front of the firing pin.

Tuttu chambered a round, then ejected it, twice, his signal to Tammy to shoot out the candle. A stream of water whisked up to the little light, and Claudia felt the cool spray drift down toward her as the flame sizzled out. The footsteps stopped as the light went out, and then a big flashlight came on, light glowing down the entryway. Pistachio shells—Puvak had found a box of packaged nuts—crackled as the intruders came around the entryway, and Claudia swore she could hear Natchiq breathe in as he set up his shot.

The person with the flashlight rolled across the doorway, arm holding out the lamp like Dante's Bertrans in Hell holding out his head. Natchiq's rifle cracked once, and the flashlight shattered out. Her shot now. Claudia flipped her eyepatch up, aimed the shotgun to the left of where the flashlight had been, a buck load in the chamber, and squeezed the trigger. The muzzle flash lit up the room like heat lightning, and she fell back behind cover just before two bullets thudded into the steel drums and books before her. She thought she heard a thud as her shot hit something, and then she heard a low groan.

Two shots from Kanayuq and Tuttu or Puvak answered back, bullets seeking muzzle flashes, and she knew how it was going to be: shoot for where you saw people firing from, and when you shot, *move*, although they had the advantage, because they could fire behind easy cover and the brigands below had to find cover.

Tuttu's poor-man's night vision goggles only worked with the first volley, because any night-sight got zapped the minute a firearm fired. Claudia thought she saw someone scuttle under the balcony, out of range, something they had worried about. If they could keep brigands from coming in, everything would be safe, but if the raiders got under the balcony and out from the open space from the second floor down to the first, the brigands would be under them and could move around at will. Tuttu didn't worry about that, because he said they'd have to go back out the way they came, and it's a lot harder to scuttle when you're dragging a fifty-pound box of deodorant.

Someone ran up the stairs to the second floor. Kanayuq put his rifle down and picked up a Mini-14, the sound of the magazine clicking in and the bolt being locked loud and distinct in the brief silence. The person on the stairs grunted something, and then screeched: a woman slipping on the marbles Puvak had littered on the steps and then falling on what the boy called "arctic pungi sticks," boards spiked with ten-penny nails laid across the treads. A light flared from the stairs, something caught fire, and the woman on the stairs tossed a torch or something at Kanayuq.

Thinking it over later, Claudia couldn't decide if the woman's rage had given her better sight, or if she had just been lucky. The torch whirled end over end toward Kanayuq's sniping post, bounced off a wall, and as she heard the glass shatter, Claudia knew what it was. A cloud of gas or diesel fuel spilled from the Molotov cocktail, catching a rack of T-shirts on fire, and raining down on Kanayuq. If he'd stayed down he would have been fine—a couple of rolls on the ground and the fire would have gone out—but when you're on fire you don't think. Kanayuq rose up, flames crawling up his arm, and in the dark he might as well have put a glow-in-the-dark target over his chest. Two shots fired from under the second floor, and the shots thunked into Kanayuq hard and fast, some kind of bullet, Claudia thought, that gave up all its energy as soon as it hit something: tumblers or dum-dums or whatever.

The flames ignited the T-shirts, and that wall began to burn. Two more bottles broke below, and then a third, a fourth, a hail of flaming bombs, and Claudia saw their strategy. They were going to smoke Oscar's Army out, and burn down Stuaqpak in the process. The woman on the stairs ran back down—Claudia hoped her foot hurt like hell—and two more people ran back to the entrance, rolling across the doorway, and out.

"Cover me!" Natchiq yelled, and he ran from his hiding place over to Kanayuq.

The point of a rifle poked around the doorway, but Tuttu fired two quick rounds and the barrel pulled back. Tammy hurled two fire extinguishers across the room to Natchiq. Natchiq grabbed one, sprayed the flames licking at Kanayuq's parka, then knelt down at his brother's side. He opened up Kanayuq's parka, put a hand on his chest, and when he held it up to the light of the flames burning at the wall, Claudia could see Natchiq's hand sticky with blood up to the wrist. Natchiq pounded his fist on the floor, looked up, grabbed the Mini-14 and fired a full magazine at the doorway, the wood splintering away from the frame.

Big long flames flared up to the second floor, thick acrid smoke curling up to them. Claudia glanced down at the first floor, over at Tuttu. He shouted something, over and over, screaming at Natchiq, it looked like. Natchiq stood, looked down at his brother, grabbed something from the dead man's neck and yanked it loose, and ran over to Tuttu.

Tammy said something to Claudia, and then through the roaring of the flames she began to hear.

"—get the *hell* out, grab everything, get to the roof," Tammy shouted.

Claudia snapped out of the fear and the shock and the light and the smoke stinging her throat. She ejected a shell from her shotgun, reached down for the boxes of shells next to her, threw them in a little daypack, and ran to Tammy.

Tammy had slung six rifles over her shoulders, looking like a girl guerrilla, two pistols stuck in her belt. She crammed box after box of shells and cartridges into a big duffel bag, hurled the bag to a ladder coming down from the roof, then crammed more shells into another bag. Little Puvak pulled a box of beans after him, and Tuttu and Natchiq were pushing a box marked TOILET PAPER—God knows what it really is, Claudia thought—toward the door. She looked around for something to save, saw a box of monofilament line, fishing hooks, lures, and other tackle, and grabbed that.

"They'll have the loading bay doors covered," Tuttu said. He had a big coil of half-inch hollow-core polypropylene rope over his shoulder.

Claudia nodded; they'd anticipated this. The second-floor stockroom door went down to a big loading bay and another stockroom. But the ladder went up to the roof, through an access hatch. Natchiq climbed up the ladder, and they started passing boxes up to him.

"Throw the food down at those assholes," Tuttu yelled, "and hang on to the ammunition."

Claudia, Tammy, and Puvak scampered around trying to salvage what they could, but the smoke got thicker and thicker, and finally Tuttu stopped them and pushed first Puvak, then Tammy, up the ladder. Claudia followed them, then paused at the top of the ladder and looked down at Tuttu.

The smoke curled up toward her, sucking up the open hole, and she could feel the heat of the flames rising toward the second floor. Tuttu stared back at the boxes they'd cached, at Kanayuq's body toward the stairs. She could imagine what he was thinking: Stuaqpak was the last link to the old world, the storehouse of everything that had connected them to Outside. As the flames licked at the television sets, the microwave ovens, the tourley knickknacks, at the cosmetics counter and the big empty meat freezers, they consumed whatever it was that had made them part of the old world, a world with a Coke can on every street corner and wads of old bubble gum on every street.

"Son of a bitch," Tuttu muttered, and he climbed up the ladder, joining her on the roof.

A southerly wind blew into their faces as they came out onto the flat corrugated steel of the roof. The smoke curled up and out of the opening, and then Tuttu dogged the hatch. Stuaqpak's roof curled down to the east, toward the arctic entry. The five of them kneeled down on the ribbed roof, the flames roaring beneath them. At the north end of the building, Claudia knew, a second-floor exit opened out to a metal staircase; someone would be at the staircase, right below them. Next to the staircase would be the freight-loading bays, so the whole north end would be covered. Tuttu looked at the pile of boxes—ten total of food, plus the two duffels of firearms and ammunition, and Claudia's box of fishing gear—and shook his head.

"Okay," he whispered, "take what you can carry and push the rest toward the edge." He pointed at the north side of the roof. "Then we'll head south and go over that way." Tuttu handed the coil of rope to Natchiq. "I'll kick the stuff over the edge and follow you."

"What are you going to do?" Claudia asked.

"Go," Tuttu said.

They rummaged through the boxes, grabbing cans of food, bags of beans, guns, ammunition, whatever. Claudia stuck some packets of hooks and lures in her little daypack, crammed her pockets full of more shells, and topped it off with a bag of pinto beans. Natchiq grabbed the big duffel bag Tammy had salvaged, leaving the second duffel for Tuttu. Tammy and Puvak followed Natchiq to the south edge, running in a crouch. Claudia watched Tuttu, waited to see what he did.

He pushed the boxes of food to the edge, and one box spilled open and rolls of toilet paper unfurled, streaming like comets. Tuttu grabbed a handful of shells and threw them over the side. Bullets pinged up at the roof, but the angle was wrong, whoever was down there couldn't get a clear shot.

"You got us!" Tuttu yelled down at them. "Let us get down safely and we'll give you what we have."

"Throw it over," someone yelled. Mick's voice, Claudia thought. Definitely a tanik.

"You won't shoot us?" Tuttu yelled.

"Of course not," Mick shouted.

Right, thought Claudia.

"Okay," Tuttu said. "It's not much." He looked over at Claudia, saw that she hadn't gone to the other end, and waved her back. "Here it comes." Tuttu started throwing cans, boxes of shells, the rest of whatever was in the boxes off the north side. The stuff thudded on the snow, and the brigands began scurrying around, shouts and yells rising up from the ground as they fought over the supplies.

Claudia ran to the south edge. Natchiq had fastened the big coil of yellow rope to a vent housing, and she looped the rope around her, looked over the edge—clear—and walked down the side of the building. Natchiq helped her to the ground. He had a Mini-14 out—the one Kanayuq had used—and watched the front of the building. They'd come down in an alley between Stuaqpak and the Arctic Slope Regional Corporation building. Puvak and Tammy were running toward the ASRC building and to the courthouse across the street.

She looked up in time to see Tuttu on the edge, throwing the second duffel to the ground. Natchiq caught it just as it hit the snow, then threw it over with the other duffel. Tuttu rappeled down, rifle slung over his shoulder, with a big huge handgun stuck in his belt.

"Here," he said to Claudia, thrusting the rifle at her. "Natchiq, take both duffels back to the qaregi."

"Where you goin'?" Natchiq asked.

"*Go*," Tuttu said.

The wind from the south kicked up, snow blowing at their backs. Smoke billowed out from the vent stacks on the roof of Stuaqpak, and flames and more smoke spilled out from the entryway. Something exploded from inside, and the brigands at the north end shouted, a great fireball gushing out from the loading bays. Someone ran across the street to the east, not noticing them.

"It's going to take the church," Natchiq whispered.

The flames from the north wall had spread out, backlighting Stuaqpak like a halo, and jumping across the street to the old white timber-framed Presbyterian church. Wind roared down the space between ASRC and Stuaqpak, pulling the fire north.

Tuttu looked at the fire, at the flames leaping at a two-story building attached to the back of the church and directly across from Stuaqpak. "Go," he said again. "Forget the church. Get to the qaregi." Claudia and Natchiq stared at him. "Now." He pulled out the big handgun from his belt. Forty-four magnum Desert Eagle, Claudia idly noticed. Her dad had had one, but she'd sold it when he died—too much gun for her.

"Where you goin'?" Natchiq asked again.

"Got to do something I should have done before," Tuttu said, slamming a magazine into the butt of the foot-long pistol. "Now go—please?"

Natchiq nodded, and Claudia helped him drag the duffels over to ASRC, and they scurried across the street to the hotel and the courthouse. Puvak had run ahead and gotten his dad, and Amaguq came up to Natchiq and helped them with the gear. Natchiq looked back at the fire, at the church beginning to burn.

"We ought to save the church," he said.

"Too late," Claudia whispered, "too late."

Tuttu ran around the west side of ASRC, up the side of the building, and disappeared. Natchiq looked at Amaguq, at Tuttu running away. He and Puvak's father stared at each other, some information being exchanged that Claudia couldn't figure, and then Natchiq slammed a fresh magazine into the Mini-14 and followed Tuttu into the roaring night.

_____ *Chapter 9* _____

LATER that night, Tuttu and Natchiq came back, soot on their faces and their beards frosted from hard breathing. When Amaguq quizzed them about where they had been and what they had done, they glared at him and said nothing. In the morning, in the brief daylight, old man Malgi took his army out to see what was left of Stuaqpak.

The red paint on the steel siding of the building had bubbled away, and the bare metal was scorched black and brown where it had oxidized. Little curlicues of smoke rose up from the big squat building, the snow melted down to gravel a good hundred feet from its edges. No one dared enter, because of the heat, because there would be nothing left inside anyway. Someday, Claudia thought, other archaeologists will sift through this and wonder what had happened and why and how it had come to pass.

Two whale ribs, old and bleached and honeycombed with foramen, still stood before where the church had been, their edges slightly charred. All the outbuildings had been connected to the main sanctuary of the church, and the fire had raced down the halls and burned everything—parsonage, church offices, social hall—to the foundation. Only scorched timbers and charred pilings poking out of the permafrost remained of the church—that and a cross that crumbled into charcoal when Malgi touched it. After the Stuaqpak fire had done its work on the church, the wind had to have shifted and blown back south, because the museum—a square building with a peaked, pyramid-shaped roof still containing some borough offices—had only been scorched on the south side.

The public health service hospital was on the other side of the borough building; except for the clinic, the hospital had been almost totally torched in the bad days right after the war day. The village graveyard curved to the east beyond the three complexes: God, government, sickness. Only the temple of politics remained—it figures, thought Claudia. There was nothing neat and orderly about the cemetery: just clumps of crosses and whale ribs and jaws stuck in the tundra and blocks of concrete holding the dead in the hard ground. North of the graveyard was the lagoon and the old sewage treatment plant and then Browerville.

Natchiq wore two rifles that day, the Mini-14 and the Ruger. They all carried an extra firearm, a sidearm or another rifle. Claudia thought they looked ridiculous and knew they felt scared half out of their hides. Natchiq squinted at a figure on the opposite shore of the lagoon, then raised his rifle and sighted through the scope. As he slid the bolt back, Tuttu reached up and pushed the rifle barrel down.

"No," Tuttu said, "not yet, not like this."

Claudia pulled out her binoculars, peered at the person in Browerville. He stared back at them, a fat man with a rifle slung over his shoulder, too. From behind a building came two more men, one of whom Claudia recognized as Mick. She thought the other could be Siqpan.

"Tuttu," she said, handing him the binoculars, "look."

He took the binocs from her, watched for a few seconds, then handed them back. Malgi moved around to Natchiq's right, Puvak to his left, Amaguq by his boy, Tammy next to Claudia. Yeah, Claudia thought, one volley and they could wipe each other out and end the game once and for all. As she took the binoculars from Tuttu, he caught her eye, shook his head slightly.

"Better get back to the qaregi," he said.

They eased back around a big mausoleum that tipped crooked out of the snow. Natchiq had dropped the Ruger in favor of the Mini-14, and they slunk back to safety. One of the men in Browerville shook a rifle at them, the steel barrel flashing at them, and Mick and his army, too, retreated.

Back at the qaregi entrance, James, Paula's husband, waved at them from a watch post at the qaregi roof, where they'd been in a trapdoor over the skylight. A wooden platform had been built on the apex of the roof, and sandbags and blocks of ice had been stacked around the railing. Over the watch post had been built a little roof, also sandbagged, to protect them from grenades or firebombs thrown onto the platform. Yellow ice draped the sides of the qaregi, to make it slippery: yellow ice from piss and used washing water. It'd stink next summer, Claudia thought, if they made it to next summer. James ducked down behind the sandbags and rapped on the roof. At his signal, Masu unlatched the outside tunnel door and, climbing over a pile of rubble and old drums protecting the entrance, they went back inside.

Tuttu's dogs had been quartered off the entrance tunnel, in a storeroom cleared out for them and blocked off by a chain-link gate. The dogs rushed to the gate as they came by, begging for scraps. Through the gate Puvak scratched the neck of a dog he called Rick, a mottled male with a hound's big head but pointy, husky ears. Masu had propped the katak hatch open and they rose up into the redoubt.

Amaguq's and Tuttu's families had been crammed into the qaregi, sleeping bags rolled up to make room during the day, boxes of food and jugs of water stashed along the sides. A low fire burned in the wood-coal stove, the room barely above freezing. James climbed down a ladder from where the skylight had been, and at a nod from Amaguq, Puvak took his post.

Masu sat on the bench by the stove, stitching a pair of mukluks. When they came in Paula started dishing out some sort of stew with mysterious bits of meat floating in it (Claudia could guess, but didn't try), and the big extended family sat down to eat, to prepare for the siege, to think the next week out.

"We've got a problem," the old man said. "Those guys

want to kill us.'' No one really had to say it, but Malgi did, anyway.

The light of two candles, and the glow from the glass window in the stove, barely lit the dim room. With the steel hatch shut over the skylight, even the meager sunlight didn't come in. Claudia looked over the faces, at the grime etched in wrinkles and folds of skins, at the bags under their eyes from little sleep, and she sighed. Somebody wanted to kill them? she thought. We're killing ourselves.

''We can hold out,'' Amaguq said.

''Maybe,'' Malgi replied. He turned to Tuttu. ''You revise your calculations?''

Tuttu nodded, tapped the ENTER key on his laptop PC, watched the numbers roll up on the little screen. ''We'll do okay. With just the food in here, on full rations, we can last three days; half rations, six days. We've got enough water for ten days, if we just drink it. That's if we play the defensive and just wait and don't go scrounging food.''

''Why wait?'' Natchiq asked.

''Yah,'' said Tuttu. ''That's what I'm gettin' at.''

''I know,'' Malgi said. ''But I think we should wait.'' He stared at Tuttu, stroked the raven's head around his neck. Authority posturing, Claudia thought. ''Grandson,'' he added.

Tuttu looked down, then up, daring the angatkok. ''I respect that, Grandfather, but we can't wait forever. Mick, Karl . . . They probably have more food than we do—they ought to, since they'll probably rob it from the rest of the village.''

''We want them to do that,'' Malgi said.

''I know!'' Tuttu yelled. He looked down, mumbled an apology. ''I mean, we agreed on that, Grandfather.''

Right, Claudia thought, the original plan: let the bullies starve their victims into rebellion.

Amaguq looked at Malgi, then at Tuttu, confused. ''I don't understand, Cousin. You don't think that plan will still work?''

''It will eventually,'' Tuttu said, ''but it's already failed.'' He shook his head. ''We thought we could defend Stuaqpak long enough for the bullies' victims to starve and come to us, see Stuaqpak as salvation. We'd then unite and crush the oppressors, right?'' Claudia smiled as the Marxist rhetoric slipped into his speech. "But it didn't work out that way—we didn't count on Mick and his gang just smoking us out, burning Stuaqpak down.''

Good point, Claudia thought. She didn't know if Mick or Karl had figured out Malgi's logic, or if they had just gone crazy. It didn't matter; that plan had failed. Without the lure of Stuaqpak's riches, they couldn't count on recruits.

"The victims could still rise up,'' Amaguq said.

"True,'' Tuttu said. "But could they rise up soon enough? Can we count on them to do our work for us before *our* supplies run out?''

"The tuvaq will form soon,'' Malgi said. "We can hunt seals.''

Tuttu shook his head, the longer hairs at his nape whipping out. "No, not while Mick's gang lays siege to us. They can pin down the qaregi, shoot us coming and going. That's what I'd do.''

"I could sneak out,'' Natchiq said.

"Too risky,'' Tuttu replied. "Besides, we have to settle this. It's a war, don't you see? It's Mick's way or ours, and if we don't take care of Mick . . . well, we have to take care of him, if we want to survive.'' He stared hard at Malgi, and Malgi smiled, then nodded.

Claudia caught the unspoken dialogue in that smile and nod. Settle it: Mick's way of greed and tanik values—wait for rescue, every man for himself—versus Malgi's way of sharing and Inupiaq values—work together, survive together.

Malgi sighed, smiled again. "I did not mean wait *forever*, Grandson.'' He held up a finger. "Wait one day, two days. Let them attack. We can hold them off—how much ammunition do we have?''

Natchiq grinned. "Boxes. Maybe a thousand rounds, various calibers.'' He glanced at Tammy. "Thanks to Little Nuna.''

Tammy blushed. "It was the nearest thing to grab.''

"Okay,'' Malgi continued. "So we take an attack or two, figure out who's in Mick's army, who he's got fighting for him—''

"I know who,'' Tuttu said. "Karl—well, he's strategy,

the boss, I guess. Mick's wife, Pat; I think Puvak's pungi sticks got her. Uh, maybe Siqpan, probably Uugaq, a couple others."

"—and then we go out and kill them."

Natchiq nodded. "Fucking ay—you got it, Grandfather." He crinkled his brow. "But, hey, Tuttu and I know where those guys are in Browerville. We can get 'em right now. Why wait?"

Tuttu clapped his cousin on the back. "Ai, I see." He smiled, a broad smile, gums spread back from his teeth. "Let them think they have the upper hand."

"Yah," said the old man.

"You know where they are?" Amaguq asked.

"Tracked 'em back last night," Natchiq said. "That bitch, Pat: she bled in the snow, and we just followed her home."

"So why didn't you take 'em then?" James asked.

"Because, Aluaq," Tuttu explained, "we didn't have them all together, in one place. I want them all, every one of them." His voice got deeper, lower. "Grandfather's right. Let them come. Let them use up their bullets. And when they think they have us"—he rubbed his palms together—"we will kill *them*."

Amaguq had the watch when the next attack came. The shrill siren they had hooked up—a smoke alarm wired to a simple doorbell switch—broke the relative quiet of muffled snores in the dancehouse. Tuttu woke up first, shaking the other men alert, and Puvak dashed down the katak before anyone else could make it up the ladder. The boy passed the five dogs back into the house—Masu took their leashes and tied them each to a corner post—and then he ran up to the front entrance. James—Aluaq, "coal," Claudia had to remember to call him, he'd finally picked an Inupiaq name—joined Puvak, and Claudia and Tammy went up top.

Claudia peered over through a gun slit, listening to Amaguq as he whispered to Tuttu. Tammy passed Mini-14s up to them, laid magazines out on the little shelves arranged around the edge of the guard post, next to gun slits. Something moved from around the pilings of the hotel, and in the quiet Claudia thought she heard boots crunch on snow.

"At least six men," Amaguq guessed. "They think they're sneaky, dashing around the Top o' the World pilings." He pointed up at the sky. "Moon reflects right off the ice and lights up the whole area."

Another figure ran out from under the hotel, around the big pilings that supported the whole structure. Chain link fence had once circled the foundation, but Natchiq had gone out the day before and cut holes in it, gaps on the Browerville side. Natchiq called it his fish trap—"Funnel them in like burbot," he said.

"Let them get into position," Tuttu said. "Puvak ready?"

Amaguq pressed a switch on a CB, spoke into it. "You ready to go to bed, boy?"

"Getting sleepy, Dad," Puvak came back. Code, Claudia remembered, in case Mick's brigands had a CB, too.

"Okay," Tuttu said. He looked around the guard tower, at Tammy, Natchiq, Amaguq, Claudia, then checked his watch. "You guys get ready. Draw their fire, hit 'em if you can, but try to wound. On three. One, two, three: fire!"

Claudia peered through the gun slit, focusing on a corner of the hotel foundation, where a stairway came up to the east entrance. Someone crouched between two posts, chain link fencing blocking the way. The Mini-14 felt light in her hands, its weight almost like a toy, but she kept remembering the holes a gun like it had put in Kanayuq. The Mini was small and the bullets light, but they could chew up a body; that was the idea. She fired on Tuttu's signal, one quick burst.

The guns of Oscar's army burped into the night, like firecrackers, yes, Tuttu's Vietnam vet uncle had it right. Like firecrackers, pop-pop-pop, a brief silence, and then pop-pop pop-pop again as two guns fired at the same time. Mick's group returned the fire, and Claudia counted muzzle flashes, six, Amaguq had been right, six flashes in the night. She kept on her target, aiming low, like Tuttu had said, to scare or wound, not kill. The attackers retreated back into the shadows under the hotel, and then Amaguq whispered into the CB again.

Puvak fired from below, not under the hotel, where he would have been firing flat on, but up, at a little white blob toward the back end of the building. Claudia had lent him her shotgun, showed him the spread and how to change the choke, and the boy had figured out the Winchester well. He hit the white blob on the first shot, hit it with number-six duck shot, and the white piece of plywood burst into splinters. The square of wood had been nailed to the roof, two ropes tied to it through holes drilled in either end. The ropes went slack and fell away from each other, and in the short silence they could hear the scrap two-by-fours thudding down the side of the hotel and hitting the snow.

Claudia couldn't see the stuff the wood was attached to, but that was the idea: neither could the attackers. At Tuttu's signal, they fired another volley, driving Mick's squad out from under the hotel and toward the netting Puvak's shot had released. The brigands ran into the black fishnet, and as they twisted and turned, she bit her lip to keep from finishing them. That hadn't been the idea, but Claudia felt the urge. Finish them off.

"Cease fire," Tuttu said, in voice loud enough to carry across the street between the qaregi and the hotel.

Their guns clattered as they laid them down. One raider squeezed under the netting and ran toward Puvak's post at the dancehouse entrance. Puvak had poked his head up, glancing back at his father. Amaguq tried to yell, but then Aluaq burst up from behind the sandbags, Mini-14 at his waist. Paula's husband swung the automatic rifle around, and the sound of bullets spitting out in one torrent told Claudia he'd put the rifle on full automatic.

Through the slit she saw Puvak turn at his father's cry, and then Puvak ducked down, shotgun raised like a spear. The attacker ran toward the boy, took a leap, and Aluaq's burst caught the man as he arced toward the entrance. The man jerked around, Puvak aimed at the sound and fired, and the boy's shot spun the man backward, three forces opposing and meeting, reaction canceling reaction. The hug of the earth conquered all, and when momentum failed the body came to the hard snow. Later, when Amaguq ran out to get the dead man's ammunition, he identified the body: a fat, fleshy man.

Siqpan.

The final attack came a night later, on a moonless night. Having figured out the trap under the hotel, the raiders worked their way around to a clump of buildings to the west. Up in the guard post with Tuttu, Claudia happened to glance over at him as he spotted Mick's brigands. Looking to the west, he raised his eyebrows, then smiled, tapped the alarm button, and reached for the CB.

"Elephant pot," Tuttu said, clicking the mike.

Elephant pot, Claudia thought. That had been their code: "elephant pot" meant east, in the direction of Elephant Pot Sewage Haulers, a big warehouse behind the qaregi, on the other side of an old frame house. "Pepe's" meant northwest, toward the Mexican restaurant adjoining the hotel. "Polar Bear" was south, for the daycare center, and "NARL" meant north. Elephant pot: an attack from the east.

Natchiq came up with Amaguq and Malgi; Puvak and Aluaq had gone back to the entrance to guard the dogs. "How many?" Natchiq asked as he came up.

Tuttu shrugged. "Three, maybe four."

Tammy followed the men up, and she and Amaguq moved to the west side, in case the movement on the east was only a diversion. The only thing Tuttu worried about was that Mick had gotten into the National Guard armory and liberated grenade launchers or mortars; they could hold off anything less. It had been a good sign the night before that all the raiders had was rifles, but Tuttu didn't trust that. "Might be testing our defenses," he said. So Amaguq and Tammy were to watch the west, and keep anyone from moving in close. Puvak's father didn't say it, but Claudia guessed that after the night before, he wanted to watch his boy, too.

Most of the house behind them had been stripped for firewood down to floor and frame, but even with the open walls Claudia had a hard time watching the attackers climb up the timbers to the roof. She raised her rifle to force one guy back—he was moving into position higher than them, and she thought it might be possible for him to shoot down into the guard post—but Tuttu stayed her hand, and only smiled at her inquisitive look.

The new moon hadn't yet risen, but the auroras flared in the heavens, green glowing filaments swirling to the east. The light from solar flares crashing into the ionosphere made the frame of the house stand out against the night, and as her eyes adjusted Claudia could see dark figures moving around the house, no more than four people.

"You got your shotgun?" Tuttu whispered to her.

She reached down, exchanged the Mini-14 for the Winchester, then showed it to Tuttu. "Yeah."

"Good." He smiled, the light from the auroras making his teeth almost glow. "Put some double-ought buck in it, and on my signal, shoot at the southwest corner post"—he pointed—"*there*, about a foot up."

"Uh, sure," she said. "Why?"

Tuttu grinned. "Just do it."

Another raider moved up into the house. Claudia thought Mick was being foolish—did he think the defenders hadn't seen them yet? And what would they use for cover once they got up there? Mick's strategy made no sense, except... She saw it now. The five attackers climbed up on the roof of the house, the plywood still intact. Someone on the second floor passed up a long, shiny thing to the raiders on the roof: a ladder. Ah, she thought. They were going to climb onto the qaregi, come down over the side of the guardhouse, down the hatch. Clever. The whispered voices of Mick's men could be heard, hardly fifty feet away. One man passed the ladder up to two men on the roof, and they slid it over toward the qaregi.

"Now," Tuttu said loudly.

Like Tuttu told her to, Claudia fired at the base of the post, the shot spreading out in a narrow choke. Malgi's shotgun fired a few feet down from her target, and Natchiq and Tuttu fired at full automatic at the center posts. The wood splintered away, the two-by-fours snapping at the base, and the house began to crumble.

Ah, Claudia thought, watching the near wall fall away from the qaregi, in on itself. Ah, that explains Tuttu's smile. The house. He'd booby-trapped the house, whittled away its frame so that a shotgun blast or two at the corners would cause it to collapse.

The house imploded, the west wall going first, tearing down the second floor and the roof as it fell, the side and back walls following. Up on the roof, the raiders slid off the smooth plywood, the ladder falling away. One man pushed free just before a wall fell, but two more were caught in the shower of snapping timbers. The sharp, easy cracks, the smooth breaks as entire walls fell in one piece told Claudia that Tuttu had notched every corner, every stress point. It amazed her that the raiders could have climbed on the house at all.

Four raiders made it to the snow, two rolling to safety, one crumbling as he hit, one bouncing on his head. They held their fire, let the two still alive help the wounded away. From Amaguq's side came several bursts of fire, one reply from a little rifle, and then silence. A cloud of dust rose from the fallen building, the wind blowing it away quickly. In less than a minute the night had grown silent again, and then the auroras flared up in a dance for them.

"All right," said Tuttu. "*All right*." He grabbed two more magazines from the ammo box in the center of the guardpost. "Natchiq, Amaguq—let's follow 'em home and finish 'em off." Claudia looked at Tuttu and he must have interpreted her glance as a request to come along. He shook his head. "You guard the qaregi with the rest," he said.

She nodded and did not argue. Crawl around in the night and commit butchery? No, she thought. For once she would not dispute Tuttu's sexism. The three men climbed down inside, picking up Aluaq as they left the qaregi, and she watched them disappear into the night.

Several hours later Tuttu and his partners came back to the qaregi, whooping and hollering, and he told them to forget about guarding, there was no need to guard, get some sleep. But Claudia couldn't get any sleep, because she kept hearing the little popping sounds throughout the night, and she kept seeing the glow on the northern horizon from burning buildings. In the morning, in the brief day, Tuttu took them out to show them his handiwork.

Hanging from the charred whale ribs in front of the church ruins were the bodies of two men, one with a droopy walrus mustache and hound-dog eyes, the other a fat pig of a man whose weight almost collapsed the rib. Because she had to know, Claudia inspected the wounds in their chests. Malgi wiggled a finger in the holes the size of a man's fist, and turned to her and smiled.

"Forty-four magnum," he said. "Yai." And he kicked Mick's body, then Karl's.

A woman's body hung between the two men, a frosted blonde, Pat—the woman Mick had flirted with that day at Stuaqpak. Her boots had been removed and the soles of each foot were pierced with little holes, holes that blood had dried around. Like Kanayuq, there wasn't much left of her chest, either, not much left of her groin, too.

"Two twenty-threes will do that," Tammy said. "Little tumblers, they give up their energy as they roll through flesh." She stared at the bodies, her lower lip clenched between her teeth, then turned away.

A few more bodies had been laid on the ground, some with their throats cut, others with horrid bruises on their heads or longbones bent at unnatural angles. Nine men, one woman, the entire count of Mick's army, Tuttu said. He'd described the final raid in vivid detail, but it had all been a blur to Claudia: following the wounded back to Browerville, picking off the stragglers, running down Karl in a leisurely chase, catching Mick in his own stronghold, burning it down . . . She didn't want to know the details, didn't care; she only wanted to know that the bloodletting was over.

"Take the bodies down," Malgi said. The old man had come to see what his army had done. He walked among the grisly display, prodding the bodies with his foot, tilting a face up with the tip of his unaaq. "Take them down, all of them. We will lay them out on the tundra and treat them with respect."

Tuttu looked up at the old man, his expression changing from the joy of battle to remorse and then—like that! Claudia thought—to shame. Good, she thought, good: it may have been necessary what was done, but we need not find pleasure in it. Kanayuq's cousin looked down, shuffled his feet, then nodded.

"As you wish, Grandfather," he said.

"It is not as I wish," Malgi said. "It is what's right. Remember that others have died, too—Kanayuq, for instance. We should bury them. Bury them all."

And so they took the bodies down, every last one, and carted them through Utqiagvik, stacked like feed sacks in the back of a pickup truck. Meanwhile, Claudia volunteered to sift through the ruins of Stuaqpak to find Kanayuq's bones. Near where he had fallen she found part of a skull, some teeth, and a few longbones. She laid what was left of Natchiq's brother in a wooden ammunition box and carried it out to the ravine south of town.

Beyond the Inupiaq bodies, by the ravine that held the other dead, the remains of Karl's army had been laid on warehouse pallets. Someone had found Edward's body and laid it next to his compatriots. Karl, Edward, Mick, Siqpan, Pat . . . all had been laid out, head to head, faces to the sky. Claudia looked at the recent bodies, stared from them over to the older bodies nearby.

"If you lay these out properly"—she waved a hand at the new bodies—"you should treat the other remains similarly."

"That's a lot of bodies, Claudia," Tuttu said.

She stared at him, nodded. "I know. If it's so easy to kill, it should be hard to bury."

Tuttu glanced at Malgi, and he nodded. "The anthropologist speaks correctly, Grandson." Tuttu sighed.

So the villagers went down into the ravine, and dragged the hundred bodies or more onto the mound at the top of the ravine, out of the trash and animal bones. As well they could, they lined the bodies out, laid out the bones, the bags of skin stretched over the bones. It took them nearly two hours of work, of horrid, disgusting labor. Good, Claudia thought. This should be hard, it should be disgusting.

When they were done, when the bodies had been placed in neat rows, all the walking villagers assembled by the bodies. The living smelled of the dead, a stench covering them: the stench of rotting flesh and the stench of their sweat and their filth. A couple of people had thrown up, but Claudia could not vomit. Her gut felt hard and her heart felt hard. She felt cold, cold from the coming winter, and cold from all the killing. The wind shifted to the south, blowing the smell away from them.

Tuttu and Natchiq and a few others walked around the bodies, splashing liberal amounts of diesel fuel on the dead. . . . The thick, nasty smell of the fuel rose up, drifted away. The villagers moved back into a semicircle. Malgi stood before them, raised his hands.

"We should pray," he said.

They bowed their heads. Claudia looked up at Malgi, caught his eye, then lowered her head. Right, she thought. Malgi had been a deacon in the Presbyterian Church. Of course.

"Dear Father," Malgi said, "we ask forgiveness of these souls. We ask forgiveness of ourselves. Out of violence and ignorance and fear these people have left this world. May they find rest in life after life, and may we find rest in our own lives.

"We send their souls to the Lord, and their bodies back to the earth and the sky and the sea that created them. In fire we cleanse them, and in cleansing them we hope to clean our own bodies, our own souls, so that we may become worthy of more life to come, of the richness of this earth."

Right, Claudia thought. Appeal for redemption, appeal to the God-that-is-the-Land. Make a bequest for that which will allow us to live on. Good, she thought. Good, Malgi, good.

"Amen," he said, and he lit a torch and threw it at the dead.

The flames burst up and the bodies began to burn in a thick, black cloud. Claudia stared at the flames, at the quick oxidation of the shells that once had held lives. Innocents, some of them, she thought. Ignorant or unlucky, in the wrong place at the wrong time. Their bodies burned, as so many bodies had probably burned elsewhere in the war. It did not matter; all bodies burned, either in quick fire or the slow rotting of dirt.

"Did you find Kanayuq's body?" Natchiq asked her.

Claudia looked up, nodded. She handed the box containing Kanayuq's bones to Natchiq. He took the box and they followed him to the other burial area, where the Inupiaq bodies had been laid out on driftwood platforms. Natchiq opened the box and laid an ivory carving inside with the bones—the carving that had been on a thong around Kanayuq's neck, the one Natchiq had recovered at the battle. Claudia caught a glance of the carving before Natchiq closed the box. A fish, Kanayuq's namesake. Next to the body of an old woman, Natchiq laid the box containing his brother's remains. Malgi said some words, and then the villagers headed back into town.

Claudia stayed behind, walked over to the bluff at the southern edge of the old archaeological site. She looked down the coast at the thick black clouds rising up from the ravine, then turned away, into the wind. The cold salt air bit at her eyes, and though the horror of the cremation and the death should have made the tears come, only the wind made the tears come. And so she went down to the beach and cried, let the wind make her cry, and hoped that someday she could find her way back to being human.

Or something.

Chapter 10

TUTTU stood at a podium on the stage in the back of the high school gym, cross-checking items from a series of lists against his laptop computer. Almost everyone in Utqiagvik milled around on the floor of the gym, clutching satchels or small boxes. Three small piles of food and supplies lay behind Tuttu. Tammy and Claudia counted the villagers, once and twice, and then compared censuses.

"One hundred ninety-five," Tammy said.

"One hundred ninety-*six*." She pointed at Tammy—"Ninety-five"—and then at herself—"ninety-*six*."

"Oh: right."

"One ninety-six," Claudia reported to Tuttu—the sum population of walking and breathing Barrow.

Tuttu nodded, looked out at the villagers. Some leaned against the walls of the gym, legs straight out, babes in their laps. The two rows of bleachers had been pushed back against the side walls, and maybe fifteen elders sat in the one row of seats that hadn't been folded up. A dozen light bulbs hung from the ceiling, barely lighting the place. One huge wood stove, section after section of shiny metal-asbestos pipe shooting up to the ceiling, kept the room slightly above freezing. Natchiq and Amaguq stood at the ends of the stage, one by an American flag, another by the

Alaskan flag, Mini-14s butt down on the floor and barrels leaning against their legs.

"Everybody who can walk here?" he asked the crowd.

A hand rose up in the back. "My wife's with auntie," a skinny man said.

Tuttu nodded. "Okay, Igaluk." He looked around the room at the little knots of people. "Anyone missing you can report when I call your houses up here. Is there anyone not here who isn't taking care of an elder or someone sick?" No more hands shot up. "All right: good."

He nodded at Natchiq and Amaguq, and they went to two doors by the front of the room, wrapped chains around the push bars, and closed the chains together with big key locks. They then went to two doors at the front of the gym, took chains from around the inside push bars, and stood waiting.

"I'll give the final warning," Tuttu said, "and then we can start." He took a step behind the podium, leaned forward, and spoke in a slightly louder voice. "This is the last call. We've met for the third time this week, and I know we're all getting a little hungry." He patted his stomach, and there was a nervous giggle through the room. "I'm going to ask you to bring up anything else you've found since yesterday, and we'll add that to the supplies." Tuttu waved at the boxes on the stage. "Meanwhile, Natchiq and Amaguq will be going around the village checking out the houses and any standing buildings they can get into. If they find any supplies beyond the lists you've given me and we all agreed would be allowed"—he waved a bundle of papers—"well, we all know the penalty."

"Confiscation and banishment," Igaluk yelled from the back.

"Right," said Tuttu. "Confiscation and banishment. Now, has anyone forgotten anything?" He glared at the villagers, his gaze going back and forth, up and down. "Are you sure?" Claudia gulped, thinking of the candy bars she and Tammy had turned in the day before. Tuttu was dead serious about this. "Okay, let's start."

Natchiq and Amaguq went out, and the sound of the chains being wrapped on the outside doors rang clear through the quiet room. Their footsteps thumped down the outside hallway of the school, and a few seconds later the exterior door creaked open, then slammed shut.

While the "peanut butter police"—Tammy's name for the two men—went around town, the rest of the village lined up to deliver the last of the supplies (Claudia hoped) they'd guiltily admitted to. Malgi had come up with a slight incentive for turning in things: for every tenth pound of food turned in, a house would get a pound added to their allotment. Tuttu argued that that was like encouraging cheating, but Malgi made a good point: a lot of the food out there didn't belong to anyone. It was old stuff left in abandoned houses, or supplies and caches long forgotten. The bonus would encourage people to search through old houses, to remember emergency stores they had left up at duck camp or out on the tundra.

Claudia and Tammy helped Tuttu with the record keeping, weighing the donations on a big meat scale salvaged from Stuaqpak's ruins. She also did a little anthropology and census taking as the heads of the houses spoke for their extended families. Using the borough records—downloaded into Tuttu's little PC, she marveled, from a disk not destroyed by EMP or cold or fire—she would cross-check her interviews later.

"Family?" she asked as the man who had spoken up earlier came to the stage.

"Igaluk's," he said.

Claudia looked up at him, a man barely Rob's age, a few years younger than Aluaq. His wife—no, a sister-in-law, Claudia thought, he said his wife was with auntie—stood next to him, a pretty woman with the tight curls of a fading perm just touching her shoulders. She wrote down "Igaluk" at the top of a page.

"What's your tanik name?" He gave it to her, and she wrote down the family name and the Christian name. She didn't care about the Christian name, but the last name would help her figure out lineage. "And your wife's maiden name, the tanik name?" That would be the sister's old family name, too, she thought.

"We're Umiaqpaks," the sister-in-law said. " 'Big boat,

ship,' that's what the name means.'' She brushed a curly hair out of her eyes, smiled with some pride. ''My great-grandfather was an orphan, his village got wiped out by flu in that epidemic, you know?'' Claudia nodded; the big one in 1914. ''He and his sister, my auntie, survived. He came on that ship, the Bear, so they called him Umiaqpak. My Christian name's Martha, my Inupiaq name is 'Masik.' ''

Gill, thought Claudia, and then she saw Masik glance at Igaluk, saw a smile flash across his lips. Gill and Fish, she thought. She looked at the couple, nodded, then wrote Masik's name down. Masik continued to recite her lineage, the auntie's names, the children's names—her niece in her arms, a toddler clutching her atigi—and the whole details of the extended family: Igaluk, the two sisters, the niece and nephew, a brother to the sisters, the old aunt, and—Igaluk's sister-in-law admitted—another boy playing in the back of the gym, her son, age eight.

''Father?'' Claudia asked. She felt cold and scientific and intrusive with the question.

The sister-in-law blushed, looked down. ''I don't know.''

Igaluk looked away, seeming not to hear the question, and Claudia figured it out. Right, a little spouse sharing, okay. Masik gave Igaluk life, the gill giving breath to the fish; did they consciously choose those names? Claudia wondered. She shrugged, wrote down ''nid,'' old cataloging shorthand for ''non-identifiable.'' One more question, though she could guess the answer. ''Any hunting, fishing partners?'' That could indicate ties she hadn't thought of, usually some sort of relation, but often just ties through friendship.

Igaluk beamed at the question. ''I fish with Aluaq,'' he said.

''Hunt?'' she asked.

Igaluk looked up at Tuttu, tapping in figures on the laptop computer. ''I'll learn,'' he said.

''Right.'' Tammy weighed their donations and wrote them out a receipt. Tuttu punched in the numbers, and Claudia turned over a new sheet to interview the next family.

It went on like that, a slow process, but the peanut butter police had even slower work. All told, Claudia recorded

statistics and lineages for thirty-two nuclear families crammed
into twenty-five houses. One-hundred ninety-six in the room,
eleven more outside too sick or old to come into the gym, or
caring for the sick. Ten of the extended families lived in
Browerville, none in the newer BIA houses. Tuttu's was the
only traditional sod house, but about half the houses had
been partially insulated with sod walls before the ground
froze solid.

About half an hour after all the latest food had been
turned in, the outer doors creaked open, and every villager
fell silent as the chains clanked. All eyes watched Natchiq
and Amaguq come into the gym. Claudia felt a collective
sigh as the peanut butter police came in, neither lugging a
box or sack. The relief was intensified by the way the two
men strode carefree into the room, big smiles on their faces.

"Did you find anything?" Tuttu asked them.

Natchiq looked at Amaguq, grinned, shrugged, and then
pulled out a small clear-plastic bag. He held it up, and the
chatter that had broken out upon their return stopped again.
Then Igaluk, who had been seated by the front, laughed at
what Natchiq had in his hand, and he whispered a word to
his sister-in-law, and the word spread and the room broke
up.

Bubble gum. Natchiq held up a bag of bubble gum.

Tuttu reached down, snatched the bag from Natchiq, and
he slammed the podium. The villagers quickly shut up.
Tuttu shook the bag, condemning the people.

"Whose *is* this?" he yelled. "Whose house does this
come from?"

Natchiq rocked back and forth on his heels, a smile still
on his face. "I don't know, Cousin. We found it under a
drum behind Igaluk's house."

All eyes turned to Igaluk. He shrugged. "Not mine," he
said, grinning, large gaps in his mouth. Igaluk tapped at the
spots where canines and incisors once had been.

"Whose is this?" Tuttu repeated. He looked around the
room, staring from old man to crone to man to boy to
woman to girl. "Whose?"

A small boy, Igaluk's nephew, looked up from the
hardwood floor, faced Tuttu, and stood. "Mine," he said.

"Yours?" Igaluk asked. "Samuel, you *know* the penalty."

"Ai, Uncle," the boy said quietly. "I found it that night after the first raid on Stuaqpak—I think one of those bad guys dropped it, or threw it away. It's not food, Uncle."

Tuttu looked at the kid, nodded. "It's not food, boy. But it is something far more precious, because there may be no more bubble gum. Ever."

"I was *going* to share it with my friends," Samuel said.

Malgi turned to Claudia. "Anthropologist," he asked. "What should we do?"

Shit, she thought, here it comes again. Do I have to decide this boy's fate? They will send him out on the tundra if they think that's what the tradition should be. And they should, if they are to learn sharing. But it's bubble gum, and he's only a boy. She sighed, answered.

"You must learn to share," she said, hoping that Tuttu caught the spin on the word "you"—second person, plural. "We"—her heart caught at the plural again—"must all learn to share, if we are to survive." There, she thought, let Tuttu do with that as he will. He looked at her, at Malgi— who nodded—and back at the boy.

"The anthropologist is right," Tuttu announced. "You must learn to share, boy." He glared at him. "You will share this bubble gum," he said firmly, but gently.

"Yes, sir." The boy looked up, the tone of Tuttu's words hitting him. "You *aren't* going to banish me?"

Tuttu shook his head. "Give one piece to every child in this room, and then return what you have left to me. We will save this for the spring. Do you understand?" He stooped, looked eye to eye with the boy, and laid a hand on his shoulder.

"Ai," he said, turning to distribute the gum.

Tuttu held a grip on the boy's shoulder. "*Samuel.* Is that a good Inupiaq name?"

Samuel glanced over at his uncle, back to Tuttu. "Uncle says that when I find my—inua?—my animal spirit, I will have a real name."

"Ah." Tuttu turned to Malgi. "Anthropologist, Grandfather, can this boy take another name until he finds his inua?"

Claudia shrugged, and Malgi nodded. "Good. Then we will call you 'Kutchuq,' to remind you of your generosity."

"Kutchuq?" the boy asked. He looked at Igaluk. "Uncle?" Igaluk smiled. " 'Gum,' " he said. "It's a good name."

The boy blushed. "Kutchuq. Az-ah." Tuttu let him go, and Kutchuq began giving out pieces of bubble gum to the children.

Kutchuq, Claudia thought. Okay, shame the boy a little. Yes, that was an old Inupiaq strategy, an old classic behavioral strategy. Make light of a transgression, but give it a name, make it long lasting, make it hard to live down. The boy would be reminded of his greed every time someone called his name, and yet he might work that much harder to prove his generosity. She knew he would work that much harder to get a real name, to prove himself as a hunter or as a fisherman, to find the spirit animal that would be special to him and dwell in his soul. Tuttu had handled it right, what did they need her for?

As Kutchuq handed out the bubble gum, Tuttu finished calculating the rations. Working from Claudia's census, he punched the names and ages of each family member, then figured out how many pounds of each supply they could take. As he input the data, as the little laptop did its thinking, a small dot matrix printer plugged into the laptop spat out sheet after sheet of decisions.

Precious equipment, Claudia thought, powered by precious batteries charged by precious fuel. Precious food. She looked over at the rations Tuttu had calculated, gasped at the numbers: each family had maybe a month's supply of food. One month.

Natchiq tore off sheets as they came out, and read out the names of the houses. The families lined up one by one, and took boxes and plastic bags. Claudia helped Tammy and Kanayuq distribute the food, avoiding the questioning stares of the villagers as they saw their bags not being filled, at what little they were granted.

"Any trading is allowed," Tuttu announced, "you can do what you will with the food." The villagers moved forward slowly, no pushing, no shoving, Claudia was glad to see. "And when you are done"—he let the words hang heavy in the air—''that will be it. Anything else we eat, or need, will have to come from the land, or what we can salvage.'' He slammed a fist on the podium, waved a hand at the boxes of food. ''This is it!'' The villagers stopped from their collecting, looked up at him. And then he whispered, almost as if he really meant it, Claudia thought, Tuttu whispered what could have been praise: ''Thanks to Mick and Karl and Edward.''

The wind howled from the northwest, a fall storm out of the North Pole, Odin's hand, Claudia thought, pushing dark and cold and ice upon them. That's how it would have seemed in Scandinavia, but in Utqiagvik the ice was the ice, not God or gods, just a great and horrible force howling in the night.

False winter's dark clouds hovered over the northern hemisphere still: the encompassing and covering clouds of dust and smoke, the microscopic remnants of cities and forests. They could still see the clouds in the brief twilight that passed for day, the sun rising low in the south, the black hood covering the sky. The sun never rose into the false winter, never rose above the clouds, but the cold that the clouds sent down chilled the Arctic that much faster.

Earlier that morning Malgi had walked along the beach with Claudia, asking her seemingly naive questions, but pumping her for knowledge as she pumped him. A chill wind blew down from the north, and to Claudia it felt like any other wind, but Malgi stopped her, and sniffed the air.

''Ai,'' he said. ''Smell that?''

She made a show of breathing in the air deeply, then shook her head. Honor him, make him feel important, she thought, but she truly smelled nothing unusual. ''What *should* I smell?''

Malgi smiled, tapped his right nostril. ''Storm smell,'' he said, ''the smell in the calm. An *electrical* smell, do you not know it? The smell televisions used to give off?''

Used to give off? she asked herself. Ah. ''Ozone?'' At the word a memory from high school came to her: slipping a glowing stick into a bottle, a long piece of wood with an ember at the end, and inside the bottle sulfuric acid bubbling away zinc. The classic chemistry experiment, making hydrogen. The air popped as hydrogen exploded, and left behind was ozone and water. She remembered that faint smell of ozone, a burnt smell, almost. Claudia sniffed again, and the smell of the arctic air meshed with the smell of her childhood.

"Yes, that's it," said Malgi. "Ozone. It is the smell of a storm." He sniffed again. "A *big* storm."

A *big* storm, Claudia thought later as she crawled down the entrance tunnel to the outside door. Snow snuck through cracks around the edges of the door, and the wind puffed in and out, threatening to take the door off its hinges. Like a freight train, she thought. That's how tornado survivors always described the sound of twisters: like a freight train. This wind, though, was more like a night of freight trains, like the hurricane she remembered from early childhood, wind that kept on and on and would seem to never end.

She imagined the wind sweeping around the side of the qaregi, imagined it sloping over its curved walls. The roof of their guard tower might not be there in the morning, she thought, but that would be okay: no need for such protection anymore. Many things might not be there in the morning. Through the cracks in the door the wind whistled, a high-pitched screech that seemed to sneak around the limits of her eardrums. She could feel the pressure on her skin, on the subtler membranes of her body, felt the crackle in the air, and smelled that ozone again, yes, like charred electronics.

Snow piled up on the edges of the drafty door, down the steps into the tunnel. Claudia had crawled down the tunnel in a big sweater, leaving her atigi behind, and regretted it instantly. With bare hands she cleared fine snow from between the cracks of the doorway, then wrapped a short length of rope around the handle, and pulled it shut tighter, cinching the end on a hook by the door. Wind still snuck through, would sneak through any crack it could find, no matter how small, she thought, but it wouldn't be enough to tear the door away. But if more storms like this one were the norm, she thought, they'd have to build a stronger door. Still the qaregi inside kept warm, the wind and cold fading in the trap at the end of the entrance tunnel.

As she turned to go back inside, she heard a groan coming from beneath the screech of the wind, a dull, insistent groan. Like boats. She remembered sleeping on a ship in a harbor once, and that had been like the sound she now heard: the groans of ships in their moorings rubbing against the dock. And yet this sound persisted, moaned underneath the high squeal of the wind. It felt like two giants crashing against each other, two steel giants' bodies grinding body into body. Claudia cocked an ear at the sound as she tried to imagine its source.

Her nerves shivered as the realization came to her. The *ivu*. A storm surge pushed great rafts of ice—old ice, sea ice—up over the new ice, the ice merging, growing, grounding on the sea bottom, and being shoved inland. Utqiagvik's great bluffs might keep the ice from climbing higher than the beach, might prevent the ivu from shearing the village surface like a galloping glacier. And then Claudia remembered the Frozen Family.

Mound 44, she recalled, Old Man Dekin's greatest triumph, an intact house found frozen—bodies and all—in the permafrost. Unlike other tombs, the house hadn't been abandoned, the bodies hadn't been buried; the house had collapsed on mother and children, the roof sealing them in the soil, the soil preserving them for centuries until a pothunter had found a foot, a human foot with skin and toenails, sticking out of the bluff. Reinhardt's memoirs had told how as crew chief he and the rest of Dekin's staff had worked around the clock to get the bodies out "until we felt as dead tired as the people we unearthed," he wrote. The general conclusion had been that an ivu, a raft of ice, had been pushed over the bluff edge and down on the house. They hadn't had a chance. The mother had grabbed a caribou skin, and put an arm around her child. They found her barely a meter from the katak, her chest crushed; she had never made it.

Well, Claudia thought, well, if the ice came, it came, and there didn't seem to be a damn thing she could do about it. She hoped the qaregi was inland enough from the bluff edge, that no great cube of ice would come skidding across the snow and onto their house. She hoped that if the ivu did come, it would kill them quickly. Maybe then the gnawing hunger inside her would end. Maybe then the great mystery of their survival would be over.

She crawled back up the tunnel, glanced back at the firmly shut entrance door, then climbed up the steps to the katak and pushed the floor hatch open. Cold, frosty air rose up into the qaregi, into the warmth of the house, she a seal, perhaps, emerging from the sea. Claudia stepped up and out of the katak, and she dogged the hatch below her.

Safe, she thought, safe. Claudia crawled into her sleeping bag, rolling next to Tammy spoon-to-spoon for warmth, and fell asleep. As the earth groaned below her, and she heard the echoes of the wind still sing in her ears, she hoped that there would be a morning to wake up to, a morning of hard cold and flat, endless ice.

In mid-November, two weeks after the final sharing, and a day after the storm, the people of Malgi's house and a handful of others from some of the other houses gathered at the old village site to watch the sun set for the last time that year—"to watch the rising and setting suns embrace," as Tammy referred to her game with Claudia and the two sticks. Claudia stood by with a final stick, and as the orange ball of the sun fell below the dark clouds, the low rays of the winter sun almost flat and barely warm, she stuck a thin stick in the sun, a few inches from the stick Tammy had set in the sun at sunrise. The sun seemed to balance on top of the stick, like a lollipop, and then it set behind it, the shadow of the stick stretching out and then disappearing.

"Night," Tuttu whispered. "The long night is here."

They filed down to the beach—because the timing seemed right and they had to know sooner or later—and walked down to a little rubber raft on wood skids loaded with sleeping bags and some food. Malgi picked up a long staff, an unaaq, and began to walk out onto the ice. Tuttu, Aluaq, and Amaguq slipped loops of rope over their shoulders, pulled on the raft, and dragged it out onto the ice after Malgi. The old man tapped every few feet, jabbing with the unaaq, jabbing, tapping, walking out onto the ice.

Claudia watched them disappear over a small ridge. She

should be out there, she knew, acquiring knowledge, learning how Malgi judged the ice to be hard enough to support weight, but she couldn't, not just then. Every time Malgi tapped she heard the cracks like rifle shots, saw the ice break away behind her, saw Rob's body cold and blue and seeming to sleep. No.

Tuttu turned, waved at her, and she clicked her citizens band radio on. More precious batteries to use up. "Breaker, breaker, good buddy," Tuttu said from the CB.

Claudia smiled. Right, the Arctic Trucker. "Come on, Hat Head."

"*Hat Head*?" Tuttu asked, then he got the joke. Caribou, Tuttu, antlers for holding hats. "Right. Uh, keep monitoring, Claudia. We'll call if we have trouble. Ten-four."

"Ten-four, good buddy," she said, watching the little raft slide over a ridge and out of sight. "Ten-four."

They built a fire and kept warm, the squelch of the CB malevolent with its implications. Tammy sat next to Claudia on a log by the fire, their backs to the bluff, the wind behind them and blowing gently off the tundra. That worried Claudia, because it could push the ice out to sea if the tuvaq hadn't formed, if the pans of ice hadn't frozen together and become landfast. The ice was scrunched together in big piles against the bluff, then flat and white out from shore, and another jumble of low mountains against the horizon. The Big Dipper hovered over the ice to the west, pointing the way north.

A shooting star rose up from the ice, bright red and then fading to white. Claudia stood up as the CB crackled in her hand. My God, they fell through, they fell through, she thought. And then against the glowing white she saw three figures walking toward shore, a dark shape behind them, and Tuttu's voice came from the CB, three quick sentences.

"We're okay," he said. "Shut the CB off. The tuvaq's formed."

Claudia rushed out to meet them then, the ice firm under her feet now, not scary or tenuous. Tammy came with her, and they took the ropes from Aluaq and Amaguq, who would let them, and not from Tuttu, who wouldn't. Claudia hugged the old man, and he patted her on the back, still tapping the ice lightly with the unaaq.

"Good ice, good ice," Malgi said. "That storm did it. The pressure ridges are almost a hundred feet high, and there's hard ice maybe half a mile out from that. Good ice, the hardest ice I've seen in years."

Tuttu glanced over at her, and she stared into his eyes and he into hers, and she saw there something she hadn't seen for a while, something warm and moist and not hard. Hope, she wanted to say, but no, not quite that. The possibility of hope. Too soon for hope, yet, but the possibility of hope, perhaps.

"The tuvaq's formed," Tuttu said, and in case she didn't understand what that really meant, he explained. "We can hunt seals.

"Maybe we *can* survive."

Chapter 11

WHITE ice, flat ice stretched from the edge of the beach to a jumbled mass against the horizon. The trail down from the qaregi to the beach had been trampled flat and smooth by the daily travels of those on honey bucket duty—whoever had to cart the day's piss and poop to the barrels at the edge of the ice. Malgi led the seal hunting party down the beach to the smooth, hard ice of the tuvaq.

Tuttu followed Malgi, of course, and then came Natchiq and Amaguq and the boy Puvak, and finally Claudia. The temperature had dropped ten degrees the night before, and Claudia had snuck a look at the thermometer, though instinct told her to remain ignorant: better not to know how cold, to not know the cold had dropped to minus thirty below.

She'd put on polypropylene underwear next to her skin, a pile jacket over a sweater and pile pants over her long johns, insulated pants over that, and topped the synthetic clothes with the sheepskin atigi she had finally gotten the stench out of. Masu had made her a pair of boots—*ugrulik* they would be called, Claudia remembered—though they didn't really have bearded seal, or ugruk, skin bottoms. Instead, the tops were of dog fur—the dog Claudia had shot—and the bottoms were rubber from old Air Force mukluks Masu had salvaged from the village dump. Claudia used half a tube of precious Shoe Goo to seal the holes and cracks in the rubber bottoms. The boots were insulated with felt liners from her shoe pacs, and stuffed with caribou fur scraps. With two pairs of wool socks and a polypro liner they were warm as hell.

A compromise, Claudia thought, looking down at her boots, at her insulated pants patched with duct tape, at her sheepskin atigi. Malgi kept asking her what the old ways dictated, how hunters might have dressed before such things as Air Force mukluks appeared in dumps, and she'd dutifully dig though her books and show him. But what it came down to was that they didn't have the materials, didn't have ugruks to make soles with, and so had to use up the modern stuff first.

The sled they pulled was a compromise, too, just like Tuttu pulling the sled instead of the dogs was a compromise. Malgi had wanted them to make a traditional toboggan sled, one of baleen, perhaps, but they didn't have baleen, the hard keratin plates that hung from the mouths of bowhead whales, so what did Malgi expect? Tuttu didn't want to use his dogs, not yet, not until he had a spring litter. Those dogs were precious and Puvak guarded them like his own children. One of the tanik schoolteachers, since deceased, had had a hard plastic sled called a pulkka, a real high-tech Norwegian thing with long fiberglass poles and a padded harness, something the schoolteacher had bought to drag his kid around town in winter. Tuttu had appropriated that from the village supplies, and piled their hunting gear into the neat little nylon bag of the pulkka.

And the rubber boat was a compromise, too, Claudia thought. They'd strapped on the half-inflated rubber raft Malgi had taken with him that day he tested the tuvaq. One of her books had talked about small boats, *umiaqluuraq*, used to retrieve seals in open water. Well, the little skin boats would have been fine, but there wasn't even one in the Barrow museum, just a large umiaq, and so they took the rubber raft.

Malgi led the way, trodding slowly over the flat ice, stabbing occasionally with his unaaq to test the ice, though even to Claudia's untutored eye the ice looked solid and firm. Good habits shouldn't be broken, she thought; she found the steady pock-pock sound of Malgi's staff reassuring. She copied his cadence with her own unaaq, walking next to Tuttu.

The refracted rays of the hiding sun bounced up into the clouds behind them, giving them some light to steer by. A low line of fog rose above the horizon, the *puyugruaq*, a cloud of gray steam below the dark clouds of black that indicated an open lead. The puyugruaq gave them something to steer for, something to head to, and indeed it was why they went out on that morning: at the open lead would be seals.

Each hunter carried a rifle strapped across their shoulders, wrapped in canvas or an old skin, the rifle resting at the small of their backs. Claudia felt the reassuring bounce of the rifle, a 30.06 she'd borrowed from the village armory, six rounds warm and wrapped in foam at the bottom of her parka pocket. Six rounds each, the day's ration. They'd catch seals with that or not at all.

Malgi stopped at something ahead, held out a hand to them to hold back. Tuttu undid the pulkka's belt harness from his waist, stepped forward cautiously to Malgi. He turned back to them, smiled, motioned to the rest of them to join him and Malgi.

The old man stood over a little dome of clear ice, a small iglu about a foot wide, a model of comic-strip Eskimo houses, a little iglu that most people thought western Eskimos really lived in. A crater of jagged ice surrounded the little dome, like the edges of a scrambled egg, and the center of the dome was black and wet.

"The allu," Malgi said, glancing up at Claudia.

"Seal-breathing hole," she said, and Tuttu smiled at that.

"A seal will come up here?" Puvak asked the old man.

Malgi shrugged, smiled back. "Not now. We have made too much noise and probably scared it off. But eventually. See how the ice is thin?" He tapped the dome lightly. "Natchiq"—he smiled at Tuttu's hunting partner, recalling the cousin's namesake—"comes here every hour or so, breaking the ice, keeping it open, taking his long breaths."

"We could hunt the seal here," Natchiq said.

Malgi nodded. "If we wanted . . . if we did not mind holding still, and waiting." He laughed. "It may come to that, Grandson." The old man stood, resumed walking, and they followed him.

Lesson over, Claudia thought, but he was right. It might come to that. Without rifles, without firearms, the long wait at the allu was a more efficient way to hunt seals, if you did not mind the long wait. She shivered, chilled from the brief stop, and walked faster to warm up.

A minor mountain range of ice greeted them at the end of the thousand yards of flat ice. Claudia imagined a tin sheet jammed against a wall, and then pushing on the tin from the edge. That's what the storms did to the new sea ice that froze and grounded against the narrow continental shelf. Malgi stopped at the beginning of the jumble of ice boulders and jagged slabs, then turned to the men. He smiled at Claudia, and she smiled back. Yes, age has its privileges.

Tuttu sighed, rummaged in the pulkka, and pulled out three axes, handing one each to Natchiq and Amaguq. The three men began chopping away at the ice, making a path through the smallest of the ridges. Claudia relieved Amaguq for a spell, but he took over after he'd warmed his insides with a swig of hot tea from a thermos. As the path grew longer, Claudia dragged the sled forward. Puvak kicked the larger pieces of ice out of the trail. Chop, chip, scrape; but the work wouldn't be wasted, as long as the pressure ridge held. It would be their escape to the lead. And the lead beckoned before them, a thickening cloud of steam just over the ice ridge.

As she pulled the pulkka over the top of a ridge and down to a narrow stretch of ice, Claudia thought that this must have been what it was like for Balboa to discover the Pacific Ocean. A new world beckoned beyond the land floe, a world of gray, thinner ice, an open lead at the edge of the new ice, and another ice pack beyond. An *uiniq*. The Arctic coast had been extended a bit farther, a new bluff created, but the lead teamed with life the way the open water held life in the summer.

Tuttu, Amaguq, and Natchiq set down their axes, stared

at the open water steaming in the twilight. Malgi came up behind Claudia, unaaq tapping, and she and Puvak helped him down onto the flatter ice, pulkka dragging behind her.

"*Ai*," the old man said. "This is it."

A little gray head bobbed up perhaps five yards from them, at the edge of the new ice. Its deep brown eyes stared at them, its whiskers frosted with water that quickly froze. The seal sniffed, a quick deep breath, then ducked under the open water.

Tuttu whipped his rifle around, unsheathing the firearm and jamming his shells in. The other two men followed him, the boy beating them in the race to get rifles ready, and Claudia unstrapped the pulkka harness from her waist. As she did so the plastic sled scraped the ice. Tuttu whirled at her, a scowl on his face.

"Quiet!" he hissed.

Malgi giggled, put an arm around Claudia, and began laughing louder. Tuttu glared at him, not wanting to admonish the old man, but his face got red, turning angrier and angrier. What was the old fool doing? he seemed to be thinking—trying to scare the seals away?

The seal bobbed up again, its brown eyes looking at the men. No wonder, Claudia thought, no man had hunted seals from the ice edge, not even Natchiq, in a decade. Little natchiq must think us mad, she thought.

She looked at the seal in the water, watching him as he took a deeper breath, his nostrils flaring quickly open as—*whoof!*—he sucked in air. Little natchiq, yes, she thought, the ringed seal, his gray and black coat spotted by doughnut-size rings. The sound of outboard motors might scare him, but this, this . . . The seal dove again.

"He hears the sled scraping," Malgi said between chuckles. "Grandson, the woman brings the seal to us."

"Good," Tuttu snorted, still angry. "Then scrape again, so I may kill it." He sighted down the rifle, watching the water. Puvak imitated him, his .22 rifle steady in his arms, cocked and ready.

Malgi sighed, gave Claudia a look she recognized well now, a "these children are so stupid" look not unlike the exasperated sigh one of her grade school teachers used to wear. Malgi knelt by the pulkka, pulled out the half-inflated rubber raft and its two plastic oars, began connecting a hose to the raft and to a foot pump.

"And how will you retrieve little natchiq?" Malgi asked. He pointed at the raft.

Tuttu lowered his rifle, turned to look at Malgi. He grinned, reddening slightly, and nodded. "Ai, Grandfather." The young hunter stepped on the foot pump, began pushing up and down, the air from the bellows hissing into the raft, and the raft growing larger like an inhaling lung. Puvak glanced at the older hunters, back at his father. Amaguq nodded, pointed with his chin at the water. The boy smiled.

The two chambers of the raft swelled to almost bursting. While Tuttu kept pumping, Malgi jerked the hose out of the raft's valve and screwed it tight. For a few strokes the hose blew air on the snow, *hoosh, hoosh.* Tuttu stopped, put the pump away, turned to the open lead.

Claudia heard Puvak suck in his breath, a quick intake of air, and she thought for the moment what his name meant: lung. She thought of all the words that came from that root: *puviq-,* to inflate; *puviun,* air pumps; *puviuraaq,* balloon . . . Lung, inflate, pump, balloon, the raft and the boy and his name. Puvak, his father had explained once, because the child screamed so much as a baby they thought him all lung; *he* had had his Inupiaq name since infancy. The boy sucked in a quick breath, and as Claudia mulled on the sound and the meaning and what that might mean, the boy's rifle kicked gently, and the dog of the sea went *whoosh.*

Whoosh, the seal took in a long breath, and the bullet cracked through the chill air. A cloud of acrid gunsmoke rose from the tip of the barrel; the barrel steamed from the heat of the explosion. Tuttu turned at the sound. The seal had poked its head abovewater, taken a breath, and with the breath came the bullet, into its skull, smashing it. The seal sank.

They rushed to the ice edge, a cloud of little bubbles rising up, and then a thicker cloud of red blood. Puvak let out his breath at the blood, grinned at his father. Amaguq squeezed the boy's shoulder, and Malgi calmly pulled out a long rope from the sled bag, unwrapped a piece of old denim from around something at the end of the rope.

"Try to retrieve the seal," he said to Puvak, handing him the grappling hook. The boy took the line and the hook, a big treble snagging hook jammed into a net float and wrapped with twine. "A *manaq*," Malgi explained.

The hunters moved back from the little hunter as he stepped toward the ice. Malgi handed him his unaaq, laid it down on the ice edge in front of Puvak, pointed at it, then his foot. Step on the unaaq to distribute the weight, he meant, Claudia thought. They watched the water, watched for the seal to rise.

It had been a good shot, she knew, a head shot, a killing shot. If he'd timed it right, Puvak had killed the seal after it had taken a breath, and the seal should float to the surface. Lungs inflated, *puvak puvinga*, the fall fat and the full lungs should bring the seal to the surface. And it rose.

Belly up, belly white, the seal came up, with a little clot of shit in its anus, and its penis stiff and erect—like walruses, the seal had a bone to keep it that way. The dead seal rose. Blood trailed from its broken skull, tongue out between its sharp white teeth, one eye flattened and pierced with bone chips.

"Azah," Amaguq's father said.

Claudia's stomach growled as she looked at the seal, at the blood, at the violence of it. Growled and rolled, two emotions crashing in her gut. Pity, at the sight of the cute little animal, so much like a puppy dog; hunger, at the sight of the meat, at the recalled taste of seal oil, of fish and meat dipped in thick, rich, fat seal oil. The cold made her body hunger for fat, for grease and butter and such horrid stuff. For fuel.

The manaq sang as Puvak whirled it through the air, the cord unreeling as the weight pulled the line loose from the boy's hand. The line cut the clouds of steam rising from their breaths, and then Puvak let go. He let the treble hook fly through the air, ice creaking below him as he shifted his weight forward. Water squeezed out from under the ice, a wave rippling toward the seal's body. The manaq fell beyond the seal, the line falling across the seal's body.

Puvak pulled the hook in slowly, drawing the cord across the seal's chest. It turned with the movement, back and forth, the line moving up to the seal's flippers, straight up like sails. The hooks hit the seal's thick skin, and Puvak pulled.

"Gently, gently," Malgi whispered to him, coaching him. Puvak snugged the hook against the sealskin, one point pressed against the side. "Now jerk, hard."

He jerked, and the manaq broke the skin, the barb sinking below the flesh. Puvak reeled in the seal, laughing and laughing, throwing the end to his father, who took up the slack from the firmer ice. The manaq turned, the seal turned, head toward shore, and father and son pulled it up on the thin ice. Puvak reached down, picked up the unaaq, and scuttled back to his father, back to the hard ice. Tuttu and Natchiq dragged the seal up onto the ice. The blood froze on the seal's coat, the seawater froze over the blood, and when it came out of the water, it had become sheathed in a thin coat of ice.

"Arriga!" Puvak said. His mouth opened wide to yell louder, but Amaguq shushed him.

"Do you want to scare away the other seals so your father won't get any?" he teased. He hugged his son.

Tuttu and Natchiq dragged the seal by its flippers to the sled, laying it on its back in the snow as the blood dripped and froze. Malgi knelt down by the seal, looked at the bullet hole in the seal's head—head on to the cerebral dome, shattering it—and patted the seal's stomach. He whispered to it. Claudia remembered something.

"Get your thermos," she said to Puvak.

The boy frowned at her, then nodded, and took out a quart-size steel thermos from the sled. He unscrewed the cap, handed the cup and bottle to Claudia. She waved a hand toward Malgi.

"Give it to Malgi. He knows."

Malgi looked up at her, squinting, asking a question with his eyes. Claudia grinned, held up her hand to her lips, miming a person drinking from the bottle. Malgi nodded and smiled back, then took the thermos from the boy.

"You must give the seal a drink of fresh water," Malgi

explained. "To thank him for giving us his . . . parka." He uncapped the thermos, poured steaming hot water into the cup, and with the seal's mouth in one hand, let the water flow down the seal's tongue. "If we give the seal a drink of fresh water, he will return to us again."

Puvak looked at the old man, looked at Claudia, and she saw in his eyes a glare that seemed to say "You're crazy, old man." The other hunters stared back at the boy, at Malgi, glancing briefly at her, and Claudia saw in their faces the same expression. Then each man's gaze flickered from disbelief to something else, some latent echo of their culture, and she felt the same shudder as the seal's soul passed through them and back into the sea.

Perhaps that, she thought, or perhaps the cold. The custom, which she knew only as custom, as old words in old ethnographies, became something else: belief, fact, truth. Puvak stared into her eyes and the eyes of his father. He bowed his head, took the cup from the old man, and gave the seal the last of its drink.

"Thank you, natchiq," Puvak said. "Thank you for my first *good* kill."

A *good* kill, Claudia thought, catching the slight inflection in the boy's words. A good, clean kill, not murder, not the kill of a soldier, but the kill of a hunter. Killing for food, killing to fill the belly. A *good* kill.

Natchiq turned to the open water, scanning it for more bobbing heads. "Let us kill more seals," he said, and she caught the embarrassment in his voice. The boy had made the first kill and now the men would have to equal it.

If they could.

No more seals came to that spot. The seals knew, Claudia thought. They could smell the blood of their brother on the sea, had heard the sound of the rifle, and had understood the sound. Even after all those years, they had learned quickly. That cracking sound meant death; stay away, little brothers, stay away from the things that shout thunder and spit lead.

The hunters waited at the ice edge where Puvak had gotten his seal, and while a few seals' heads popped up out in the lead, none came close enough for a good shot.

Amaguq shifted nervously on a foam pad—hard and cracked in the cold—and it was all he could do to keep from pacing around. The other hunters waited no better, except for Malgi. The old man, Claudia observed, had never lost that essential Inupiaq trait. He sat still, knees straight before him, rifle on its open case across his legs, scanning the sea.

No seals came, and after what seemed like an hour, Malgi finally stood. At the movement, the other men and the boy got up, and Claudia stretched with them, stamping the cold from her feet. Natchiq uncapped the thermos and passed around a cup of still-hot tea. Malgi took the last sip, smiled as the warmth passed through his lips and down his throat, then handed the brown-stained cup back to Natchiq.

"Your inua does not honor us," Malgi said. He glanced at Claudia, raised an eyebrow, and looked out to the uiniq.

She followed his gaze, peered into the gloom of the dark sea. The sun had never risen above the horizon, of course, but refracted rays had bounced up from the south, giving them enough light to see by for a few brief hours. Those hours were ending; even that light faded. Claudia guessed what Malgi thought as he looked out at the open: even if a seal rose up feet from the ice edge, would they have enough light to make a good shot?

"We should go back," the old man said.

At his words the hunters gathered up their gear. Tuttu deflated the raft and laid it on the pulkka. He gently set Puvak's seal in the raft, and strapped everything tight. Tuttu told Puvak it would be a great honor to drag the sled back by himself, but the boy laughed off the suggestion.

"I should share the honor with you, Uncle," he said.

Amaguq clapped his son on the shoulder, beaming at his good humor, and took the harness for himself. All the way back the older men and Claudia traded off pulling the pulkka. Holes parted in the dark clouds and the light of the Big Dipper helped guide them home. Except for the huff of the hunter working as human sled dog, and the scrape of the plastic sled across the ice, the tuvaq was silent.

Claudia felt warm in her parka, felt warm from the exercise. The pull of the harness actually was pleasant, the extra effort resulting in muscles straining and cooking, the exertion warming the blood and pumping it though her extremities. Natchiq pushed the sled behind her as she climbed up the high ridge of the landfast ice. She let Puvak take the sled when they came to the end of the jumble of old ice and the flat plain of the tuvaq between the ridge and shore opened up.

Utqiagvik glowed to the northeast. The old man walked next to the young boy, whispered Inupiaq words into Puvak's ear. The boy picked up the pace as the rhythm of the words beat through the night. Claudia let the words roll over her ears, smiled as Malgi translated the song for the boy.

"I have caught my first seal," he said.

"I am strong and a good hunter now,

"My family will eat my first seal.

"I give my first seal to my *aana*.

"The seal that came to me that I shot.

"I thank you, *natchiq*, for honoring me.

"For letting me become a hunter."

The hunters returned home.

Chapter 12

A FEW days after Puvak got his first seal, the hunters went out on the ice again. Malgi's arthritic knees had been visibly paining him. When the old man made preparations to come with them, Tuttu asked him to stay behind and "commune with the seals and ask them to come with us." Malgi admitted that they would need all the help they could get, since they were "lousy hunters," and the face-saving suggestion worked.

Claudia set out with Amaguq, Natchiq, and Tuttu. Since Puvak had killed his first seal and proven himself as a hunter, the boy was welcomed; Natchiq thought he might bring good luck. Puvak pulled the pulkka across the flat tuvaq and up to the little mountain range where the ice pack pushed up against the landfast ice.

They'd left the village early, when the night was pitch black and the ice glowed like a scratched mirror. A steady southeast wind had blown snow across their old trail. Still, they easily picked it out by looking for the hard-packed path the weight of the seal-heavy pulkka had made on their last trip. The deep black canopy of the dust cloud still covered much of the sky, but holes had begun to appear in it. Some brighter stars poked through the inky cap over the sky. It seemed to Claudia that the cloud of dust had shrunk, too; the sky was clear from the horizon to a declination of fifty degrees, so that only the constellations around the North Star were obscured.

The hunters climbed over the ice ridge and down to the edge of the uiniq, the open lead. Claudia knew no sun would rise for them still, but they'd learned from the earlier trip to arrive at the ice in complete dark, and wait for the sun to rise near the horizon, the rays bouncing off the atmosphere and granting them a brief twilight. Puvak took off the sled's harness, pulled out the rubber raft, and began pumping it up. Amaguq smiled at his son. He smiled at Claudia, nodded. She remembered that the pumping had brought the seals before, and grinned at his gesture: the boy would bring the seals to the men and allow them the first shot, allow them to do what he had done on the last trip.

A dim glow spread out from behind them, the light like a city on the horizon, giving the chunks of ice relief and definition, making it easier to distinguish little round heads from floating icebergs. She looked at the open water, but saw nothing yet, nothing beyond the pack to the north and the cold, dark water between.

Claudia picked up a flat piece of ice, set it down quietly near the ice edge. She took her borrowed rifle out of its case, unwrapping the two-foot-square piece of foam padding from around the Ruger, and sat down on the pad. She laid the rifle across her thighs. In her parka pocket she felt the cartridges, warm and ready to be slipped into the rifle. Tuttu, Natchiq, and Amaguq had already loaded a round into their rifles. Whoever saw the seal first would have first shot; Claudia and Puvak would then load their rifles and back-up the shots, if necessary.

She didn't think this ice edge sealing would work. The night before she and Malgi had discussed the merits of it with Tuttu. No one had any real experience with winter seal hunting, except Malgi, and that had been more than a decade before the war. Malgi argued that ice edge sealing worked if hunters could range up and down the open leads, going from one spot to another and following the seals when the rifle shots scared them off. It had worked well with snowmachines, Malgi said, but they couldn't waste the gas on the snowmachines, not then. It had worked well before

that with dog teams, but they only had the five dogs Tuttu
had saved, and he didn't want to risk the dogs until the
bitches had a spring litter. Malgi argued that without
snowmachines or dog teams such sealing would be worthless.
Better to spend the time waiting at the allu, the seal-
breathing holes, like the polar bears did, he maintained.

Maybe he was right, Claudia thought, but they should
still give ice-edge hunting another try. If they got one more
seal, Tuttu told Malgi, that would be one more seal than
they had. Claudia knew what bothered Tuttu, though, and
why he wanted to hunt at the open leads. The wait. Good as
they were at waiting, Tuttu was right in guessing that no
one had the stamina to wait for hours at a time in subzero
weather, for a seal that would or would not come.

"This seal will come," Tuttu had said earlier that morning.
"I dreamed a great seal rose from the ice edge and that my
shoulders ached from pulling it to shore."

The twilight grew brighter. Some of the dimmer stars
faded away. The cold water turned from deep black to
almost blue, and they could see the ice and the things that
moved among the ice clearly. Claudia watched the far edge
of the lead, watched where the ice began again, a distance
of maybe half a mile.

Something seemed to rise at the other side of the lead. At
first Claudia thought it was a shadow cast by an iceberg
against the pack ice, but as the light changed slightly, she
felt that it was definitely something other than ice. Perhaps
a whale, she thought. Would the bowheads come by here
this late? That would be a boon; perhaps they could change
their tactics, dredge up old whaling guns and harpoons and
go for bowheads.

Perhaps it was even agviqluaq, she thought. She remembered
seeing the whales the day her world ended, remembered the
gray whales rising and falling. Hadn't there been some gray
whales caught in the ice off Utqiagvik once? When she was
just a girl she remembered the story. It had been on TV
nightly for three weeks and become the talk of her fourth-
grade class. They had all saved milk money and sent a
check to the "Eskimos at Point Barrow" to pay for the
rescue effort to free the whales. That had been when she

had first heard of Barrow, of Eskimos and whales and the Arctic. Could that thing be a gray whale?

No, she thought, any gray in these waters this late in the year would be dead, or should be dead. Only the bowhead, only agviq could survive ice. Agviq had already gone on, would not return, if he returned at all, until the spring.

The thing across the water seemed to shimmer, to change shape. As the twilight increased, as the sun came closer to the horizon, not quite rising above it, dark shapes became clearer and icebergs became more like icebergs. Claudia watched the whale shape move, become clearer. For a moment it seemed distinct and obvious, an object clean and not rounded, two straight lines perpendicular against the ice, with a straight line across the top, and a rectangular shape on a curved shape, like a box on the back of a whale. But then the light shifted again, and the whale thing changed again. She saw it for what it was: an iceberg. It had only been an iceberg. Claudia laughed at herself, at the things cold could do to the imagination and to eyes. She felt glad she hadn't mentioned the thing to the others, and they hadn't seemed to have seen anything.

But out from the lead a light *did* flash at them, a blinking light, a strobe, a quick pulse for every heartbeat. It should not have been there, not on the ice. Nothing so mechanical, so human, had a right to exist there.

"What the hell . . . ?" Tuttu asked.

He turned from the light to the sled and quickly undid the raft from the pulkka. The twilight had dimmed the stars, but could not dim the steady blinking of the strobe. By no stretch of the imagination could the strobe be seen as anything else but something artificial, something made, something *other*.

Amaguq helped push the raft to the edge of the open lead. Tuttu took the oars from the raft bottom, and set them in the locks. He got in the raft, quickly turning around to sit. Natchiq and Amaguq reached forward and shoved Tuttu and the raft into the water; the edge was firm and it held both their weight.

Breaking through new, thin ice, Tuttu rowed out to the light. The current pushed the light toward them, and Claudia

wondered if that meant the pack ice would close the lead.
Maybe. The raft and Tuttu disappeared against the black of
the sea, but the hunters could hear the steady splashing of
his oars. The sound of his rowing grew more and more
distant. Claudia tried to estimate how far away the beacon
flashed. Five hundred yards? A thousand?

Puvak rummaged in the bag of the sled and pulled out a
Peak camp stove—*my* camp stove, Claudia thought. No,
ours, she quickly corrected herself. He set the stove on a
piece of scrap plywood, and Claudia went to help him.

The wind kicked up slightly, blowing from the northwest,
and it brought a chill with it. Cold snuck into the gaps
between her atigi and her mittens, around the ruff of her
hood and against her face. Puvak had extended the legs of
the little Coleman camp stove and had started to pump it,
bringing the gas up to pressure. As he screwed the pump
tight and slipped his gloves back on, Claudia took over.

Damned Peak stoves always need priming, she thought.
She spread a squiggle of precious priming paste on the
generator, cupped her hands and lit the paste with her
pocket lighter. The little high-tech system—lighter, paste,
stove—impressed her, but depressed her at the same time.
They might have disposable lighters for a long time—Tammy
had saved a whole box at Stuaqpak—but the gas and the
paste would give out soon. And then how would they boil
water at the ice edge in the middle of winter?

The paste flamed and the thumb tip of her left polypro
glove melted back. She pulled her hand away, slipped off
her other mitten, and then while the generator was still
warm, turned the lever on the gas and lit the stove. Yellow
flames licked up around the gray metal of the burner. With
her right hand she quickly pumped the stove. As air mixed
with gas the flames turned from yellow to red to orange to
blue, and the trusty camp stove roared like an engine.
Claudia grinned at the fire, held her hands over the warmth,
then slipped them back in her mittens.

Amaguq helped them and brought over a blackened pot,
and dropped chunks of blue ice—ice chipped from the
ridges back from the lead—into the pot. The stove roared
and the pot shook and steam rose up from melting ice.

Claudia and Puvak tended the stove, and it wasn't until Natchiq tapped her on the shoulder that she realized Tuttu had come back.

The beacon flashed closer, now appearing, now disappearing behind some shape. As Tuttu got closer, she saw that he towed something behind him, and the beacon was on that thing. He rowed with the wind. Wind and current pushed Tuttu and the raft up the ice from them. Natchiq and Amaguq grabbed unaaqs and ran to meet him.

The two men snagged the guylines of the raft with the gaff end of the unaaqs, pulling Tuttu up on solid ice. He jumped out, reached to the stern of the raft for a rope tied to the thing behind, and yanked it up behind him. Natchiq and Amaguq helped him drag the thing up onto hard ice.

It looked like an orange seal, perhaps an ugruk, with three-fingered hands, broad feet. A white face stared up at them from inside an orange head, and the beacon flashed from the crown of the head. Green stripes reflected light back from the strobe, stripes running across the thing's chest and around its shoulders. Claudia stood over the thing as the three men pulled it out of the water.

Between heartbeats of the flash she stared down at the orange seal, and then she saw what it was. A pale face stared out from the shadows of the hood, blue eyes, lashes frosted with rime; a thin mustache and short beard, also frosted; long nose, thin lips. A man. She touched the fabric of his survival suit, felt the neoprene fabric yield with the pressure of her fingers. Claudia yanked off her mitten with her teeth, slipped a hand under his hood and to his neck. Cold. His skin burned with cold, but she felt a pulse from his carotid artery.

"He's alive," she said, "but severely hypothermic."

"The seal I dreamed of," Tuttu said. "It was orange. I couldn't figure out why it was orange."

Puvak came up with a mug of hot water. She took it from him, held the cup to the man's lips and poured it in him. His lips licked at the water, opened for it; a little color seemed to come to his cheeks.

"We should get him back to Utqiagvik," Tuttu said.

Amaguq brought over the sled. He'd taken out a sleeping

bag, laid it open on top of all their gear. Puvak held the still-warm pot in his hand, took an empty thermos and poured the rest of the water in it. He put the pot under the bag, next to the collapsed stove. Amaguq and Natchiq lifted the man onto the pulkka. In his survival suit he was too big to fit in the closed bag, so they just wrapped it around him, then lashed him to the pulkka.

"Who is he?" Puvak asked.

The men looked at each other, shrugged. Claudia leaned down to tighten the ropes around him, then noticed lettering across the visor of the man's hood. She spelled out the letters—an "r," a "p," a backward "n"—and made no sense of it until she noticed the style of the lettering, and the little red star above the lettering. Cyrillic.

"*Grigoriopol*," Claudia whispered.

"What?" Puvak asked. "Greg-what?"

"Grigoriopol," she said. "A city in the Soviet Union. A—"

"Russian," Tuttu said. "A Soviet."

The hunters stepped back from the man, and first Natchiq, then Amaguq, pulled their rifles out and pointed them at the Soviet, as if he could spring up and snap their heads off. Natchiq chambered a round and aimed his 30-06 at the man's throat. The man's eyes fluttered open, then focused on Natchiq and the rifle. His hand rose up, got tangled in the ropes of the pulkka.

"*Nyet*," he said.

Claudia stared at Natchiq, watched his eyes, watched him sight down the rifle. His finger pulled back, and she remembered that the Ruger had a hard pull; midway through, at the sound of "no," Natchiq's finger relaxed, and slid back through the slit of his mitten and back to warmth. The hunter lowered the rifle.

"No," he said. Natchiq turned to his cousin. "I'm sick of this kind of killing."

The other hunters looked at Natchiq, at the Soviet, nodded, and put their rifles back into their cases, over their shoulders. Claudia stood, and Puvak handed her her rifle.

"This man's cold," Tuttu said. "Should have brought the CB, to get help." He turned to Puvak. "Run ahead."

He waved a hand in the direction of the village. "Tell Malgi to fire up the stove, and start boiling water. You hunters"—he jabbed at Claudia and the men with stiff fingers—"you hunters take this man back." Amaguq reached for the raft and slung a rope from it around his shoulder. "Go. *Go!*"

Even the inside of the entrance tunnel felt warm, and the air grew warmer as she climbed up to the katak. Tammy stood in the open hatch, coming down the stairs to meet them. Claudia shooed Tammy back out of the open hatch. Natchiq and Amaguq pulled the Soviet into the tunnel. Claudia moved aside as the men swept by her, Natchiq walking backward up the ladder and into the house. Tammy reached down to help him.

"Who"—she looked down at the Soviet, expecting to see one of the hunters, Claudia guessed; her mouth dropped open at the sight of the orange-suited stranger—"the hell is that? Puvak said someone was hurt, had fallen into the water."

Claudia helped Amaguq push the Soviet into the house. Tammy let go of the man, stepped back, looked at Claudia. The Inupiaq woman's lower lip trembled. The man *did* look frightening, Claudia agreed: the orange survival suit, the pale face, the eyes.

"A Russian," Claudia explained.

Tuttu came in behind them, and Malgi shouted something from by the stove. Natchiq and Tuttu tore their parkas and boots off and were stripping to bare skin. Amaguq threw the damp sleeping bag aside and was yanking at the zipper of the Soviet's survival suit.

Masu pushed her way to the man, waving a circular bladed knife, and with the ulu cut the orange suit open. Claudia stared at the blur of activity, then realized what they were doing. She went to her corner of the qaregi and started grabbing sleeping bags: hers, Tammy's, Rob's, any bag in sight.

The Soviet groaned as Masu pulled the survival suit off him, like peeling a shrimp, Claudia thought. His teeth chattered and his arms and legs shook violently. Masu cut away the submariner's light coverall, pulled off his boots and the rest of his clothes. The two hunters stood buck naked over the stripped Soviet. Claudia threw the bags at them. They lifted the Russian up and into a bag, then climbed in next to him, Inupiaq on either side of the man, four bags wrapped around all three.

Puvak had gone down into the entrance tunnel, came back in, holding the thermoses from the sled. Malgi took the thermoses from the boy, and went over to the Soviet. Someone had already put a huge log onto the fire and started pots of water boiling. Tammy stood to the side, still shocked. A stranger, Claudia thought, the significance hitting her. Someone totally new to the village. There hadn't been a stranger in Utqiagvik since the day of the war.

"A *Russian*?" Tammy asked.

"A *Soviet*," Claudia said as she moved toward Malgi, and began helping him pour hot water and tea into hot water bottles. "From a *ship*, Tammy." She pointed at the ripped orange survival suit, then tried to think how a Soviet sailor could wind up so far from Siberia. "Maybe a submarine."

Tammy stared at her, the words starting to make sense. "Oh," she said. "Oh, *shit*."

The naked Inupiaq men climbed out of the sleeping bag, went to the men's side of the house and changed into dry, warm clothes. Claudia knelt next to the Soviet, felt his skin. Some more color had come back to him, but he still looked clammy, cold, almost dead. Tammy passed another hot water bottle to her. She laid it against his groin, across his stomach. In a hospital, the thing to do would be to get warm fluids in him, immerse him in warm water, perhaps. Claudia had even heard of blood-warming machines, or respirators snaked down into the lungs blowing hot air into the system. Anything to get heat into the body.

But they didn't have that, they just had hot water bottles— another odd bit of salvage from Stuaqpak—and naked men. Masu said something to Tammy, and then the lesbian tapped her on the shoulder.

"Our turn, Masu says." Tammy pulled her turtleneck over her head, her jet black hair falling out of the neck like tentacles of an aberrant anemone.

Claudia stripped, crawled inside with her friend. The Soviet's cold skin drew goose bumps from her body, made her nipples rise erect. She put an arm around him, hugged him to her. His belly to her belly. Tammy straddled the man's back, and across his neck grinned at her.

"A Commie sandwich, huh?" Tammy asked.

Claudia nodded, grinned. "A *submarine* sandwich, Tammy," she said.

Masu pulled out the cold water bags, replenished them with fresh hot water from the wood stove. The stove creaked as the steel expanded, the pipe pinged as flames roared inside. The old woman picked up Claudia's damp clothes and hung them from the clothesline strung between posts.

She felt her body warm from the heat of the stove, from the insulation of the sleeping bags. Tammy's warmth seeped over to her, and she felt a glow spread through her, not just warmth, but something else. Claudia stared at the sailor's face, at his eyelids shut and sleeping, at the wheat-blond short hair falling across his forehead. The stranger. His penis rubbed against her thigh, but she didn't think of that. It wasn't that he was a man, not that, Claudia thought. It was that he was not of Barrow, not of the Arctic coast, that he had come from someplace else. He had survived, too.

Hugging the cold man, feeling her warmth pass from Tammy to her to the Soviet, Claudia wondered what the man would think if he were to wake up suddenly and see her, a naked blond woman—somewhat attractive, she liked to think—pressed against him? What would he think if he turned to see Tammy? What would he think if he woke up between two men? Perhaps he would like that, perhaps not. The smooth touch of the man, the warm touch of Tammy, the heat blazing from the stove as the big log Malgi had tossed in caught . . . Claudia felt the cold of the hunt, finally, and exhaustion from the pure effort to be outside, and then remembered the joy of Puvak's kill. She fell asleep.

A great steel whale ripped through the sea, bending like a serpent, thrashing the ocean behind it into froth with its flukes. It spat harpoons back out at whalers, roared fire

from its mouth, and whipping glass hung from its upper
jaw, rows and rows of shining swords. The whale came to
her, its eyes gleaming red, a beacon flashing from the steel
whale's skull. She floated in the ocean, naked and trembling.
As the whale came to her, jaws open, as it came to her and
bit down on her, a great light flashed across the sea, and
Claudia woke up.

A log caught fire in the wood stove. Flames shot up the
glass window of the stove, heat expanding the iron. Yellow-
white light flickered out a crack of the door where asbestos
sealing had rubbed away. Water steamed from a pot on the
wood stove, a chunk of blue ice sizzling into its primal
form.

She rose. Tammy lay on the other side of the Soviet, an
arm across his shoulder and his face nuzzled into her hair.
Claudia slipped out of the sleeping bag, shivered in the
slightly colder air of the qaregi, and looked up at Masu
sitting on a bench sewing, and watching over them. The old
woman's fingers fell and rose, fell and rose as she quickly
pushed a needle through a pair of pale blue coveralls. Masu
nodded as Claudia caught her eye, then jerked her chin at
Claudia's underwear and socks hanging from the clothesline.

A light bulb glowed from the rafter above Masu, two
wires twining around each other to a big black 12-volt
battery on the floor. Claudia remembered vaguely some idea
of Natchiq's to rig up a light for the old woman, to recharge
the batteries using a DC generator on a windmill. The rest
of the house was in darkness, and from the side of the room
where the men slept, someone snored.

The polypro underwear felt dry and warm as she pulled it
down from the line, but it stank of her sweat. It scratched
against her skin, the plastic fibers snagging on the hairs of
her legs. Dimly Claudia remembered a day when she had
cared about smooth legs, when the feel of nylons felt sexy
against her thighs, in some place and time where it made
sense to walk in skirts under a sun that burned and in air
that did not chill. She pulled the long johns over her cotton
briefs; her ears crackled with static as she slipped her head
through a turtleneck and shook out her hair. The blond

strands fell in her eyes and she swept it back over her shoulders.

"We saved you some seal," Masu said. She pointed with the tip of her needle at the stove.

Claudia buttoned up her wool pants, slipped a sweater over her head, happy and warm and rested. On the back of the stove was another pot, lid closed tight. She lifted it up and stared down at a lumpy hard mass of brown meat.

"Liver," said Masu. "From that seal Puvak got. The men ate but Tuttu said to save some for their hunting partner."

She smiled at that, glad that Tuttu and the others had remembered her help. Too bad they hadn't gotten a seal this time. Claudia tried to think how the meat would be divided if the partners had come from other houses, but the point was academic: they all lived in the same qaregi and would share together.

Dipping her fingers into the warm meat, Claudia snagged a hunk and lifted it, steaming still, to her lips. She thought of the first time she'd had seal years ago, had liver, and had almost gagged on the smell. She still almost gagged when they'd feasted the day before, but her stomach won out then as it did now, reminding her how long it had been since she'd had a filling meal. Too long, too many days of subsisting on old cans of tuna, stale Pilot bread, or greasy spam. A great spoonful of peanut butter would taste best, she thought, but Tuttu had hidden the last jar, saving it, he said, "for something worth celebrating."

She chewed on the strong meat, greasy from the seal oil it had floated in in the pot. The oil slid down her throat like crankcase oil, a strong flavor, yes, but satisfying. Claudia ground the meat down hungrily, and reached for another piece. The oil seemed to catch fire in her stomach, fuel for her fat-famished body. Masu poured her a cup of tea from a thermos by her feet.

"Good," Claudia mumbled from around the meat.

Masu smiled. "Good seal. The boy did well."

He had, Claudia thought. She looked over at the men sleeping, noticed Puvak sleeping soundly next to his father, his father's arm across his son's chest.

The Soviet stirred. Claudia looked down at him. His color seemed to be back in his cheeks, and his lips were no longer pale pink but red. The orange survival suit had been hung from a nail from a post, one end ragged where Masu had cut the suit open. Other than the reflective tape and the ship's name across the breast, there were no other markings, no other insignia on the suit.

Masu held up the coveralls she was mending, checked her stitching. Claudia glanced over, noticed the Cyrillic letter on the breast pocket. She turned to Masu, reached up and looked over the coveralls. Strips of Velcro had been sewn over the right pocket of the coveralls and on both sleeves, but they were only the backing, the burr side of Velcro. The Soviets had picked up a trick or two from us, she thought. The Velcro had probably held insignia and a name, but those had been ripped away to keep the man from being identified. The only marking was the word GRIGORIOPOL again. Why would they leave the name but not anything else? Old-fashioned Commie disinformation? It didn't figure.

Masu inspected her sewing, nodded, turned the coveralls over to work on a tear on the back. "Had to cut it away from him," she said. "I thought he might need it."

The Soviet stirred, and the movement caught her eye. He rolled over, pushing Tammy away, and his right arm shot into the air, pushing something back. He sat straight up, one sleeping bag falling in a heap off of him, and then his eyes blinked open, and he screamed.

The scream broke the subdued quiet of the house, startling Claudia with its violence. She knew that scream, had heard screams like that before. She remembered the scream of her sister's nightmares, the nightmares Susanne had every now and then after her rape. The sailor's scream was the same kind of animal scream, a scream that rose from the lungs and came forth from the back of the throat, tongue flat against lips and teeth bared back.

Tammy rolled over at the sound, away from the sound, and pushed at the man with her left arm. He fell back, rose up, Tammy pushed him back, and he rose up again. Tammy woke up then, Claudia at the sailor's side, and the two women held the man until his screaming stopped and he quit shuddering.

"Who is he?" Tammy asked.

"Grigoriopol," Claudia said.

She looked at the Soviet, dressed in his coveralls, a borrowed sweater over them. At the name, the man looked up, shyly staring over a cup of steaming tea. He smiled at Claudia, sipped more tea. Masu had given him a plate of the seal liver, and the way the man tore into the meat—not flinching at the smell, smiling, even—told her that he was no stranger to the Arctic. A tanik, yes, a gussik, Yupik Eskimos would call him. Gussik. Cossack. It wouldn't be the first time a Russian had come to these shores. White, blue-eyed, sandy-haired, yes, but the Soviet knew Native food.

"Ask him who he is, where he comes from," Tuttu said. The Soviet's screams had woken the house, and now everyone sat around looking at him, curious at this alien.

"My Russian's lousy," Claudia said.

"*Ask*."

"*Tovarisch*," she said. Was that the right word? Comrade? Friend? "*Gde vy zivete?*"

"Grigoriopol," he said. He smiled, sipped his tea again.

Shit, Claudia thought. Has she asked the wrong question— where do you live? She thought again. "*Kak imja?*" What is your name?

"Ah," he said, smiling. "Grigor."

She shook her head, sighed, then smiled. Why not? It would be a common enough name, Grigor. The coincidence wasn't that odd. Grigoriopol. If that's what he said . . .

"Grigor, then."

"Does he speak English?" Puvak asked quietly. Amaguq moved to admonish his son, then laughed. No one had asked the Soviet. "Well?"

"*Vy govorite angliyskaya?*" Claudia asked.

"*Da*," he said. "Yes, I do."

He spoke English with an accent that was flat, neutral, with little trace of the Slavic twang native Russian speakers had. The accent was American, maybe Midwest. Claudia felt that chill she'd felt on the ice. Even during the Gorbachev era, not just anyone could go to America and learn to speak English with a Midwest accent. He had to have been someone . . . special. She glanced at Tuttu, caught his eye, and shook her head slightly.

"Ah," Tuttu sighed. "That makes things easier. Your name is Grigor?" The man nodded. "And your ship, it was named *Grigoriopol*?" He nodded once more. "What kind of ship? An icebreaker? A destroyer?"

"A submarine," Claudia said, thinking of her guess. He had to have come on a submarine.

"Yes," Grigor said. "A submarine."

"A submarine?" Tuttu glanced at Claudia. "Okay. A sub. Where is it now?"

Grigor shrugged, sipped some more tea. "I do not know. The crew threw me overboard."

"*Why* did the crew throw you overboard?" Tuttu asked.

"They did not like me. We did not—what is your expression?—we did not see eye to eye."

"So they put you in a survival suit?"

"Yes."

"And threw you overboard? And then the submarine went away?"

"Yes. Yes."

Amaguq followed the conversation, listening. His eyes lit up, and then he nodded. "Your submarine, Grigor? What kind could it have been? A boomer, perhaps?"

Claudia looked at him, remembered Amaguq saying back during the siege that he had worked with a submarine patrol in the Navy. Of course he would know submarines.

"A 'boomer'? I do not know the term," Grigor said.

"A nuker," Amaguq said. "A ballistic missile launching submarine."

"Oh." Grigor shrugged. "I do not know these things. I could not tell you anyway."

Tuttu stood, his face red and his fists balling open and shut, open and shut. He slapped the mug of tea out of Grigor's hands, grabbed the Soviet by the collar and yanked him up.

"The war's over. We saved your fucking life, asshole. It

was a boomer, right? A fucking nuker, right?'' He shoved the sailor down to the floor.

Grigor picked himself up, started to stand, thought better of it, then sat back down. "Yes," he said. "The *Grigoriopol* was a boomer, as you say.''

"Thank you," Tuttu said. He sat back down across from the Russian. "Well. Now that we have that settled . . . How the hell did you wind up here?'' He motioned to Masu, and she poured Grigor another cup of tea.

The submariner nodded to the old woman, took the tea, and sipped it again. "We were trying to get back home," he said. And he told his story.

"No, we did not fire our missiles," Grigor said first, holding up a hand. "You think that we would?" Tuttu glared at him. "Our mission was deterrence, you see? If we had to fire our missiles, we would have failed in our duty."

"I've heard *that* before," Amaguq said. "Standard nuclear Navy propaganda."

Grigor risked a smile, then sipped his tea again. "But it is *true*, comrade. Still"—he shrugged—"we did not fire our missiles.

"I think you know of the war, yes?" He smiled a silly grin. "Even in these far-off reaches, word must have come to you."

"We know about the fucking war," Tuttu said. "Get on with it.''

"Well, imagine what it must have been like for us. Our patrol was the north Pacific, to strike fear in the hearts of your brave generals. The *Grigoriopol* could hit any of your cities on the West Coast—any city in Alaska. Any *village* in Alaska, you understand?

"We went in and out through the Bering Strait like it was our very own house—as it, indeed, is, in a way. You do not keep as many listening stations here, like you do in the Atlantic. We have never understood this. The Soviets rule the Arctic Ocean, it is our Pacific, our Atlantic. With our thousand icebreakers we can go anywhere at any time on the surface, and with submarines—you see, the ice does not bother us. You Americans do not seem to understand ice, seem to fear it." Grigor looked at Claudia when he said that.

"We are Alaskans," Tuttu said. "We are Inupiaq. Do not scare us with talk of ice."

Grigor smiled over the lip of his mug, nodded. "No offense. I was speaking only of your motherland, not of you. And so, as I was saying, the Soviet Union ruled the North Pole, and we could go anywhere we wanted at will. If we so desired, we could sneak down your coast—your very backyard!—and enter that vast Pacific and do what we would. Of course, we have Pacific ports as well, and Siberian ports, and icebound as they may be, they are no matter. Not for the *Grigoriopol.*

"No one ever caught us, not your antisubmarine forces at Adak"—he grinned at Amaguq—"not anyone. Unless we *wanted* to be found. We would do this, you know: let you find us, let our great submarine surface just off the coast of California. Ah, would *that* strike terror into your hearts!"

"We would do the same," Amaguq said.

"Yes, of course, comrade," Grigor said. He smiled. "It was all the game we played. But when push came to shove—is that the idiom?—when your forces and our forces went on alert last summer, why, we went under. We hid. We waited. What did you hear of the war up here? How did you know?"

"The radio told us," Tuttu said. "Our 'emergency broadcast system.' A full-scale Soviet attack." He glared at Grigor. "How could we respond? You got Prudhoe Bay—the oil fields. We heard *that* one here."

"We struck first?" Grigor shook his head. "Impossible. It is not our policy; our Premier swore a doctrine of no first use a decade ago, and we have not changed."

"You struck first," Tuttu said. "That is what the radio said."

Claudia looked at the two men, thought of the dud Soviet missile that had hit the camp at Tachinisok Point. She remembered what the radio had said, could hear clearly the shrill voice of the announcer ticking off all the names of the cities that had been hit. Something had bothered her about that . . .

Grigor shook his head. "I do not want to disagree with those who have saved my life, but—no, we could not have launched a first strike. My orders weren't—" he stopped, suddenly aware of what he said.

"Your orders?" Tuttu asked. "*Your* orders? You would get the orders?"

"Or execute them," Amaguq said. "That 'no first use' is bullshit. You don't have a 'we are happy' system."

" 'We are happy'?" Tammy asked.

"American submarines constantly receive a 'we are happy' signal. If the signal stops, something's wrong, and they launch their birds. The Soviet subs don't work that way. They're first strike weapons." Amaguq glared at Grigor. "*Comrade*. That's what they told us in the Navy, anyway. Or what we heard."

"I did not receive any first-strike orders," Grigor said.

"But why would *you*?" Tuttu asked again. "What was *your* role?"

Grigor sipped from his tea again, then mumbled from behind the cup. "KGB."

"KGB?" Tuttu asked. "*KGB*?"

He nodded. "Political officer. My job was to make sure the *Grigoriopol*'s commander properly executed his orders. *All* his orders. I got no such orders, friends. You will have to believe me."

"I believe you," Claudia said.

"Thank you," he replied.

"Maybe you shouldn't," she said. She sighed, rubbed her eyes. She understood now. Something had bothered her about the dud missile that had killed Natchiq's sister, but hadn't exploded. Something had bothered her about the radio announcement from KBRW. Maybe . . .

"Natchiq," she asked. "Were you at KBRW when the emergency broadcast system came on?" He nodded. "And did you get a list of the cities that had been attacked?"

"Yes. Someone from Anchorage. And then Anchorage went off the air. We figured out what that meant."

"But the cities back East? You heard about those over the emergency system?"

"Yes."

"No one guessed at those?"

"No. Why? Should they have?"

"Yes," she said. How would the announcer at KBRW *know* the lower-48 cities had been attacked? She thought. That's what had been bothering her. She couldn't figure it out, didn't understand. Now she did.

"The emergency system lied," she said. "No one could have known. The system itself should not have worked, could not have worked. The EMP? You know the EMP?" Grigor shook his head.

"Electromagnetic pulse," Amaguq explained. "The big zap?"

The Soviet nodded. "*Da*. The thing that destroys electronics. Yes, of course. That is why we use vacuum tubes in so many of our systems."

"The EMP would have destroyed any civilian communications. Maybe the military systems would work."

"Probably not," Amaguq said. "It's a big hole, they don't like to talk about it."

"Yeah," said Claudia. "Anyway, beyond that, with a full attack, enough to wipe out all those cities supposedly hit, the stations themselves would be nuked. We couldn't know, not if the Soviets hit first."

"But if they didn't . . ."

"There might be a warning. Or someone might lie." Claudia felt the muscles in her neck tighten, felt her head grow light, felt the life seem to drain from her body. Goddamn them all, she thought. Goddamn my country for starting this thing. "*We launched the first strike.*" The men looked at her, stunned. Grigor smirked. "But don't be so noble, Grigor. You would have launched a first strike, too, if we hadn't beat you to it."

"Us? Never. You said—"

"We beat you to it." She pointed at him, then waved her arm toward the stove. "Down the coast, south of here, there is a tower of some sort. Part of the Alaskan warning system, you see? On my way up here—I will tell you of this later, these people know what I mean—I passed by this tower. The tower had been destroyed. Two cabins nearby had their windows blown out. A woman—Natchiq's sister—was killed from a blast, a missile, I think, that crashed but did not explode. The force of the crash knocked the tower down, and broke the glass of the windows, and the flying glass killed Natchiq's sister. But it did not go off."

"A warning tower?" Grigor asked. "You see—it could not have been a first strike, for surely we would take out cities?"

"True," she said. "But while it was not a first strike, it was a first-strike attack. Why would you destroy warning systems if you had already been fired upon? Or if you had no intention of first use?"

"That is what I mean," Grigor said.

"*You do not know what you mean*," Claudia yelled, "and don't tell me what you mean. I am an archaeologist, *comrade*, I analyze events and artifacts and they do not lie. An attack on a warning system tells me one thing: you intended to launch a first-strike, for the first thing you would hit in a first strike, the only reason anyone would launch a first strike, would be to disable any early warning system. You launch a first strike because you don't want to get caught with your pants down and you want to catch the other guy with his pants down."

"But you said the Russkies *didn't* launch a first strike," Natchiq said. "I don't understand."

"You're right, they didn't," Claudia said. "And I think that's true. But the Soviets—your people, Grigor—would have programmed all their computers, all their systems, for a first strike. That's what the attack on the tower says. Even after a first strike is useless, you wouldn't have taken the time to change everything. You'd go ahead and use your old attack scenario, launch a retributive wave as if it were a first strike. Warning systems first. Command and control centers next. Intelligence and computer systems following. Then cities. Am I correct, comrade?" Grigor nodded. "You probably took out Tachinisok—or tried to—from the *Grigoriopol*. You bastard, you would have gotten Barrow if that nuke had blown." She stood, the hunters stood, only Masu sat, still sewing, quietly listening. They circled the Soviet.

"*No!*" Grigor said. He stood, fists clenched before him.

"No, we launched nothing! I swear it! We could not! The crew—the other officers"—he looked down—"they would not let me."

"*You*?" Tuttu asked.

"Well, not me alone," he said. "The commander and me."

Grigor sighed, taking a breath, and then spat out the words almost without a pause. His English is *damn* good, Claudia thought. "When we surfaced, we did not hear anything. It is as the sailor said"—he pointed to Amaguq—"we do not have a constant signal. So we must check. And if we hear nothing, we are to surface, at great risk, and attempt communication. We surfaced. We understood what happened. I had my orders, the commander had his orders, and the two of us were to do what duty demanded. But the crew intervened. They locked us up, kept us from launching the missiles.

"Out in the Aleutian trench, they discarded the missiles. The commander—well, you saw how I was? That is what they did to him. They set him adrift in a survival suit, somewhere near the Aleutians. Perhaps your southern brothers found him, as you found me. They kept me with them, in case we came across any other survivors—I would naturally be contacted in such a case—until they made it to the Arctic. And up here, they set me adrift, off your coast."

"And the sub? What happened to it? Did it sink?" Claudia asked.

Grigor shrugged. "I do not know. The last I saw of it was when they threw me onto the ice. My comrades were very forgiving; they let me have my Kalishnikov and several magazines. What happened to them? Perhaps they went home, to make their own lives. I do not know. I drifted, made it to the ice pack. All I remember was trying to cross the open water, to get to your side, and passing out in the water, and then this hunter"—he pointed at Tuttu—"pulling me to shore."

"*But I did not launch any nukes*," Grigor said firmly. He bit his lower lip, glanced down. "It would have been my duty to do so, and I would have been not ashamed to do that, but the crew did not allow me. You must believe that." He looked up again.

Claudia stared at him, looking in his eyes. Grigor blinked his eyes, opened them, caught her glare, stared back at her. He looked to the men, at Tammy, finally at Malgi. Malgi nodded.

"I believe him," he said, and sat down. They all sat down. The old man looked at Claudia, then nodded at her. "And I believe you, anthropologist. I believe that our country started this thing, and that this man's country finished it, and that they would have liked to start it, but we did not give them the chance.

"It does not matter now, does it?" Malgi asked.

"No, Grandfather," Puvak said, "it does not."

"Good, boy," he said. "Gussik, eat." Malgi waved at Masu, and she put down her sewing and got the seal pot from the stove. "What happened cannot be changed, but what will happen can be." Masu ladled out a hunk of seal liver, handed Grigor back his plate.

"Eat, 'comrade,' " the old man said. "Eat hearty."

Chapter 13

THE dome of the seal hole, the *allu*, glinted in the low light of the false dawn on the flat plain. New ice had built up seaward of the ridge of the landfast ice, pushing the open lead a thousand yards farther out. Inside the snug darkness of her hood, the allu was a dot at the end of a tunnel, a point of reflected light. Claudia sat with her legs bent before her, one foot against the knee of the other leg. Her rifle laid across her lap, the stock resting on a thigh. She sat on a square of ensolite foam, the foam stiff and hard in the bitter cold, but still insulating her somewhat from the packed snow and ice beneath.

She had sat like that for what seemed like an hour. That morning, on the way out, Claudia had put on every piece of clothing she seemed to have: two thicknesses of underwear, her wool pants, wind pants over that, turtleneck shirt and pile jacket and the atigi. A balaclava Tammy lent her. Heavy mittens. Still, with all the warm clothing, the cold had seeped into her bones, it seemed, chilling her almost as she sat. Cold: deep cold, numbing cold. She had never felt it possible to feel cold like that, not even the summer of her first trip to Barrow when she had joined the infamous Polar Bear Club—a quick dip into the sea, dodging small icebergs and plunging below the surface, rising up with a yelp and running through new snow to warmth. This, this was far, far colder.

Spread out along the ice, she knew, the other hunters waited in equal misery. They had separated at the ice ridge and spread out to find allus. The seal holes had not been hard to find in the new ice, the flat ice: like pimples on the fresh skin of a vain teenager, the domes were obvious and apparent if you were looking. Even Malgi had come with them, shrugging off his stiff knee and letting Tuttu know that no other Inupiaq alive could wait out the cold any better.

She had walked with Malgi to his hole, and he had shown her how to wait for the seal. He had shown her to sit crosswind to the hole, to calculate where in the dome the seal would poke his nose, to figure out where his head would be. He had shown her the angle to hold her rifle, and told her when to raise her rifle into position, and when to shoot. And then he had pointed out an allu a thousand yards distant, the allu she now sat before.

Malgi had said not to watch the hole, but to listen, to crouch in the darkness and warmth of her hood and wait for the seal to come back to its hole, and breathe. "Listen for the first breath," he had said, "and then prepare." So she sat before the hole, listening and staring at the glint of light at the end of the tunnel of her hood. As she waited, she thought.

It was as if she had shut her conscious mind down, the way one would drift off to sleep with an alarm clock ticking beside the bed. The clock would tick and the mind would ignore the sound, but some shred of awareness listened throughout the night for the ringing. The ear would not be ready for any other sound than the alarm sound; it would know, it would alert the brain, and the brain would wake up. As she dreamed while she slept, so she thought as she waited.

She thought first of the dwindling supply of food in their qaregi, and how other houses surely must be coming to the limits of their allotments. The master stores at the gym grew smaller and smaller. Tuttu had punched some numbers into his laptop a few days before, and had come up with various scenarios based on full rations, half rations, quarter rations, and so on. None of them had been encouraging; even the tenth-ration scenario had them running out of food well before spring. They had not calculated for the Soviet before, but it didn't matter: Tuttu had calculated for a minimum death rate of three villagers lost over the winter, though he hadn't advertised that consideration. Already four people had died, Igaluk's old aunt, two other elders, and one small child. Grigor's presence balanced Tuttu's calculations.

Of course, Claudia thought, Tuttu's figures had been based on them getting nothing from hunting—a worse case scenario—and already they'd slipped from gloom to hope, slight hope, with Puvak's seal. Three other houses had gotten seals, too. Someone had found a rotting walrus, dead from the fall, with fresh polar bear tracks around it. The bear hadn't come back but that hunter had salvaged the meat for Tuttu's dogs; Tuttu had promised him a bitch from the spring litter.

And two of Tuttu's dogs had swollen bellies and tits popping out, the two he called Libby and Susan. A third bitch, Roxy, was coming into heat, her vulva swollen and oozing yellow scent. When Roxy began presenting herself to the males, Tuttu said he'd let both males have a shot at her, just to mix up the gene pool as much as possible.

Claudia smiled at the thought of the last two male dogs in Utqiagvik getting to be studs. In dog yards she'd seen among mushers down south, it had only been one or two males who got such rights—unless some male slipped his chain. Let there be a thousand dogs, she thought, and may the seas swim with seals.

Or at least this hole, this seal.

Shifting her leg slightly, her leg scraped the snow. Almost right at the noise something rasped from the allu. Claudia tilted her chin up, letting her hood fall back off her head, and then got a better look at the icy dome. Something had darkened the dome. It rasped again, a deeper rasp. Second breath, she thought. She clicked off the safety of the rifle—a round had been chambered when she first sat down—and brought the butt up to her shoulder. The seal breathed a third time, and Claudia squeezed the trigger.

Sing! she thought. Sing, bullet, sing through the air! Her mind had gone numb from the cold, the breaths of the seal had been a roaring sea in her ear, and the bullet flying out of her rifle became a bee humming to the head of the seal. Sing, she thought, and sing death.

The crack of the rifle came next, and a cloud of steam rose from the heat of the rifle barrel. Claudia stood and rose through the steam, the moisture sticking to the hairs of her ruff and her blond hairs poking out from under her wool cap. Sing, and cry! She set the rifle down on her foam mat, grabbed her unaaq and jabbed toward the shattered allu with the hook end of the staff.

Cracked ice littered the edge of the hole, and water splashed around the smashed dome. The seal floated head up in the short tunnel leading down through the pack ice, blood dying red the black water and the white snow and the blue ice. She smiled, then grabbed for the seal with the unaaq, and pulled its head up onto the ice.

The seal's body jammed in the short tunnel, a tunnel cut only wide enough for its head and upper body. Claudia grabbed a short length of rope, a rope like a fish stringer with a sharp spike of metal at the end, and threaded the rope through the hole made in the seal's head by the bullet. She pulled the metal through, tied it around the rope, and then looped the rope around her right foot. She held the seal to keep it from falling back down to the sea, to keep the sea current from pulling it away.

Her shot had hit just behind the seal's left orbit, between the eye and the ear. A clean shot, a good shot, but only by chance. The bullet had to have cut through the ice dome, would have been deflected by the ice, and landed where it had. Claudia whacked at the allu, widening the hole. She wrapped the end of the rope around her foot and pulled the seal out farther. Chip the ice, pull the rope, squeezing it out. A polar bear would just crush the seal with one blow, she knew, and pull the whole thing out, bones broken and the seal but a bag of flesh. That's what Nelson said in one of his books. She had to widen the hole, ten minutes of steady chipping.

The exercise warmed her, the elation of the kill warmed her. She yanked the seal out of the ice and the sea, and as she did it it reminded her of the violence of birth, the birth of Susanne's daughter, the daughter fathered by the man who had raped her. Violence and joy. Susanne had cried at the joy of her new child, had screamed at the man who had done this to her and at the state that would demand she bear the child to term. Violence and joy. Claudia had seen that child come into the world, had watched it leave Susanne's arms and off to some happy husband and wife. The child had been blond and blue-eyed. Claudia's first niece? Where was that niece now? Had she survived, too?

She pulled the seal out of its hole, out of the water where it got nourishment, back into the air where it got life. She chipped away at the ice, widening it to allow the seal's hips to come out. Pull and yank, pull and yank, the edges of the ice bloody, the head of the seal bloody, the body of the seal bloody. Blood and violence and nourishment. Joy. Claudia brought the seal up onto the ice, laid it out on the ice. It rasped a breath—air trapped in its stomach?—and laid still.

Joy! The excitement of the kill and the recovery warmed her. The thought of food for her house warmed her. She had made a kill, she, a woman, something a good Inupiaq should not do. But she was not Inupiaq, she thought, she was a tanik, and they were not Inupiaq, not really. Meat! She had killed this thing, this seal. How old was it? A year? Two? It looked to be barely a pup. She had killed some mother's child so she could live. The seal had killed some mother fish's child so *it* could live, and on it went. She had understood the process before, had grasped it intellectually. Kill to live.

The dogs on the beach had been something else: reaction to danger, a quick response. Defending the store had been something else, too, the same as the dogs: kill or be killed. This seal was different. She had deliberately waited for the seal, had *hunted* the seal, had consciously and with no regret set forth to take its life. The seal had come to her, she thought. It had come to her and taken three breaths and she had taken it, Claudia felt glad. She felt joy. This, this was her first real kill since the war, her first deliberate hunt.

"Aaaairrrrigaa!" she shouted, the Inupiaq song of joy. The sound echoed against the ice ridge, bounced off the small mountains and to the sea. Thank the seal, she thought.

Thank it. As if in response, a rifle shot cracked through the still air just north of her, from the direction of the village. The seal had come to someone else.

Quickly, while she still felt warm, she stripped her mittens off and opened up the thermos from her pack. Warm water steamed out of the stainless steel flask as she poured a cup. The seal lay on its belly, mouth slightly open and the rope strung through its upper jaw. She kneeled down and poured the cup of water into the seal's mouth, as they had done for Puvak's seal. Give it a drink of fresh water. Let the seal's spirit know that they were grateful to it for letting them have its body, its parka.

Frozen crystals of blood fell into the cup, melted in the little bit of water on the bottom. Claudia held the cup to her lips, swallowed it, the melted blood and briny seal's breath. It tasted salty, bitter, warm on her throat. She poured another cup of water, a full cup, drank, felt the water rush through her gullet and into her stomach. Warmth.

Claudia replaced the thermos in her pack. She undid the knot on the rope, retied it, slipping a loop around the seal's neck. She put the rifle back in its case, the foam pad in her pack, tied the rope to her pack and slipped the pack over her shoulder. She slung the rifle across the top of her pack, its long loop falling across her chest, around her breasts, the belt of her pack snapped through the strap. Lean forward and the rifle would follow over her head, instantly ready. She set out back to Utqiagvik.

On her walk back to the village, Claudia heard at least two more shots—four shots total, counting hers. Tuttu met her at the trail over the ice ridge, dragging a seal behind him. Ah, she thought, good. His seal was bigger than hers, almost twice as large—an old bull male, she decided. He nodded at her as she walked up.

"Did you water your seal, anthropologist?" he teased.

"The seal was thirsty." Claudia shrugged, smiled. "It seemed the right thing to do." She pushed her hood back, looked at him, motioned with her chin at his seal. "And you?"

"Hah! Superstition," Tuttu said. He looked down, then

back up, and grinned. "But maybe you and that old man are right, so I gave my seal a drink. You think it worked with Puvak's seal? That spirit must have told his brothers we were worthy of them." He pointed at her seal, then back over her shoulder to someone else coming up behind her.

Claudia whirled, still fearful of the tug of nanuq on her kill, as she'd heard polar bears did—grab the seal from a hunter, and who would argue with that? But behind her came either Amaguq or Natchiq. No, not them, she saw, they didn't have a white atigi with wolverine trim around the bottom. Malgi! The old man pulled a seal behind him, too. He strained with the weight, a seal at least twenty pounds more than Tuttu's. Azah, she thought. *Azahah*.

Malgi wheezed as he came up to them, but his steps were strong and sure. He stopped, flipped back his hood, and smiled at them through an ice-crusted mustache. The old man bit on the icicles frozen to the fine hairs, bit them off and sucked at his body's breath.

"*Two* seals?" Malgi asked. "You see, Grandson? You see why we should wait for the seal, instead of chasing him? Was I not right? And look at this seal"—he waved at his—"I did not think I could lift it out of its allu. You see?" He tilted his head back, laughed. "You see! Three seals! Three, now!"

Claudia smiled, happy at the old man's joy, at her joy, at Tuttu's joy. "I heard four shots."

"Amaguq?" Tuttu said, pointing beyond Malgi.

Claudia took her Nikons out from a parka pocket—she'd remembered them this trip—and scanned the twilight. Someone in a white atigi, coming from the southwest. Who had come with her, with Malgi? Yes, Amaguq: Natchiq had gone northeast with Tuttu. Puvak had stayed back at the qaregi.

"Amaguq," she said. She focused tighter on the dim figure. "No seal—but he's carrying something."

The hunter, the wolf, came up to them, held up the thing as he approached. He waved the thing at them, a thing about two feet across, arms thrust out in eight different directions, body like a triangular wedge. A crab! Hah, she wanted to shout, We got seals, you got a crab. The man laughed at the sight, Amaguq laughing with them.

"You shot that?" Tuttu said.

"Did you give it water, too?" Malgi joked.

"Yah," Amaguq said. "It was a fierce fight! He bit the cup!"

The hunters chuckled, packs came off and they all pulled out thermoses. Malgi poured tea from his thermos into their cups, and they stood, rocking on their feet, sipping on tea while Amaguq caught his breath and told them his story.

"I shot a seal—I did!" he said. "An ugruq, I think."

"Bearded seals don't use allus," Malgi said.

"Well, as *big* as an ugruq. Anyway, as you told us, I quickly tied a line to the seal, held the line with my foot. I was reaching over to get my unaaq when something pulled on the seal. I grabbed the rope, thinking maybe the current had the seal, or maybe the seal wasn't quite dead."

"You should loop the rope around your foot right off," Malgi said. "Tie a circle in the end. That current can get strong."

"It wasn't a current!" He sipped his tea, shook his head. "I had the rope in my hand—I hadn't put my mitten back on, so I had a good grip—when something pulled, hard. I pulled back, and it pulled harder!"

"The seal woman," Malgi said, nodding. "She wanted the seal back." He smiled, to show he was joking.

"No, no, not her—oh! Anyway, I pulled, something pulled harder. I figured out that something was eating the seal, biting at it. So I yanked hard, thinking it was a fish—I don't know, it acted like a fish. And the thing pulled back real hard, disgusted at the game, I guess. It pulled my hand down into the water of the broken allu. Yai, that was cold! But I held on." Amaguq tapped his chest. "It wasn't going to get *my* seal."

"*Something* did," Tuttu said.

"Yes," Amaguq said, "something did. So when that thing yanked, I got smart"—he tapped his forehead—"and thought, okay, better not keep getting wet. I slipped my unaaq through the loop on the rope, and let that thing pull the rest of the rope down into the hole. I figured I could pull the seal back up after I got my mitten back on. I took off my wet glove liners, slipped my hand back in the mitten.

"I watched that stick wobble back and forth. The thing pulled on the rope, yanked and pulled. I thought it was going to break the unaaq, just pull the whole thing through the hole, it pulled so hard. And then it yanked real hard, one big pull, and the unaaq bowed in the middle, and bounced back out. I grabbed the unaaq, pulled back on the rope, and brought up—this!" Amaguq held up the crab.

"That crab ate the seal?" Tuttu asked, eyebrows raised in mock astonishment. "Azah, he must have shit a lot already! How big is his stomach? Did he puke on you?"

"No, no," said Amaguq. "An *aaglu* ate the seal—a killer whale. I was about fifty yards from the lead. After I pulled the crab up, I heard a *whooshing* noise out from the open water. I looked out there and saw this huge fin cutting through the sea, and then the whale spouted again, and dived, like he was giving thanks to *me*."

"The killer whale?" Claudia asked. "You think a killer whale took your seal?"

"It could happen," Malgi said. "Once I saw a polar bear lying in the sun, on a little ice floe. Out of the water this aaglu rises up, pulls nanuq into the water, and eats him in about two bites. The wolf of the sea—he knows his brother, Amaguq."

Amaguq shrugged, as if to say, believe me or not. "I think the aaglu left a little meat on the end of the line, and the crab took it. So I got the crab, at least." He held it up again, and the hunters laughed at his story.

Claudia smiled. Three seals and a crab. But better, they had a story. The thrill of the hunt, the joy of the kill, and the laughter of Amaguq's story washed through her. What did it matter that Amaguq got a crab? The bond, that was what counted: he had hunted well, even if he hadn't completely succeeded. They had all hunted well. *I hunted well*, she thought. This is what matters. *We have hunted, I am a hunter*.

Chapter 14

ON January the twenty-third the sun rose for the first time in sixty-five days. Claudia and Tammy were out drilling for water on the freshwater lake, walking around and around a long auger bit, when Claudia glanced to the south and saw an orange arc rise up above the horizon. The battery on her digital watch had died a month before, its crystals freezing and fading in a lethargic dance; she had no idea of the time when the sun rose, but later calculated it to be about one o'clock in the afternoon. Claudia slowed on her side of the auger. Tammy glanced up.

"Look," Claudia said.

"Ah," Tammy said, "azahah. The sun. It's that day?"

The anthropologist nodded. "I'd forgotten. The night's over—the twilight, anyway."

The great orange ball rose over the frozen lake, the windswept lake. Drifts and mounds on the ice cast long shadows toward them, and Claudia turned to the north and saw her own shadow pointing to town. Three satellite dishes, like hubcaps on cones, pointed straight across the tundra, almost flat to the horizon. The sunlight caught the dishes, making them glow pink, the ends of the receivers glinting. Tuttu and Natchiq had been messing with the satellite dishes, trying to get one to work, she remembered—

trying to fix the satellite that picked up signals from Anik II, a Canadian telestat. The dishes, too, cast shadows. Shadows!

Overhead, the sky was clear, a dark blue that faded to pale, the color of new ice. A wisp of a cloud swung from horizon to horizon, as if the sea had raked the sky with foamy fingers. But no dark clouds blotted the dome of day above. No ash swirled in the upper atmosphere. All was clear, the winter of war gone with the winter of night.

The sweat at her back grew moist and cold and clammy. Claudia and Tammy looked up at the sun, then resumed their work, drilling through the new ice to the water below. Water from the lake tended to be more brackish, fouler tasting than the clean, pure water from piqaluyak ice, but Claudia thought it easier to get to than hiking all the way out to the landfast ice ridge. The auger broke through into unfrozen water, and they heaved the bit up just as a buzzing noise hit them.

Something that sounded like an angry mosquito hummed to the north, just beyond the satellite dishes. Claudia searched for the sound, trying to place its origin and location. It sounded familiar but ancient, a sound, like the New York Philharmonic playing Beethoven's *Ninth*, she knew but had not heard in a long, long while. Her memory played with the noise, put a tag on it, and then she made the connection. She heard the throaty roar of a motor coming from the satellite dishes down the road. She looked for the thing with the motor and saw a light bob down the road toward them. ATVs. Four-wheelers.

She half expected to see Jim and Horace and Oliver roaring up on ATVs; Claudia hadn't heard a four-wheeler since Ataniq, right after she and Rob had emerged from their fallout shelter and started their walk to Wainwright. But of course it couldn't be Jim or anyone from Ulguniq; despite trying, no one had heard from Wainwright since the war, not over the CB, not over any sort of radio. If anyone lived in Wainwright, they'd have to wait until spring and the water cleared enough to boat down to find out. The gas for a trip by snowmachine couldn't be spared, and who'd want to hike down there?

Claudia and Tammy laid the auger down, and watched

the light grow larger. They noticed another light follow the first light. Two ATVs, then.

"Who's that?" Tammy asked. She pushed the hood back from her atigi, ran a hand through the shorter hairs on the top of her head. Claudia smiled at the gesture, thinking of Tammy's obsessive attention to her appearance. Unlike Claudia, with her shabby bangs hanging down in her face, Tammy kept the vestiges of her punk cut neatly trimmed. No one else in the qaregi shared her obsession. Tammy kept teasing Claudia about her unkempt hair, threatening to "whack that shit" out of her eyes some night when she was asleep.

"Got me," Claudia said. "Didn't know anyone could get gas. Natchiq guards it like gold."

The two ATVs turned off the road and onto the lake. Tuttu and Amaguq. Tuttu drove out on the ice, and pulled up to them, the four fat wheels of the ATV skidding and whipping the machine around. He kept the engine on idle.

"Been lookin' for you, anthropologist. Something's come up." Tuttu patted the seat behind him. "Get on."

"What's going on?" Claudia asked. Why would they waste precious gas searching for her? she thought. A chill went down her spine. Someone hurt? Had Malgi or one of the elders died? "Anything wrong?"

He shook his head, smiled to reassure her. "No. Something else—it's easier to show you. Let's go."

Amaguq stopped his ATV behind Tuttu, smiled at Claudia. Tammy ignored the two men and had begun pulling water out of the ice hole with a hand pump and filling two five-gallon jugs. Claudia jerked her head at Tammy, turned to help her.

"Got to get some water, Tuttu," she said. "Since you came out all this way . . . ?" She pointed at the pulkka sled, two ropes attached to the sled and tied to waist belts.

"Tammy can bring the water back," Tuttu said. "We got to go."

Tammy looked up at her name, glared at Tuttu and his suggestion. Tuttu sighed, killed the ATV's engine, and took the pump from her. He pushed the pump handle up and down in swift, firm strokes, quickly filling both jugs. The hunter lifted both jugs onto the pulkka, threw the pump and auger in with them, strapped everything together and tied the drag lines to the back bumper of his ATV.

"Okay," he said, kicking the machine back on. "*Now* can we go?"

She nodded, and Claudia climbed behind Tuttu, groping for the foot pedals with her mukluks. Tammy got on behind Amaguq, and the two ATVs roared up the road, toward town. It was the same road Claudia had walked on when she first came into Utqiagvik, the same road that went by where Kanayuq's remains had been laid out.

Claudia hugged Tuttu's stomach, leaned her head against his shoulder to get her face out of the wind. Coarse brown hairs from Tuttu's wolverine ruff tickled her cheek; it felt warm against her face, his body felt warm against her chest. The wind whipped his thick brown hair into her wavy blond hair, and mixed the two together, brown and blond swirling around in the chill breeze.

Turning her face out of the wind, Claudia glanced over at Tammy. Tammy gripped the seat of Amaguq's ATV with her thighs, clung with her hands to the black luggage rack. She leaned back from Amaguq, head raised up. Her hood had slipped back and the stiff hair on her crown ruffled in the wind, like the hairs on Tuttu's wolverine trim. Qavvik, Claudia thought, the wolverine. Tammy said they should call her that, but no one had; Tuttu still called her Nuna, if he spoke to her at all. But, yeah, the wolverine would be right, Claudia thought: fierce and independent.

The ATVs came into town, zoomed by the qaregi, passed by the ruins of Stuaqpak, past the ashes of the Presbyterian church, and around on a road that paralleled the lagoon. Tuttu steered the ATV into a street across the road from the older school, the junior high school, and stopped at a two-story building with gray steel siding; a sign read BARROW CABLE COMPANY on the front of the building, and various microwave relay towers and antennae poked out from the roof. Across from the cable building Claudia glimpsed the burnt hulk of the old KBRW station, its plate-glass window through which the deejay had watched the world pocked with bullet holes. Still standing, though, was the Barrow

National Forest, a small sign proclaiming the fact; the "forest" was a frayed piece of baleen stuck on the end of a stick, probably the most widely photographed piece of baleen on the North Slope.

As they got off the four-wheelers, Natchiq came running out of the building, his shouts drowned out by the noise of a diesel generator rattling in an insulated box by the arctic entryway. More fuel wasting? Claudia thought. He motioned them inside and up a set of stairs just inside the door.

"The broadcast's starting again," Natchiq said. They came into a room crammed with video monitors and electronic equipment. Natchiq waved at a bank of television screens, the same image repeated on ten 19-inch screens and one large 32-inch screen. "See?"

Claudia froze at the image, the video monitors lighting the room. Big boxes of esoteric electronics hummed and blipped. She pushed her bangs back from out of her eyes, watching the screens in awe. *Television.* She had thought she would never see television again.

On the screens flickered a head-and-shoulders shot of a man in his mid-forties, image after image repeated. The man wore a royal blue suit with narrow lapels, a thin red tie, and a white shirt that seemed to glow on the monitor. He had gentle blue eyes, a kindly face, like the face of one's favorite uncle or grandfather, and a neat, graying mustache. His hair had been swept back from his face in smooth brown waves, with a touch of gray at the temples and sideburns. As he spoke a smaller image flashed on the screen behind him: a map of a country shaped like a curved sword.

"It didn't play this far before," Natchiq said.

The face . . . Claudia had seen that face before. Some kind of newscaster, that was obvious, but who? Natchiq turned a knob on a control panel, raising the sound. The camera cut from the talking head to brief scenes of archaic-looking helicopters flying over tropical jungle, then to a shot of the jungle turning into flames, and another shot of two soldiers carrying a man on a litter to a waiting helicopter. The medics hunched low in the kind of walk that people who worked around whirling blades soon developed. The grandfatherly man's face came back on the screen.

"Who's that?" Tuttu asked. "You know, Claudia?"

She listened to the man, tried to put a tag on his voice. The voice sounded familiar, a soothing, slightly bass voice, with a slight accent—Midwestern? Northeastern?—she couldn't quite place. *Vietnam*—he was saying something about Vietnam. My God, she thought, did the world survive only to get in *that* mess again?

". . . and that's the way it is," said the newscaster, "for January twenty-third, nineteen sixty-seven. This is—"

"*Walter Cronkite*," she said.

"Walter Cronkite for CBS News. Good night," he said.

"Walter Cronkite?" Natchiq asked. "Didn't he retire in . . . I don't know, I was a kid then."

"Nineteen eighty, eighty-two, something like that," Claudia said. "He used to do specials, though. Walter Cronkite. I remember him from some old science programs I saw in high school. But he didn't look that young."

"You heard the date: one twenty-three, sixty-seven," said Natchiq. "It's a tape. Right day, wrong year."

"How'd you pick it up?" Claudia asked.

"Tuttu, Amaguq, and I have been monitoring for the last week. Shortwave, AM-FM, VHF, UHF, anything we could get working. We just reconnected the satellite dishes today. I think it's a feed off one of the RCA satellites."

Electronics, Claudia thought. The electronics worked. That wasn't supposed to be, though. "What about the EMP?" she asked.

Natchiq shook his head. " 'Lectromagnetic pulse didn't get us. It's a high-altitude effect," he explained. "Got to blow a nuke at least sixty miles up to create it. The Soviets would try to blanket the lower-48 states, but that wouldn't get the Arctic. We'd have tried to hit Central Siberia, but might miss their east. Anyway, the EMP didn't get us, I guess."

As Natchiq explained, Claudia remembered he'd worked for Barrow Cable before he'd gone back to hunting—he'd learned electronics in the Army. "And the other guy," she said, pointing at the screen. "Where's the feed come from?'' She tried to remember what she could about satellite broadcasting. Someone had to broadcast from the ground and shoot up to the satellite. Satellites just didn't broadcast on their own.

Natchiq shrugged. ''Anywhere; it's hard to calculate.''

Anywhere, Claudia thought. Anywhere. Somewhere out there someone had gotten hold of a satellite transmitter and a bunch of old CBS news tapes and was broadcasting to the world. ''So we're not alone,'' she said.

Tuttu nodded. ''We're not alone.''

Natchiq had taped the broadcast and was rewinding it. He started it again, and Claudia stared at the screen as the news for January 23, 1967 played once again.

''Why wouldn't he—she—just broadcast live?'' Tammy asked. ''Why wouldn't they let us know where they are, what's going on there?'' Natchiq shrugged.

Claudia listened to Cronkite, watched the images—commercials and all—of a time before she was even born. Why just broadcast old Cronkite tapes? she asked herself. Why—because of Cronkite, that was why. She remembered her mother talking about those times, about that awful war, and how the stability of Walter Cronkite—that gentle newscaster breaking yet another tragedy to them—had helped America get through. Why? That was why, she thought.

''Cronkite,'' she said aloud. ''Whoever's alive wants to send us hope—not the hope of today, but the hope of a time past. Anyway, they've already sent the most important message they can.''

''Someone else made it,'' Tuttu said, grinning slyly.

''Yeah, someone else made it,'' Claudia repeated.

''So maybe we can, too,'' Tammy said.

Claudia smiled. ''Right. Maybe we can, too.''

And maybe we *can't* make it, Claudia thought. She wanted to say it, too, but dared not. Thinking could make it so, but saying would make it so. So she kept quiet as they sat in the high school gym.

Natchiq had rigged up a video monitor to show the Walter Cronkite broadcasts to the villagers. There had been five transmissions since January, five over the last two months. That night's had been particularly gruesome: a plane crash, a segment on the Biafra war, and more Vietnam footage. The gloom of the old news matched their gloom. Tuttu had done a new calculation of their supplies, and announced it after Natchiq turned the monitor off and the glow of the tube had faded.

"Doesn't look good," he said. "We're running short of store food—and we haven't gotten any seals."

At first, all the houses feasted well, once the hunters had learned the hard secret of sitting in the cold and waiting for the seal to come to the allu. The seals they had caught so easily had been divided and shared—a piece to some elders, a share to cousins, another share to the Honkey House, as everyone called the group of whites who'd banded together. It had all gone quickly. But on subsequent trips they got fewer seals. On the latest trip—a long wait made endurable only by the blessing of the lengthening sun—of fifteen hunters spread up and down the ice, not one had even seen a seal.

"The ice has frozen too hard," Malgi explained. "Though there are leads open here, they must be closed further down, between us and the seals."

"We could go further down then," Aluaq, Paula's husband, said. "Hike to where the seals are. Find them."

Malgi shook his head. "What if they are not there? You will have hiked for nothing. And how long would you hike? And how much energy would you waste getting there? We should wait for the seals—or the leads to open."

"We may not be able to wait, Grandfather," Tuttu said.

He read off his figures, based on a new inventory—and another round of scavenging—of all the houses's stores: rations enough to last the whole village perhaps one more month. At the words, Claudia felt the old hunger roar in her stomach again. Was this what life would be from now on? Continuous hunger?

But Tuttu had *some* good news. He said that Natchiq had figured out how to recharge a bank of big 12-volt car batteries off a wind-powered generator, like he'd done with Masu's reading lamp in the qaregi; as long as the Cronkite broadcasts kept coming, they could watch them.

"We have some fuel left," Tuttu said. "Some gas, some diesel oil. We'd have more if Edward hadn't blown the barge." He frowned, and Claudia recalled the barge blazing, Edward's body ripped with bullets. "Maybe we could use some of it to go down the coast in boats when the leads clear. Or out on the tundra on sno-gos." He shrugged, then smiled. "But the *best* news . . . Puvak?" He waved at the young hunter.

Puvak rose up from the back of the gym, holding up two squirming pups barely bigger than his hands, one jet black, one almost blond. "Two litters of pups," he said. "Out of Libby and Susan. Libby had the first litter, but Susan had more. Both out of Rick. We should have teams by fall!" He beamed as the little dogs wiggled in his hands.

The villagers laughed as one pup yipped, and Puvak was surrounded by kids and elders who wanted to hold and stroke the puppies. He handed one pup to Masu, Malgi's wife, another to Masik Umiaqpak's aunt. The two crones held them gingerly, smiling at fluffy balls of fur, the way they seemed to want to crawl everywhere to forever. Masik's son, Kutchuq, petted the black pup, and it reached to suck on his finger. Claudia grinned. Soon, with more litters, every child in the village would raise her own team, every child would learn to build sleds and weave traces and run dogs.

"The pups are more mouths to feed," Malgi said. "And how are we to feed our own mouths?"

"The dogs can share my ration," Puvak said, a slight edge of anger in his voice. "Grandfather," he added out of respect.

Malgi nodded at the boy, smiled. "You are a good enough hunter that you will feed us all." The Angatkok sighed.

"Malgi," Amaguq said. "Tuttu said we have some fuel. If the leads open enough, we could drag the boat out to the edge of the tuvaq, and run down the coast."

"Ai," he said. Malgi smiled. " 'If the leads open.' They will not do that soon enough. But even if they did . . . why waste our precious gas? And roam around chasing little seals?"

"Better that than starving," Tuttu said.

Claudia stared at Malgi, at Tuttu, listening to the exchange. The old man was right, of course, so often right. The seals had gone elsewhere, and they couldn't hunt them from the breathing holes, or even the local ice edge. They would have to go find them in boats. But why *not* hunt them from boats? she thought. Why should he object to that?

They had the boats. They had some gas they had carefully rationed. There was even a tattered skin boat in the museum they could use—Malgi's old boat, in fact. If they had to paddle, they could do that. What was the old man getting at? He looked up at her, caught her gaze, and nodded, tapping his chest. She looked down between her breasts, at the whale amulet dangling on a cord from her neck. Absently, she had been stroking the carving, the carving she had found the day her world had ended, and Malgi had noticed the gesture.

Agviq, she thought. Yes. The thought crept through her. Of course. Dare she say it? She frowned at Malgi, furrowed her eyebrows. He pointed a finger at her, opened his mouth, moving his lips in silent supplication. Speak, he seemed to say. You speak.

"We could hunt . . . something bigger," she said.

"Bigger?" Tuttu asked, whirling to face her. "Like the ugruk? Like the walrus? Ai, that's an idea. But they have not come yet."

"*Bigger*," she said. "Something worth our time, worth the gas, that could feed an entire house—our entire village."

Malgi stood, and everyone in the gym turned to him. "Agviq," he said. "We could hunt agviq."

There! she thought. There! He has said it. The whale.

"The whale?" Natchiq asked. "You want us to hunt the whale?" He shook his head. "With *what*? Thirty-ought-six rifles?"

"No, not rifles," the old man said. Malgi reached under a bleacher seat and pulled out a six-foot-long roll of green canvas. He unrolled the cloth, and held up a long lance, a staff with a barbed head like a missile. A thin rod poked out from the tip of the staff. "With this," Malgi said, holding it above his head. "With my father's old darting harpoon."

"*That?*" Tuttu scoffed. "That is a museum piece. It would not work. Do you have the bombs for it? Do you know how to work it?"

"*I killed two whales with this!*" Malgi shouted, "Before the government told us we could not whale anymore, I killed two whales. I have used it. As for bombs . . ." He shrugged.

"I could make bombs," Grigor said from Claudia's left, down at the end of a bench. The Soviet stood. "May I see it? I knew of Siberian whalers who used something similar. You have gunpowder?"

Tuttu punched a few keys on his laptop computer, and nodded. "Twenty pounds, at least."

"I could make a bomb then," Grigor said. "In . . . in the Spetsnaz"—he blushed at the mention of his duty in the Soviet special forces—"I . . . I learned to make such things."

Tuttu stood, took the darting harpoon from Malgi, held it out to Grigor. "Could you, Russian? If you could"—he smiled—"we could forget who you were and call you Inupiaq. Hah! If we could kill a whale, if the whale would honor us, we could call all of us Inupiaq!" He smiled, a smirk of a smile that Claudia had seen often—the smile he made when he thought something absurd and stupid. "But Grandfather, indulge this stupid boy. Is it not too early to hunt whales?"

Malgi nodded. "In the old days, it would be too early, but things have changed so much, who can tell?"

"Can we last until the whales come, though?" Claudia asked.

Tuttu sighed, tapped some figures into his little computer. "If it's six weeks—barely," he said. "We'd do better if we could get even one seal. Perhaps a polar bear—anything."

"Then it's settled," Malgi said. "We can prepare to hunt whales while we wait."

Tuttu shook his head. "Kill a whale? I doubt it. But if we could . . . Ai, what the hell. We have no choice, do we?" Tuttu patted his stomach, and Claudia understood. To really survive, to endure, they would have to catch whales. It was the essence, the true test of being Inupiaq. "Let us try, then," he added. "Let us try." He took the darting harpoon from Malgi, and raised it with one arm raised high. The villagers cheered. A whale. They would whale!

Tuttu stared down at the ground then, and Claudia caught his gesture. Try, she thought, try.

Or die.

Chapter 15

CLAUDIA climbed the steps of the weather tower at the edge of town, and looked west to Utqiagvik. The sun had risen at a respectable five in the morning, and now cast Claudia's shadow and the tower's shadow across the softball field toward town. High noon. Her steps echoed on the cold steel treads winding up one side of the tall building, and then she came to the top.

The weather tower reminded her of Tyco Brahe's observatory in Copenhagen, a place she'd visited when she was sixteen. Brahe's tower had a ramp winding inside, wide enough to drive a carriage up, should the King want to drop by and gaze at the stars. On top of Brahe's tower was a little room, with a railing ringing the roof. On top of the weather tower was a white dome, and a railing around the dome. Both towers were the same height, the same general dimensions, though the weather tower really wasn't an observatory, but a high shed for inflating and launching weather balloons. Still, she climbed the weather tower for much the same purpose as the Danish astronomer: he, to peer into the past of stars' ancient light; she, to look into the past of Barrow's recent ruins.

Soon, she knew, village children would climb these same steps to look out at the ice and watch for the opening of the uiniq, the lead—perhaps even to see the misty plumes of agviq's return. Now, Claudia climbed these steps to see the plan of the town, to see where streets had been and houses had been; to see where to begin digging for treasure.

At the top of the tower she paused to catch her breath, then took out her binoculars and scanned the town. She looked at the town not as her home of some months, but the way she would look at a site. She looked at it to find things. She looked to see where houses would be, buried under the drifts, to correlate her street map with addresses and house locations.

Claudia looked for whalers.

Days before, she had pored over various books and reports still intact in the museum director's office. That had been a start. In the museum Malgi had pointed out the guns, the tools, the artifacts he remembered as being useful for whaling, but most of the tools had been broken and useless— why else would they wind up in a museum? In the office they had found something equally valuable: all the old references, the classic texts of ethnography and history, archaeology and anthropology, stories and accounts. Helen Hughes's whaling survey—with names and addresses of whalers—had proved invaluable. Claudia interviewed the surviving elders, interviewed Malgi, until she had come up with as many possible locations of old whalers. And now she stood on the roof, trying to figure out whose homes still stood, where the rubble would be of homes that had collapsed or had been looted. She tried to figure out who lived where and where they might find working tools and weapons, or the logbooks and maybe even journals of old whalers.

A brisk wind rattled the steel panels of the building, robbing heat from her bare fingers. No matter. Claudia had long ago learned the trick of working with her hands in cold and rain. She marked block locations and house locations on her map with a big yellow marker. There, a neat green house almost directly across from the weather station: Igaluk's mother's family, whalers for six generations. At the edge of the site, the log home that had been robbed for firewood: Amaguq's uncle, a big man in the corporation who had moved to Anchorage a few years back, a great whaler. And so on.

The wind blew across the town, blowing in from the sun,

throwing the snow into drifts. Houses and old cars and piles of junk became teardrops in the plain, round lumps covered with snow and spreading drifts like comet tails. Smoke rose from homes scattered around the town, beaten paths connected the houses to each other and to the gym, to the cable station, to the pack ice. Many of the old streets remained covered, discernible only as long open lines empty of structures. The tiny village clung to the edge of the sea, on a spit of humanity between ocean and the vast emptiness of the land. This could be all there is in the world, Claudia thought. There could be no one else.

It could be like long ago, when the Inupiaq and their ancestors had only dim knowledge of people beyond their cognitive horizons. They would have known of others like them or similar to them, down the coast and inland, because it was from those people that they acquired goods they could not make or find: steel points in their later years, beads from the Russians, jade from the Nunanimiut far inland. This land and this place would be their center, she thought. It is now our center. The world cannot revolve around Washington or New York or even Tokyo anymore; those places did not exist anymore. It was only them, and whoever sent them Walter Cronkite. And the Soviets, if Grigor could be believed. And who else? she thought.

Who else?

"Ah—here," said Malgi. He pointed at a drifted-over house with his unaaq. "Simeon's house, my father's brother. He died long ago, but his daughter lived here, until . . . we never found her body."

"He was a good whaler?" she asked.

"Ten whales in his lifetime, the first when he was but eighteen. My father and Simeon crewed with their father and then together when Grandpa died and I crewed with them." Malgi scratched at a depression in the drift, on the leeward side. Claudia had marked the house on her map, but Malgi took her straight to it.

She turned to Tuttu and Amaguq, to Aluaq, and smiled. She was on her turf now: boss lady of an excavation. "Dig," she said. "Find the door and we'll go in."

The three men moved snow off the side of the house, and quickly hit something hard and shiny. Ice? Claudia stopped them and crawled through the little tunnel they'd made. With her trowel she scraped at the snow, the old muscles burning in her palm and fingers. A trowel! The touch and texture of it thrilled her. She was back in her element. She scraped away packed snow and loose snow, layer upon layer the way drifted snow built up, then hit hard ice, solid ice. The tip of the trowel wouldn't yield and squeaked against the ice. She frowned, pushed harder, trying to understand this new thing. Claudia smiled then at the realization. Glass.

"It's a window," she said. She crawled out, looked at Malgi. "You want to save the glass or go right in?"

"Save it," Malgi said. "They don't make glass anymore, you know?"

She nodded and said, "Then we need to find the door." Figure the house used plywood siding, she thought. It would be in four-by-eight dimensions. Two pieces of plywood end to end between the door and the wall, toward the middle of the house. Put the door in the middle? It made sense. "It would be"—she paced out two strides, about eight feet—"about right here."

The men dug, and when they tired briefly, Claudia took over. Close in work. She used the little folding shovel brought up from Pingasagruk, the one she had tried to bury the dead blond woman with at the ravine, the one who looked like her sister. The point of the shovel hit something solid. She slammed it in again, pulled the shovel out. A bit of packed snow with a splinter of wood stuck to the cold steel.

"Bingo," she said. "Go at it, guys."

Tuttu smiled, and began whaling away at the entrance. The way he swung the shovel, the way he raised the blade up and down with such earnestness, reminded her of Jules, another undergraduate student she'd worked with a few summers back. She had just started her master's and Jules was finishing up his bachelor's. Unlike Rob, Jules hadn't been shy or intimidated. They'd had an intense affair that dig, and then he went off to do Meso-American stuff and she'd stayed with Arctic.

Big pyramids suited him better, she thought, watching the powerful but cavalier work of Tuttu. Jules could never catch on to the concept of digging in narrow levels of ten centimeters. Unwatched and unrestrained, he could dig to sterile in two days, permafrost or not. But he'd been hell on piss-filled entrance tunnels.

Tuttu swung down with his shovel, and suddenly he pitched forward and rolled down the angled hole to the door. He came up laughing, rubbing his head. He handed the shovel to Claudia. She took it, laid it down. Tuttu held his hand out and pulled her down.

"It's open, Nivakti," he said. Her old nickname. Digger. Cute, she thought.

She flicked on a flashlight and followed him into the cold house. Tuttu helped Malgi down into the house. It was one of those old government houses, either a BIA tin box or one of the ones brought up by Karl's company that cost two hundred thousand dollars and had the insulation of a wasp's nest. Claudia shined the flashlight into corners of the house, impressed by the bright beam. Lithium batteries, she thought. Good old Natchiq had found a stash at the cable company—for camcorders—and rigged up a recharger. Bless him.

At first she thought the house had been abandoned and never lived in, so neat and sterile was it. No pictures on the wall, save an old North Slope Borough calendar and a dime-store Jesus print. One couch and two chairs. She moved toward the kitchen. A bloodstained piece of plywood lay against one wall, a set of two ulus hung on nails next to the sink. Nothing else but a few pans on the stove. And there, on a plastic cutting board, three pieces of red meat and black stuff like candle wax stuck to it. A microwave oven door had fallen open, and on a platter was another piece of the meat. The black stuff confused her for a moment. She turned to Malgi, padding softly behind her, his unaaq tapping on the linoleum floor. Tuttu stood by his grandfather. She shone the light on him and back on the meat.

"Maktak," he said.

Whale flesh and whale blubber. That shouldn't be. All the whale meat should have been eaten before the last time the whalers could go out for whales. Or maybe some had been saved when Malgi's Uncle Simeon had found out he couldn't go whaling again. Maybe it had been the last. Maybe his daughter had found it in her freezer, and had been going to thaw it and eat it because the war had come. Something had stopped her...

Claudia whirled the flashlight beam around, toward what would be the backdoor of the house.

"Azah," Malgi said.

"Shit," said Tuttu.

"We never found her body out on... on the tundra," the old man said. "Things came up. There were so many others to look for, we couldn't look for everyone."

Claudia shined the light on the dead woman, crumpled by the door. A small hole pierced the little window of the backdoor, cracking the glass into a spider's web. A small hole bored through the woman's chest, the bullet pushing her against the wall opposite. She didn't want to turn the woman over, didn't want to seek the origin of the brick-brown stain on the floor. She didn't want to find where the bullet had wound up. It didn't matter. Malgi's cousin had gone to answer the door and been shot. Or maybe she had just been standing by it, hit by a stray shot flying through town.

Tuttu pulled a curtain down from the window over the sink—what a silly honkey idea, Claudia thought, a window over the sink—and covered the woman with it. "We'll bury her in the summer," he said. "I'll—I'll wait in the other room."

His face seemed paler—pale, perhaps, not at the death itself but the deaths it recalled, Claudia thought. She felt herself go cold from the house and the body, and thought, Yes, we will find many more under the snow and bury many bodies in the summer.

She shone the light back around the kitchen, moved down a hallway to a bedroom. One room was almost empty, bare but for an unmade bed and a small bookshelf holding child's toys. Malgi had said his cousin had a son who had joined the Army, been kicked out, and wound up in Fairbanks. The boy had never come back. He said the son had been found hypothermic in the street, with a blood alcohol level of 25 percent. To the other room . . .

A double bed, two big reindeer hide skins over it. A woman's atigi hung from a hook next to the door. Claudia touched it, ran her fingers over the embroidery on the covering. The hairs of the ruff fluffed against her touch, and the sheepskin hide felt thick on the inside of the parka. She looked at Malgi, and he nodded.

"Masu might like that," he said.

A massive dresser stood against the right wall, more like a big chest than a dresser. A hutch, actually, she thought. For fine china. On the shelves and behind the glass doors, though, row upon row of tiny white figurines shone like teeth. Ivory. Carvings. She slid back the doors and ran the beam of light over the carvings.

Polar bears and seals. Musk ox. Walruses. Four cribbage boards with scrimshaw scenes: a racing dog team, a village scene, and two whaling scenes. One scene showed a skin boat coming up on the whale, harpoonist with darting lance raised; the other showed a group of people pulling the whale out of the water. And whales. Dozens of whales. Whales sounding. Whales diving. Mother and child whales. Two whales copulated face-to-face, snouts raised and flukes down, fins hugging each other. And a large whale, lines etched in it like a butchering diagram. Exactly. She picked it up, showed it to Malgi.

"Ah, the shares," he said. He ran his fingers over the lines, squinted at tiny words etched in an odd cursive script. "The names of them. I'd forgotten." He smiled, slipped the carving in his pocket.

They began opening drawers, sliding doors back. On a lower shelf were maybe twenty artifacts, mostly harpoon heads and points. Small points, for seals. Barbed points, out of antler, for arrows. Some heads had empty slots, others had ground purple slate points set in them. There were two massive harpoon heads bigger than her hand, each inset with shiny steel blades. Whale harpoons. At the base of one head had been etched twelve sketches of whales, the early ones crude and simple, the later ones more fluid, more lifelike.

"Here," said Malgi. She turned the light toward him.

He stood by a gun case, the same Colonial style as the hutch. Probably mail order from a furniture store in Anchorage, Claudia thought. Malgi had unlocked the doors—the key still in the lock—and held out an odd-looking gun. The barrel of the gun was smooth, about eighteen inches long, and ended in a squat action. The stock of the gun was an open trapezoid, the butt rounded for the shoulder. Malgi clicked something on the action, and opened the barrel of the gun like a breech loading shotgun.

"Pierce bomb gun," he said. "I had one just like it, but on my last hunt it fell overboard. Someone in an aluminum boat ran into us." He frowned, the remembered hurt and loss and anger flickering across his face. He hefted the bomb gun, and grinned. "If my uncle had bombs . . ." He rummaged in drawers at the bottom of the cabinet, pulled out two pointed rods the length of the barrel that looked like Fourth of July skyrockets without the stick. "Ah. Ah." Malgi's grin grew larger as he slid a bomb into the gun.

Someone came down the hallway after them, and Claudia saw the light of a flashlight bobbing around corners and then come into the room. Tuttu swept the flashlight before him, stopped it on the old man. Malgi held the bomb gun with both hands, raised it over his hand, and laughed.

"Grandfather?" Tuttu asked. "I heard noise . . ."

"Airigaaa!" Malgi said. "Look at this, Grandson. Look at this! Now! Now we can hunt the whale!"

"Grandfather," Tuttu whispered, seeing the gun, the ivory carvings on the case, the points and lances and harpoon heads and the atigi hanging by a hook on the wall. He raised his eyebrows and smiled a grin to match Malgi's. "Such treasure . . . Ai, Grandfather. Perhaps we can hunt the whale now."

Perhaps we can, Claudia thought to herself, adding a silent prayer. Perhaps we can—if the whale lets us.

Chapter 16

CLAUDIA looked up at the weather tower, to Grigor standing at the railing with the darting gun in his hand. He attached the gun—iron, bomb lance, and wooden staff—to two pulleys on a wire that sloped down from the tower and to a mound of packed snow. Village kids had shaped the mound of snow to look something like a whale, but not *the* whale, not agviq, but more like a storybook whale: all head and little tail. Inside the snow a sheet of plywood with foam tacked to it had been buried.

She stood well back from the mock whale, with Amaguq and Tuttu and the rest. Grigor, Natchiq, and Malgi fumbled with the darting gun from up on the tower. Malgi had decided that Natchiq would be the whaling crew's harpoonist, since he was the best shot with a rifle and had the best eyes. Grigor took a special interest in the test, because he had, after all, loaded the charge that would explode the bomb.

Tammy bobbed nervously next to Claudia, shifting her feet left, right, left, right in the cold. Their breath rose in steamy clouds and fell into a small fog over the swampy land to the northwest. Kids ran squealing across the field, climbing up and down on the "tail" of the target, away from the wire.

"Ready?" Tuttu yelled up to Grigor.

The Soviet finished clipping the darting gun to the wire, and shouted back to Tuttu. "Ready."

"Get those kids out of there," he said to Tammy.

She scowled at him, then sighed, and chased the five or so children back to the watching group. About thirty villagers had come out to watch the test of the darting gun, many of them convinced it would not work, some eager to see its spectacular failure. The people quieted, the children tittered nervously, and Grigor released the gun.

The shaft fell down the wire, the wire that guided the gun down to the mound of snow. The cable went through the snow and to a post pounded in the ground beyond. As the darting gun fell, Claudia thought that that would not be the way it would fly toward agviq. Natchiq would throw the harpoon into the hard skin of the whale. Gravity would do part of the work, true, but not like this. The real thrust would rely on human muscle and human aim and human skill, not on a wire guiding the bomb to some kid-carved whale's brain. This was a test. It was only a test, not of someone's skill at throwing harpoons, but of the powder, the bomb, the technology.

The pulleys sang as they rolled down the wire. Tuttu glanced at his watch, at the Rolex he'd recovered from Karl's body, and he counted the seconds as the lance hit the snow. "One," he said, as the harpoon head slid into the packed powder. "Two," he said as the firing rod followed the head of the iron. "Three, four, five—"

Smoke and mist billowed from the packed snow. The wooden shaft shot back out, spinning around the cable in a wobbly spiral, the cable itself whipsawing back and forth, rattling the side of the weather tower where it had been attached, rattling the post on the ground. The villagers ducked as the cable threatened to work loose, but it held.

Out shot, too, the darting gun itself, a unit two feet long set on top of the harpoon shaft that held the iron and fired the bomb. On the hunt the darting gun would be attached to the shaft, Claudia knew, and the darting iron would be tied to floats. Now everything was attached to nothing, free to fly on its own. And it did. The darting gun broke loose from the shaft and flew out end over end. The villagers ducked lower. Claudia glanced quickly to see that the bomb had come loose, that its charge had fired the bomb free from the gun. It had.

Claudia imagined the bomb, and the nearest analogy she could think of was model rockets. As a young girl she and her father had made and fired model rockets for a joyous few years before she realized teenagers did not do nerdy things like that. You could buy the engines from some place in Colorado, and the engines were like big firecrackers, like the bomb charge in the darting gun. One charge burned out a ceramic nozzle in the back of the rocket engine. A thin sliver of powder burned through the engine after the initial propellant had exhausted itself. Waiting at the head of the engine was another charge, a brief burst of powder to explode the rocket's nose cone loose, to pop out the parachute and bring the rocket safely back to earth. Waiting at the head of the darting bomb was the second charge, the killing charge.

It was like gun and grenade together, she thought. One charge shot the bomb into the whale, and seconds later a larger charge, the grenade charge, went off.

Tuttu counted off the seconds still. "Eight," he said, "nine, ten—"

A section of snow in the target flew out in chunks of ice and steam. The villagers fell to their knees as the ice flew overhead. Then a puff of foam pellets roared out of the open hole, plastic melting and singeing and smoking as the foam tacked to the plywood flew out. The plywood followed, slivers of flaming toothpicks. Claudia relaxed, smiled to herself.

It had worked. It had gone off just as it should and—

Out from the plywood came the darting iron, three feet of steel rolling end over end. The villagers hit the snow. "Twelve," Tuttu continued, as if this was perfectly normal, "thirteen, fourteen—"

Thunk, the harpoon hit the side of the weather tower, tip imbedding in the steel door, then hitting something hard and solid—finally—behind. The iron thrummed in the air, whipping side to side as fast as the wire whipped. When the iron quieted and the bomb quieted and the smoke and steam and blazing foam had settled, the observers rose. They dusted off their pants and parkas and stood. Their voices were like the chittering of ravens. Claudia met her fellow hunters at the harpoon.

The point of the harpoon had been buried up to but not beyond the first barb. Tuttu easily pulled it out and turned it over and over in his hands. Sleek and almost aerodynamic, the head of the harpoon was a wedge of curved steel, with one barb inches back from the head, a second barb even farther back. The head swiveled on a shaft on the iron, in theory toggling open. If it had toggled open, it would have stuck in the plywood and foam "skin" of the fake whale.

"It didn't open," Tuttu said.

Malgi came down the stairs, and walked up to them with Natchiq and Grigor. Tuttu held out the iron for the old man's inspection. Just behind the swivel of the head was a small hole drilled through head and shaft. Claudia could see a wood peg stuck in the hole. Malgi took the harpoon from Tuttu and pointed at the peg.

"I thought that might happen," he said, grinning. "I couldn't remember what kind of wood to use. I know you're not supposed to use oak or stuff, because it won't break." Malgi worked the head of the harpoon, showing how the wood kept it from toggling back. "My old man used wooden matches." He reached into a pocket and pulled out a wooden match. With thumb and forefinger he tried to snap the match, but it would barely bend. "*Good* matches, huh?"

"Got to use crummy matches, Malgi," Tuttu said.

"Yai. Crummy matches."

Grigor had gone over to the mound of snow and dug for the exploded harpoon bomb. He came back with a shredded and twisted half-cylinder of steel. "It works," the submariner said. He grinned. "*Real* well."

Claudia thought of the bomb driven deep into the whale, thought of the damage a big "bullet" like that would cause, then imagined the bullet exploding. Azah, as Tuttu might say. The right shot—into the brain, into the heart and lungs—it could kill a whale instantly. And then she thought of how big the whale could be, and how even a bomb like that would be no worse than a pellet gun on a grizzly bear. Still . . .

"Yah, it worked real *whale*, Russkie," Malgi said. And the women and men and children broke up laughing at his joke, the poor Soviet standing dumbfounded.

It worked real whale, Claudia thought. Holy Mother Mary: we might just be able to pull this off.

A boat. Well, yes, Claudia thought, We're going to need a boat. Some days after the test of the darting gun harpoon, she stood in the lobby of the Utqiagvik museum staring up at Malgi's umiaq, hung from the second floor railing. The skin boat had been displayed top side up, paddles and sealskin floats lashed to the gunwales. Natchiq and Amaguq leaned out over the umiaq, tying new ropes to the seats and unscrewing the boat from the bolts that held it to the railing. When they had the boat undone, Aluaq and some other men helped lower the boat to the floor.

Ten years of hanging from the ceiling of a museum had not been kind to the umiaq. As it came down to the ground, Malgi reached out with his tough old hands and guided it down. He ran his hands over the smooth wood gunwales, over the rough walrus hide covering, over the tight stitches. What he saw Claudia guessed had been diluted by memory, but what she saw was a boat in sorry shape.

Malgi had told her that he'd given the boat to the museum when the government had ordered the Inupiaq to stop whaling. "I could not stand to see my boat rot away by my house," he had said. "Better it should rot away in a museum, so my grandchildren can learn what I once had done."

While Malgi's umiaq hadn't gone the way of the other boats in the village—bleached wooden frames hardly worth firewood—it clearly could not touch water without major repairs. The thick hide skin had cracked and broken in several places. Where old women had long ago pieced together the skins to make the covering, the stitching had stretched and expanded. Claudia knew that a new covering should be made; in the old days, the skins would be good for at the most two years. But where would they get walruses, or ugruk, the bearded seal?

Malgi walked around his umiaq, touching it and inspecting it and probably remembering it, she thought. His eyes seemed to cloud a little, maybe even mist a little, and the old man's face had the childish laxness she'd seen in people that meant they had gone somewhere else and were not rooted to the reality of the moment. He shook his head, breathed a long sigh, then bit his lip.

"We should make some new skins," Malgi said. He glanced at Claudia. "Would that not please agviq?"

Ah, she thought. There it is: the new standard. It should please agviq. Claudia nodded, hesitant.

"Is that not true, anthropologist?" The old man looked around at the other men, and they all turned to Claudia for her learned opinion.

Shit, she thought. This is what they wanted me for all along. This is the deal I made with Malgi when I first came to the village. This is my part of the bargain, the reason why they have taken me in. I must tell them how to be Inupiaq. They do not know! They do not think they know! And what do I know? she asked herself. What can I tell them? I never whaled, as Malgi did. I never went out on the ice and watched the steaming leads. I never pulled on the lines and dragged the great beasts out of the water. I never flensed and butchered the whale, never decided shares and portions and rewards for this or that. I only tasted the briny maktak. I know nothing! Who am I to tell this man, this umialik?

All I know is what I have read in books, she thought. Murdoch, Rainey, Nelson. Van stone. Reinhardt, Cassell, Dekin, Hughes and all that. All whites, all taniks, visitors to this culture who tried to report the facts objectively. And what could *they* know?

"Well, Claudia?" Malgi asked, breaking her thoughts. "Is that not correct? Would it not please the whale to put on a new skin?"

"Yes, Malgi," she said. "Agviq chooses who may take him, who may have his 'parka.' He looks at the covering of the boat, sees the bottom of the skin, and the crew with the cleanest hides, the crew that has thought properly of agviq, who has made the right preparations—that is the crew agviq will honor.''

''If we are so worthy,'' Tuttu said. ''But how can *this* honor the whale?'' He waved a hand at the tattered hide, the holes gaping in the old boat.

''Ah''—Malgi smiled, put an arm around Tuttu—''we can fix this. We can make this boat worthy of agviq. Perhaps we cannot do this in the old way''—he glanced at Claudia, and she nodded, *yes, yes, help me out, old man*—''but maybe we can do it in such a way to please the whale. Perhaps agviq will understand, and forgive us.''

''I think . . . I think that would be okay,'' Claudia said. Go ahead, she thought. Go ahead, Grandfather, send me out on a thin limb with a roaring chainsaw.

Tuttu smiled. ''If all we need to do is fix the boat, and make it look good for agviq . . . I think we can do that.'' He motioned to Natchiq and Amaguq, and Aluaq and the rest. They picked the boat up and took it out the double doors of the museum, back into the world.

A preponderance of garages was available for the taking in Utqiagvik, but Tuttu settled on the old Public Safety Office Building, across the street from Pepe's. The fire trucks and rescue vans had been driven out during the chaos right after the war, and the burnt hulks of the trucks lay in the parking lot by the Mexican restaurant and the Top of the World Hotel. Aluaq took a perverse pleasure in stoking a stove they'd set up in one garage of the building. He'd fueled the stove, he said, with criminal records from the PSO office—starting with his own ''and working right through the alphabet.''

They dragged the umiaq up Kiogak Street to the garage on a *kamotiq*, or Greenland-style sled. Originally used by dog teams, the heavy wooden sled proved equally adaptable for being pulled behind iron dogs—snowmachines. As she leaned into a band of canvas webbing sewn into a loop of rope, Claudia wished they had come up with a lighter version. The eight-foot runners—two-by-six lumber curved at the ends—and three-foot one-by-fours nailed crosswise could stand up to sea ice, she knew, but she wasn't sure *they* could stand up to *it*.

Natchiq had said he would generously allot some precious fuel for a four-wheeler to drag the sledge. Tuttu—the self-righteous jerk, Claudia thought—had said, no, let his crew pull. "Good for their muscles," he'd said. We'll pull soon enough, she thought, so I guess we should start now.

Inside the PSO garage they set the umiaq on old pallets, keel side up. Aluaq threw a fresh bundle of records on the fire—"We're up to the Rs," he said pointedly to Natchiq. Four rusty pots of marine fiberglass and paint sat by the fire, condensation steaming away from them. Masu stood as they came in. She smiled at Malgi and he smiled back. The old crone held up an ice pick and a clean white spool of heavy fisherman's twine. Yes, thought Claudia, the old seamstress. Agviq would approve of *that*. There was none better in the village.

Malgi followed his wife into the garage, a roll of something dark brown and rank-smelling in his arms. He set the roll down on the cold concrete floor, untied it, and spread it out. The thing was a circular blanket of four thick skins stitched together. A thick rope had been threaded around the edge. Shallow cracks marred the surface of the hide, but unlike the umiaq skin it was in good condition.

"The *mapkuq*," Malgi said. "For the blanket toss. When we had the whaling festival years ago twenty of us would grab the edge and toss young men and women high in the air."

"Grandfather," Tuttu said. "Not the blanket skin . . . Surely there is something else to use?"

Malgi shook his head. "I could find no other skins." He shrugged. "It is a sacrifice. It is necessary." He nodded to Masu, who took out her sharp ulu, sizing up the mapkuq. The old man smiled. "There are not so many of us now, so we do not need as big a skin." Masu squatted over the edge of the blanket, began cutting around the rim of the four hides, cutting the rope and the handholds away. "We just need a *little* hide for the boat. If we have something to celebrate, the small skin will do."

Tuttu stared at Masu as she cut. He looks like someone

just cut off his arm, Claudia thought. Had he jumped on the skin as a boy? she wondered. He managed a smile, then sat down next to the old woman to help, holding the hide up as she cut.

Masu cut the piece of hide into six-inch strips, wide enough to cover the gaps between shrunken skins on the boat. Her gnarled fingers flashed, the awl whisking in and out the tough hide, and she repaired the holes. Small holes got patches inside and out, seams were reinforced, tears repaired. The skin covering of the boat did not look new, but it looked like the umiaq could float. Masu tied off the last stitch, looked up from her work.

She shook her head. "It's the best I can do."

Tuttu helped the woman up, put an arm around her. He ran his hands over the patches, over the new seams. Malgi smiled at his wife, moving to her and hugging her from the other side. "It is fine, you have done a good job." Husband and grandson squeezed the woman, and she beamed.

Natchiq brought over an open can of fiberglass paint, the piercing smell of toluene or whatever stinging Claudia's eyes. He stirred the paint, mixing clear liquid with white powder. The powder dissolved into a milky yellow, the paint seeming to loosen up. Natchiq dipped a ratty paintbrush into the can, pointed with his chin at the umiaq. "Well?" he asked.

The rest of them turned the umiaq over and grabbed more paintbrushes. Each hunter chose a section of the covering— the bow for Natchiq, the stern for Tuttu, the middle for Claudia and Malgi and Amaguq—and they splashed wide strokes of clean paint on the covering. As the paint went on it covered the aged surface of the old skins. It looked like new wood coming out from under a weatherbeaten surface, Claudia thought, the way the wood of their paddles had emerged when they had scraped them clean earlier. Clean wood and new paint: it should please agviq, she hoped. It should please the whale.

Chapter 17

AND then in early May, just as the hunters had made the last preparations of their gear, Puvak went out to the end of the tuvaq in search of piqaluyak ice. The young boy had gone to the ice ridge "to get a drink," he said, because he had tired of the cloudy water they got from Freshwater Lake. It had been a sunny day, just barely under freezing despite the warmth of the long day beating down on the ice. Even before he got to the ridge he said he had seen steam rising to the north.

"The polynya?" Grigor had asked him when he told the story later.

"The *puyugruaq*," Puvak had said proudly, using the Inupiaq word for open water.

Puvak had climbed the ridge of jumbled new and old ice, looking for the telltale blue of pure ice. He had worked a little ice chunk loose and sat for a moment to rest, staring out to sea. The morning sun warmed his back, casting the ice ridge's shadows across the new ice at the flaw edge. The boy squinted at the calm, flat water.

He said he saw the little white whales first, the belugas, leaping in a narrow lead of freshly broken new ice. "My blood stirred at the sight," he said, "but it roared at what I saw next." Ahead of the belugas, in a small pod, two great black whales broke up through the thin ice, cracking it to

—213—

bits, "and rising up with their heads, battering the ice with the thick knots on their foreheads."

"Agviq!" Puvak had yelled from the ice edge, but at the great distance from the village, even with his strong young voice, no one heard him. He said he yelled all the way back to the village. When he got where he could "smell the woodsmoke," Puvak said, Masu heard him.

Claudia had been in the qaregi adding a sawn chunk of two-by-six lumber to the stove when Masu came up the katak and into the house. The old woman was half out of breath and panting, but her eyes blazed with wonder and she had a smile that threatened to eat her ears.

"Puvak," Masu said, panting. "Puvak saw . . . saw—"

"Sit, catch your breath," Malgi said from a bench by the stove. He laid down a length of rope he had been braiding onto a beachball-size orange float. "The boy? Is he okay? What did he see?"

"Agviq," Puvak announced, coming up behind her. He stepped through the katak and lowered the trapdoor behind him. He caught his breath, smiled, and handed a white bucket with a small chunk of blue ice in it to Claudia. "Two whales, and *sisuaq*, the little white whale."

Malgi grabbed Puvak by his shoulders, held him very still. "Agviq? You saw the whale?" The boy nodded. "Describe it."

"It had a large head, with a big bump on the top, and white at the tip of the head and under the jaw." Puvak caught his breath, continued. "The two whales broke through the ice, and the white whales followed them."

"Agviq," Malgi said. "It *is* the whale. The gray whale could not break through the ice—besides, it is too early for them." He grinned. "The whale! He has come back!"

Come back! Claudia thought. She had not known. How could anyone know? They could only guess. What had the war done to the oceans? What had the long night done to the seas? Would it have killed the plankton that fed the krill that fed the little fish, all of which agviq ate? Would the radiation have destroyed them as it must have destroyed other animals? No one could know. They could only hope, and guess.

Agviq, the boy said, had returned.

Malgi pulled on his kamiks and atigi, and grabbed the fishing float and line. "We must go," he said. "We must tell the others, the crew." The old man raised the katak door and went down. Claudia put on her own boots and parka, and followed him.

A crowd of people had come from the other houses. They clustered around Malgi as he came out, shouted questions at him, at the boy. Malgi yelled something, waving them away. "Get your own crews," she thought she heard him say.

It had been a matter of pride with Malgi. While others in the villages had at first been excited by the idea of whaling, no one really believed that the whales would come back. Sometimes not even she believed the whales would come back, Claudia thought. At first, other villagers had been excited by the idea of hunting whales. But as they saw the work involved, many had begun to tease Malgi and his whalers. As Malgi's crew continued their preparations, the other houses, the other hunting groups, began to pressure Malgi into giving up his plans. He had not; he had stubbornly believed. He had thought that if he believed, the whale would come; it would come because he believed it would come. It had to do with faith, and trust. Who was to say he was wrong? she asked herself—not the last time she would ask that question of herself.

Most of the villagers had been for hunting seals, and small parties had gone out, with a little success. Others had been for using what fuel they had left, exploring the outlying villages, and seeing what food remained—raiding other villages, if there were people still there who would resist sharing their food. Malgi had been firm. *He* and his partners would prepare to hunt for whales. Igaluk and a few had gone along with him, but most had given up the idea. Too much work for too little a chance.

Now the whales had come. And everyone wanted to join Malgi's crew. He would have none of it.

He stormed off down the street to the Public Safety Office, Claudia hurrying to keep up with him. Puvak laughed and talked with the villagers. He turned and saw

Malgi walking away, the bright orange float bobbing on his back. The boy waved off a question, and ran to follow Malgi and Claudia.

Malgi burst into the PSO garage, where Tuttu and Amaguq worked on the umiaq. The final coat of fiberglass had been applied the day before, and the room still reeked of the bittersweet-smelling paint. Tuttu wound a length of rope along the gunwales while Amaguq lashed the seats tight to the frame. Malgi threw the big float into the umiaq, then wandered over to the pile of whaling gear laid out on a pallet.

"Load the umiaq, Tuttu," he said. "We must hurry."

"Grandfather," Tuttu asked. "What . . . ?"

"Agviq!" the old man said, whirling to face him. "Puvak saw the whale! Two of them, well south of the point. We must hurry! Who knows if there will be other whales?"

"Agviq!" Amaguq asked. "It is true?"

Puvak had come inside, practically dancing with his excitement. Claudia had not seen him as proud since the time he had killed his first seal. "*I* saw the whale," he said. "Out in the lead, a narrow lead."

Malgi frowned at the boy, quickly glanced at Claudia, giving her that inquisitive look again. She would see that look often, she thought. She could almost guess his question.

"Should we be so proud of that which the whale lets us do?" Malgi asked.

Claudia did not bother to answer directly; it was another of his damn rhetorical questions. "Agviq honors those who are worthy," she said. She noticed her voice had that tone it would get when she had taught Anthropology 101, a sort of snotty teacher tone that did not altogether displease her. "Perhaps someone should not boast about such honor." Malgi glared at Puvak, and Claudia looked over at the young man. She smiled, nodded slightly, encouraging him.

Puvak blushed, looked down. "'Agviq let *someone* see him," he said. "Someone is honored that he should be granted this blessing."

Good boy, she thought. Refer to yourself in the third person. Good boy.

"The whale," Tuttu whispered. "Grandfather, is it time then? Are we ready?"

"If we are worthy," he said. Malgi bowed his head for a moment, then looked up. "Get the gear and umiaq ready, Tuttu, and pull it down to the bluffs." He turned to Claudia. "Go find that young hunter, Aluaq, and the Russian. Meet us on the beach." The old man opened wide the garage doors, and the bright morning sun shone on the gleaming white boat. A chill breeze tickled at the ruff of Malgi's hood. He turned into the wind, facing Claudia by the door. "Agviq!" he said. "We will get a whale." He caught Claudia's eye, grinned, and shook his head. "If the whale so blesses us."

The whaling and camping gear had been piled inside the umiaq, and the umiaq strapped to the heavy kamotiq sled. Natchiq and Tuttu jogged ahead to clear the old trail through the ice ridge, while the rest of the crew pulled the sled down the bluff and onto the flat sea ice. Puvak had argued for harnessing the young pups, to get them used to pulling with the big dogs, but Malgi gently dashed his enthusiasm. "Plenty of time for the pups to learn next fall," he said, "and we don't have enough big dogs anyway." So Claudia, Puvak, Grigor, and Aluaq became human sled dogs. Again, Claudia thought, thinking of the pulkka sled she had dragged while sealing. Half my life feels like it's been spent walking, hauling sleds like a dog.

Claudia had been the only woman allowed to come on the ice, not just because Malgi had decided she would advise them on the proper whaling methods, but because the men thought she was not menstruating. Malgi had been sure of that taboo, that women in the midst of their monthly bleeding could not be on the ice. It would not please agviq. In the close quarters of the qaregi, everyone knew that Masu and Tammy were in their periods. But she spotted only a little, and she hid her pads and tossed them in the fire when no one was looking.

As she trudged across the ice, Claudia adjusted the padded rope that crossed over her shoulders and under her left breast, and leaned into the line. On the flat, smooth ice of the tuvaq they could get up some speed, keep their momentum going. But the winds had blown snow across their old trail, and hitting the packed snow was like wading through sand. As they came closer to the high ridge of ice that had been pushed up at the edge of shallow water, the tuvaq became buckled and rough. After a few steps, she realized that they also struggled uphill.

Then, the movement of the kamotiq became not one smooth glide, but a series of jerks. Lean into the harnesses, yank the sled forward until some obstruction stopped them. Pause, take a breath, jerk the sled forward again.

A hundred yards or so away she heard a chainsaw whine. Natchiq, eternal guardian of sacred petroleum products, had grudgingly consented to ration a gallon of gas so they could cut a path through the ridge with the chainsaw. His decision had been made easier when Malgi had told him he and Tuttu would be cutting the trail. As she helped pull the sled, Claudia wished Natchiq had been assigned to her duty. Perhaps he would have then consented to a few more gallons for a sno-go.

Over the ridge ahead of her the steam rose, just as Puvak had described it, though the steam seemed wispy now. In the clouds a band of dark blue hovered almost directly overhead—the water sky, Claudia realized. The clouds reflected the lead below, and the nearness of the water sky meant that open water was just beyond the ice ridge.

By the time they caught up with Tuttu and Natchiq, the two men still hadn't opened the trail through the jumbled blocks of ice that formed the ridge. Well, Claudia thought, she couldn't be too critical. Even with a backhoe it might have taken them days to make a perfect trail. The narrow trail so diligently broken through the winter had drifted over with blowing snow; in some parts, chunks of ice had broken loose and fallen on the trail. Too, the trail that had been just right for the smaller pulkka sleds was hardly wide enough for the big kamotiq. They rested at the crest of the ridge.

From the top of the ridge they could easily see the open lead snaking between the flaw edge and the pack ice beyond. They'd been lucky: the uiniq, the lead, came close to the grounded ice, and they would not have to venture too far out on the ice edge. While thanking the luck, Claudia also considered the fickle conditions of spring ice. Another lead could lie beyond this one, and that might be the one the whales took. Or, the wind could blow, shutting off the lead, or breaking the edge loose.

A couple of the men went down to help break trail. Claudia shrugged off her harness and started to help, but Malgi tapped her on her shoulder. "Let's see those binoculars of yours," he said.

She reached beneath the folds of the white covering over her atigi, and fumbled for the Nikons dangling around her neck, underneath the atigi. Claudia pulled the cord of the binoculars over her head and out from under the two braids over her breasts. Malgi took the binoculars, squinted through them and scanned up and down the open lead.

Claudia searched, too, looking for fountains of spray as the whales exhaled, or the splashes as they dove. Nothing. Malgi stopped for a moment, focused on something, then shook his head. He handed the binoculars back to her.

"Agviq has gone on," he said. "The chainsaws may scare the whales off. Maybe we shouldn't run them . . . ?"

Claudia shrugged. Of course they shouldn't. But if they didn't use the saws, it would take that much longer to make a path. In any case, the whales had already been scared off, so they might as well finish. Still . . . She did not say these thoughts, though.

"Well, the harm's done now, anyway," Malgi said, answering his own question.

Natchiq cut the chainsaw off and waved up at them. The path was now clear enough down to the flat ice. Small chunks of ice still littered the trail, but they had moved away the larger boulders that could break the sled runners or grab at the fabric of the umiaq. Claudia put the Nikons back around her neck, inside their case, and shrugged on her harness.

They swung the ropes around to the side of the kamotiq, in sort of a reverse fan hitch. Gravity pulled the sled down, they guided it. The hunters leaned back into the lines, kicking their heels in. Natchiq laid the chainsaw down and joined Tuttu at a line at the rear. The two men pushed at the back of the kamotiq, it slid forward, then everyone held on as sled, umiaq, and gear roared down the slope. And then they were on the flat ice.

Camp went up quickly, because it had to be taken down quickly if the ice moved. Tuttu unlashed the umiaq from the sled and the men picked it up and carried it to the ice edge, bow forward. Claudia helped Malgi and Puvak with the sled, turning it so one side faced a northeasterly wind blowing up the coast, parallel to the lead. They set up a wall tent next to the sled, so the sled would make a bench and table for their camp. The other hunters carried boxes and bundles into the tent, putting a Coleman gas stove on the sled. Natchiq went and got the chainsaw. Quickly, under Malgi's scowls, he cut a pile of snowblocks from a packed snowdrift. He and Tuttu laid the blocks behind the sled and around the lead side of camp—a blind.

"To keep agviq from seeing us," Tuttu explained.

In the umiaq Malgi helped Tuttu arrange the whaling gear. At the bow of the boat would sit Natchiq the harpoonist. Malgi set the darting gun point skyward, the trigger rod well away from any accidental bumping. A line ran from the harpoon to a coil of rope behind the bow seat, and three orange fishing floats were attached to the harpoon line. One paddle lay across the bow seat, two paddles lay across each of the three middle seats, and an eighth paddle was set across the stern seat. Bailing buckets, extra paddles, more lines, a whaling iron, and a large canvas bag of miscellaneous equipment had been lashed or secured under seats or to the deck. Behind the harpoonist's seat was a small ax hanging by a loop in its handle, blade and ax head resting inside a plastic bottle lashed to a thwart. The umiaq was ready.

Claudia took out her binoculars, Puvak started melting a pan of blue ice on the stove, and the other hunters settled in to wait. Agviq will come or he will not, and all we have to do is wait, she thought.

Just wait.

She did not know how long they waited, because only Tuttu had a working watch and he had left it on shore. Long enough for the cold to seep into her toes, Claudia thought.

The sun rose high to the south and slid low to the west, so she knew it had to be getting late in the day. Such light made seeing better, though: the low light scattered flat across the open lead, making anything in the water seem to leap up from the slightly choppy surface.

Her toes felt numb and her fingers felt numb but the spring cold did not pierce through her like the winter cold. It did not turn her into one seeming hunk of ice, and she knew that all she had to do to warm up was get up and walk around. Malgi said that if any of them got cold, they could get up one or two at a time and walk to the top of the ice ridge. If they were quiet, he said, they could even work on the trail.

Claudia had gotten up to stamp the cold out of her toes and join Aluaq up on the ridge when the young man shouted down toward her. She yelled up at him, and then saw that he was pointing at something far out on the other side of the lead. Claudia turned, snatching for her Nikons. Twisting and turning the lenses, trying not to breathe on the binocs and fog them, she looked. And she saw it.

A plume sprayed up from what at first seemed a small volcano on a black island of ice. Claudia focused the binoculars. The island undulated, rolled forward into a low hill, and disappeared. Next to it, another such island rose, and the whale exhaled a cloud of sea spray. And then a *third* whale rose behind the second, and blew.

She dropped the binoculars as she ran to the ice edge. Her yells had merged with Aluaq's and with Tuttu's and the whole crew's. Natchiq got into the boat first. Amaguq and his son jumped in behind him. Grigor had risen from a nap and was madly tying up his boots. Aluaq ran down from the ice ridge, still screaming "Agviq! Agviq!" Malgi slowly, gracefully, climbed into the stern seat, the umialik's position, his face serene and composed. The old man rubbed the raven's head around his neck, and muttered something as he waited for the crew to board.

Grigor hopped over to the boat, one boot still untied, and leapt in. Aluaq hit the gunwale with his hip, swung his legs over with the momentum, almost kicking Puvak in the back. Claudia stood by the stern with Malgi and Tuttu, the two men on the starboard side, Claudia to port, and Grigor forward at the middle starboard seat.

"Go," Tuttu whispered.

Grigor shoved the umiaq from his side, and the bow slid down the ice edge into the water. Natchiq held on to the darting gun, kept the point still straight up. As the white boat fell into the water, Claudia suddenly thought that they hadn't even tested it. They had been so eager and excited they hadn't even tried the boat to see if it floated. She bit her lip as the water rose up the sides of the skins, almost to the gunwales. The men clung to the rope around the edge of the boat, and it rocked as it hit the water. Grigor jumped in, and then Claudia and Tuttu jumped in as they gave the umiaq one last push.

Malgi's umiaq wobbled in the cold water, thudding against a small chunk of ice. She realized she had been holding her breath the whole time, from when they slid the boat into the water until she had jumped in. When she realized no water leaked through the seams and cracks of the old skins, Claudia let out her breath in a *whoof* like the whale, and smiled.

"Azah," Tuttu said, "it floats!"

Malgi looked at his grandson, frowned at him, then laughed. "Fortunately," he said.

The crew took up their paddles and rowed quietly, softly, through the water. Natchiq lashed the darting gun with a slip knot, took up his own paddle, and directed them toward the whales. He pointed at the far side of the lead, at a point almost straight across.

"The whales swim about four knots," Malgi said quietly. "If we paddle hard and fast, we can intercept them." He pointed at where one of the whales rose—with his left hand, at an angle to port—and then to a high ridge of ice across from them—with his right hand, straight on.

It took some minutes for them to coordinate their paddling. Tuttu steered at the stern, paddling from either port or starboard, while Natchiq made slight course corrections at the bow. The rest of the crew stayed to their own sides, digging in with the paddles. Claudia tried to remember her old Girl Scout training, paddling canoes at summer camp.

How did it go? Plant the paddle in, pull back? Amaguq and Puvak switched sides two seats ahead of her—compensating, she realized, for her weakness. She blushed. They couldn't have two weak paddlers on the same side, could they? But she was glad to stay on the left, since her stronger arm was on the left.

Old skin or not, the umiaq held together. It slid through the water like a dolphin, barely making a wake. They made no sound but a quite *hunnh* as each paddler breathed with each stroke: *hunnh*—breathe!—stroke, *hunnh*—breathe! —stroke. The water flowed through and around and behind them, as if they were pushing the open lead and the umiaq stayed still. Pieces of ice thudded against the skin of the boat, bumped it slightly, the skin yielding to the force and pushing the ice back and away. Natchiq pushed big chunks of ice out of their path, or steered them around larger bergs.

Claudia kept her eyes on the prominent chunk of ice opposite them, across the lead, not looking. Natchiq would look, he was their eyes. She concentrated on paddling straight, on keeping the rhythm. She was a gear in the machine, a body and not a mind. Dig and pull, dig and pull. It had the same beat as groveling in the soil, digging in the thawing permafrost.

You slanted the trowel into the soil, pulled it to you, pushing the dirt up. Down, slice, pull, up. A good archaeologist made her hand a machine, the trowel gripped slightly, feeling with the edge of the steel. You felt for the things that were not dirt, not smooth and easy to push aside, or too easy to push aside, like rootlets clumped around a point. When you felt it, you stopped and looked to see what you had. Dig and pull.

As she paddled, Claudia remembered what she had been, where she had been. She got that feeling she sometimes got, when you were in a place alien to what you were used to, and wondered to yourself how you had managed to be where you had come to be. She should not be there in the Arctic, Claudia thought, not in the spring. She never came to the Arctic in the spring. Archaeologists didn't do that. They were summer people and they spent their springs planning for the next expedition, madly scrambling to line up money. She should be in Binghamton, she thought, defending her thesis. She would have written it up, would have passed it through Cassell, and now they would be fighting off the slings and barbs of the committee. She would pass. She would get her degree. And then she would come back here.

But she was here, she thought. Binghamton might not be and Cassell might not be and nothing she ever had known might not be, but this ice, this water, this boat, her: this was now and she was there and that was all the *to be* in the world she could possibly know.

Something rolled down her cheek from her eyes. She licked at the briny liquid and tasted it and imagined that agviq had blessed her with his sweat. That was what some old-timer told her once: our tears are agviq blessing us with his sweat. That is why you give agviq a drink, the old-timer had said. Our water is our sweat and it is like tears to agviq.

Water, she thought with a start. We did not water the boat. She wondered if it would displease the whale. She wondered if her menstruating would displease the whale.

They paddled forward, slowly, but faster or as fast as the whale. Natchiq held up his hand, and Malgi whispered, "Stop." The whalers brought the paddles up, held them tips up and handles down, the seawater dripping down the clean wood and onto their hands. The umiaq coasted, bumping aside a small hunk of ice.

It rose. Black like fine obsidian, the whale rose up, no more than twenty yards from them. Claudia did not think it could be so huge. The whale stretched at least as long as the umiaq. It rose farther, arching its back. At the bow of its head, two nostrils flared, two teardrop-shaped depressions on the smooth black back. Agviq exhaled, spraying a plume of misted sea spray down on them. Its exhalation was a roar, a great sigh, and the noise stirred them. Natchiq unlashed the darting gun, and Malgi shouted, "Dig, dig!"

The whale flapped its flukes, the great black flukes, and pushed forward. Agviq raised his chin and head, and she could see the white spots, the bare white from where the old-timers said the whale had rubbed against ice. The whale did not seem to notice them, or if it did, took no bother. Did this whale know it could be hunted? Was it old enough to remember days when the Inupiaq had come out in boats to receive his blessing? Was it like the whale Claudia had read about once, a sixty-foot old whale killed in '81 and found with an ivory harpoon head in its side?

They dug in, struggling to keep up with the whale. How long would it stay on the surface? Claudia thought. She could not remember. She only knew that they had to catch it just before it took a breath, kill it with air in its lungs so it would float to the surface. They paddled, their strokes furious and mad. It did not matter now if the whale heard them. Of course he heard them. "Dig, dig!" Malgi shouted from the stern.

And she remembered the word for "digger," the nickname Tuttu sometimes called her: Nivakti. Little digger. Dig. Nivak? Was that the imperative verb? Or should it be "you will dig," *nivakniaqp*? Whatever. Dig, though. Dig for treasure, little girl. Dig for the whale.

She felt the ivory whale against her skin and around her neck, and wished that this whale would become that whale, that he would bless her. She prayed to the whale and heard Malgi next to her mumbling his own prayers. Come to us, agviq, she thought. Honor us. Let us take you. Give us your parka so we may live.

"Slow," Natchiq said from up front.

Claudia glanced over and saw that they had come up next to the whale, that the paddlers ahead of her had to pull their paddles out of the water to keep from hitting the whale. They coasted next to agviq, skin of the umiaq against skin of the whale. She stroked harder to keep pace with it, the tip of her blade barely passing over the whale's tail. Agviq was not just as long as the umiaq, but twice as long, perhaps forty feet. A ton a foot, forty tons. How much meat could that be? The boat wobbled and she looked up to see what had disturbed them. She saw Natchiq rise.

Natchiq let out a length of rope attached to the ring of the iron on the darting gun. The rope, the whale line, was connected to three coils of rope in tubs and three orange floats beside the coils. Natchiq leaned into the gunwale, bracing one thigh against the side of the boat, pushing with his left foot. He raised the gun, held it poised over the edge of the boat, harpoon head pointing down at two ridges behind the blowholes, at the whale's neck. He held the pose, waiting, waiting.

One flick of agviq's tail, Claudia thought. One flap of his fins, a kick of his flukes, and that's it. They would be thrown over into the water, far from their camp, and they would drown or freeze. The whale held still, barely moving, and they held still, barely moving. Why does he wait? she asked herself. Why doesn't he get it over with?

Natchiq stared down at the whale, she saw. He looked at the whale's blowholes. She saw what Natchiq looked for, then, and watched as agviq sucked in air, saw the edges of the holes dilated, pulling in water and spray. Agviq breathed. And as agviq breathed, Natchiq threw the darting gun at the whale, momentum driving the harpoon in.

First, the harpoon head hit the skin. The weight of the darting gun and the shaft and the throw drove the point of the blade in. The paddlers on Claudia's side pulled their blades out of the water, quietly setting them down on the umiaq's bottom. Next, the head disappeared into the skin, and a foot of harpoon shaft followed. Claudia looked for the rod, the trigger rod. Natchiq had thrown the harpoon in and the rod would come next. The rod hit. She saw the orange painted tip touch the whale's back and then the bomb lance exploded.

The water erupted. At the touch of the harpoon agviq dove, taking the harpoon with him, and it was as if the harpoon pushed him and the bomb pushed him. The charge fired the bomb into the whale, the bomb lance shoving the gun away from the whale and back out of the water.

Natchiq fell into his seat, still grasping in his right hand the rope that held the gun to the boat. The motion of the gun through the air jerked the rope taut from Natchiq's hand, pulling him to the side. His left arm whirled as he flailed for balance, the arm whirling like an amputee helicopter blade.

The lines sang! From the tubs in the bottom of the boat where the lines had been coiled, the lines whipped out. One long line pulled the other three lines out of the boat. The aft line flew away, snatching a paddle from Malgi's grasp and wrapping around his arm. The line to the last float wrapped around a cleat on the boat, so that the whale dragged the first two floats and the umiaq, and the umiaq dragged Malgi. As the line fouled on the cleat, it shook the umiaq, paddles flying out of Grigor's and Puvak's hands.

Tuttu sat to her right, his lips moving as he counted. Claudia remembered how the bomb would work. First, it would blow free from the gun and into the whale. Then, the second charge would explode. Five seconds. She watched Tuttu's lips. One. Two. Three. The float line pulled the old man from the boat, and as he splashed into the water Claudia heard a bone crack. Malgi fell into the water, the boat wobbled, and Tuttu quit counting.

Tuttu reached over the side to grab his grandfather, but the whale pulled the old man down. Claudia could see a white thing dragging behind them, held underwater by the force, and she could see two of the three orange floats streaming across the water ahead of them. The line between the first two floats and the third float—still in the umiaq—began to pull the cleat's screws out of the gunwale. If the cleat came free, it would yank the remaining float away, and agviq would take Malgi down with him. Claudia saw this and yelled.

"Cut the line! Get him!"

In the bow, Natchiq pulled out the ax. He raised the ax to cut the line between the whale and the cleat, so that the line holding Malgi would remain with the boat, and the rest of the line would be taken by agviq. But as the ax fell, the cleat snapped free. The third float popped out of the umiaq. Tuttu caught the last length of line as it went by, but the rope burned through his fingers and he let go. Cleat, line, float, and Malgi went away with the whale.

And then, like a kid farting in a bathtub, the bomb exploded ahead of them, from the flesh of the whale. A huge bubble of air burst below and rose to the surface—a red bubble. The orange floats suddenly slowed, then stopped. They watched the pink froth on the sea, looking to see if the whale came up.

But Malgi sputtered to the surface, his white atigi rising full of air, like a skirt around him. Natchiq put the ax back in its sheath, then reached over with a grapple to pull in the last float, still attached to the sundered line. He passed the float back to Tuttu, who quickly tied it to the stern cleat, and threw it to Malgi. Malgi reached for the float, grabbed it. They began hauling in the line, the float, pulling the old man to them.

Someone remembered to paddle and then Claudia got her paddle and they pushed the boat to the old man. Natchiq reached over, with one arm yanked him in, Amaguq and Puvak scuttling aside to make room for the old man. Amaguq pulled off Malgi's parka and put his own over the old man. Grigor and Puvak reached overboard and recovered their paddles, while the two floats drifted away.

Tuttu shouted for them to "Dig! dig!" but no one had to be told to do that. Claudia dug in, glancing at the man almost turning blue, trying not to look at the white bone sticking out of his arm. In front of her, Grigor pulled in the last of the nylon line. He held up the end of it, frowned at the frayed ends, the ends burned into little blobs of plastic.

"The bomb was too big," he said. "It must have killed the whale." Everyone looked at the flat sea, but they could not see the whale's body floating to the surface. They had killed him too well, and he had sunk.

Claudia looked at the broken line, at Malgi dripping wet but alive. Thank God, she thought. Thank God the bomb was too big.

Chapter 18

THEY tried the CB to get help, but either Tammy or Masu wasn't listening, or one of the radios was broken. So, Natchiq ran toward town to get a sno-go while the whalers got Malgi warm. Claudia didn't think they should dare set his broken arm while out on the ice, but the sight of the clean, white bone sticking out of Malgi's skin scared her. Grigor showed them how to bandage and splint the fracture—he seemed to know a fair amount of first aid, too, in addition to his bomb-making skills. Before they set the arm they stripped his wet clothes off, and put on dry clothes brought out for just such a catastrophe.

While they waited for Natchiq to come back with the snowmachine, the wind had started to shift. Malgi, barely conscious, had made a point of warning them to watch the wind, to be ready to break camp in a hurry; then he had passed out.

Just as Claudia began to wonder how long it could possibly take Natchiq to come back, she heard the roar of a sno-go, coming fast across the flat ice toward them. Gingerly, Natchiq brought the snowmachine over the ice ridge. He towed a metal sled behind a big, long-track military snowmachine, one of the sno-gos the Eskimo Scouts used. Grigor got on behind Natchiq, while Claudia held the old man in the bottom of the sled, on top of a foam bed and sleeping bag Natchiq had taken the time to throw in.

Claudia held Malgi as they went back over the ridge and then bounced over the slight humps of the tuvaq. The old man winced at each bump. The cold air pushed her atigi hood back against her neck, and loose hairs from her braids whipped around her face in the wind. Malgi mumbled something.

"Shh," she said. He felt light and fragile in her arms. It dawned on her then that he was a small man, a small, old man, though he had always seemed so much larger: bluster and age could make little men seem bigger than they really were.

"Did we kill the whale?" he asked.

"Yes," she said, because it was true. They *had* killed the whale, at least wounded it enough that it probably would die soon, somewhere under the ice. She hoped he wouldn't ask the next question, but of course he did.

"Did you *recover* the whale?"

"No." She held him tighter as she saw the sno-go hit a bump and first Natchiq, then Grigor, bounce up. Malgi hissed as the trailing sled flew through the air and then bounced on the ice. "No, the bomb was too big; it must have killed the whale and the whale sank." Claudia smiled. "*Fortunately* for you, though. The line broke and agviq didn't drag you under."

"He must not have liked me," Malgi said.

"I can see why. You're a tough old coot."

He nodded, then drifted off to sleep. They came up to the bluffs, rode along the beach edge and toward the part of town where the bluffs sloped down to the beach and it was easy to drive up into the village. Masu came out of the qaregi as they came to the entrance. Tammy followed her and between the four of them they got Malgi inside and laid out on another mattress. Claudia helped Grigor take his pants off to examine Malgi's knee. It had become swollen, and Malgi winced when they touched it, but it didn't seem broken or anything. Grigor wrapped an ace bandage around it, the best he could do without a brace.

Masu had started boiling water on the stove and Tammy

had dragged out a medical kit. They sent Paula over to the medical clinic, and she found more gauze and tape and even a box of plaster of paris. Tammy came up to Malgi with another rarity, a nearly full bottle of Jim Beam whiskey. She held out a glass, opened the top of the bottle, and began to pour a shot for Malgi.

"No," he said. He stared at the whiskey and Claudia thought she saw his good hand shake as it moved out to take the glass and then fell away. His lower lip trembled. "Not even for this."

"Then take this, husband," Masu said. She held out a strip of something black, turned it over to show pale pink on its underside. "Someone found this in an old frost cellar."

Maktak. "I . . . I cannot," Malgi stared at the blubber in her hand. "I am not worthy."

"You are. You are worthier than any man I know."

Grigor took Malgi's broken arm then, gently, by the upper shoulder, and Claudia reached over to hold his chest. Masu put the maktak between Malgi's teeth as he opened up his mouth to cry out. He looked at his wife and she looked at her husband. He nodded and bit down on the hard, cold black skin. Grigor pulled his broken bones apart and began to set them. By the time the Soviet was done, the old man had chewed the maktak down to a little strip of mangled flesh. He swallowed the last bit of maktak, a smile on his face, and fell asleep.

After Claudia helped Grigor wrap the last strips of wet plaster around Malgi's arm—making a cast—she went outside to clear her head. Tammy came out with her. The two women climbed up the ladder to the roof of the qaregi, to the old watchtower. Over the jumble of the flaw the sun slid down to the horizon, the jagged ridge casting long shadows toward them. A stiff wind blew from the southwest.

The wind shifted, she thought.

Somewhere beyond the ridge was the whaling camp, Claudia knew. She had brought her Nikons up with her, her good old battered Nikons, and scanned the ice out of habit.

It occurred to her that she should have left the binoculars at the camp. Take 'em back tomorrow, she thought.

A shadow moved from behind a ridge. Claudia quickly focused on the shadow, but the glare from the direct sun made it hard to see. Another shadow moved out from the jumbled ice, into the shadows cast by the ridge, and she could see what they were: the whaling crew. Two, three more men moved along the path, dragging the big umiaq on the kamotiq.

"Tuttu's coming back," she said, handing the binoculars to Tammy.

Tammy squinted through them, gave the Nikons back to Claudia. "Why?"

Claudia shrugged. "I hope . . . I don't know."

The two women rushed down back into the qaregi, out the entrance tunnel and down the bluff. Masu looked up at them as they went out; Claudia had quickly told them she was "going to meet the whaling crew," and left.

They met Tuttu and Amaguq and the rest halfway on the flat tuvaq. Claudia took Puvak's line at the sled, relieving the boy; he scurried back to take one of the guy lines that kept the umiaq from tipping over. Tammy walked behind Claudia and Tuttu at the bow, pushing at the boat as it came to rough spots in the ice.

"What happened?" Claudia asked Tuttu.

"The uiniq closed," he said. "The wind shifted and the lead closed. We would have waited for it to open again, but the wind started to move the ice at the flaw edge—move us."

"Shit," she said.

"Yeah, shit." Tuttu grunted as he leaned into the harness, yanking the sled over a slight warp in the ice. "Anyway, we climbed to the ridge and saw that a lead had opened beyond, and that whales were in it." He shook his head. "But we couldn't get across the rotten ice between us and the lead: too thick to paddle through, too thin to walk on. We came back."

"The wind may shift again."

Tuttu glared at her, grunted again. "Yeah. Maybe."

* * *

So they waited. On the ice, on the shore, cold or warm, it didn't matter, Claudia thought. They waited. They dragged the umiaq and the gear back into the PSO garage, and fixed the things they should have fixed first.

In the garage, Tuttu passed out shares of blame instead of shares of meat. First, he berated Natchiq up and down for putting the brass cleats around the top of the gunwales. "Those damn cleats almost killed the old man!" he screamed. "What a dumb-fuck idea! You should have known the lines would foul on them."

"I didn't, Cousin," Natchiq said. "And why didn't you know?"

Why didn't *I* know? Claudia asked herself. She should have. She'd read the whaling books, the reports, the accounts. She should have known, too.

Tuttu snorted at Natchiq's reply, turned his wrath to the Soviet. Grigor had come up to the garage to help when he'd heard the whalers had returned. "And you!" Tuttu yelled. "Crazy Commie! You said you knew bombs? What do you want to do—nuke us?"

Grigor turned red, stamped his foot. "Fool! The bomb blew! I am not used to your powder—it is gunpowder, I do not know the proper charge. You would not let me test the charge, you did not want to 'waste powder,' you said. I didn't, and we wasted a whale! Blame yourself! The cartridge worked, anyway." Grigor turned, crossed his arms, ignoring Tuttu.

"And *you*," Tuttu said, turning to Claudia.

Here it comes, she thought. The greater share of blame. It is all my fault, of course, me, the anthropologist—the woman.

"Anthro-POL-o-gist." He spat the word. "You told us nothing of our traditions. Do you know them? What ceremonies should we perform? How should we act toward agviq? Perhaps the whale turned from us because we insulted him. Perhaps the wind shifted because of you!"

Claudia faced him, lips clenched. "I—" *I*, she thought. What can I say? I know the traditions, yes. I should have known. And we did not give the boat a drink. We did not pray to the whale. We did not do this, did not do that.

But those are old traditions. What of the old should we use? What should we abandon? Can I say? she asked herself.

Worse, she thought, I went out on the ice in my period, a clear taboo. Can I tell them that? I dare not; they could not forgive that. Still, perhaps that was all superstition after all. What did she know? What did any of them know? She said that. "I . . . I do not know."

"I should have known," Malgi said. They turned to face the old man. He hobbled into the garage on Puvak's arm. Natchiq got a chair and the old man quickly fell into it, propping his bad leg up on an empty drum of kerosene—the knee that had been wrenched when the whale yanked him out of the umiaq. "All the blame rests on me, not her, not the Soviet, not Natchiq. Was I not the one agviq lashed out at?"

"Grandfather, you did no wrong—" Tuttu said.

"*I did wrong.*" The old man glared at Tuttu, and the grandson looked down. "We all did wrong. How could any of us know? You are not whalers—I am the only one who ever went out, ever hunted. I am an old man and have forgotten much. I should have known that the lines have to pull free. The aft tub—that was stupid to put one tub behind all of us. The cleats. What do we need cleats on the gunwales for? And the bomb. I watched my own father make his own bombs, measure the powder and make the bombs. I should have remembered." He tapped his forehead. "And the traditions. You blame the white woman? If not for her, we might have no traditions. We forgot them, did not teach them to our children. If we taught them to her, or the other anthropologists, sometimes we lied." He smiled. "My own grandfather lied, he told me. He thought it was a joke and that the anthropologist would get it. But that guy—I forget his name—he wrote it all down, jokes and all." Malgi chuckled.

Claudia blushed. Yes, that old problem, she thought. How can you trust informants?

"So," Malgi said. "Did we ask for a ceremony? None of us did. We were so eager to get the whale. *We did not think*. And so we did not get the whale. We were not worthy of it. Can we become worthy of it?"

"Yes," Tuttu whispered.

"That was a rhetorical question," Malgi said. He smiled, and the other whalers laughed at his little joke. "But 'yes' might be a good answer. Now"—he reached over to a tray of tools by his chair and picked up a screwdriver, and held it out—"*how* shall we become worthy?" Malgi looked at them, and they waited for him to answer his own question. "Perhaps we should begin, Natchiq, by taking off those damn cleats."

The wind still did not shift; it kept blowing steadily from the southwest. Other villages took their failure as a sign that whaling was worthless, a stupid idea. Unable to defend their stubbornness, the whalers waited inside the qaregi, hoping they were right, but fearing they might be wrong.

Grigor sat in one corner, looking over some transcripts of interviews Claudia had found: old whalers talking about how they made bombs. She should have looked for the reports before; when she thought of it later, she found the reports not in the museum director's office, but in the Office of History and Culture, in the oral history files. Tons of information. Amaguq sat next to the Soviet, helping him with the difficult words. Numbers, that's all that counts, she thought. How much powder should be crammed into an eight-gauge shell? How big should the charge be for the bomb?

The wood stove had been fired up high, and the weather outside had turned mild, so the inside of the qaregi was hot, almost sweat bath hot. A bucket of ice melted on the stove, and over a big tin tub Tammy poured more hot water into the soapy water left by Claudia, Paula, and Masu, who'd bathed before her. All the men and the boy, Puvak, had stripped to jeans, their white bellies and chests contrasting with the deep tans of their faces. Masu had washed, but kept her undershirt off, wearing only long johns.

Though her face had become lined and her chin had seemed more pronounced, the way chins of old Inupiaq women sometimes did, Masu's breasts remained firm. She

sat at the end of a bench, close to the fire, while Paula—
Belinda, Aluaq's wife—combed Masu's damp, long hair
and braided it into two plaits—French braids. Claudia chuckled
at the cultural incongruity, at the tight braids woven into
themselves at Masu's temples and joining at her nape. Masu
turned around, facing Paula, and Paula took a pair of
scissors and quickly trimmed the little half-moon of bangs
across Masu's forehead. She handed the scissors to Masu,
and the old woman reciprocated, trimming the young tanik's
bangs, too. With her dark brown hair, the other tanik
woman in the qaregi looked more Inupiaq than her, Claudia
thought. Paula turned around and Masu began arranging
Paula's hair in the complex braids.

As she watched the women, Claudia remembered when
she had been a young girl and such braids had been popular,
how she and her friends would sit for hours arranging each
other's hair. Masu's gnarled fingers flashed in the light
streaming down through the gut-skin skylight, Paula's damp
hair gleaming in the old woman's hands as she finished the
last braid. The tanik stood, smiled at the old woman, and
got up. Masu caught Claudia looking at her, nodded, and
pointed at Claudia's head, then patted the bench next to her.

Claudia walked over to the old woman and took Paula's
place. She pulled a T-shirt over her bare breasts, hesitating
for a moment as she came toward the men. Should she
remain shirtless like them, her fellow crew? No, she thought,
she would not bare her breasts to these men. Tuttu looked
up at Claudia, grinned as she pulled the shirt down. Well,
Claudia thought as she tucked her shirt into her pants, well,
maybe she'd bare her breasts for *some* of these men. She sat
down before Masu, who began running a comb through her
hair.

The comb snagged and she winced as Masu pulled it
through her hair. Standing in the big tin tub Tammy scrubbed
her bare body and washed her long black hair. A cleansing.
Masu had bathed and then Paula and Claudia and now
Tammy. Then they'd change the water and the men would
bathe, even Malgi as well as he could around his cast, even
the boy. Malgi had thought it might be a good idea to be
clean, and discussed the idea with Claudia. "Would it

please agviq?" he had asked her, and she thought, Forget the whale, it will please *me*. None of them had had a real bath since Puvak had killed his first seal; they couldn't spare the water, or the fuel to make water.

"Yes," she'd said though, with a growing smile, "yes, it would please agviq if we became clean."

Their white atigi snowshirts hung on a line outside, bleaching and airing in the sun. Their mittens lay in a pile by Masu to be patched. Puvak wiped his hide mukluks with grease, oiling them. Maintenance, Claudia thought, things that should have been done that in their haste they neglected. While they waited for the wind to shift, for the whale to come, if the whale came, they cleaned and patched and repaired all their gear, because "it would please agviq," as Malgi had said, but also because it was right.

Masu ran the end of the comb across the top of Claudia's forehead to one ear, then the other, parting the bangs from her crown, and then she ran the comb to her nape. The comb's teeth scraped her scalp, and Claudia could feel the hair parting down the back of her head, straight and even. Masu pushed Claudia's head forward, and her scraggly bangs dangled before her eyes and onto her nose. She felt Masu pull the hair on the right side of her head in and out, yanking each strand tight, felt the hair being woven into a braid like the leaves on a cactus palm, down over her ear and to the nape. Again she thought of being young, and the memory merged with the moment; the bond she had felt with her long-ago friends—adolescent girls on the cusp of womanhood—became the bond she began to feel with these women.

A hand, Tammy's hand, Claudia saw, came up to her face, lifting her bangs between thumb and forefinger. As Tammy pulled the bangs up, Masu pulled the hair at her neck down. The women rocked her head with their movements. Tammy smiled and held up a pair of scissors. Claudia grinned, then nodded, the brief motion causing Masu to jerk her hair tighter.

Tammy took her own comb and ran it down Claudia's bangs, pulling the hair straight over her forehead. The lesbian brought the open tips of the scissors up to the space between her eyebrows.

"Not too"—the scissors rose, settled against the middle set of wrinkles in her brow, an inch below the hairline—"short," Claudia said. She sighed as Tammy closed the scissor blades.

The hairs fell down to the bare wood on the bench before her, between Claudia's legs straddling the bench. Tammy clipped the bangs from the middle, first to the left, then to the right, and through the disappearing curtain of blond fringe, she saw Tammy, grinning as she leaned back, squinting at her. She set the scissors down, combed out the short bangs.

"Now you can see the whale," Tammy said.

Claudia's forehead felt cold, exposed, the way skin always felt when covering hair had been removed away from it. She rubbed the wrinkles on her forehead, felt the clean edges of the shorn hair. Tammy held up a hand mirror, and she looked at herself.

Young, Claudia thought, forgetting how young she really was, compared to Masu, compared to Malgi. The shorter bangs made her look younger, the neat blond fringe square across her eyebrows. And the hair wasn't in her eyes, like Tammy said. Her mother would be proud, Claudia thought.

Masu tapped her on the back, finished with the braids. Reaching back, Claudia felt the cool surface of the plaits, the way the strands wound around each other in valleys and ridges. She stood, switching places with Tammy, and Tammy sat in front of the old woman and the old woman began combing out the young Inupiaq's black hair. Tammy handed Claudia the comb and the scissors, then ran a hand through the black brush at the top of her head.

"Clean it up," Tammy said. "Pull it up about an inch with your fingers and cut across the top of your hand, all one length."

Claudia did as Tammy asked, snipping a clump and moving her hand back through the hair like a mower. The stiff black hairs fell on the bench between them, mingling with her blond hair, with Masu's gray hair, with Paula's dark brown hair. They had shared the same house, the same air, the same food, even the same bathwater.

We are unrelated, Claudia thought, two Inupiaq women, two taniks, and yet we are sisters. Trust and sharing. We put our souls in each other's hands, and we must trust each other. The men surrounded them, their brothers, yes, but we are sisters. Sisters, she thought, as Masu pulled the braids tighter on Tammy's head, and the bonds grew tighter.

Chapter 19

"TIME for Walter Cronkite," Tuttu said.

He sat straight on the bench before Malgi as the old man drew a razor across the crown of Tuttu's head. Tuttu had been looking through Murdoch's book, and seen pictures of nineteenth-century Inupiaq men with shaven patches at the crown of their heads—Eskimo tonsures. So all the Inupiaq men in the qaregi, even the boy, Puvak, decided they should shave the crowns of their heads, leaving fringes around the edges. When Tuttu had told her of this, Claudia had hoped to herself that he didn't get to the chapter on tattoos and labrets.

Malgi mumbled something, and wiped away the lather from around the pale, stubbly white circle on Tuttu's scalp. The younger man rubbed his head, the way Claudia remembered an old boyfriend had rubbed his newly shaven head the morning before he had the brain surgery that killed him on the operating table. Tuttu stood up, patted Malgi's own bald spot, and they both chuckled.

"Cronkite's coming on?" Malgi asked.

Tuttu nodded. "Time for Cronkite, yah."

She couldn't figure out how he did it, Claudia thought, but ever since that first Cronkite broadcast had come in, Tuttu knew when the next would be coming. There was no predictable pattern, no way to know—it wasn't like they had *TV Guide* mailed to them each week—but, bang, Tuttu would get a funny buzzing in his teeth. Sure enough, they'd check with whomever had TV duty that day, and Cronkite would be coming on. The little black and white monitor—plugged into the village cable network, 12-volt DC battery powering the tube—would go from no-signal snow to the big CBS eye. Everyone would go over to the gym to the big color TV, and fifteen minutes later Cronkite would come on.

Natchiq damped down the stove and the people of Malgi's qaregi pulled on boots and pants and shirts and trooped down the katak, out the entrance tunnel, and to the gym. As they passed by other houses, Puvak or maybe Amaguq would pop his head into the door and yell "Cronkite." Soon, they led a procession of villagers, old men and women and children and the other surviving taniks, down Nachik Street and over to Momegana Street and to the old school gym.

Up on the roof the long blades of a wind generator whirled in the steady southwesterly breeze, beating like the wings of a condor. A wave of cold air rolled over them as they entered the short hallway to the gym; they didn't keep it warm inside because no one spent enough time in there to bother. Tuttu lit a candle lantern hanging by the door and went up to the stage, where they'd set up a huge Mitsubishi television screen. He fiddled with some switches, the set warmed up, and soon the CBS eye looked down at them, the unblinking black and white eye.

In the glow of the set and the ruddy glow of the sunlight barely shining through grimy skylights, the villagers assembled. No one talked, Claudia noted again, not at first. The big eye on the screen and the dim gym—their eyes slowly adjusting—and the strangeness of a television broadcast from decades ago and no one knew where created the feel of a religious occasion. Seeing Cronkite was like going to Mass and taking the wafer and having God transmuted within you. Well, not *quite*, she thought. But close.

Tuttu fiddled some more with the TV set, just the way her father would fiddle with the TV set when she had been very young, Claudia remembered. Men always did that, even if the signal came in perfectly, probably to assert their control over technology or something. The CBS eye blinked out and the purple-gray of the faded tube stared in its place. A sigh, a wave of exhaled breaths, rolled over the villagers, disappointed shock at even this brief loss of the modern world. Some began to whisper. Tuttu held the lantern high, looking down at something behind the set. He displayed a loose wire, did something to the connector at the end of it, then touched it, Claudia surmised, to the bank of batteries behind the television.

The screen came back on just as Walter Cronkite's head filled the frame. He jumped right into his broadcast, the lead story having something to do with the Vietnam War, some battle for a strategic rice paddy or piddly-ass hill. That led into a piece on Nixon, a younger Nixon, just into his presidency, no bags under his eyes and his really serious lies a few years away. Claudia paid no attention to the words, the words meant nothing. She watched the images, the flickering phosphenes of not only a time she knew was gone, but also a place.

Richard Nixon with his baggy suit, his heavy eyebrows, his wife with her prim smile and neatly coiffed hair, their daughters looking like princesses, pink and tidy . . . The soldiers in the Vietnam piece looking so young, so vulnerable. One moment they would be heading out to battle in clean fatigues, clean-shaven and waving peace signs at the camera, and the next frame would show them bloodied and filthy and sweaty, and dead.

But it was the images of the commercials that amazed her, the world depicted. Medicine ads up the wazoo, over-the-counter cures for cold sores and colds, hemorrhoids, menstrual cramps, constipation. There was a Clairol ad showing white, joyful blond women romping on the beach and running through the surf, their hair teased into respectable bouffants that never rustled in the ocean breeze. "Is it true blondes have more fun?" the announcer asked, and several of the villagers turned to look at Claudia, tittering. Tammy nudged her, pointing with her chin at Tuttu. He grinned at Claudia and she blushed.

Claudia looked at the Clairol blondes running in the waves and thought they looked like seagulls, the ends of their hairdos flipping up like wings. She tried to imagine Tammy and Masu, even Paula, running in the Chukchi Sea with hair like that. She shook her head. Another world.

Cronkite moved into the lighter segments, some piece about hippie homesteaders getting back to the land in Oregon. That seemed realer, somehow: about the tribes of long-haired men and women building yurts and domes in the coastal rain forest. She'd seen people like that farther south in Alaska, even a few years ago. "Bush hippies," the old-timers called them—the sons and daughters of those '60s flower children, people her age, living in cabins and running dogs in Talkeetna and Trapper Creek and Homer.

Another aspirin commercial and then Cronkite let Charles Kuralt close with an "On the Road" piece from Twin Snakes, Florida, something about an old codger who collected cypress knees he thought looked like Jesus Christ that Claudia thought looked like cypress knees.

"And that's the way it is," Cronkite ended, "May seventeenth, nineteen sixty-seven. For CBS News, this is Walter Cronkite. Good night."

Good night. The date stuck with her, today's date, but a different year from previous broadcasts. When they'd first seen the Cronkite tape it had been 1967, but the right date, and then the broadcasts skipped around: '66, '68, '65, '68, '68, even a '70. No one knew why. Claudia figured whoever had the tapes couldn't find a tape for every day in one year. They jumped around, the only common thread that they all had something to do with Vietnam. There was always a Vietnam piece. But wasn't that the way it was? she thought. Hadn't her father told her that, her uncles? Vietnam up the wazoo, too, just like the medicine ads. A national obsession for at least ten long years.

The credits rolled, the image of Cronkite faded, and the TV screen jumped to the big eye again. Then the CBS logo blinked out, the snow came on, and the set hissed static, the static of the only other broadcast around, the hum of the unaltered electromagnetic spectrum. The villagers rose and began to leave the gym, onward to an uncertain future.

And *that's* the way it *is*, Cronkite said in her mind.

* * *

A few nights later some noise woke Claudia up. She sat up on her mattress. Tammy snored next to her, a gentle rumbling more like the thrum of a fan than the roar of an engine. In the darkened corners of the qaregi the people of Malgi's house slept, Masu and Paula with their husbands, Tuttu and the rest of the men on the other side of the house. One of the puppies slept at the foot of Puvak's mat; Puvak had gotten permission to start bringing one puppy at a time into the house, to get them used to people. A log popped from inside the stove. Claudia nodded, and thought, A log cracking, that's what the noise was.

Still, awakened, she couldn't go right back to sleep. From the pile of boots and mukluks by the fire, she found her own boots, put them on, and went up the roof hatch. The sun had dipped low over the horizon, of course, but did not set. Utqiagvik spread around her, smoke rising from houses the main indicator of what was occupied and what wasn't. Many of the abandoned houses poked through the melting snowdrifts, and some of the garbage in the streets had begun to reappear. Bodies might reappear, Claudia thought, shuddering at the thought. Summer might be gruesome, if they survived to summer.

She stared out to sea and the wind blew the loose hairs at the back of her neck around and into her face. The ice ridge seemed to grow higher in the low sunlight, and a fog bank hovered between it and the sun. Claudia sucked in her breath, touched the loose hairs with one hand, shaded her eyes with the other. She looked again. Fog between the sun; wind at her back. The wind had shifted. Steam hung over the ice. The lead? Had it opened?

Someone lifted the trapdoor at her feet, and she looked down to see Puvak climbing up, the puppy in his hands. "Dee-Dee was whining to go out," he said. "I heard someone up here."

"Puvak—go get my binoculars. They're hanging by my mat." She reached down to take the puppy, and Puvak popped back down into the house. Claudia stroked the little dog, felt it squirm in her hands. She set it down, and the pup waddled over to a corner of the platform, peed in a patch of snow.

"Here," Puvak said, coming back up the ladder. "You see something?" He handed her the Nikons.

"The puyugruaq," she said. Claudia looked through the binoculars, focused beyond the ice pack. Ah. It is open, she thought. She could see the water gleaming, a narrow band just beyond the ice pack. Steam above, sky water in the clouds: the uniniq.

"Go," she said to Puvak. "Wake your father, tell him you're going to the ridge. The lead—it should be open. Take these"—she handed him the binoculars—"and get a CB from Natchiq."

"Wake Natchiq?" Puvak asked. She knew what he thought: the harpoonist hated to be woken.

"Wake the house! The wind's shifted! The lead's opening! The whale . . . agviq may be coming!"

Puvak grinned, slipped the Nikons around his neck, and went down below. Claudia picked up the puppy, held her close to her chest. Dee-Dee whined, nestling its nose in her breast. She stroked the dog's back. Maybe. Maybe they would get one more chance.

Someone had stoked the fire higher, and the warmth seemed to revive them, restore their spirits. Masu stirred a big pot of oatmeal, next to a pot of water boiling on the stove. The whalers got ready. While Claudia tied up her boots, Tammy braided her hair, nothing fancy, just two braids over her shoulders. Malgi sat next to the CB, tuned down to squelch. Low static hummed from the radio. Amaguq had told his son to report when he got to the lead, about a half hour walk, maybe. Malgi glanced at Tuttu's watch, looked up, shrugged.

Natchiq sat on the bench next to Claudia, a harpoon laid across his lap. In his hand a file flew over the edge of the iron, quick strokes going down, down, a *whitt, whitt* noise blurring with the hum of the radio. As Natchiq worked, a line of clean metal crawled up the edge of the blade. Natchiq looked up, saw Claudia looking at him.

"No one will go swimming this time," he said, looking over at Malgi. "The iron will go in deep and straight."

Right, she thought, and smiled at him. They had decided

to set a harpoon first, to a separate line, and follow up with a darting gun with no iron. The harpoon will attach a line to it, the gun will wound the whale. Grigor had said he made the bomb less powerful, but they cannot risk it, cannot allow the possibility of losing this whale, of the charge destroying the line. Set the iron; wound. That will be the way.

Tuttu held a clipboard in his lap and drew figures in it. Claudia tried to see what he wrote, but could only see the outline of an umiaq and words next to the drawing. He scowled, crossed something out, wrote something in. "Anaq," he muttered.

"What's wrong?" Claudia asked. Tammy pulled the braid tighter, jerking her head back.

"We're short one paddler," he said. "Look"—he showed her the plan—"there's Natchiq in the bow, the harpoonist. Puvak and Amaguq behind him. Grigor and Aluaq in the middle seat. Malgi with you next, then me at the stern. But Malgi"—Tuttu looked away as his grandfather glanced up at his name—"can't come. We need someone with you."

Tammy pulled her braid tighter once more, and Claudia's neck jerked back again. Claudia laughed inside. "Why not Tammy?" she asked. "She's been hunting with us. We could take her."

Tuttu stared over her shoulder at Tammy. "The woman who loves women? Another woman on my crew?" He snorted. "I'll find some boy, don't worry."

"If *one* woman is okay, why not two?" Claudia asked. Tammy finished braiding her hair, and set her hands on Claudia's shoulders. She reached up, took the Inupiaq woman's hands in her own. "Why not?"

"Grandfather?" Tuttu asked.

Malgi looked up from the CB, stared with his hard blue eyes at Tuttu. He smiled. "Would it please the whale?"

"Would it please the whale?" Claudia repeated. "I do not know. Why did you let me hunt before?"

Tuttu grinned. "You're a good shot. Is little Nuna a good shot?"

"Qavvik," Tammy said. "If you're going to call me an Inupiaq name, call me the right one." She ran a hand through the bristle at the crown of her head, bleached redder by the sun. "The wolverine."

"Claudia is the anthropologist," Malgi said. "We need her to advise us." He looked at her. "And she is a good shot."

"Should little *Nuna* come along?" Tuttu asked. He spat out the name, glaring at Tammy.

"Would it please agviq?" Malgi looked at Claudia. "Anthropologist?"

"Women have hunted before," she said. "They have been on whaling crews before. I interviewed a woman who had been on a crew back in the 1980s."

"Should *this* woman take my place on the crew?" He glared at her now, and she knew the question he asked. "Would having her on the crew please agviq?"

"No woman could take your place, Grandfather," Claudia said. "No *man* could possibly take your place. You will be on the ice, if we can use the sno-go again"—she looked over at Natchiq—"and your spirit will be with us on the water. Can this woman help the crew?"

"Yes, that is the question," Malgi said. "Can she help the crew better than someone else?"

"I was an Olympic kayaker," Tammy said. "Would have been in those Olympics we boycotted." She squeezed Claudia's shoulders, and she felt the strength in her hands.

"She is my partner," Claudia said. "She is my sister." Claudia crossed her arms across her breasts and took Tammy's hands again. Then she smiled. "And, as Tuttu says, she is a woman who loves women. Doesn't that make her something like a man?"

"Do you love *her* like a man?" Tuttu asked.

And Claudia saw it then, saw the source of his displeasure. He was jealous! He saw the closeness between them, knew that Tammy could love Claudia like Claudia could love Rob—or Tuttu. She nodded her head. She saw it. Tuttu wanted to know. She looked at Tuttu and he looked at her and blushed.

"I love her like a man loves his brother, or his cousin, or his fellow hunter," Claudia said. "I sleep next to her but I do not sleep *with* her, much as she might like that. I would

sleep with a man, if I could find a man I was worthy of."
There! she thought. Let him know!

Tuttu smiled, and he nodded. "Perhaps it would be okay.
But does Tammy still bleed?" He glared at Claudia. "You
know we cannot have women in their period on the ice."

"I am beyond my period," Tammy said. She pinched
Claudia slightly. "All of the women are beyond our periods."

"So," Tuttu said. "Well. I don't know . . . Perhaps it
would please agviq to have such a strong paddler on our
crew then." The young umialik grinned. "I know it would
please me to have two such fine women in front of me."
The men laughed at that, even Claudia and Tammy giggled
a little. "Qavvik, you may crew with us. Perhaps you can
teach your partner how to paddle!"

Malgi held up a hand, quieting them, and he fiddled with
the dials of the CB radio. He turned the volume up, adjusted
the squelch, and they heard Puvak's tinny voice coming
from the speaker.

"Grandfather, Grandfather!" he shouted. "I am sorry to
not call sooner but I had to shoot a polar bear!" Claudia
shook her head at the boy's luck.

"Go ahead, Puvak," Malgi said.

"Grandfather, the lead has opened but it is narrow. It
extends to Walakpa, maybe farther. And Grandfather, I saw
plumes, six of them!

"Agviq," the boy said, "the whale has returned!"

Chapter 20

A ND so the whalers set out on the ice once again. No
one knew how many whales would pass or if there
would be any left by the time they'd dragged the
umiaq and gear back out. They had to hurry. Natchiq
consented to letting them use a snowmachine—and a few
gallons of gas—to drag the kamotiq and skin boat to the
lead. Malgi said he'd walk out on his own, despite his
bad knee and broken arm, and the whalers said, no, he'd
ride. They boosted him up into his boat. With his crew
guiding the sled over rough ice and the sno-go moving
slowly, Malgi sat in the center of the boat, proud and
beaming.

A quick camp was set up again, the sled parallel to the
edge, the umiaq bow forward—darting gun and harpoon
pointing to sea—and the tent back from the ice. Puvak
greeted them as they came over the ridge, and dragged his
father to see nanuq, the polar bear.

Puvak said he hadn't wanted to shoot the bear—"I didn't
want to scare off agviq, if he was there," he said—but had
to when it surprised him. Amaguq's son had rounded a
boulder of ice on the trail, and there the bear had been,
coming toward him. "I didn't think, just brought my rifle
forward and fired." His .22, Claudia noted. He'd killed the
bear with two perfect shots to the heart and lungs.

The boy had already skinned out the bear and eviscerated

it. With the skin off, the bear looked like a man, a tall man.
Nanuq had already begun to regain his summer fat; his
flanks had some marbling in the muscle, and a layer of fat
spread across the bear's pelvis. Death had caused the bear
to ejaculate, his penis engorged and poking out of its
sheath. Definitely male, Claudia thought. And it had
survived the winter. Probably, it had been feeding on
carrion—maybe dead whales, seals. Nanuq, like the whale,
had survived. Would survive, though Puvak had killed
this one.

Puvak helped Malgi out of the umiaq. He had scraped the
hide clean of blood and tissue, and laid out the skin fur side
up on the sled. "Sit, Grandfather," he said. "This hide, the
bear, is for you and Masu." Malgi smiled, let the boy help
him sit down, and grasped Puvak's shoulder firmly, the way
he would a man.

Malgi gestured for the whalers to come stand before him.
The six men and two women moved over to the old man,
stood in a semicircle before the sled. "We must do this
right," he said. "We need a ritual. Anthropologist?"

"What kind of ritual?" Claudia asked.

"Something to honor the whale. I don't know . . . Something."

Claudia glanced at Malgi, turned, looked to sea. There
were so many rituals, so many things they could do. What
did the Utqiagvik whalers do in the past? she asked herself.
What would be proper? She touched the ivory whale around
her neck.

"We must give the umiaq a drink," a woman said from
behind them. They turned. Masu had followed them out,
carrying a small wooden bucket. She held the bucket up.
The wood of the bucket was old and glossy, the way wood
got when it had been handled and rubbed by many hands.
"I forgot to give the umiaq a drink. My mother used to do
that for my father's boat, and agviq honored him many
times."

Claudia smiled. She had forgotten that, then thought of it
when they struck the first whale, and had forgotten it again.
Malgi looked at her and she nodded at him.

"Pull the umiaq out," he said to them. "Pull it onto the ice."

Natchiq went to the bow, lifting the darting gun and harpoon out very carefully. They dragged it back from the edge, toward where the old woman stood with her bucket.

"I forget the words exactly," she said. "But I think it goes like this"—they bowed their heads—" 'Umiaq, carry these whalers safely over the water. Help them honor agviq so that agviq will honor us. We thank the skins of the animals that gave us their parkas for this boat, and we offer them water so that their thirst will be quenched.' " Masu raised the bucket to the bow of the umiaq, and poured it on the thick hide stretched over the forward part of the keel.

"I must go back now," she said when she was done.

"Wait," Claudia said. She looked to Malgi. "There is another ritual I remember." Malgi nodded. "We must put the boat back in the water and get in. Masu—the umialik's wife—you stand at the ice edge."

The old woman nodded, her eyes flashing. She smiled. "I remember! Yes!"

"In the boat," Malgi said to them. "Go, go!"

The whalers got in, Natchiq at the stern, the rest in their places. Claudia told Natchiq to get the harpoon, to stand ready with it. They paddled out, away from the camp, from the white tent and the kamotiq and Malgi sitting on the sled.

"Tell them to head back in," Claudia whispered to Tuttu.

"Head to shore," he said.

Masu stood at the edge of the ice, slightly stooped, her gray braids hanging over the front of her atigi, a flowered cover over the hide parka. She held her hands at her sides, feet bowed slightly out.

"Natchiq," Claudia said, "when you get up to Masu, raise your harpoon to her, and get ready to throw it."

"You want me to throw it at her?" he asked.

"No," she shouted. "No. At the last minute, dip it into the water. It's as if she's the whale and . . . how do I explain it?" She looked back at Tuttu.

"Don't," he said.

The whalers paddled, the blades digging in, slow, smooth. Claudia glanced over at Tammy to her right, and saw her shoulder and arm muscles bulge through her atigi, watched the quick, sure movements. Not jerky, she saw. Like a machine. The umiaq came through the water, the sun now in their eyes, as they moved closer to shore. Natchiq raised the harpoon, pulled his arm back.

Masu stood straight and immobile on the shore, staring at the whalers, at the glint of the steel point of the harpoon, a broad smile on her face. Natchiq let his arm fall and dipped the point of the blade into the sea, then raised it up. He sat back down, the paddlers pulled their paddles blade up, and the umiaq coasted up on the ice, stopping inches before Masu. As the umiaq came to her, she knelt down, head bowed before the whalers. Masu rose, turned her back on them, and walked back to the village.

Malgi got up, hobbled over to the crew as they got out of the skin boat. They turned the boat around, setting it up as before. Puvak and Amaguq went to the old man, supported him on either side.

"One more ritual," he said. He pulled out the dried raven's head from under his shirt. For the first time, Claudia noticed that the head had been wrapped to an old Christian cross, and she remembered that back before the war, long ago, Malgi had been a deacon in the Presbyterian Church. "We must pray."

Pray to what? she asked herself. To the God that had been supplanted on the old Inupiaq belief system, or the beliefs that had been supplanted on the old God? "Was the Whale Jesus?" she had asked an anthropology professor once, and he had answered with a question, "Was Jesus the Whale?"

They bowed their heads. Malgi said something in Inupiaq, but the words were clipped and spoken fast, recited, and she had trouble recognizing them. And then they came to her, familiar in their meter. Her Inupiaq had never been good, she had only passing knowledge of nouns—verbs baffled her—but this poem she remembered. How could she forget?

And then, as if to confirm her guess, Malgi spoke the translation.

"Our Father, Who art in Heaven.

"Hallowed be thy name.

"Thy kingdom come, thy will be done

"On Earth as it is in Heaven.

"Give us this day our daily bread.

"And forgive us our debts.

"As we forgive our debtors.

"And Lead us not into temptation.

"But deliver us from Evil.

"For thine is the Kingdom, and the Power, and the Glory.

"Forever."

"Amen," Malgi said.

"Amen," the whalers said, even Grigor, the godless Communist.

And why not? Claudia thought. Heaven was the sea and God was the whale and Jesus was the whale and the daily bread was the whale. If they spoke in the words of an ancient sect of wayward Jews, well, why not?

They waited again. Malgi lit the Coleman stove, using more precious kerosene, and they started a pot of tea going. The sun rose almost directly overhead. All eyes stared out at the lead, down the lead. Up on the ice ridge Puvak scanned with the Nikons. And they waited.

Claudia imagined the whale coming up the lead, following its ancestral route. Agviq has always come north to the Arctic, come to feed on the plankton and krill, she thought. The whale has always come to breed in the Beaufort Sea to the east. It must round this point, must pass Nuvuk and Utqiagvik. The whalebones in the old houses, the huge harpoon points in the houses, offer proof of how long the whales have come. They have seen whales earlier, she thought, and the whale will come.

Huge and massive, she thought of it swimming through the cold water. If ice stood in its way, agviq would burst through it. The bowhead knows the path, knows where to go. Claudia sent her thoughts out to the whale, lurking unseen down the lead from them. Come, agviq, come to us who are unworthy. Give us your parka so we may become worthier. Come. Come.

A shout! Puvak uttered only one syllable in his excitement. "Ag"—he scrambled down the ridge—"*viq*"—the last syllable lost in his tumbling fall down. "There! There!" He pointed across the lead, and down the lead.

Claudia took the binoculars from him, focused on a plume of misty breath rising. Yes, the whale, she thought. One, no, two. Two plumes. "Two whales." She handed the binoculars to Tuttu.

"Too far," Tuttu said.

"We will chase," Natchiq said. He moved to the umiaq, climbed in, looked back. "*We can catch it.*"

"No," Tuttu said. "Wait."

"Come, paddle for me." He pointed at Tammy. "You, Qavvik, you are a strong paddler. Paddle for Natchiq."

Tuttu glared at Natchiq. "*Wait*, Natchiq."

Natchiq sighed, nodded. "I will wait *here*," he said, crossing his arms across his chest.

The whalers stood by the edge of the ice, looking again for whales. Now that Puvak had seen the two across the uiniq, perhaps more would come. They watched the water, some, like Tuttu and Amaguq, looking straight across the lead. Others, like Grigor or Aluaq, scanned the edges. Look, look. Come to us, agviq, Claudia thought again.

"Azah!" Amaguq shouted. He pointed frantically at a shape moving barely ten yards down the lead, behind a little point of ice between them and the umiaq.

"Quiet," Tuttu said.

Puvak helped Malgi stand, and the old man looked around the edge of the windbreak formed by the sled. He smiled. "Ah, it will round the point. Tuttu," he whispered, "get the crew behind the umiaq."

Tuttu nodded, waved at the whalers. They scurried around to the boat, taking their stations at the gunwales. "Get in?" Tuttu asked.

Malgi stood with his weight on one leg, leaning against an unaaq staff. He shook his head. "When agviq comes near, push the boat toward it, with just Natchiq in the boat.

Push the boat onto the whale, and Natchiq can strike it with the harpoon—Now! Now!''

The seven whalers leaned into the gunwales, shoving the skin boat across the ice and into the sea. Natchiq stood, raised the harpoon as the umiaq coasted across the five yards of water to the whale. Agviq rounded the little point of the ice edge, rose before them, one eye staring sideways at them. He does not see us, Claudia thought. He does not see the white boat, the white atigis. We have fooled him!

They pushed the boat almost right onto agviq's back, the bow of the umiaq intersecting the whale. Natchiq pulled his arm back, pulled the shaft of the harpoon back, and thrust. The iron and the shaft sailed barely ten feet, a coil of rope unwinding out from behind it. The point caught the sun, glinted in the bright light, and the flicker of light met the reflection of sun on the whale's glossy back. It hit, point of steel hit hard flesh, the steel parted the flesh, cut into the skin, and the rope jerked the shaft back. The iron held, the bit of wood in the head snapped, and the toggle flipped back. A strike! Claudia's heart soared at the thunk of the harpoon hitting, at the shaft of the harpoon sticking straight up from the whale's back.

Natchiq threw out the big orange fishing floats. One, two, three, the lines snapped out and the floats splashed into the water. The umiaq coasted to a stop, dead in the water. In the water, the lines uncoiled like snakes, and then the whale dragged the pink and orange floats behind him, billiard balls across the felt of the open lead. He took the floats with him, out into the lead, a thin trail of blood behind him.

"Get the boat, get the boat!" Tuttu yelled.

The harpoonist sat back down, grabbed an oar, and paddled back to them. Amaguq reached out, pulled the umiaq up to the ice edge. He and Puvak climbed in behind Natchiq, and the others quickly took their positions. Tuttu swung the umiaq around, stern to the ice, gave it a shove, and got in behind Claudia and Tammy. Malgi hobbled up to them, carrying something wrapped in white canvas that he'd pulled out of the tent.

"Take this!" the old man yelled. He threw the object at

Tuttu. He caught it, set it down in the boat. He turned back to Malgi, waved.

"Agviq will not get away!" he yelled.

"Don't lose it!" Malgi said. "Chase it, tire it, and then"—he held up his arms, mimed the firing of a rifle—"finish it!"

Tuttu looked down at the canvas-covered object, smiled.

Claudia turned around, picked up her paddle, and concentrated. At the bow, Natchiq called out commands. "Forward, faster, faster," he shouted. The whale had not dived yet, and still towed the big orange floats behind him. He must be tiring already, Claudia thought; the other whale had moved faster than this. They dug in, dug with the blades. Tammy set the pace for the crew, her strokes hard and deep and powerful. Next to her, the woman grunted, breathed, grunted. Her nostrils flared with each breath, each breath blowing on the men in front of her. And they paddled harder.

"We've got him!" Natchiq shouted. "A little to port" —Tuttu corrected the direction at the stern—"now, now, up on him, up on him."

They pulled alongside, between two floats trailing behind agviq. Natchiq raised the darting gun, the gun without an iron, only a line attaching it to the umiaq. He glanced back at Tuttu, and Tuttu nodded. Strike when you're ready, the glance said, Claudia knew.

Agviq exhaled, and a fine mist sprayed them, a clear mist. The whale sucked in air, and she heard the noise again, like a tub draining the last bit of water. Natchiq leaned forward, let fly the darting gun. It arched, came down just behind the whale's blowholes, and the trigger rod hit. The gun fired its bomb into the whale a full two feet from where the iron stuck up, on the other side of the backbone. Out and away the bomb kicked the darting gun. Natchiq yanked back on the rope, pulled the gun out of the water. When the bomb hit, thrust down into the skin, agviq dove.

The end of the harpoon shaft disappeared beneath the waves. The floats were pulled under. The whale kicked its flukes, splashing the umiaq. Behind her Claudia heard Tuttu counting quietly, "One thousand one, one thousand two, one thousand three, one thousand four . . ."

And the bomb exploded again. A column of bubbles burst to the surface, first clear, then pink, then deep red. Claudia turned to Tammy, and they smiled at each other. "Ariggaaa!" Natchiq shouted. Grigor turned back to Tuttu and grinned.

"Too much, you think?" the Soviet asked. Tuttu shook his head.

"Just right." He pointed at the end of a line of bubbles moving ahead of them. "Now, follow, and we'll get agviq when he surfaces."

They paddled ahead, watching the bubbles, waiting. A float popped up, then another. The third float came up, and then the whale, the great massive whale, surfaced. It stretched longer than the umiaq, twice as long. Sixty feet, Claudia thought, sixty tons. *My God, that's enough meat for a year, maybe.* Agviq floated in the water, kicking slowly with its flukes, flapping lazily with its fins. He looked up at them with one eye, the eye distant but not dead.

Claudia felt something wet run down her cheek, wiped at the briny water, the tear. She stared at the whale, felt pity and sadness that they had to kill such a great thing. The whale stared back, blinked its eye—she thought—at her. Agviq turned its head down, ducking its great head below the water.

"Finish it," she said. She turned to Tuttu. "Put it out of its misery. Take it. *Take it.*"

He nodded, reached down for the thing in the white canvas, unwrapped the object. Tuttu ran his hand over the smooth metal of the object, down the eighteen-inch barrel, over the action, along the open-trapezoid of the stock. He clicked a button and swung the barrel forward, took something else from the canvas pouch, and slid another bomb—like the darting gun bomb—in.

"It's Malgi's grandfather's," he explained. "A Pierce bomb gun—1922, in case you're wondering, archaeologist." Tuttu clicked the barrel shut, turned off the safety. "You sure this will work, Grigor?"

The Soviet shrugged. "Malgi said it's the same bomb as the darting gun. That worked, didn't it?"

Tuttu nodded. "Too well."

The whalers paddled the umiaq up to the whale. Tuttu raised the butt of the bomb gun to his shoulder, sighted down the barrel. Agviq raised his great head, turned to face the umialik.

"What if the bomb blows up?" Tammy asked.

Tuttu hesitated, looked up at her, scowled. "It would not please agviq for the bomb to blow up in my face," he said. "Shut up, Qavvik." He aimed again. Agviq begs for the bomb, Claudia thought. He begs for death and the chance to honor us, we who are so worthy.

Tuttu fired.

The bomb, too, like the darting gun bomb, flew through the air, through the water. It hit the whale in the backbone, severing the spine, Claudia saw. Four seconds later and the second charge blew. She watched agviq's eye the whole time, watched it watching her. When the second explosion hit, agviq shuddered, and the light in his eye faded. He flapped one fluke, kicked briefly with his fins, rolled halfway over, then back, and settled in the water.

"Azah," Tuttu said. He wrapped the bomb gun up again.

"We did it," Natchiq said. "We did it!"

The great whale floated in the icy water, a black iceberg, a floating mountain of flesh. Blood streamed out from his wounds, from the harpoon. They did it. They had killed a whale. Claudia felt the tears stream down her cheeks now, rivers of water, tears for agviq, tears for themselves, tears of sadness at the death that had just come and the life that death would bring.

Tuttu reached down toward the whale, took a long knife and cut a hole in agviq's lips. He tied a line through the hole in the lip, cinched it to a cleat under the stern seat. "Now, paddle!" he yelled. "Pull agviq to the ice edge."

Dig, Claudia thought, dig. Behind her, Tuttu began to sing. The melody and the beat hit her before she comprehended the words. When the words came, though, she laughed and joined in, and everyone joined in, even Grigor.

"I am the Captain of the Pinafore!" Tuttu sang.

"And a right good captain, too!" the whalers responded.

"I'm very very good and be it understood, I command a right good crew!"

"He's very very good and be it understood, he commands a right good crew."

Gilbert and Sullivan, Claudia thought. What would Reinhardt think? What would the anthropologists say? They had killed a whale.

They had killed and *recovered* a whale.

Chapter 21

THE whalers turned the umiaq and the whale toward the shore, putting the sun at their backs. They strained at the paddles, digging in hard. Claudia concentrated, focusing on Aluaq's neck; the younger man's muscles bunched in tight cords as he pulled back on his paddle. On the shore, Malgi waved a flag—an American flag—on a staff.

Natchiq took a flare gun from a seabag at the bow, and fired a shell toward the camp. Malgi waved the flag more furiously as the flare parachuted toward him. The flare burned out, but something else flashed from the top of the ice ridge, sunlight reflecting on metal. Claudia took out her binoculars and checked.

"A boat," she said. "Another crew's coming out."

Tuttu took the Nikons from her. "Igaluk," he said. "He has to have gotten together a crew."

Igaluk or whoever put the boat in the water, an aluminum boat, and they began paddling toward Tuttu's crew. Four men, Claudia saw through the binoculars. No motor. The skiff came closer to them, and Tuttu hailed them as they got in shouting distance.

"We got a whale!" he shouted.

"You need help towing it in?" a man in the bow shouted back. Igaluk, Claudia saw—right, Masik's brother-in-law, the man she thought might have fathered a child with his brother's wife. He'd been one of the few not to ridicule Tuttu about whaling.

Tuttu glanced over at Claudia. "We'll have to share with him, won't we?" he asked.

Claudia nodded. "Yeah. But you still get the best share."

Tuttu grinned. "Okay!" he shouted back.

She smiled, too. Okay. They'd need help getting the whale out of the water anyway—need help butchering it, hauling it to shore, she thought. The whole village has to help. One crew alone couldn't do it all.

Igaluk pulled beside Tuttu's umiaq, reached down to the whale's lips and attached another line through the whale. The crews talked back and forth across agviq, telling how they'd chased it. With the heavier boat and the smaller crew, Igaluk and the three other men wouldn't keep up as well, but they did lessen the load slightly. The two boats paddled closer to shore, and then they saw a *third* boat coming over the ridge.

"They'll believe me, now," Tuttu said to Claudia. "See? We'll take many whales."

When they got to the ice edge, the crew of the third boat waited for them to come in. Someone had begun pounding four heavy car axles into the ice. Malgi hobbled around, shouting orders. He dragged out a heavy block and tackle from the tent, and someone took it from him and began to attach it to the stakes. Malgi pushed the line round and round the block, one end stretching toward the ice ridge, the other toward the water.

Tuttu jumped out of the umiaq as they came broadside to the ice. He untied the lines to the whale from the boat, held them in his hand. Malgi hopped over to greet him, and Tuttu half caught him, half hugged him as they met. "Grandfather," Tuttu said, "I got a whale."

"Ai, Tuttu." Malgi waved his arm out to sea, out to agviq. "That you did." He picked up the loose line from the block and tackle and walked over to the stern of the boat. "Help me in the umiaq," he said to Claudia. She shrugged, and with Tammy boosted Malgi up into Tuttu's seat. The old man held the rope from the block and tackle, wrapped it loosely around the stern cleat. Natchiq had started to climb out of the boat, but stopped at Malgi's signal. "Paddle over to the whale."

Natchiq nodded, got back in, and they moved the boat around to the whale's tail. Malgi took a long knife, leaned over the side of the skin boat, and cut off the very tips of the whale's flukes. He handed the tips to Claudia, then took the line and tied it around the whale's flukes.

"Now, back in," he said to the crew.

Back on the ice, all the crew got out. The two women helped Malgi out. Claudia handed him the fluke tips. Malgi took a bit of string, and tied the tips of the flukes to a paddle. He gave the paddle to Puvak. "Take this," he said. "Run to the village. Tell everyone to come out here, especially the old people. Tell them we got a whale!" Puvak smiled, nodded. "Run, Puvak! Go!" The young man turned, dashed off over the rough ice ridge.

Less than an hour later, the villagers came. Old men, old women, toddlers in diapers, the entire town tromped out the path and to the whale. As the villagers arrived, each body got drafted into mule duty. In a tug-of-war with agviq, they grabbed the haul rope and dragged the great whale up onto the ice, until only the tip of his jaw remained in the water.

Claudia could not keep track of the butchering after that. Malgi sat on the kamotiq, a stack of machetes and long knives before him. He took out the carving showing how the shares would be apportioned and used it to show Tuttu how to butcher the whale, how to share it. As the crews butchered the whale, the old man sharpened the knives. Men in hip waders walked over the whale's back, hacking at the thick skin. When a sizable enough chunk of the whale had been cut away, the villagers leaned into the rope again, pulled the whale out more, again and again.

It went on, faster than she thought possible. Sixty tons! The blades flashed, the hunks of meat came flopping down onto the snow. Tuttu ran around, jotting figures and numbers on a clipboard as people from other crews hauled the meat to shore. Somewhere in the midst of it all Igaluk asked Tuttu and Malgi if he could borrow the whaling gear, and damned if he didn't go out with a small crew and get *another* whale.

Sometime around midnight, when the sun had fallen to a point just above the western horizon and all the meat had been stripped from agviq, the whalers stood exhausted and bloody, staring at their work. The baleen had been removed from the whale's mouth, the great horny combs that had the consistency of plastic. Yankee whalers had once taken the bowhead only for the baleen, and used the black plates to make corset stays and buggy whips. Now the Inupiaq whalers would use the baleen for toboggans, for baskets, Claudia thought.

The ribs and vertebrae, the jawbones, all the bone but the skull and some of the larger backbones, had been hauled away: ribs for sled runners, vertebrae for chopping blocks, bone for carving, bone for tools. When they had taken all they could use from agviq, the whalers pushed and shoved and heaved on the skull, and returned the whale to the sea. Food for crabs, Claudia thought, food for plankton, food for other whales.

As the skull of the first whale sank below the ice, it occurred again to Claudia what they had done. Agviq had blessed them; they had taken a whale. Two whales. She looked out at the setting—no, near-setting—sun, and realized what had happened, what truly had happened. They had taken a whale. And that, she thought, might mean they could survive forever.

The puddles on the ice grew larger, the edge of the tuvaq fell away in great pans, and soon even the ice ridge itself broke loose from the shore and floated away. By late May the temperature had risen to above freezing. Drifts dwindled to anthills of packed snow, and soon only in the shade did the snow linger. In Malgi's qaregi the entrance tunnel became flooded as the surface ice melted, and they had to abandon the winter entrance and come and go through the roof. Puvak's puppies had grown big and fat, and smelly. When the tunnel flooded, he moved them to a pen outside.

Three whales total did the village get. Tuttu and Malgi's crew struck the first whale, and then Igaluk got the second, and a crew led by some old guy from Browerville got the third. New ice cellars were dug near the whalers' houses,

264 · MICHAEL ARMSTRONG

and they filled the cellars with fresh meat. Tuttu did some calculations on his laptop and figured the whales *might* last them through the winter, if they got a few seals.

In June, a month after they had struck the first whale, Tuttu and the other whaling captains hosted Nalukataq, the whaling festival. Claudia conferred with Malgi on the celebration. Luckily, most of the articles they found, most of the pictures, showed the festival and not the actual whaling. That made sense, Claudia thought. Whalers wouldn't be likely to take photos while whaling, and yet tanik photographers wouldn't be likely to go out on the ice—they might not have been welcome. But Nalukataq was held on land, in early summer. Besides, she thought, anthropologists always loved festivals.

First, they had to prepare the festival area. Malgi said that in the past they'd held the festival in many different places in town, but he had always liked the field by the community center, across from the hotel and where the bluffs became lower and met the flat beach between Utgiagvik proper and Browerville. Malgi's crew dragged his umiaq down to the festival area, and they turned it on its side, back to the wind. They set up the aluminum boats the same way, though Malgi said that those used to get the other whales didn't look as good as his skin boat.

"But we'll make many more umiaqs this summer," he said.

All the villagers made it a point to put on clean clothes, their fancy parkas if they had them. In the qaregi they had another bath. The men shaved their tonsures clean, and the women braided their hair again. Claudia had found a can of the foam hair dye Masu had used on Belinda when she became Paula, and she was about to dye her hair jet black when Tuttu stopped her. She wanted black hair, Claudia told him, so she could feel more Inupiaq, look more Inupiaq.

"Silly woman," Tuttu said, taking the can from her. "What would you do next? Inject silicon into your eyelids? Grind your molars flat?"

Claudia looked at him, looked at the can of dye, and for

some reason she could not understand, climbed up out of the house and ran down to the beach. Tuttu followed her, caught up with her along the bluffs, below the house that had burned when Edward had shot up the barge.

"Claudia!" he yelled.

She turned at her name, saw him, ran away again. He caught her, turned her around, held her firmly but gently by the shoulders. Tuttu had brought a blanket from the house, and he put it over her shoulders; she had not bothered to put on a parka when she ran out.

"Claudia." He touched her cheek with his finger, wiped the tear streaking down it. "You cry? Why do you cry? Agviq has blessed us and we have meat in the cellars."

"I . . ." she thought of Belinda, Paula, the dark-haired tanik who Masu had taken under her wing and treated like a daughter. She thought of Tammy, Inupiaq in blood but no more Inupiaq than she. "I am not Inupiaq, I do not belong here."

"You *are* here," Tuttu said. "You know as much about us as we do. You can hunt, have hunted. You helped us get the whale." Tuttu shook her gently. "Isn't that enough?"

"It . . . I don't know." She turned her back to him, pulled the blanket tight around her. "I have never understood this land, never understood this place or these people—you. I have spent my whole life trying to understand it. Sometimes I think I do. And then you'll do something and I just get confused."

Tuttu turned her around to face him again. "*I* get confused. *Malgi* gets confused. Why do you think he needs you?"

"Needs me?"

"Needs you. Confirmation. He is an old man, he forgets. You help him remember. You support him. He needs you. We all need you." Tuttu looked down at the beach, looked up at her shyly. "*I* need you." He reached out, combed his fingers through her damp hair.

She shivered at his touch, cocked her head back. "*You* need me?" Claudia smiled. "A tanik?"

"A real person," he said. Tuttu ran his hand through her hair again, down her neck.

She opened up the blanket, pulled it around him, and

drew him closer. Claudia held up her neck, and Tuttu kissed it, ran his lips over her skin and down to her breasts. She let her knees collapse, fell under his weight, and they rolled to the sand.

"*Tuttu*," she said.

Claudia rolled over on top of him, the blanket over her back, the ends of the blanket enveloping Tuttu like a tent. He reached up, unbuttoned her jeans, and pulled her pants and underwear down to her knees. She reached down, undid his belt, unzipped his pants, and opened them. Tuttu smiled, reached up to her, ran a finger along her nose, down her sternum, down to her crotch. Claudia bowed her head, her wet hair falling into her face and into Tuttu's face, and in the sand, below the bluff, the two hunters made love.

Later, they sat side by side staring out at the ice and the sea. To their left the hulk of the barge and the ribs of the tugboat, like the ribs of the whale, sat in the shallow water and the rotting ice. Tuttu put an arm around Claudia, the blanket wrapped around both of them. His blue baseball cap had fallen off in their lovemaking, and Claudia ran her fingers up from the nape of his neck through the fringe of his thick black hair, across the bald spot shaved clean on his crown. The afternoon sun shone down on them, and Tuttu's untanned scalp gleamed white, like fresh bone. She traced the faint white line of a fading scar that cut straight across the top of his head.

"Malgi cut a little too close with the razor when he gave you a tonsure?" she asked.

"No," Tuttu said, smiling shyly. He pushed her hand away and put his cap back on. "Some poor ass shot aimed a little too high with her shotgun."

Claudia looked at him, looked over at the barge, looked at his hat. The hat—Edward's hat. She remembered shooting the red hat off of the guy who had blown up the barge, remembered thinking that Edward's scalp should have had cuts on it if he'd really been shot at by her, but it hadn't.

"You got that cut when I shot at you," she said. "*You* blew the barge?"

He glanced at her out of the corner of his eyes, grinned,

then scowled when he saw she didn't smile back. "I blew the barge, yes," Tuttu said, nodding.

"And you killed Edward? Shot him?" He nodded again. "Why? Why did you blow the barge? We could have used that fuel—that food."

"I did some figuring," he said. "On my laptop computer, you know? And I figured out, with the food on the barge, in the store, if we all shared we might last the winter and this summer. But then I thought, what if we don't share? Many might die. And what would we do after that? There wouldn't be another barge, Claudia. You knew that. We all knew that. Maybe someone's alive out there—whoever sends Walter Cronkite, you know?—but they weren't going to come soon enough to help us. So I had to make it hard. I had to force these people to do what they should do, to become hunters. Kanayuq knew, he was the only one. I blew the barge and wore Edward's hat and parka so it would look like Edward did it if someone saw me."

"You bastard!" she yelled, suddenly standing up. "I almost killed you!"

Tuttu stood, untangling the blanket, and wrapped it around her again. "I know. I didn't think about that. As it happened—well, putting that shot over my head made it look like Edward had blown the barge—those holes in his hat."

"Shit." She turned from him, shook her head.

"You won't tell anyone?"

"I could have died. We could have all died."

"We didn't," he said. Tuttu touched her shoulder, and she turned back to face him. "You didn't."

"No, we didn't." Claudia smiled. "Christ, *you* blew the barge. Jesus." She shook her hed. "Next you'll probably tell me you've been broadcasting Walter Cronkite."

"Well . . ."

"*No.* You couldn't have." Claudia pushed him with both arms, teasing. "Come on? Those broadcasts? You didn't."

"Not me . . . I think I know who did, though. You know that time you saw me go by at Tachinisok Inlet?" Tuttu cocked his head at her.

"Right. Malgi said you'd come to look for me."

"Malgi was spooking you. I went down to Wainwright to

see if anyone was still alive. They were alive, all right. I guess you met Jim, huh?''

Claudia nodded, thinking of the guy in the sea otter cap who'd forced her and Rob away from Ataniq. ''Mean as nails Jim. I knew him.''

''He told us about you and Rob, said he'd kicked you out. Well, he didn't like me much better. He said Ulguniq didn't want anything to do with us. When I asked him how we'd know if they were still alive, Jim said that 'maybe Walter Cronkite would tell it on the news.' ''

''*Shit*. So they're alive, too?''

''That's what those broadcasts tell us. No one knows, though. After the first one came on, I almost told Málgi, but then I thought about it further. It should remain a mystery. Not every little string has to be tied up, you know? If no one knows where those broadcasts came from, they might think there's a world still alive there—a world beyond even Wainwright, Ulguniq. It gives us hope. You saw that: those broadcasts gave us hope. If I'd said they came from Wainwright . . . it wouldn't have been the same.'' Tuttu shrugged. ''I guess it doesn't matter now.''

''No.'' Claudia smiled. ''Let's keep it a secret, all of it.'' She put her index finger to his lips. ''Shhh.''

Tuttu ran his finger up her chin to her mouth, and she closed her lips over his finger and licked his bare skin. It tasted like maktak, she thought, like agviq, like her tears.

''My lips are sealed,'' he said.

Tuttu pulled his finger from her lips, traced four lines up and down her chin. ''You're a woman, Claudia,'' he said. ''Maybe we should give you a tattoo.''

Claudia smiled. ''You been reading Murdoch again? Maybe we should give *you* a labret.'' She poked his cheeks, once, twice.

They put their arms around each other, she wrapped him in the blanket, and they walked back to the qaregi. On the roof of the house, just before they went in, Tuttu smiled at her, touched her chin again.

''Hey, Claudia,'' he said. ''I've been meaning to ask you: what does *Claudia* mean?''

"*Wise*," she lied. *Claudus*, lame, she thought. Not the best Latin name.

"Like the snowy owl?" he asked.

"Like the owl."

Out to the festival grounds the villagers went. From a staff behind each whaling boat flew flags: an American flag over Malgi's umiaq, a Soviet flag over the boat to the left, and an Alaskan flag over the boat to the right. The whalers placed hunks of flipper and maktak and slabs of meat on pieces of plywood before each boat. Much meat already had been eaten, and much more would be distributed over the year, but Tuttu and Malgi—with Claudia's help, of course— decided that for the ceremony they should distribute a sizable portion. Puvak organized some of the older boys into a wood-gathering expedition, and they built a huge fire beyond the shares of meat. Masu and Paula stirred several pots of boiling whale steaks. No one knew quite how to prepare the meat, but Masu said that "we have the whole winter to learn," when someone pointed this out.

In an open area beyond the fire the mapkuq, the blanket toss skin, lay on the ground. Masu had stitched a new edge for the skin, and had put a new loop of rope around it. When all the villagers had come and the old ladies and old men were made comfortable in the shelter of the boats, Malgi organized the blanket toss.

Claudia looked at the skin, remembering the tradition. The idea had been that hunters would toss someone up in the skin to scout the horizon. This explanation had always seemed suspect to her, some old guy pulling a honkey's leg. How well could anyone see when leaping in the air? She thought people did the blanket toss because it was fun. Even Inupiaq, she knew, had to do things for the pure joy of it. Anthropologists always thought people did things for reasons— they never could think that people did things just for the pure hell of it, the fun of it.

The villagers grabbed the edge of the skin while Malgi stood back and shouted directions. Grab the edge with both hands. Tilt forward, move back. Forward, back. Malgi threw a basketball onto the mapkuq, and the hunters and whalers and men and women bounced the ball up and down, pulling in and out. Then Malgi stopped them, got onto the skin. Knee's better, Claudia thought, but if that old fool breaks another arm . . .

Malgi jumped up and down, bouncing with the skin, and the villagers laughed at him flying up into the air. Around the edge of the tossers little children squealed as the old man flew higher and higher. Malgi reached into the folds of his sling, and threw out candy and bubble gum—hidden all these months, the sneak, she thought—and the kids ran around gathering up the treats. She remembered, then, Kutchuq and his gum and what Tuttu had told him, and she saw the boy pick up a piece of bubble gum, start to unwrap it, then hand it to a little girl.

Now that Malgi had shown him how, Tuttu got up on the skin. He should have had first toss, Claudia thought, because he got the first whale, but then she smiled to herself. Malgi was out there on the second trip as surely as he had been on the first. Tuttu bounced up and down, stumbling at first, but soon getting the knack of it. She watched him, learning from him. Keep the knees straight. Let the blanket toss you. Tuttu got fancy, scissoring his legs back and forth, even doing a flip at the top of a high bounce. He, too, tossed out goodies to the crowd: shotgun shells and rifle cartridges, cigarettes, bags of tea, packets of fishing hooks, even—the women giggled—tampons.

Natchiq took his turn and then Amaguq and Puvak. Finally, Tuttu pushed Claudia out onto the skin. He thrust something into her hand to throw, and she looked down at the shiny yellow objects. Ivory, small pieces of carved ivory, whales and seals and polar bears that Tuttu had carved. She nodded at him, mixed them in with the artifacts she and Rob had found at Pingasagruk. Old ivory and new ivory, talismans of luck. They would carve many more such talismans, many more tools: harpoon points with steel blades, arrows and darts, old tools and new tools out of whatever the land and the old civilization could give them. A new culture, she thought, not like the ancient, not like before the war. Something else, Claudia thought, like the vision she had seen on the beach at Pingasagruk on the day her world ended.

The villagers pulled back at the skin, and she bounced up a few feet, up and up, remembering trampoline lessons from when she had been in grade school in Florida, a Florida that no longer was. Up she flew, and when she got the swing of it, Claudia whirled around, her braids flying out from her head, the carving of agviq flying out from the thong around her neck. She leapt and spun, leapt and spun, and the world swirled around her: tundra, village, ice, tundra, village, ice.

Holding the edge of the mapkuq, Tuttu laughed up at her. "Ukpik," he yelled, giving Claudia her name. The snowy owl. "You are Inupiaq now."

"Real People!" she shouted down at him as she flung the amulets out at her village. She stopped, and Tuttu helped her down. Tammy climbed onto the skin, and the villagers tried their best to upset the lesbian, but she only bounced higher and higher.

"We are all Inupiaq now!" Ukpik yelled up at Qavvik. She brushed a blond hair out of her face, and wiped a slight tear off her cheek as she thought of her old world that would never be and the new world that was becoming. "Only the Real People live here!"

_____ GLOSSARY _____

WHERE known, Inupiaq words in _Agviq_ have been spelled using the orthography of Edna Ahgeak MacLean in her _Abridged Inupiaq and English Dictionary_ (Fairbanks, Alaska: Alaska Native Language Center, 1980)—an excellent source for readers who would like to learn more about the Inupiaq language. Jana Harcharek of the North Slope Borough Inupiat History, Language, and Culture Commission also made corrections to this glossary. Place names have been spelled using the U.S. Geological Survey official spellings, but corrected to the proper Inupiaq orthography if known. Some additional non-English words have also been included.

General Terms

Aaglu—killer or orca whale (_grampus rectipinna_).
Aluaq—coal; name for James, Belinda's husband.
Amaguq—wolf (_canis lupus_); name of Puvak's father.
Angatkuq—Eskimo shaman.
Anorak—(from Greenland Eskimo _anoraq_); pullover jacket with a hood.
Agviq—bowhead whale (_balaena mysticus_).
Agviqluaq—gray whale (_eschrichtius glaucus_).
Atigi—parka.
Iqaluk—fish; brother-in-law to Masik.
Iglu—house.

Iglugruaq—Point Barrow type semi-subterranean sod house.

Inua—Yu'pik (southwest Eskimo) word for "spirit," especially an animal spirit.

Inupiaq—literally, "the real people"; North Alaskan Eskimo, generally living in the area from Unalakleet, Alaska north to the Canadian border; the language of the Inupiaq people.

Kamik—boot.

Kamotiq *or* kamotiqiluuiak—Greenland-style sled.

Kanayuq—four-horn sculpin fish, or bullhead; Inupiaq name of Arnold, Marvin's (Natchiq's) brother and Simon's (Tuttu's) cousin.

Katak—literally, "to fall." The hole in the floor of an iglugruaq in which one enters the house.

Kuspuk—Yu'pik name for a woman's dress.

Kutchuq—gum; Samuel, son of Masik.

Maktak—skin of whale; black, chewy, sometimes called "Eskimo bubble gum."

Malgi—arctic loon (*gavia arctica*); name for Tuttu's grandfather. Also, a twin.

Manaq—retrieving hook; thrown out in water to pull in seals.

Mapkuq—sewn together seal skins used in blanket toss.

Masik—gill; Kutchuq's mother.

Masu—edible root; name for Tuttu's grandmother and Malgi's wife.

Mukluk—Eskimo name for a knee-high boot made of skins.

Naataq—gray owl (*strix nebulosa*).

Nalukataq—whaling festival held each June at the end of the whaling season.

Nanuq—polar bear (*ursus martimus*).

Natchiq—common name for any seal of the genus *phoca* (*p. largha, p. hispada, p. fasciata*); Inupiaq name for Arnold's (Kanayuq's) brother, Marvin.

Nivak—to dig.

Nivakti—digger; archaeologist.

Nuna—earth, land; derisively, dirt; Tuttu's name for Tammy.

Paula—literally, "soot"; Inupiaq name for Belinda.

Piqaluyak—year-old or older blue sea ice in which the salt has been leached out; freshwater ice that can be drunk.

Puyugruaq—steam that rises over open leads in the ice; in Russian, *polynya.*

Puvak—*lung; name for Amaguq's son.*

Qaregi—*dancehouse, like the iglugruaq, only much larger.*

Qavvik—*wolverine (gulo gulo);* name given to Tammy.

Sigpan—stove blubber; name for John, a crony of Edward.

Siksrik (sometimes *siksik*)—onomatopoeic name for arctic ground squirrel (*spermophilus parryi*). Also known as "parka" squirrel, for use as fur for fancy parkas.

Sisuaq—beluga whale (*delphinapterus leucas*).

Stuaqpak—Inupiaq name for the main village store in Barrow; literally, "big store."

Tanik—white person. Sometimes used to refer to any non-Inupiaq person.

Taniayaaq—person of mixed Inupiaq and non-Inupiaq heritage; usually refers to someone half-white, half-Inupiaq.

Tourley—tourist (Inupiaq slang).

Tuttu—caribou (*rangifer tarandus*); Inupiaq name for Simon.

Tuvaq—landfast sea ice, an ice shelf along the coast that has frozen nearly to the ocean bottom and is safe to walk on.

Ugruk—bearded seal (*erignathus barbatus*).

Ugrulik—kamiks made with ugruk skin soles.

Uiniq—an open lead in the ice.

Ukpik—snowy owl (*nyctea scandiaca*).

Ulu—women's knife, shaped like a quarter of a circle with a handle at the pointed end.

Umialik—traditionally a boat captain; rich man (one who can afford an umiaq).

Umiaq—boat; sometimes used to refer to an *umiapiaq*, an open boat made of skins stretched over a wooden frame.

Unaaq *or* unaaqpauraq—a staff with a pole at one end and a hook at the other; used to probe ice and retrieve game.

Place Names

Ataniq—abandoned village south of Pingasagruk, at westernmost tip of Peard Bay.

Atqasuk—village south of Barrow.

Birnirk (Pigniq)—archaeological site north of Barrow, near the Naval Arctic Research Laboratory.

Eluksingiak Point—eastern point of land at mouth of Kugrua Bay.

Ipiutak (Ipiutaq)—archaeological site discovered by Froelich Rainey near Point Hope, Alaska (Tikigaq).

Kaktovik (Qaaktugvik)—Village on Barter Island, in northeast Alaska, at the edge of the Arctic National Wildlife Refuge.

Kugrua River—river that flows into Peard Bay.

Nalimiut Point—point just southwest of where the Seahorse Islands meet the mainland; on Peard Bay.

Nulawik (Nullagvik)—hunting camp about halfway between Barrow and Peard Bay.

Nunavak (Nunavaaq)—hunting camp between Walakpa and Barrow.

Nuvuk—literally, "point"; old village at Point Barrow.

Pingasagruk (Pingusugruk)—archaeological site and ancient village north of Ataniq, south of Point Franklin, on barrier island between Peard Bay and Chukchi Sea; Claudia's site.

Tachinisok Inlet—inlet immediately east of where the Seahorse Islands meet the mainland; due east of Nalimiut Point; hunting and fishing camp near an airstrip and DEW line tower.

Ukpiagvik—"where the snowy owls are"; name for the general area around Barrow, including Browerville.

Ulguniq—Wainwright, Alaska.

Utqiagvik—"the high place"; name for Barrow, specifically the bluff area but not including Browerville. Also spelled Utkiavik (Dekin 1981), Utkiavwin (Murdoch 1892), Utkiavie (Brower 1942).

Walakpa (Ualiqpaa)—archaeological site south of Barrow; place where Wiley Post and Will Rogers died in a plane crash in 1935.